KATASTROPHE

BY THE SAME AUTHOR

Spoils of War

Finisterre
Aurore
Estocada
Raid 42
Last Flight to Stalingrad
Kyiv
Katastrophe

DI Joe Faraday Investigations

Turnstone
The Take
Angels Passing
Deadlight
Cut to Black
Blood and Honey
One Under
The Price of Darkness
No Lovelier Death
Beyond Reach
Borrowed Light
Happy Days

DS Jimmy Suttle Investigations

Western Approaches
Touching Distance
Sins of the Father
The Order of Things

Enora Andressen

Curtain Call
Sight Unseen
Off Script
Limelight
Intermission
Lights Down

FICTION

Rules of Engagement
Reaper
The Devil's Breath
Thunder in the Blood
Sabbathman
The Perfect Soldier
Heaven's Light
Nocturne
Permissible Limits
The Chop
The Ghosts of 2012
Strictly No Flowers
Acts of Separation

NON-FICTION

Lucky Break
Airshow
Estuary
Backstory

KATASTROPHE

GRAHAM HURLEY

HEAD
ZEUS

An Aries Book

First published in the UK in 2022 by Head of Zeus Ltd,
part of Bloomsbury Publishing Plc

9 7 5 3 1 2 4 6 8

A catalogue record for this book is available
from the British Library.

ISBN (HB): 9781838938369
ISBN (XTPB): 9781838938376
ISBN (E): 9781838938390

Printed and bound by CPI Group (UK) Ltd,
Croydon, CR0 4YY

Head of Zeus Ltd
First Floor East
5–8 Hardwick Street
London EC1R 4RG

WWW.HEADOFZEUS.COM

À Danielle
notre prof inestimable

'The purpose of propaganda has never been to instil convictions, but to destroy the capacity to form any'

– Hannah Arendt

January 1945.

Just occasionally, one of the guards would arrive under cover of darkness with a tiny morsel of rotten venison, wrapped in newsprint. He was a Ukranian, Borys. He had a distinctive cough, a rasp deep in his throat, and if you had the ears for it you could hear him coming. Werner Nehmann had the ears for it, and also the luck to occupy one of the tier of wooden bunks nearest the door.

The cough. Then the dry squeak of snow beneath the approaching boots.

The *Vory*, the gangster *zeks* who ran the hut, were playing cards beside the stove and never lifted their heads. They didn't have to. They knew that the offering was for them, settlement for yesterday's use of the strangling towel on the hated ex-NKVD *zek* who'd complained about the tiny splinters of soap in the bathhouse once too often. Little Nehmann, the Georgian with the crooked smile, would play the postman, meet the guard at the door then bang it shut seconds later, keeping the icy wind at bay. Then would come the moment when he deposited the ten grammes of weeping venison carefully beside the fan of cards on the quilt the *Vory* used as a table. One or two of the faces would glance up, watching Nehmann as he stepped away. Not with a shaving or two of the meat, but with the soiled sheet of newsprint.

Next day, the paper dry, he'd return from the mine and stamp the life back into his sodden feet and hoist himself up to the top bunk where the freezing air was a degree or two warmer. He was still in his working clothes – cap, padded coat, pea jacket, felt trousers. He'd sleep like this, his hands thrust between his thighs, trying to conjure warmth from the icy darkness, but for now he listened to the chatter of the *Vory* while he used a carefully torn length of newsprint to roll himself a cigarette.

His fingers, swollen from hunger and hopelessly bent from a year and a half at the unforgiving end of a shovel, took a while to coax every last shred of tobacco into place, but then he lay back, the cigarette between his ruined fingers, enjoying the anticipation of the struck match, the tiny flower of flame and then the harsh bite of the *makhorka* tobacco. Not just that but also the taste of the printing ink from the news sheet.

Had he tried to make sense of the columns on this page of the paper? Of course he had. One of them listed the output of tractor parts from a factory in nearby Magadan. Another celebrated the performance of a Shostakovich symphony at the concert hall in distant Novosibirsk. Did he believe a word of either story? *Nein*. But that wasn't the point. The point was the tang of printer's ink on the very tip of his tongue.

Did he invent this taste? Was it just another of the fictions that had sustained him for most of his working life? And in any event, did it matter? Of course not. Anything, he thought. Anything to mask the sour camp breath of sweat and old clothing, of the thin *kasha* that was never warm enough, of jerking awake like an animal night after night, disturbed by the faintest noise, his hair already frozen to the roughness of the filled sacking that served as a pillow, his ear instantly tuned to the howl of a wolf beyond the treeline.

Everything happened very slowly in the Gulag, he told himself. But even last year's news, the knowledge that something out there in the real world had happened and been recorded, kept him sane. First you invent a story. Then you see it into print. And then, if you're very, very lucky, you get to smoke it.

One of the *Vory*, the oldest, had abandoned the card game for the brief comforts of his concubine. The *Vory* called him 'Zoika'. He was young, no more than a boy. He had the body of a ghost and he occupied the bunk below Nehmann. He offered a range of talents and in spring, for some reason, his keeper celebrated the melt by auctioning shares in Zoika to anyone with enough tobacco. Now, in the depths of Nehmann's second Siberian winter, there was no sharing and by the time the *Vory* had noisily finished and rejoined the card game, Nehmann's cigarette was nothing more than a wet stub. He looked at it a moment, then let his hand dangle over the side of the bunk. Moments later, the stub had gone.

'*Guten Appetit*,' he murmured. The little waif would eat anything.

*

Nehmann's war had come to an abrupt end in Stalingrad, almost exactly two years ago. With the city in ruins, and the Russians accepting the surrender of General Paulus' Sixth Army, 91,000 German troops stumbled into captivity. One of them, taken prisoner in a church, was Werner Nehmann.

Technically, he wasn't a soldier at all but a journalist, working for Joseph Goebbels' Ministry of Propaganda. This distinction was lost on the Soviet arresting officer who handed him over to an NKVD apparatchik, who took one look at Nehmann's stolen greatcoat, and his Russian leather boots, and promptly assigned him to one of the work parties digging out foundations for a primitive war memorial.

This was to be raised on one of the cliffs overlooking the still-smoking deathscape that had once been Stalin's city beside the Volga, and in this respect – as in so many others – Nehmann was lucky. He'd suffered no wounds. Neither had he succumbed to frostbite, or dysentery, or the multiple outbreaks of typhoid that had crept into dugout after dugout as the German advance stalled. On the contrary, thanks to his comrade in arms, a gruff *Abwehr* spy hunter called Wilhelm Schultz, he'd been generously fed and watered, a blessing that earned him murderous looks from the endless lines of ravenous prisoners he passed at dawn every morning as his work party, bent against the driving snow, struggled up the bluff towards the memorial site.

By the time the excavations were done, it was early spring. Nehmann's last glimpse of Stalingrad was late in the afternoon of a cold, grey day. He stood briefly in the last of the daylight, the sweat cooling under his tunic, awaiting orders from the piratical Kazakhs who served as escorts. The city lay beneath him, as pale and still as a corpse, not a hint of movement, and he remembered lifting his head in time to catch a single shaft of sunlight on the far horizon where the city gave way to the interminable steppe. He was looking west. Berlin was thousands of kilometres away. Should he give the Kazakhs the slip? Should he start walking? Might there be an alternative to sleeping on the bare earth, surrounded by coils of barbed wire, aware that his luck was fast running out?

The answer was no. Next morning, along with hundreds of other prisoners, the Kazakhs shipped him across the river, marched him to the railhead and threw him into a cattle wagon. For the next eight days, it was standing room only, the prisoners huddled together for warmth, pissing through gaps in the planked floor as more of the steppe rolled slowly past. The journalist in Nehmann wanted to find out about these broken bodies. He asked questions the way most men drew breath. His curiosity was instinctive, ungoverned, insatiable. Where had they come from? What did they make of the last three months? What next for the Führer's all-conquering armies? But these whispered enquiries, however deftly he dressed them up, fell on deaf ears.

Once a day the train would stop. The door slid open and unseen hands tossed loaves of black bread into the stink of the cattle wagon. There was a bucket or two of water as well, but Nehmann had counted eighty-seven heads at the start of the journey and the food and water was never enough. Dawn on the third day revealed three corpses, all of them still standing, denied even the space to collapse. With rough impatience, a huge Sergeant from Saxony managed to force the door open. All three men were stripped of anything remotely useful – clothing, boots – and rolled onto the trackside. No one said a word, no muttered prayers of farewell, and not for the first time Nehmann understood the vast indifference of death. It went, he thought, with the landscape. These men had simply given up, surrendering to hunger, and disease, and the rank bitterness of defeat. Three naked corpses and the featureless steppe were a perfect fit.

Towards the end of the journey, Nehmann fell to thinking about Schultz. In so many respects, in the madness of Stalingrad, they'd been made for each other. With his tiny team, Schultz had commandeered parts of a bus station as *Abwehr* field headquarters. The building gave them shelter and a degree of warmth, and down in the basement he'd been happy to find room for Nehmann, newly arrived at the front.

Pre-war, in Berlin, the name Stalingrad had meant nothing, and it was here that the two men had first got to know each other: Schultz the fast-rising star from Army Intelligence, part street brawler, part poet; Nehmann, the little Georgian genius rumoured to have the ear of Joseph Goebbels. They shared an appetite for beer and schnapps in a certain kind of bar, for tradeable gossip from the bedrooms of the Nazi elite, for women with class, and appetite, and a sense of humour, for anything – in short – that punctured the strutting self-importance that went with ministerial office on the Wilhelmstrasse. Long before the war had got properly underway, they'd agreed that the Thousand Year Reich was one of God's sillier jokes, destined for an early grave. Not that anything in peacetime Berlin had ever prepared them for this.

Schultz and Nehmann had been arrested together in a church on the eve of Paulus' surrender. Outside, it was nearly dark. Both men were facing a line of heavily armed Soviet soldiers, and both expected to be shot. Instead, on a grunted order from the officer in charge, they were searched and then separated. Nehmann had a last glimpse of Schultz as he was pushed towards a waiting truck. The big *Abwehr* man shook off his escort and threw Nehmann a glance over his shoulder.

'Tante Gerda,' he growled. 'First through the door buys the drinks.'

Tante Gerda was a bar in Moabit, much favoured by those few Berlin scribblers who still refused to take the Nazis seriously. For once, Nehmann struggled to reply and by the time he opened his mouth, Schultz had gone.

*

The journey from Stalingrad finally came to an end. Nehmann had been counting. Four days on his feet. Four days without a shit. Four days when his brain had slowly given up the battle to make sense of what was going on. More dead bodies. More sips of icy water from the circulating tin mug. More whispered rumours that so and so, the thin guy pinioned in one corner of the cattle truck, would be lucky to make it through.

The train juddered to a halt. Mother Russia, thought Nehmann, could stretch no further east. Beyond here, the train would surely topple off the edge of the known world and end up in the sea. Men outside were shouting. The wooden door was pushed open and the faces peering up recoiled at the pile of more naked bodies readied for disposal. Nehmann was a Georgian and his real name was Mikhail Magalashvili. He spoke Russian, understood the Cyrillic alphabet, but staring out at the trackside sign in the marshalling yard, he was none the wiser. Krasnoyarsk? Where on God's earth was that?

It was the dead of night. Open trucks took them through the deserted city centre, the bald tyres whispering on the packed snow, the driver lurching left and right to avoid the bigger potholes, the prisoners still on their feet, every back turned to the bitter wind. Already, on the dig in Stalingrad, the Russians had taken to calling them 'zeks'. Nehmann had heard the term before and knew what it meant. 'Zeks' were the cast-offs on whom the Revolution depended for the latest Five-Year Plan. 'Zeks' dug canals, felled trees, tamed hostile stretches of the taiga, burrowed into the frozen earth in search of precious minerals. 'Zeks' fed the great industries evacuated east of the Urals, safely removed from the German onslaught. Another name for 'zeks' left nothing to the imagination. 'Zeks' were camp dust.

Nehmann still thought they were close to the ocean, but he was wrong. The journey went on for six more days. Every four hours the truck would stop. Bread would appear from nowhere, and huge buckets of a thin, cold, buckwheat gruel called *kasha*, and guards would gesture for the men to exercise, drive the cold from their bones, empty their bladders or their bowels in the frosted roadside tussock. This small improvement on the days and nights in the swaying cattle truck sparked brief exchanges of conversation, and on the last night Nehmann found himself beside a gaunt figure who must have been in his fifties. He had a Moscow accent, and the delicate gestures of someone used to a life indoors.

It was the middle of the night. The road had narrowed and now it wound upwards into the mountains. The endless pine trees were mantled with snow that feathered in the slipstream as the truck rumbled past. The sky was cloudless, brilliant with stars, and many of the men gazed upwards, their eyes moist in the icy wind. The old man beside Nehmann lifted a weary arm.

'The Dipper,' he murmured. 'It's in the wrong place.'

Nehmann followed his pointing finger. The man was right. The Big Dipper was the constellation of the Great Bear, Ursa Major. Nehmann had grown up in the Caucasus, and on nights like this, perfect visibility, his father's thick finger would often trace the tell-tale outline from star to star. The Great Bear, he warned, was Russia. The Red Army had only recently crossed the mountains and pitched their tents in Tbilisi, their presence visible on every city street. The image of the Bear over Georgia had stayed with Nehmann ever since, an astral placard, proof that Communism had terrible consequences, but those stars had always been in the north, high over the mountains. Now, it was down near the horizon, no less impressive, no less portentous, but mysteriously rehomed. God again, he thought grimly. Capricious. Forgetful. Tidying the Dipper into a corner of the night sky where it didn't belong.

*

That first year, 1943, was Nehmann's first taste of the region they called Kolyma. His first camp lacked even a name, and his first hut, like all the huts that followed, had been thrown up in a hurry. Every plank in the four walls had made an enemy of its neighbour. There were gaps everywhere, a nightly invitation for winter to make itself at home among bodies desperate for sleep. Warmth from the single stove never reached beyond the nearest tiers of bunks, and in any case the wood had always run out by mid-evening.

Curled up in the aching cold in his bunk, Nehmann would sometimes open one eye and watch a fellow *zek* creep across the rough wooden floor and settle a stolen potato in the embers of the stove. The mouldy pebble of starch would offer a couple of barely cooked mouthfuls at the very most, but the *zek* would stay beside the stove for hours, standing guard, his gaze fixed on the tiny mound of cooling ash. Occasionally, when the guard arrived before dawn to bang his hammer on the hanging rail to ready the hut for another day's work, the *zek* would still be there, his patience a testament to hunger and perhaps optimism. Even then, Nehmann knew that the harsh metallic clang of the hammer, steel on steel, would stay with him for the rest of his life. It was implacable. It brooked no argument. In the muddle of lightly fevered dreams that served as sleep, it elbowed everything else aside.

Nehmann's first working party, twenty souls, took him away from the camp and up into the mountains. An hour or so on the ice-crusted muddy path and he was looking at one of the patches of bare snow among the pine trees worn thin by a winter of the hardest labour. Whether by axe or a rusting two-man saw, cutting down trees drained starving bodies of their last gramme of energy. Then, in the chill sunshine of early spring, the shadows would lengthen, and the guards would check their watches, and the *zeks* would muster to drag the fallen trees back down the mountain. The guards, duty bound to be back in camp in time to attend their late-afternoon propaganda sessions, would urge their charges to still greater efforts, the stripped tree trunks on their shoulders as they fought for balance on the packed snow.

Because he was a recent arrival and something of a novelty, Nehmann always seemed to end up with the heaviest end of the tree, and he quickly learned to skip sideways on the steeper corners of the path, all too conscious that a fall – with the crushing weight of the tree on top of him – would probably be fatal. This little circus manoeuvre seemed to work, and to his quiet satisfaction others in the work party began to copy him.

Back in the hut, he found himself talking to a political prisoner from Leningrad who'd made an enemy of powerful elements in the Party. A professor of literature from the State University, he'd brought both logic and passion to the pointless, self-serving *Obkom* committee debates that – in this man's account – often lasted until daybreak. In the end, as he'd half expected, he'd paid a terrible price for his honesty and his talents, falling foul of Article 58 of the regime's penal code, but even now he didn't seem to care.

'Maybe I should have watched where I put my feet,' he told Nehmann. 'Much like you, my friend.'

There were other moments, too, when the numbing shocks of camp life began to lift, and Nehmann sensed the possibility of light in the darkness. The felling area in the mountains was surrounded by stands of dwarf cedar. The first time Nehmann laid eyes on them, they lay prone, half covered in snow, yet more victims of the pitiless winter. Then, one dark, cloudy morning, one of the little trees roused itself, animal-like, shaking the snow from its branches. How and why this happened was a mystery but within minutes, as Nehmann watched, other dwarf cedars sprung to attention. Nehmann's laughter attracted the attention of one of the older *zeks,* a former mayor from a Moscow suburb, another of the camp's Article 58 politicals. He struggled across through the drifts of thick snow and told Nehmann that spring was only days away.

'They know,' he gestured at the little trees. 'Don't ask me how, but they do.'

Nehmann, a journalist to his fingertips, trusted no one, but the next morning there was a flicker of heat in the sun and when they made it up the mountain to the felling area, every dwarf cedar was on parade. Nehmann, who'd loved conjuring tricks all his life, was delighted. More to the point, when the ex-mayor presented him with a handful of cedar nuts, he slipped them into his pocket. He loved the smoothness of the nuts between his fingertips, and the sight of them reminded him of another kind of bean, back in a previous life, when the sound of the grinder, and the taste of fresh coffee, were pleasures he'd been foolish enough to take for granted.

*

Never again. In the Gulag, food dominated everything. Basic rations boiled down to meagre helpings of pea soup, buckwheat *kasha*, pearl barley so tough it was known as 'shrapnel', and bread that would put a stopper up your arse for five days. Just getting by on a diet like this, especially in winter, was near-impossible, but to eat better – under the quota system – you had to work harder. Nehmann had no trouble following this logic but meeting a decent quota meant having enough food in your belly, at which point any sane man would start looking for ways of cheating the system.

The hut's orderly, that first spring, woke up one morning to find a dead body in the bunk below. The man had died in the night but the orderly kept the news to himself until the day's rations had been delivered. That way he got double rations for the day, trading half of the dead man's allowance for tobacco, and everyone agreed that providence had smiled upon him. This incident made a profound impression on Nehmann, who began to ponder ways in which he, too, might profit from a little free enterprise.

There were a couple of dozen horses in the camp. They were used to haul logs and Nehmann knew that they were even more vulnerable to the Siberian winter than *zeks*. And so Nehmann made it his business to keep his eye on the oldest beast, which was beginning to shiver and gasp for breath. Temperatures that week froze your spit before it hit the ground, and late one afternoon word went around that the horse had collapsed. In his home town, as a fourteen-year-old, Nehmann had worked in the local abattoir and still remembered how to butcher a carcass.

After dark, he borrowed a knife from one of the *Vory* on the promise of choice cuts, slit the animal's throat and then opened its belly. The *Vory*, ever suspicious, joined him beside the steaming carcass, gazing at the rich spill of intestines, then dipped his little finger with its long nail into the warm soup of blood and guts. That night, before the guards came, Nehmann had time to slice off parcels of meat, which he hid in nearby drifts of snow. The rank stench of the opened beast brought wolves into the camp that night and they feasted on the remains of the horse, but a handful of Nehmann's cache of precious protein survived and the episode won him a quiet round of applause from his fellow *zeks*. The camp authorities were less impressed. Three days later, Nehmann was transferred.

*

Gold had never much featured in Nehmann's life, but this never-ending war was full of surprises, and a day in the back of yet another truck took him and dozens of other *zeks* north along the Kolyma Highway. The highway, built by *zek* labour years before the Great Patriotic War, was also known as the Road of Bones. Nehmann had first come across the phrase only weeks before and was struck by the neatness of Soviet thinking. First you laboured day and night to build this gravelled highway. Then you died of exhaustion and became part of its foundations.

The new camp was a ninety-minute trudge across the green sprawl of the taiga to the gold mine. An army of *zeks*, now helped by American-supplied bulldozers, had taken a huge bite out of the hillside above the River Kolyma. The innards of this vast quarry looked like a child's painting, crude daubs of heavy greys and blacks, glistening from the overnight rain. Half close your eyes, Nehmann thought, and you might be looking at the remains of a gigantic fire, left to cool overnight. Slurry the colour of ash. *Zeks* struggling with wooden wheelbarrows loaded with rock, their faces the colour of death.

The work was brutal, far worse than Nehmann's earlier dalliance with timber felling. By nine o'clock, in the first fitful rays of the sun, he would be hauling a stone-filled cart, the horse collar biting into his bony shoulders, his thighs and lower back on fire as he struggled to make it to the waterside site where the minerals would be crushed and sieved. Other *zeks* watched, passive, incurious, while he took a shovel to the stones in the cart, adding them to the pile, grunting with the effort, the taste of blood in his mouth from his weeping gums. The cart empty, he'd return for another load, and then another, each journey a little slower than the last, oblivious to the laughter of the guards. Nehmann, they'd concluded, was a 'wick'. Wick meant goner.

Months went by. A prisoner of the quota system, Nehmann knew that he'd only get through by working harder, by earning more rations, by submitting to this pitiless regime, and so he forced what remained of his body to still greater efforts until the guards began to view him in a new light. Then came the evening when he limped to the bathhouse, utterly exhausted, only to find that some camp sadist had found a full-length mirror for the use of the *zeks*.

He paused in mid-step, his cap in his hand, stared at the image in the pitted glass, took stock. The torn pea jacket, the filthy buttonless military shirt, a dirty body latticed with scratches from louse bites, rags around his fingers, rags tied with string around his feet, a mouth full of inflamed gums and loose teeth, and not a gramme of spare flesh on the scaffold of bones. Back in the previous camp, he'd learned the hard way about the dangers of losing all sense of direction in the sudden whiteouts on the mountainside. Now, eyeballing the scarecrow figure in the mirror, the feeling of panic, or perhaps resignation, was very similar. He'd lost his bearings. He no longer knew where or who he was. To grow old in the Gulag was an oxymoron. Kolyma was eating him alive.

Redemption arrived in the shape of the *zek* who occupied the bunk below him. He was an old man by the standards of the Gulag, itself an achievement, but his lungs were slowly filling with some nameless infection and he knew that he hadn't long to live. His name was Lev. During the civil war, he'd carried a radio for the Bolsheviks, and in what little time was left to him, perhaps as a legacy, he wanted to teach Nehmann Morse code. Nehmann said yes, only too happy to keep his brain alive, and tap-tapping lessons on the rough, unsanded wood of the bunks lasted late into the evening. Nehmann, to his delight, mastered the alphabet within weeks. Lev died one August evening, coughing his life away in the fetid shed that served as the camp hospital, and back in his bunk that night Nehmann tapped out a final message in the belief that he might still have been listening. 'Twenty-six words a minute,' he sucked at his sore knuckle. 'Thanks to you, my friend.'

The summer melted quickly into autumn. Nehmann's face, raw and swollen from mosquito bites, began to recover. Both hands had moulded themselves around the pick and the shovel and the handles of the wheelbarrow, but he watched others eating and learned to pinch the stem of his soup spoon with the tips of his calloused fingers. Writing was another challenge. He'd relied on pen and paper all his working life but now he had to wrap a length of torn rag around the shaft of the pen and the pencil to get the right purchase. The truth, he knew, was that his living hand, the right one, the one he relied on, had become a hook, an artificial limb, and there were moments of despair when he wondered about a drop of oil, or – if that failed – a crosscut saw. But then he remembered the quota system again. One-handed, he'd never earn enough food to stay alive.

And so, like every other *zek*, he simply resigned himself to the numbing routines of camp life. The six o'clock starts. The ten daily roll calls. The four questions you faced hour after hour, from guard after guard, a deliberately tireless reiteration of your place in the camp pecking order: first name? Family name? Offence? Sentence? Nehmann never fully understood the revolutionary logic that tied these four facts together, but he knew that wasn't the point. The questions were framed to make you feel utterly helpless, and unless you were stubborn enough to keep a part of your inner self well hidden, it worked.

From time to time, very occasionally, there came moments of near relief. An accident in the mine left the maintenance gang a man short and for three giddy weeks Nehmann found himself helping to lay and re-lay the heavy planks of wood that took the weight of the wheelbarrows and the stone carts en route to the washer. There was variety in this new challenge, and with it came the opportunity to spread the physical stress to different corners of his body. The quota system was different too. Nehmann was good at the work, nimble when it mattered, and towards the end of the month, with second helpings at the evening meal, he even put on a kilo or two of extra weight. Back in Berlin, Goebbels had given Nehmann a nickname. *Der Über* was short for *der Überlebender*, but only now did Nehmann realise how prescient the Minister of Propaganda had been. *Überlebender* meant 'survivor'.

After the planking, another assignment. Barrowloads from the mine had to be washed and sieved for the little tell-tale specks of yellow among the slurry. This, after all, was the whole point of the vast pit beside the river: to deliver gold for the Revolution. The work was horrible. You pulled rubber galoshes over bare feet and stood in the freezing water for an entire day, desperate to earn your quota. In this godless corner of Kolyma, gold was the basic unit of everything, the one elusive commodity against which you measured production, a less empty belly, a night's sleep and the prospect of another day on God's earth. If the sieve was your friend, you made it through. If it wasn't, then you began to falter.

Nehmann never faltered. Not physically. Not in ways that immediately mattered. Not that summer, nor the winter that followed, nor the long year thereafter. Keeping track of the passage of time turned you into an animal. Without a watch, or a radio, or access to regular newspapers, you began to keep an eye on the passage of the seasons, of the days when the green sprawl of the surrounding taiga turned first yellow, then a briefly radiant gold. You sniffed the air like a dog, scenting hints of frost. You watched the thin daylight disappear earlier and earlier. In short, you became a plaything of the elements, of the weather, of the ever-changing truce between darkness and light, utterly removed from the world that had first shaped you.

Nehmann had always had a talent for introspection, for taking a good look at himself, for mustering as much honesty as he dared about his own ability to cope in any situation, but he knew that two long years in Kolyma exacted a heavy price. The curtains had closed on memories of pre-war Berlin, of the Führer's triumphant return from crushing France, of the love affair that had brought a half-Jewish pianist called Maria into his life, of the reckless *pas de deux* he'd conducted with Hitler's Minister of Propaganda, even of his friendship with Willi Schultz. Most of Stalingrad had gone too, an experience Nehmann once swore he'd never forget, and all that was left was a world of thin *kasha*, and frozen spitballs, and a misplaced Dipper that – on cloudless nights – never failed to make him feel profoundly alone.

All the stranger, therefore, to awake one winter morning much earlier than usual with a face in the darkness peering up at his bunk.

'Herr Nehmann?' His German accent was excellent. '*Kommen Sie mit.*'

2

Tam Moncrieff had been at his desk in St James's Street for less than an hour when Ursula Barton tapped briefly on his door and stepped in. Unusually for this time in the morning, she was wearing her ancient grey cape, pebbled with raindrops. Moncrieff had closed the file he'd been studying, a reflex reaction. Now he reopened it.

'Been out?' He was looking at the brown manila envelope in her hand.

'Late, I'm afraid. Shameful, I know, but Alice has been poorly again. I had to stay overnight this time, do a little shopping first thing. Thank God she's got four bedrooms. And thank God for Mr Witherby.'

'Mr Witherby?'

'Stall near the back entrance to the market. Homemade rabbit pies and very relaxed when it comes to ration cards. I think he's the nicest man I've ever met. He's even civil to Alice when she bothers to get down there.'

Alice was Barton's ex-mother-in-law, a relic from the collapse of her long-ago marriage. Moncrieff had met her only recently and had disliked her on sight. She lived in Clerkenwell and employed domestic help, but no one had ever stayed longer than a month or so. Barton didn't much like her either, but she always answered her frequent calls for help. In her private life, as here in MI5, Ursula Barton had always suffered from an implacable sense of duty.

She studied Moncrieff for a moment, and then carefully laid the envelope on his desk. The flap had been neatly ungummed with something very sharp. Barton again. Neatness is all.

'This arrived from Broadway last night. Downing Street have also been on, by the way. The PM wants to see you. I gather it's a thank you for Yalta but that sounds far too sentimental for even him. Beware subtexts, my dear. Hidden reefs.' She nodded down at the envelope. 'I suggest you read that first. To be honest, it's a pathetic offering but forewarned is forearmed, *nicht wahr?*'

Moncrieff smiled. 54 Broadway housed the London headquarters of MI6, also known laughingly as the Secret Intelligence Service, a source of constant irritation if you were even half serious about winning the war.

Barton was already making for the door. Then she paused and tapped her watch. 'Half past ten. Apparently he's in the gloomiest of moods. Good luck.'

Yalta. Moncrieff reached for the envelope, and then sat back. It was thanks to Ursula Barton that he had found himself at an Oxford college on a nine-month intensive language course, thanks to her that he'd been able to win a reasonable degree of fluency in Russian, and finally thanks to her that he'd been assigned to the Crimea ahead of the recent conference. At Yalta, the Soviets had spent three furious weeks preparing for the hundreds of Western delegates that were about to descend on the once stylish Black Sea resort, and it had been Tam's job to monitor the security arrangements at the clifftop Vorontsov Palace, assigned to the British delegation.

To his quiet satisfaction, Moncrieff's Russian had been more than passable. He'd been fluent in German since his university days and spoke good French, but the Cyrillic alphabet and the mysteries of Russian syllable accentuation had been a real challenge. All the sweeter, therefore, to be able to kindle a handful of friendships in the warm Crimean sunshine that might one day prove more than useful. Which was doubtless Barton's intention from the start.

He opened the envelope. Inside was a single sheet of paper. In keeping with these occasional Broadway tugs on the arm, the intelligence was unsigned and carried no other indication of authorship. He supposed that the phone number scrawled in pencil across the bottom invited further discussion if required, but there was little attempt at proper context or any kind of authentication. Simply the passing-on of a rumour. Scuttlebutt, Moncrieff thought. He'd picked up the term from an American he'd met in the Crimea, charged with making President Roosevelt's palace safe for democracy. Scuttlebutt meant information that might – or might not – be true.

In two brief paragraphs, the MI6 note offered an alert to developments in northern Italy. Moncrieff already knew that the Allied thrust north had come to a temporary halt. An entire German Army Group had dug in under the command of *Generalfeldmarschall* Kesselring. Now, with the Americans over the Rhine at Remagen, and the Russians poised for a final drive towards Berlin from the east, the war for the Germans was plainly lost. Hence, perhaps, a series of messages from an SS General, Karl Wolff, to an American outpost of the Office of Strategic Services, the OSS, in Bern, in Switzerland. Wolff, it seemed, was a realist. If negotiations proved fruitful, he appeared to be offering the surrender of all Nazi forces in northern Italy.

Moncrieff reread the note and reached for his pen. The Office of Strategic Services was an American organisation, largely covert, charged with stirring up trouble in occupied Europe. It was led by an exuberant figure who might have stepped out of

Hollywood, a much-decorated Colonel who'd won his spurs in the Great War. Moncrieff had only met him on two occasions but had seen enough of the man in person to know why they called him 'Wild Bill' Donovan. His impatience with paperwork and the constraints of partnership in a much-tested alliance was legendary. As was his closeness to the man in the White House. Roosevelt put enormous trust in him. Which might – or might not – be important.

Moncrieff scribbled a brief note to himself before checking his watch. Downing Street would be a twenty-minute stroll through the thin drizzle. Umbrella, he thought grimly, remembering his brief week in the Crimean sunshine.

Arriving a little early at Downing Street, Moncrieff was parked in a corner of the main hall until the Prime Minister was ready to receive him. He'd first met Winston Churchill in 1938, the year before war broke out. Already an old man by then, Churchill spent a lot of his time at Chartwell, his country home down in Kent, bent over a raft of paperwork on the terrace overlooking the gardens and the lake, and the day Moncrieff arrived to brief him about developments in the Sudetenland he was struck by the old man's vigour and sheer reach. Even then he seemed to have half the world at his beck and call, and once the war was properly underway Moncrieff had met Churchill a number of other times, mostly in connection to Rudolf Hess, Hitler's deputy, who'd arrived unannounced in Scotland four years ago.

Now, Moncrieff nursed the dampness of his overcoat, watching the comings and goings of uniformed couriers and senior military, doubtless bringers of good news and bad, all of them stoking the furnace at the heart of the coalition government.

'Major Moncrieff?'

The voice took him by surprise. People seldom addressed him by rank any more. He stood up, plucking at the creases in his corduroy trousers, and followed the woman through a warren of passageways and down a flight of stairs to one of the Garden Rooms. Churchill was sitting behind a desk, the pinkness of his cherub face side-lit by the wash of grey light through the window. By mid-morning, still clad in a silk dressing gown, he'd yet to get dressed, and Moncrieff caught the scent of *eau de cologne* in the stale air.

'Has anyone attended to you?' Churchill waved him into the vacant chair beside the desk. 'Tea? Coffee? Some of that filthy vodka we were all obliged to bring back?' He harrumphed at his own joke, not taking the enquiry any further. He was obliged, he said instead, for all Moncrieff's efforts on his government's behalf. Yalta was undoubtedly the worst place in the world to have convened a meeting of any sort, let alone a gathering of the Mighty, and he fancied he still had the evidence to prove it.

'We had a sitrep every morning, myself and Sarah. Counted the little *cadeaux* the buggers left. My record was nine, all of them on the ankles. You?'

'Sir?' Moncrieff was lost.

'Bedbugs, Moncrieff.' He hoisted one slippered foot onto the desk, peering at the pale, hairless flesh. 'Gone now, thank God, though Sarah thinks she's scarred for life.'

Moncrieff, at last wiser, murmured his sympathies. Sarah, one of Churchill's daughters, had accompanied her father to Yalta.

'Another thing.' Churchill hadn't finished. 'The *look* of the bloody place. Did you ever see anything like it? Balmoral at the front. Marrakesh at the back. Never mix water and wine, Moncrieff. The delicacy of Islam? Bullied to death by a helping of Victorian Gothic? Same principle. Buildings are like religion, best kept pure both in body and spirit. And that garden at the back of the place. You know what I thought when I got up that first morning? How warm it was? How everything was growing fit to bust? It put me in mind of Provence. Then you take a proper look, go out for a little stroll, and everything's too big, too close, too *oppressive*, the mountains, the crags, those bloody cypress trees. It was like waking up in the middle of a funeral. This was a landscape that breathed all over you. It took liberties. It reeked of intimidation. It...' He broke off, reaching for a cigar from the silver box on the desk, the frown lines on his face suddenly transformed. 'Forgive me, Moncrieff. This is an old man speaking. You're right, the whole thing was a huge adventure. A dicky bird tells me our Soviet friends wired the gardens with microphones, as well as every last room in every last palace. Might that be true?'

'It would, sir.'

'You checked it out? You *know*?'

'I checked the grounds at the Vorontsov. I also talked to Sergo.'

'Lavrentiy Beria's boy?'

'The same.'

'And?'

'I asked him about a couple of the microphones I'd noticed. Omni-directional. Decent range. I thought I put it in the Briefing Notes.'

'You did, Moncrieff, you did. And we were duly grateful. But tell me this. At Livardia, I'm told they cleared several paths in the garden for Mr Roosevelt's wheelchair. That's where he *had* to go. And that's where they ambushed him with all those microphones. True?'

'Yes, sir.' Moncrieff nodded. 'I'm afraid so.'

'Bloody clever.' Churchill was stripping the cellophane from the cigar. 'Obvious, perhaps, but still clever. We underestimate our Soviet friends at our own peril, don't you think?'

Moncrieff nodded, said nothing. Lavrentiy Beria was the head of the NKVD, the huge security empire that was the real source of Stalin's power. He had a reputation for sadism and a talent for mass murder, and Moncrieff had run into him twice at Yalta as the Russian arrived with a sizeable escort to check last-minute alterations at the Vorontsov Palace. Small in stature. Fleshy lips. Bulging eyes slightly magnified by the lenses of his pince-nez. His son, Sergo, had thankfully been spared his father's appetites. In charge of the transcription teams installed at Yalta, he'd been understandably reticent when it came to details, but Moncrieff had grown to admire his quiet diligence.

Churchill wanted to know about bomb shelters. At Stalin's palace, the Great Man was protected by seven feet of newly poured concrete, enough – said Churchill – to withstand the direct impact of a thousand-pound bomb. At Livardia, Roosevelt had been presented with a bespoke hidey-hole offering similar protection.

'And we poor Brits, Moncrieff? Supplicants at the table? Nothing. *Rien.*' He held Moncrieff's gaze for a long moment, as if MI5 might be to blame for this oversight, and then struck a match and applied it to the cigar before the space between them filled with smoke. The room suddenly smelled, Moncrieff thought, like a gentlemen's club, or perhaps a casino.

'I took it up with them,' Moncrieff said. 'But time, alas, had run out. To be fair, sir, none of you lacked the kind of protection that would matter.'

'Good God, no. That's not my point at all. That road up through the mountains? The one from the airfield to Yalta? Fifty miles, I'm told. And sentries every hundred yards presenting arms. Hard to tell the men from the women, but that's probably my eyesight. The hotel grounds, too. Security men everywhere, hard not to trip over the buggers. No, we were all duly grateful and we all raised a glass, night after night.' He paused briefly to contemplate the smoke curling up from his cigar before returning his gaze to Moncrieff. 'Ever meet Stalin, by any chance?'

'Never had the pleasure, sir.'

'Shame. Guy Liddell has every faith in your judgement, especially when it comes to people.'

'Really?' Guy Liddell headed MI5's 'B' Section and was the one figure to whom Ursula Barton showed any deference. This compliment, albeit second-hand, came as a genuine surprise.

'Indeed, Moncrieff...' Churchill was frowning now. 'Anthony thinks he's the cruellest man he's ever met. Can you credit that?'

'Guy Liddell?'

'Stalin. Uncle Joe. Anthony says he has a hint of murder in his eyes, always there, day or night. I know Anthony's one for the great phrases, and all those state trials probably bear him out, but at Yalta I have to say he was the perfect host, quiet, reasonable, and good company after a glass or two. We had to weather the odd tantrum, especially when it came to Poland, but on the whole he was commendably well behaved.' Churchill paused, his eyes still fixed on Moncrieff. Anthony Eden was the Foreign Secretary. 'Some of our American friends, Moncrieff, believe the Russians view peace as simply a breathing space between conflicts. They also believe they want to set us at each other's throats, us and the Americans. Divide and rule. Appeal to our darker angels. So very oriental, Moncrieff. Might you have a view?'

At last Moncrieff began to glimpse the real reason for his summons to Downing Street. This wasn't about Yalta at all but about the two brief paragraphs he'd just read from MI5's cousins in Broadway. He knows, Moncrieff thought. And Ursula Barton, or perhaps Guy Liddell, probably told him.

'Well?' Churchill was expecting an answer.

'I'm not with you, sir. You want my opinion on the Soviets?'

'I want your opinion on what happens next. Yalta was supposed to address that. All too sadly, I suspect it won't. We have our interests, Moncrieff, but alas we have no money. Our American friends are well aware of that, as are the Soviets, which makes the months and years to come somewhat tricky.' He suddenly mimed his two wrists manacled by circumstances beyond his control. 'This brings a harvest of the richest irony, of course. On the one hand the Americans are doing their level best to dismantle our empire, while on the other the Soviets are making Herculean efforts to build their own. Unless we are extremely clever, and extremely *alert*, both may succeed. We went to Yalta, like we went to war, to give the Poles a proper say in their own future. This is a sore we can never leave alone but the Americans are indifferent, and in any event the entire bloody country, *le tout* Poland, is now in the hands of the Soviets. *Force majeure*, Moncrieff. The first principle of Russian diplomacy.'

Once again, Moncrieff could only agree. Last week's parliamentary debate on the Yalta Resolutions had sparked a revolt on the Tory benches. The Prime Minister had gone to the Crimea in search of a fair post-war settlement in Eastern Europe. He'd returned, in the eyes of many, with a fistful of empty promises, much like Neville Chamberlain before him.

Churchill knew this. Moncrieff could see it in his eyes, in the hunch of his shoulders, in those tiny signals of defeat in his otherwise indomitable frame. This, he realised, was a moment of extraordinary intimacy, all the more surprising for being so unexpected. But Churchill hadn't finished. He put the cigar carefully to one side for a moment then leaned forward over the desk. He had the most beautiful hands, Moncrieff realised:

slender, with perfect nails and a triple-banded signet ring on his little finger.

'That first proper day at Yalta, Moncrieff, Uncle Joe took us all by surprise by turning up early at Vorontsov. I like to think we mustered courtliness and a degree of good cheer. We told him fibs about the accommodation, how wonderful everything was, and then I showed him the Map Room. You know our travelling map room? The one we take abroad? The one we use to keep ourselves au fait with events? It's an exact facsimile of the real thing. We adjust it hourly, by the minute if necessary. So there it was, our pride and joy, and I took Uncle Joe across the room for a look-see. And you know what happened? I wanted to make an early point, *entre nous*, about the Poles. How we all owed them a decent future, a fair outcome to all the blood and suffering, some kind of post-war parlay that would leave them a free people in a free land, mistress in their own house and captain of their soul. And so my finger was hovering over Warsaw, poor Warsaw, and Uncle Joe shot me a look, and then did a little pointing of his own. Not a word between us. Just fingers. Where was he pointing? Which city put that ghost of a smile on his face? Landsberg, Moncrieff. Landsberg an der Warthe. And Landsberg, as you doubtless know, is in Germany. Not only that but it had fallen to the Red Army just a couple of days before, and already they were moving on...' Churchill broke off, shaking his head, and for a moment he seemed near to tears, then he visibly stiffened, in control again, but his voice had sunk to a murmur, as if he was talking to himself. 'The following day we commenced negotiations. Everything happened in the ballroom at the Vorontsov Palace. It was the coldest, emptiest room you can possibly imagine, except there were hordes of us inside, around that table, all of us trying to have our say with those interminable pauses while the interpreters get to work. The

Soviets, Moncrieff, have a reverence for the samovar. There's nothing, no international crisis, that will resist the properties of Russian tea. And so the waiters come and go through those huge double doors with more tea, and more tea, and yet more tea until your bladder gives out and you hoist the white flag. The facilities were outside, along the corridor, and coming back, I found myself pausing, watching yet another waiter, laden with tea, and plates of those tiny pastries, and he hesitated outside the double doors, scarcely daring to make a noise as he turned the handle, and it suddenly occurred to me that this was a death scene, that there was somebody dying in there, and you know who that somebody was? It was Poland, Moncrieff. We arrived to make a peace. And instead we'd probably administered the last rites. Sad. Inexpressively so.'

This time, to Moncrieff's faint embarrassment, he did cry. From the pocket of his dressing gown he produced a handkerchief and mopped his eyes. Moncrieff could do nothing. From the floor above came the sound of a telephone ringing, then the scrape of a chair, then silence again. Churchill cleared his throat, muttered an apology for blubbing, and then half turned to stare sightlessly out of the window, and as he did so an enormous explosion rolled over the city, sending hundreds of pigeons into the grey March morning above Horse Guards Parade.

Churchill was staring at the window. Moncrieff was already on his feet, heading for the door, meaning to intercept any intruders, but when the door opened he found himself looking at the two Special Branch plainclothes bodyguards responsible for the Prime Minister's safety. When they stepped into the room, Churchill waved them away. By now he was on the phone.

'Another V-2, Moncrieff.' He had his hand over the black Bakelite mouthpiece. 'Bane of our bloody lives.'

*

Minutes later, Churchill insisted on Moncrieff accompanying him into the walled garden at the back of the house. Both men stood in silence on the wet grass, the Prime Minister still in his slippers, watching a column of smoke billowing above the rooftops to the north-east. The situation was confused but it seemed that the rocket had registered a direct hit on a busy indoor market. Fire engines and ambulances were already racing to the scene and Moncrieff caught the faintest clanging of bells, a grim coda to their Yalta musings on this suddenly glum March morning.

Churchill had ordered a car to be readied to take him to what he called the seat of the atrocity, and was about to get dressed. Moncrieff suspected that he'd like to be there at once, in the thick of it all, among the rubble and the bodies, but one of his private secretaries joined them in the garden and persuaded him to wait an hour or so until his presence would be better appreciated.

'I suppose you're right, Jock,' he grunted.

Alone again, just the two of them, Moncrieff hunted for a change of conversational subject, anything to lighten the Prime Minister's mood. He knew that Churchill had only yesterday returned from a brief tour of the front line in Holland where a British Army Group were preparing to cross the Rhine and push into Germany. Was everything in order for this historic moment?

'*Tout va très bien.*' The question had raised a wan smile. 'History can sometimes be kind as well as cruel, Moncrieff. I'm glad to say that Monty is as unbearable as ever, which is definitely what the Germans deserve, and I'm even more pleased to say that I was able to do my own little bit to keep the Hun in his place.'

'Sir?' Once again Moncrieff was lost.

'We paid a visit to the Siegfried Line,' the smile was broader, 'and I was able to relieve myself on just a little piece of Herr Hitler's barbarous concrete.' He glanced sideways at Moncrieff. 'I have a name for you, my dear. Wilhelm Schultz. An acquaintance, perhaps? Or even a friend? Some kind of comrade in arms?'

'A friend.'

Churchill nodded, contemplative, giving nothing away. Willi Schultz was a spy catcher from the *Abwehr*, streetwise, fearless, with interesting connections among the many elements in the Reich who'd never fully reconciled themselves with the Nazi madness. Moncrieff had bumped into him in the war's darker corners and held him in some esteem.

'You've been in touch with him?' Churchill asked, 'Recently?'

'No, sir. To the best of my knowledge he's still in Germany, though the *Abwehr* is under new management these days, which may have clipped his wings. On the other hand, he may have been killed. Willi always had a hunger for action, an appetite that might not have served him well.'

'I see.' Churchill nodded. 'And if I were to tell you otherwise?'

'Then I'd be glad.'

'Excellent.' The smile again. 'Then I suggest you talk to Mrs Barton. It was she who appears to believe that this friend of yours is very much alive, and more to the point she also suggests that he might know a great deal about all this nonsense with the Americans in Bern. A conversation, Moncrieff? Before the Germans make yet more mischief? Might that be in order?'

*

Moncrieff left Downing Street minutes later. The rain had stopped and en route back to St James's Street he took a long detour through the park to try and muster his thoughts. He'd always had a wary regard for Ursula Barton. German by birth, she'd married an English diplomat and served in the British Embassy in The Hague until her husband's philandering and – in her words – general uselessness had led to a divorce. With her native German and quick intelligence, MI5 had snapped her up and she'd moved to a small, slightly neglected semi-detached in Shepherd's Bush by the time Hitler's tanks rolled into Poland and war was declared.

As Moncrieff now knew, Barton had always nursed a *tendresse* for him, a characteristic mix of professional respect and perhaps something else. She recognised the steel that years of service with the Royal Marines had implanted in his soul, and she thoroughly approved of his linguistic skills. She'd put a number of opportunities in his path, some of them frankly hazardous, and after one of them nearly killed him she became the careful guardian of his convalescence. When other agencies came beating at his door, she sent them packing. And when he finally returned to St James's Street, she ensured that the paperwork crossing his desk was both challenging and worthwhile.

With the Red Army turning the tide of the war at Stalingrad, it was Guy Liddell who first suggested Moncrieff's crash course in Russian as a down payment on MI5's role in whatever followed the current hostilities, but Ursula Barton was the one who pushed it through the several committees who'd had their doubts. Moncrieff himself had loved those busy months in a draughty suite of rooms at Balliol. He'd revived an all too brief relationship with a classics lecturer called Ivor Maskelyne, and wrestled Russian verb endings to the mat. As importantly, perhaps, his rapport with Ursula Barton, the Queen of St James's Street, had matured into a real friendship.

Ursula was nearly a decade older than Moncrieff. With her neglected perm and her wardrobe of cardigans, she had neither the time nor the interest in making the most of her looks. Her sole concession to womanliness was a slash of scarlet lipstick for occasions that seemed promising, and in company she trusted – when she gave life a chance – she could be surprisingly funny. Moncrieff, as it turned out, was company she trusted, and over the last few months they'd begun to spend a little time together, sometimes in favourite restaurants, occasionally for an afternoon or even a whole day, at her semi in Shepherd's Bush where she stood guard over an enormous library of opera discs. This was a relationship that Moncrieff had begun to cherish, and the knowledge that this wary affection was mutual became in some ways a kind of consolation.

A year before the war began, Moncrieff had lost his heart to a woman called Bella Menzies. They'd met in Berlin, where she was employed at the British Embassy, and their relationship had somehow survived her defection to Moscow. Since then, thanks to the fortunes of war, they'd managed to meet on a number of occasions. The last, four long years earlier, had brought her briefly back to England before flying out to Kyiv in the company of a legendary Soviet bombmaker called Ilya Glivenko. That assignment had led to her death, and it had fallen to Ursula Barton – years later – to break the news. She'd handled this challenge with a sensitivity and grace that had taken Moncrieff by surprise, yet another factor in this new relationship of theirs.

He found her at her desk in St James's Street. He had a number of questions he wanted to ask about an SS General making contact with the OSS spooks in Bern, and about Willi Schultz, but one look at her face told him that this wasn't the time for either. She stared up at him as he carefully closed the door and took the empty seat at her desk. Ursula Barton never cried. Ever.

'What's the matter?' he asked.

'You heard the explosion?' She was staring at him, her face a mask, her fist closed around a ball of handkerchief.

'Of course. I imagine everyone did. Any news? Any details?'

She shrugged, said nothing. Then she shook her head as if she wanted rid of something inside.

'Farringdon Market,' she said tonelessly. 'That lovely Mr Witherby. Probably gone.'

3

It was beyond puzzling, beyond inexplicable, beyond a miracle. Winter savagely rationed daylight in Kolyma, a few precious hours – normally sunless – was all you ever got, but this was a different kind of illumination. The voice in the chill darkness of the hut belonged to an NKVD officer who quietly introduced himself to Nehmann as Leon. It was he who accompanied him out to the warmth of the waiting ZiL, who pointed out the armed escort in the back of the limousine, who filled the many hours on the Road of Bones heading south, and who finally conducted him into the Hotel Tscentral in Magadan, again with the escort in tow. By now, it was dark again.

A key was waiting in an envelope on the unmanned reception desk. All three men rode the noisy elevator to the seventh floor. The carpet in the emptiness of the corridor was cratered with cigarette burns. The escort ripped open the envelope and handed the key to Leon, who opened the double-locked door to Room 761 and stepped aside.

'The aircraft leaves at dawn. Be ready for us by seven o'clock. *Schlafen Sie gut.*'

Nehmann nodded. He was looking at a change of clothes, neatly spread on the double bed.

'So where did you learn your German?' He half turned in the open doorway.

'Berlin.' Leon was pocketing the key. 'There are sandwiches on a plate in the cupboard behind the door. *Weisswurst*, Mikhail Magalashvili. Your favourite, we understand.'

A gentle push took Nehmann into the room. A murmured assurance from Leon told him that the escort would be standing guard outside the door all night and would respond to any reasonable request. The single window, should Nehmann have the urge to try, was designed not to open. Then the door closed and there came the sound of the key turning twice in the lock, leaving Nehmann still dressed as a *zek*, as unwashed and unkempt as ever, staring down at the huge bed. My proper name, he thought. He knows who I really am, where I come from, which kind of sausage I like. How? And, most importantly, what next?

He peered into the bathroom, tested the hot water tap, fashioned an ill-fitting plug from the scrap of threadbare towelling that served as a flannel. Lying in the bath, with the hot tap still on, he worked up a grey lather from a pebble of soap he found on the floor. After two years of abject submission, of bare survival, Nehmann knew he was back in the world of political calculation. Leon badly wanted to be his new friend, that much was obvious. But why?

By his own account, this man held the rank of Colonel. He spoke flawless German and, it seemed, French and Spanish too, but where on earth could he possibly belong in the gallery of impassive NKVD faces Nehmann had encountered since Stalingrad? The thick pebble glasses? The bookish stoop? The playful intelligence in his blue-grey eyes? On the road south from the camp, he'd talked of nights on the Ramblas in Barcelona, of skiing parties in the Obersalzberg, of a memorable Christmas in an English country house overlooking the Thames. How on earth had the Revolution mustered the wit and good sense to come up with someone so cultured, so fluent, so *likeable*?

This was a question Nehmann couldn't answer but he realised at once that it didn't matter. When he was a child he'd sometimes sensed a presence in the mountains of Svaneti that dominated his native town, something he couldn't quite name. An older brother he'd consulted thought it might have been God but Nehmann wasn't convinced, and nothing he'd experienced since leaving home had brought him any closer to the Almighty. On the contrary, the hand of God had done nothing to stand in the way of Hitler's Reich and everything that had followed.

God, probably in his own interest, had ignored the work of the *Luftwaffe* over Warsaw, and Rotterdam, and London, had looked the other way when the SS plunged into countless ghettos and the Jew wagons clanked east, and He'd very definitely taken extended leave when hundreds of thousands of grown men reduced Stalingrad to rubble and each other to anonymous parcels of flesh and broken bone. But here He suddenly was, in the otherwise godless wastes of Kolyma, rescuing some nameless *zek* from an eternity of near-impossible quotas. Relax, Nehmann told himself. Understand a miracle, and you're probably dead already.

*

He awoke early, no idea of the time, still dark outside. Last night, before collapsing between cleanish sheets, he'd decided to leave the sandwiches as a down payment on the weeks to come. If they were really there in the cupboard behind the door, it meant that he hadn't imagined Leon, that yesterday had really happened, and that some kind of future without bedbugs, and wheelbarrows, and filthy rags tied around his bony feet, might even be possible. Carefully, with a blanket wrapped around himself, he opened the cupboard door and peered inside. Not just a plate, not just four thick sandwiches with an overflowing spill of *Weisswurst*, but a generous curl of mustard on the side. If friendship with Leon brought blessings like this, then Nehmann was very happy for him to audition for the role of God.

For the next ten minutes, with no idea what time it might be, he dragged a chair across the room and sat beside the window, staring down at the empty street, wolfing the sandwiches. No *Vory* demanding their take. No fellow *zeks*, pleading starvation. No fizzing nerve braced for the clang of the hammer. The sandwiches gone, Nehmann carefully rubbed his calloused finger around his gums and teeth, extracting every last particle of *Wurst*. When he looked at his finger before a final lick, he saw that it was smeared with fresh blood but the knowledge that his gums were still swollen and bleeding didn't matter. Escaping Kolyma was said to be impossible. You had to be dead to be shipped out. Yet here he was, en route to – of all places – an *airfield*.

From the hotel, in the murky half-light of dawn, they drove for perhaps half an hour. It was a biggish plane daubed in the colours of war, brown and green, two engines, sleek fuselage. Nehmann had never seen anything like it. The airfield was primitive. The grass runway was dusted with snow and a bitter wind off the mountains was playing havoc with the shredded remains of the windsock. A windowless wooden shack and a big military-looking tent offered passengers protection from the weather, and from the comfort of the ZiL Nehmann watched them hurrying across the frozen grass towards the plane. Most of them were in uniform, no less shabby than the handful of civilians, and everyone was carrying at least two bags. A huge man stood guard beside the open door, his face half hidden beneath an enormous beard, and he watched the pile of bags grow as the passengers hopped onto a crude wooden box and scrambled into the plane itself.

'There's room for us?' Nehmann nodded at the plane.

'*Kein Problem.*' Leon was rolling himself a cigarette. 'I reserved the best seats last week. It's better than it looks, believe me.'

'It looks wonderful.' Nehmann was thinking of the brief days and freezing nights on the long-ago journey east. 'Where are we off to?'

'Moscow, my friend.' He lit the cigarette. 'As long as the gods are with us.'

A brusque wave of a gloved hand from the figure beside the bags summoned the two men to the aircraft. Nehmann stepped out of the car, unprepared for the icy blast of the wind. Mystery hands at the hotel had supplied him with a pair of trousers, a shirt and a heavyish jacket, as well as thick socks and a pair of decent leather boots. The trousers were worn, and a little on the thin side. He'd found a handful of kopeks in one pocket, and he could definitely have done with a proper coat, but he marvelled at how quickly he'd lost his resistance to the cold. Two years in Kolyma should have turned him into a polar bear. Wrong.

The giant with the beard turned out to be the pilot. The plane, thick with the harsh tang of *makhorka* tobacco, bumped over the turf towards a line of stones that appeared to be the perimeter fence. The bags left outside were now piled in the aisle between the rows of seats. A handful of passengers were standing up at the back of the aircraft, but if you were lucky enough to have a seat, the bags were shoulder-high.

Nehmann was sitting beside the window, and as the pilot bounced the aircraft into the sky, the engines howling, he watched the snowclad taiga slowly recede. The pilot levelled off early, flying low beneath the grey corrugations of cloud, following the line of a river. Even here, barely minutes away from Magadan, there was no sign of human habitation, and for a while Nehmann did nothing but stare blankly down as the aircraft bucked in the rough air and the bareness of the landscape unfurled. The engine, with its blur of propeller, looked close enough to touch. The wing behind the engine was streaked with oil, and Nehmann's eye tracked the lines of tiny rivets that held everything together. The cackle and roar of the engines swamped everything else except the growing realisation that this was for real, that the prospect of Moscow was more than a fantasy, and that his days of sieving gold from exhaustion might truly be over. In the end, numbed by the noise and the hot fug of the cabin, he went to sleep.

*

'Magalashvili?'

A face swam into focus. Nehmann tried to rub his eyes, but nothing happened. His muscles were glue. He had a bad taste in his mouth. He was desperate to talk, to explain himself, but the gap between the wanting and the words was simply too wide.

His name again, prefaced this time with Mikhail. It came with a leer that softened slowly into a smile. Goebbels, he thought. The blackness in his eyes. The gauntness in his face. And just a hint of concern in that thin smile. Had Hitler's dwarf, the High Priest of the Big Lie, the club-footed cripple on the Wilhelmstrasse, somehow ghosted onto the flight? Had the *Reichsminister*, in some rich conspiracy, grown impatient with his own lies – too small, too obvious, not *bold* enough – and despatched himself to the freezing Gulag to scrabble around on his hands and knees for copper, or tungsten, or those tiny flecks of gold that could madden the sanest man? Had Berlin finally seen the end of him? Had Goebbels, like millions of other *zeks*, become camp dust?

'You want soda?'

A different voice. Nehmann at last managed to open his eyes. He could feel the bulk and warmth of Leon's body beside his. The Russian was nodding at a huge woman who'd emerged from the cockpit. From a burlap sack she was producing glass bottles of something pink and fizzy and tossing them down the aircraft towards a forest of raised hands. Leon managed to catch one and handed it on. Nehmann was grateful but what he really wanted was something to eat. They were only three rows of seats away from the cockpit. He struggled to his feet, managed a painful half-crouch in the swaying aircraft, caught the woman's eye, asked for bread, *kasha*, anything to silence his empty belly.

'Sit.' It was Leon again. Nehmann did his bidding, mumbled an apology. Maybe not *kasha*. Maybe just bread.

Leon laughed, then a hand from behind appeared in the space between the two seats, and Nehmann knew at once that this was another of the NKVD man's little conjuring tricks. First, the miracle of his deliverance from the camp. Now, a black bread sandwich, something fishy, half a raw onion, even a hard-boiled egg.

'For me?' Nehmann had already grabbed the food.

'For you.'

'And...?' Nehmann tried to twist in the seat, to strain upwards, take a look at the face behind him, but the effort was too much.

'Eat,' Leon murmured. 'We need to deliver a happy man.'

'We?' It had dawned on Nehmann that this little miracle was anything but.

'We,' Leon agreed. 'The Revolution was never perfect, but we always make plans.'

Nehmann gave up. One escort left in the ZiL at the airfield, he thought. Another waiting for him on the aircraft, pre-positioned, fully provisioned, awaiting his cue. Leon reached for the bottle and popped the stopper. First the fizz of escaping bubbles, then a light, pinkish froth. Leon licked his fingers, exactly the way everyone else around them was doing, took a mouthful or two, and then handed it across.

'You want a sandwich?' Nehmann asked.

Leon shook his head. No need. The hand again, this time with an apple and a chunk of cheese. Nehmann stared at them. He'd seen neither for two years, not a single piece of fruit unless you counted the berries they scavenged from the taiga, and certainly not cheese.

'The apple's for you?' Nehman couldn't resist asking.

'Yes.' Leon was amused. 'You want to taste it?'

'I want to touch it.'

'Why?'

'To make sure it's real.'

The food made Nehmann sleepy again. He could feel it filling the space beneath his ribcage. I'm a balloon, he thought. Stick a knife in me, and the whole plane, the whole world, will stink of fish and onions. He smiled at the image, remembering the face in his dreams, the bloated lies he'd pushed across Goebbels' desk, those brief months of glory he'd enjoyed in the warm Berlin sunshine, the Minister's mischievous little imp, Goebbels' treasure, the freedoms he'd enjoyed, the liberties he'd taken, the fictions he'd invented, the show-off stories in the *Völkischer Beobachter*, his monthly column in *Das Reich*, and then those darker weeks and months when no lie on earth could save him from the cripple's wrath.

'Interested?'

It was Leon again. He'd found a tattered book pushed down the side of his seat. Nehmann swallowed the last of the soda, wiped his mouth with the back of his hand and then licked it dry before peering at the title. A handful of stories? By Lev Tolstoy? He half closed his eyes, shaking his head, mumbling – yet again – his thanks.

Of all the deprivations he'd suffered in the camps, all those needling moments when his sheer helplessness had so nearly got the better of him, none had hurt him more than the absence of books, of stories, of the right words in the right order, of the comfort of knowing that he was in the hands of a stranger, and that some form of closure, or perhaps redemption, awaited on the final page. Books had always offered Nehmann solace but the people who ran the camps must have known that because the written word was scarcer than hope itself. Having a book, especially the wrong kind, could put you in some snowdrift with a bullet in the back of your neck. Best, therefore, to try and forget the doors in your head that only certain kinds of books could open.

He dropped the crumpled food bag between his feet, picked the crumbs from his lap and settled back, his shoulder against the quivering window, the pale wash of light falling on the faded red of the book's cover. A minute or so with the view had already told him that nothing had changed – more snow, another dark carpet of pine forest, a slightly wider river – and so he opened the book, flicking through the well-thumbed pages until he found a story that seemed familiar.

The Kreutzer Sonata? He half closed his eyes. The little school at home in the mountains of Svaneti, he thought, and a draughty classroom full of near-feral adolescents with absolutely no interest in books. Half of them, he suspected, didn't know how to read, while the rest, fearful of the Orthodox priest in charge of the class, did their best to feign interest. He smiled, plunging into the first long paragraph, hopscotching from word to word, picking up speed after a long absence from the printed page, knowing already that he was right.

This was the story about the priggish civil servant with the handsome, wayward wife. He sires five children but for his wife the joyless mechanics of mere conception is never enough. And so she surrenders herself to a lover, a handsome violinist with a taste for well-cut suits with diamond studs, and takes advantage of her husband's absence to make music with her new beau. The end of the affair is predictably melodramatic but alone in the class, only Mikhail could surrender to a yarn like this and embellish it with countless details, most of them near-pornographic, dredged from the shallows of his fevered imagination.

To his regret, Mikhail Magalashvili took the priest's invitation to pen an essay on the real meaning of Tolstoy's story at face value and was thoroughly thrashed for his efforts. The beating hurt like hell but afterwards he understood the real significance of this episode: that the right words, in the right hands, could enrage as well as enthral, and that a gift for putting this stuff on the page could take you anywhere. Assuming, of course, that you held your nerve.

*

By the time the pilot began to throttle back and lose height, it was nearly dark. Nehmann had nodded off again but a cough from one of the engines brought him upright in the seat. Checking out of the window, he saw a huge expanse of water, almost black in the last of the light.

'Lake Baikal.' Leon was looking, too. 'Here we stay the night.'

The landing was a repeat performance of the take-off, the pilot bullying the big aircraft onto the lumpy turf the way you might school an unruly dog. The plane finally stable, he taxied towards a cluster of tents. Beside one of the tents were three horses. They looked, thought Nehmann, like the animals he'd seen in Kolyma and in the early months at Stalingrad before most of them were eaten: thin, listless, their heads down, their breath clouding from time to time in the freezing air. The aircraft came to a halt and the pilot cut the engines. In the sudden silence, Nehmann could hear nothing but a high-pitched whine. Then he felt a light pressure on his arm.

'A word, *tovarish*.' It was Leon. 'We sleep here the night. Now we can get out, walk a little, do whatever we must, take a breath or two. It's possible to sleep in one of those tents, or here in the plane where it's warmer. Our friend behind us will be taking care of you. Maybe when we go outside, he uses his handcuffs. Maybe not. Your choice, Mikhail Magalashvili.'

'Not.' Even after two years in the camps, Nehmann had a horror of pissing or shitting in public.

'Then we have to trust you, *tovarish*, but a word before we set you free. Never try to escape, and you know why? Because first we'll chase you, wing you with a shot or two, enough to bring you down. Then we'll bring you back inside, and bandage the wound, and warm you up with a little tea, and all that will happen before we take you outside again and have you re-shot. Properly.' A thin smile. 'We understand each other?'

Nehmann felt himself nodding. He'd been around more than enough people in his life to understand that this man wasn't joking. Beneath the bonhomie, and his easy saunter through remembered European cities, he was carved from the same unyielding timber as every other NKVD officer. More importantly, something Nehmann recognised at once, he had an intelligence and command of language that made him truly dangerous. 'Re-shot' was masterly. 'Properly' evoked a multitude of nightmares. Nehmann had no intention of making it this far, only to bolt towards the fantasy comforts of the nearest treeline.

'I'm in your hands,' he said, holding Leon's gaze. 'You have my word on that.'

*

They took off again at dawn. Nehmann had slept fitfully, wedged against the window as the intense cold of the smallest hours stole through the packed fuselage, half listening to the mumbles and snuffling of the bodies around him. A soldier in uniform in the seat in front had cried out in his sleep, begging for his mother and waking up the civilian beside him. An apology had done nothing for his neighbour, and in the scuffle that followed a knife had evidently been pulled. The NKVD guard who had the food in the seat behind clambered over the mountain of bags to restore order and Nehmann had watched as he punched the young soldier unconscious, returning to his own seat with blood on his knuckles. Leon appeared to have slept through this entire episode, though Nehmann had his doubts. You didn't get to the rank of Colonel in the NKVD, he told himself, without an awareness of when to let good order take care of itself.

Another half-day in the air took them to a biggish city which Leon announced as Krasnoyarsk. Here, he said, the battle for knee room and some place to hide from the incessant roar of the engines would finally come to an end. A vehicle would be waiting for them. The train left in the early evening. Five more days, maybe six, and they should be in Moscow.

An American Jeep, brand new under a thick pelt of viscous mud, took them to the railway station. Nehmann gazed up at the tall, domed entrance. The war had evidently never penetrated this far into Soviet Russia and the yellow wash on the plastered walls above the big, grey pillars looked untouched.

'They built it back in the last century.' Leon had anticipated his question. 'The past is a place where no one dares trespass, not any more, but sometimes you get to wonder. Handsome, is it not?'

Nehmann was still staring at the big Cyrillic capitals that announced the station's name. This was where the cattle trucks from Moscow dumped us, he thought. This is where we stumbled into the cold and spent countless more days in the back of an open truck. Look for the Gulag's front door, and here it is.

Leon was waiting for him on the pavement. Nehmann got out of the Jeep and all three of them climbed the steps to the station's main entrance. It was bitterly cold in the wind and Nehmann was glad of the enveloping warmth once they were inside the enormous concourse. Marble floors. A scatter of passengers. Everything spotlessly neat. Nehmann was staring at the wooden destination board. The first of the evening's two trains left for Moscow in an hour and a half.

'Come.'

Leon, it seemed, knew the station well. On the first floor, in a kind of galleria, Nehmann found himself settling at a table laid for two. The NKVD guard from the plane had already left on some errand or other. There were no menus, but an underdressed waiter was already arriving with two glasses of beer and a bottle of what looked like vodka. The food, he said, would be coming soon.

'*Prosit, ja?*' Leon reached for one of the beers. Nehmann did the same. It was the first time he'd drunk proper alcohol in more than two years. Not the punishing hooch they brewed from stolen peas and rotting potatoes in the Gulag, but alcohol from a bottle, well-behaved, dependable, a drink that wouldn't rot your stomach or turn you blind. Nehmann took a cautious mouthful, then another. Leon, watching, raised an eyebrow.

'You drank *chifir*?'

'Everyone drank *chifir*. The best stuff gives you the weirdest dreams. The place was surreal already. You didn't need *chifir* to tell you that.'

Chifir was brewed from loose-leaf black tea. On the coldest nights, from a batch you trusted, it could be a blessing.

'So a little of this, perhaps?' Leon was already uncapping the vodka. The waiter had left two shot glasses. The biggest of the measures Leon pushed across the table.

'So what shall we call you?' he asked.

'We?'

'Me.'

'Nehmann. Werner Nehmann. Magalashvili was a long time ago. I left him behind in Georgia, along with all the other nonsense.'

'Such as?'

'A father who wanted to nail me to the floor. A mother he never talked to. Grown men killing each other in family feuds. A world that stopped at the bus station.'

'So what did you do?'

'I got on the bus and went as far as my money would take me. What choice did I have? Home was a bloodbath, especially in the winter. And if we got bored with killing each other, there was always another enemy at the gate.'

'You mean us?'

'Of course. You can't pull a knife on an entire army – even Georgians aren't that foolish – but I knew some men who tried...' Nehmann reached for the shot glass. '... *prosit*. Long life and no more trespassing.'

'On?'

'The past. Yours...' Nehmann shrugged, '... and mine, too. What do you really want to know?'

Leon studied him a moment, saying nothing, then swallowed the vodka in a single gulp. Nehmann did the same, closing his eyes and enjoying the burn of the clear spirit as it scorched down his throat and coiled into his belly. He was aware of a slight moistness, a tiny loss of focus, when he opened his eyes again, but his hand was already reaching for the chill of the beer.

'Well?' Nehmann took a long pull from the glass. 'How often does the war give you privacy like this?'

'More often than you might imagine.' Leon was refilling the shot glasses. 'You worked for Goebbels, am I right?'

'You are. Is that what this is about? My ex-boss? The guardian angel who read the death tallies from Stalingrad and put me on the next plane east? The fucking Reich's favourite undertaker?'

'Do I hear anger?' Leon might have been talking to some third person at the table. 'Maybe we should be expecting that.'

'Maybe you should.' Nehmann was staring at him. He wanted more beer, more vodka, more of everything. 'I understand the system, *tovarish*. I understand cause and effect. I understand the malice, the sheer fucking evil, that took me to Stalingrad, and then to some godawful camp in the mountains, and then the gold mines, which were even worse, and because we speak the same language, you and me, I can even give that evil a name.'

'Goebbels?' Leon, when he chose, had the lightest touch.

'Of course. But it's complicated, isn't it? I bent the truth for that man because that's what he wanted. I did it willingly and I did it well, better than anyone else he'd ever met. This is him talking, not me, and for once I haven't made it up.'

'But did he?'

'Did he what?'

'Make it up?'

'Ah…' Nehmann sat back, reaching for the shot glass, nursing it in his cupped hands, his little pebble of fire. He gazed at Leon for a moment, surprised and slightly aghast at his own passion, his own vehemence, his own – yes – anger. It should have taken a great deal more than a shot of vodka and a glass of beer to unbutton him like this, and yet it had happened. Maybe Leon had sensed the poison boiling inside him, two whole years of fermenting resentment, and tapped into it. Simple, really.

'So?' Leon was still waiting for an answer. 'What did Goebbels really think? Of you? Of those talents of yours?'

'He thought I was a genius. His word. Not mine.'

'Because?'

'Because I got people's attention and kept it. Because I could make them laugh. Because I took risks. Because I was much, much bolder than any other journalist on the street. And because I could make these people *believe*.'

'In what?'

'In the cause. In all the Nazi shit. Does that make me an accomplice? Of course it does. Did I believe any of it? Never. Did it bring me a nice apartment, and a cellar full of French champagne, and a vision who played in a nightclub in Moabit and had the good sense to fall in love with me? Yes, and yes, and yes again. And did any of that matter? As long as the tanks moved forward and we were killing the right people? Of course it didn't.'

'And now?'

'Now is different. Now is now. Give me a wheelbarrow and a powerful reason for staying alive and a bowl or two of *kasha* in my belly, and I can meet any quota you care to name. That's because we Georgians are survivors. We come from the toughest stock, *tovarish*. We're bred to make it through. And we also have luck on our side. Not fate. Not the Thousand-Year-fucking-Reich. Not the Revolution of the Proletariat. Luck. That's all you can rely on. Life's a gamble. You throw the dice and try very hard not to think about the odds. At Stalingrad, I worked with a man called Schultz. He was German. He caught spies for a living and he never let me down, not once. Willi Schultz. The only man in that tomb of a city who could lay hands on a fresh chicken and a bottle of this stuff when the guys in the forward shell holes had started eating the dead. I loved that man. He's probably dead himself now but if there's a fresh chicken in hell, he'll find it.' Nehmann paused while his hand curled tighter round the shot glass. Then he tipped his head backwards and emptied the vodka down his throat without bothering with the courtesy of a toast.

'So what about you, Leon. What do you make of all this?'

'All what?'

'This.' Nehmann's gesture took in the entire station. He was drunk now but he didn't care. 'The war. Where we all end up. How we cope. The war. Your war. Your peace, for that matter. Killing people. Millions of people. Shooting them. Beating them to death. Starving them. Tell me about that.'

'All wars are voracious,' Leon said mildly. 'Without victims, they die.'

'Very pretty. My guardian angel would love that. Warrior or philosopher? You have to make a choice.'

Leon declined the offer with a regretful shrug. When he wanted to know more about Goebbels, about what Nehmann had done for him, and specifically about what kind of relationship might still be left, Nehmann shook his head.

'No,' he said, reaching for the bottle of vodka.

'No? You're serious?'

'I am. I'll tell you anything, but only when you tell me what happens next.'

'Here?'

'In Moscow. I want to know why you came looking for me. Why you put me on that aircraft. Why I'm not at the fucking gold mine, doing my bit for the Revolution. That's all I ask, *tovarish*. What *use* am I to you? It's the simplest of questions.'

Leon nodded. He seemed to understand. At length he refilled his own glass and leaned forward across the table. It was a gesture, Nehmann thought, laden with promise. It meant that this man was taking him seriously. In a world where nothing was quite what it seemed, it hinted at complicity.

'*Krysha*,' Leon murmured, 'is the Russian for "roof". You'll know that already, and what you'll also know – in Moscow, in Russia as a whole, and especially in the Gulag – is that *krysha* also means "protection". Without *krysha* you can probably count your days on the fingers of one hand. I, Mikhail Magalashvili, I am your *krysha*.'

Nehmann nodded. Said he understood. One more question. Then he'd shut up and behave himself and get peaceably drunk.

'Of course.' Leon made a tiny placatory gesture with his hand. 'Go ahead.'

'What happens in Moscow?' he asked again. 'Assuming we ever get there?'

Leon gave the question some thought. The restaurant had begun to fill but the adjacent tables were still empty. He was still leaning forward over the table but now he gestured Nehmann even closer.

'A word about the *Vozhd* might be helpful,' he said.

'Really?' Nehmann blinked. The *Vozhd* was the Great Leader, the Chosen One. 'What are you telling me here? What does Stalin have to do with any of this?'

'That I can't tell you. Not because I don't want to but because I don't know. Stalin is someone you'll recognise. Stalin is a gangster. Stalin is a tireless, dull, lost-for-words Georgian bandit. He trusts his dog, *tovarish*, and for whatever reason he trusts me. Which is why we're sitting here together.'

'So you can do what?'

'Take the measure of you. Work out when you're lying and when you're not. And then, when the time is right, it may be my pleasure to drive you out to the Kuntsevo dacha and deliver you in one piece.'

'To who?' Nehmann frowned. 'Whom?'

'The *Vozhd*, of course.' Leon refilled Nehmann's glass, then sat back, clinked glasses, and offered a toast. '*Udachi*.' Nehmann judged the smile to be genuine. 'Good luck.'

4

Moncrieff insisted on accompanying Ursula Barton to what remained of the Farringdon Market. Nearly twenty-four hours had passed since the rocket had blown the building apart. The V-2 carried a warhead containing nearly a ton of an explosive called amatol 60/40. The rocket was supersonic and none of the hundreds of shoppers, tradesmen, and passers-by would have heard it coming. The rocket was unguided. It could have fallen anywhere. That it exploded in the middle of a weekday, at the moment when the market was at its busiest, was – in the words of a local pastor – beyond human comprehension. Moncrieff had long ago abandoned the last shreds of his belief in a God, benign or otherwise, but he knew that Barton, raised a Catholic, still attended services in her local church.

The market was now a mountain of charred timber, much of it still smoking. Uniformed constables ringed the site to keep the public at bay, while searchers – many of them soldiers from a nearby barracks – dug among the ruins in a desperate search for survivors. According to the Major in charge of the troops, the vast majority of traders had been accounted for, either dead or tallied as casualties.

By now, the death toll was in three figures. An underground railway line ran below the market in a shallow cutting, and the sheer force of the explosion had collapsed the floor of the building into the void below. Many of the dead, having survived the blast, had tumbled onto the line and perished from impact injuries or electrocution. Rescue crews had worked through the night evacuating the wounded and tidying the remains of the dead onto stretchers. Three bodies, all of them shrouded in blankets, still awaited collection.

Barton wanted a list of the dead, the missing and confirmed survivors. At first the Major shook his head but she took him aside from the crowd of onlookers and Moncrieff watched as she explained herself. After five years of war, he thought, London was no stranger to scenes like this. People had got used to the sweet stench of ruptured sewers, to uniforms dusted with falling ash, to faces blank with exhaustion and shock, and to the shrill pipe of the search leader's whistle demanding silence as his men bent to the rubble, listening intently for any sign of life. These glum dramas had unfolded year by year, street by ruined street, but Moncrieff sensed something else this morning that hadn't been evident before. People knew that the war was coming to an end. And that made the sudden violence, and the countless bodies, even harder to bear. By now, Londoners should feel safe in their own homes, yet the carnage went on and on. Worse still, thanks to the dark arts of German rocket science, there appeared to be nowhere to hide.

Moncrieff's gaze strayed to the shrouded bodies on the stretchers. Beside them was a line of bird cages, most of them damaged in one way or another, and when he took a proper look he realised that each cage contained the body of a canary, stone dead among a scatter of bird seed. They must have come off a speciality market stall, he thought. Maybe there were more pets under all that rubble, hamsters, and rabbits, and a tortoise or two, all of them felled by the blast of the explosion, but there was something very English about the neatness of the line, about the care and effort that somebody must have taken to retrieve these broken little bodies. It spoke of a thousand sitting rooms, all of them brightened by the chatter of a little bird. It spoke, in a way, of the nearness of peace.

Barton was consulting some kind of list in a notebook the Major had produced. Her finger strayed from page to page until suddenly it stopped, and she looked up, and nodded, and turned away to rejoin Moncrieff at the kerbside.

'He survived,' she said briskly. 'Whitechapel Hospital.'

*

The hospital was nearly as chaotic as the scene they'd just left, staff and relatives milling about in the cluttered space that served as a reception area. At first the woman behind the desk refused to admit them but once again Barton found the right official at the right level, played her MI5 card, and gained entry. A harassed nurse took them to a small, cheerless room at the end of a corridor at the back of the building. A bunch of early daffodils in a jam jar had begun to wilt in the heat from the big cast-iron radiator, while a poster on the wall warned them about listening ears. Under the circumstances, given MI5's duty to keep the nation safe, this might have raised a muttered comment and maybe even a smile, but Barton seemed oblivious.

At Moncrieff's insistence, she took the plumper of the two armchairs, crossing her legs, nursing her battered handbag, and staring into nowhere.

'Is he badly injured?' Moncrieff enquired after a while.

'I've no idea. That's why we're here.'

The comment didn't invite further conversation. Moncrieff studied her a moment, the pursed lips, the tiny nerve-flutter beneath her left eye, the pallor from a life spent largely indoors, then shrugged. Like everyone else at St James's Street, Barton was familiar with this kind of violence both first hand, especially during the Blitz, and almost daily in the flood of interview transcripts that came across her desk. Refugees claiming to have fled countless Nazi atrocities. Whole families, often Jewish, betrayed by watching neighbours. Alleged survivors from the Gestapo torture suites. It was one of MI5's jobs to sieve through the wreckage of the war in Europe in the search for duds and phonies, and some of the finer print, whether invented or real, was frankly shocking in its barbarity. Was this why Ursula Barton had so suddenly turned her face to the wall? Or was there something Moncrieff had missed?

'How well do you know this man?' he asked.

'Not at all well. Which, I suspect, is rather the point.'

'So...?' Moncrieff still didn't get it.

'You're right. My Mr Witherby is a stranger. He sells me pies. He has the nicest smile. He seems to treat everyone like a member of his family, and he never cheats on the change. You might think it's not much to ask but from where I'm sitting, he's beginning to feel the exception to the rule.'

'Which is?'

'Every man for himself. And every woman, too. Dog eats dog these days. War is supposed to bring out the best in us. I'm no longer sure that's true.'

Moncrieff nodded. Part of him knew exactly what she meant. Wherever he looked, whenever he listened to passing conversations, he sensed a growing selfishness, which was odd. The better the news from the front, the less kind and less patient people seemed to be to each other. In both friends and strangers, he'd noticed a grim determination that when the war was finally over, there'd be no going back to the old ways. Deference and good manners could take a society just so far but after this amount of blood had been spilled, there had to be a very different settlement.

'You think we're doomed?' he said lightly.

Barton seemed to flinch at the crassness of the question. Then a hint of a frown clouded her face before she turned for the first time to look Moncrieff in the eye.

'I think we're in deep trouble,' she said. 'Especially in our line of work. It's nothing we haven't discussed before, but soon it might truly matter.'

Moncrieff nodded. This wasn't about Mr Witherby and his pies at all. This was about the latest quarrel between rival intelligence agencies, about the oceans of bad blood that had lapped against the battlements of St James's Street and Broadway.

Barton wanted to know whether Moncrieff had phoned the number on the single sheet of intelligence about the Bern episode that had arrived from MI6.

'I did. Of course I did. I told you last night. After we discussed Willi Schultz.'

'And?' The frown had deepened. 'Remind me.'

'The number took me to some apparatchik. She was worse than useless. She said the intelligence had come in from the Americans. She had no idea of its value or its exact provenance. She'd simply been asked to pass it on in the usual spirit, and that's exactly what she'd done.'

'Usual spirit?'

'I gather that was Broadway shorthand for co-operation. We might see it differently. Bluff would be a kindness.' Moncrieff was frowning now. 'Obfuscation, making life tough, would be closer.'

'You think they're trying to throw us off the scent?'

'I think they're telling us to stick to our knitting. If a scent exists, it's none of our business. What is or isn't happening in

Bern is very definitely happening abroad. Abroad belongs to them, always has done. It's turf, territory. That's what these people are really about.'

Barton held his gaze for a moment, then nodded and stared down at her hands. Last night, once she'd shifted the weight of the day's paperwork, Moncrieff had spent nearly an hour trying to press her about Willi Schultz. Winston Churchill, he'd pointed out, appeared to believe her when she said that Schultz was alive and still in post in Germany. He seemed keen for Moncrieff to make an enquiry or two, track the man down, have a conversation. This he was willing to do, not least because Churchill was his Prime Minister, but he had to know a great deal more about the old *Abwehr* bruiser. What was the strength of the intelligence? Where had Barton got it from? How did she *know* Schultz was back in play?

Last night, Barton had mentioned Birger Dahlerus, a Swedish businessman who'd once acted as a conduit between *Generalfeldmarschall* Hermann Goering and the British government. Goering's bid to open separate peace negotiations before the war erupted with Hitler's whirlwind descent on France had come to nothing, but it seemed – years later – that this backchannel through Stockholm was live again with an approach from Willi Schultz. Before he'd left the office last night, Moncrieff had pressed for more details, but Barton had shaken her head. She planned to put another call through to Dahlerus. Then a sensible way forward might become a little clearer.

Now, Moncrieff wanted to know whether she'd managed a second conversation.

'I did, yes.'

'And?'

'He was evasive. Not at all the old Birger. To be frank, I think he's gone lukewarm on us, and to be even franker, I think

I know why. Our friends in Broadway have been whispering in his ear. And he, poor soul, has been foolish enough to listen.'

'He told you nothing? About Schultz?'

'Only to confirm that they might be having conversations.'

'Might be?'

'Yes.'

'About?'

'He wouldn't say. I mentioned Bern twice and the fact that he wouldn't comment, I take as a yes.'

'Meaning Schultz is involved in the Bern business?'

'Up to his neck, says little me. Do I have proof? No. Would we be remiss not to find out? Yes. And do you, Tam Moncrieff, represent our best chance of doing just that? I'm afraid the answer, once again, is yes.'

Moncrieff leaned forward, wanting to know more about this proposition, but there came the lightest knock on the door before he looked up to find a young man in a white coat gazing down at them both.

'My name's Carter,' he said. 'I'm one of a team of doctors looking after the people from the market. You're interested in...?'

'His name's Witherby,' Barton said at once.

'And you are?'

'A friend. Or maybe an admirer. His first name's Stanley, if that helps.'

The doctor nodded. He'd met Stan Witherby's wife only an hour ago.

'And?'

'I'm afraid he's not at all well. Multiple contusions, broken ribs, damage to his pelvis, and that's not the half of it. We'll get him through one way or another but it's going to take a while.'

'Is he allowed visitors, by any chance?'

'I'm afraid not. The surgeons took his legs off first thing this morning. He's still very poorly.'

Moncrieff was looking at Barton. The news that he'd spend the rest of his life a cripple took a moment or two to sink in. Then, with a visible effort, she got to her feet and smoothed the pleats on her skirt and offered the young doctor the brightest of smiles.

'I imagine he's a lucky chap to be alive,' she said. 'Thank you for looking after him.'

They shared a taxi back to St James's Street. A burst water main had sent the traffic on a long detour through Clerkenwell and when it became obvious that their route was going to take them back past the ruins of Farringdon Market, Barton leaned forward and told the driver to take another diversion left.

'Cost yer, ma'am.' The cabbie gestured at the meter.

'It has already,' Barton snapped. 'Just do as I ask.'

Back in the office, she was suddenly brisk. Moncrieff lingered briefly by the open door, awaiting what he fondly imagined might be orders, but when he asked whether he needed to pack a bag and prepare himself for some kind of expedition, she shook her head.

'We need to know a great deal more,' she said. 'Your friend Ivor phoned first thing. I suggested a late lunch at the hotel.' She glanced at her watch. 'He should be there by now. By all means send me the bill.'

*

St Ermin's Hotel had been a hive of spies for most of the war. MI6 had established an early presence on one of the top floors, while SOE – Churchill's cherished Special Operations Executive – pitched their tents a floor or two lower. The restaurant became an unofficial and wildly overpriced canteen for men who traded in secrets, and every year the maître d' took a quiet pride in acquiring the first August grouse before any other hotel in London.

Moncrieff found Ivor Maskelyne on a barstool next door. He was a big, untidy man with a fierce, restless intelligence who taught classics at Oxford and was frequently the guest of choice on high tables across the university when votes were cast for provocative company.

Moncrieff had first met Maskelyne when he was keeping wicket for the team Kim Philby fielded at Glenalmond, the St Albans outpost of MI6's Section Five, and they'd shared a companionable ride back to London in Maskelyne's Alvis. More recently, a real friendship had developed after Moncrieff's arrival at Balliol College. Mastering Russian in just nine months was never going to be easy, but Maskelyne's company in the back bar of a dowdy pub called the Antelope had turned a challenge into a delight.

'Ivor.' Moncrieff extended a hand. 'How are you?'

'Same as ever.' Maskelyne reached up for Moncrieff's shoulder and gave it a squeeze. 'Nothing changes, I'm afraid. Once upon a time I thought this bloody war might turn us all into heroes. It's good to be wrong sometimes, but not always. What Oxford needs is a bit of youth, a golden splash or two of innocence, something truly callow in the way of ignorance. But we're all too fucking old, and all too fucking *clever.*'

'You came up specially?'

'I came up because that delightful woman of yours suggested it would be in your interest. Might a silky Margaux be in order? She's tasked me with buying at least one bottle, but I think she meant two. To be honest, I'd no idea that state funds could stretch so far. What does the Treasury know that we don't?'

Maskelyne called for the sommelier from the restaurant and ordered the wine. Moncrieff settled on a glass of dry sherry to warm proceedings before they ate. The bar was beginning to fill, and already Moncrieff recognised a number of faces, most of them florid and blotchy but no less watchful after five busy years behind MI6 desks. As the sherry arrived, Moncrieff beckoned his guest closer.

'Was this hotel your choice?' he asked.

'Hers. I suspect is we're here to be seen. I know it's far from subtle, but La Barton knows us Broadway types prefer it that way. Your good self lunching with the enemy in plain sight? A bold move, if I may say so.'

'They've extended your contract?'

'My guess is they've forgotten to cancel it. Either that or the bloody thing never existed in the first place. Rule one in Broadway? Never write anything down. The Germans live and die for paperwork. We make everything up as we go along and leave no trace behind. This at least has the merit of spontaneity. Catch the enemy on the hop. Attack him when and where he least expects it. *On s'engage. Et puis on voit.* Sound advice in the right hands but, alas, there are no Napoleons at Broadway.' He smiled. 'Are we getting the picture here?'

Moncrieff nodded. MI6 had developed a habit of inviting top academics into the world of intelligence gathering, and Maskelyne was part of this spillage from Oxbridge high tables. At first, Moncrieff had wondered what he brought to the Broadway feast apart from a raging thirst and an acid wit, but his months at Balliol had taught him a great deal about the man's integrity, as well as his intellectual courage, and he could imagine circumstances when the wiser souls at MI6 might listen to his advice and act accordingly. Maskelyne had always argued that both intelligence services wasted a great deal of the nation's time and effort exploring cul-de-sacs that led nowhere and, after six years with a front-row seat at this circus, Moncrieff could only agree. Which left one key word on the table.

'Bern?' Moncrieff enquired.

They'd moved from the bar into the restaurant. Maskelyne had insisted on a table at the back of the room where they could rely on a degree of privacy.

'Bern, my friend, is a mess. You'll know already that the OSS are bossing this. Broadway fancy they have the measure of the Americans, but nothing could be further from the truth. It's not just Bern, incidentally, it's Zurich, too. Allen Dulles runs the OSS operation out of Bern but keeps a special apartment in Zurich, and that's where episodes of special interest tend to happen. Because Dulles, of course, calls the shots.'

'Karl Wolff?'

'Interesting character. Came to the Party at a sensible time. Had the good sense to get alongside Himmler, who knew talent when he saw it. There's a lovely shot of a little group at the Berghof in May 1939. The photograph is in colour, which is a treat, and Himmler is there and so is Heydrich, but Wolff is definitely the grown-up on the terrace. He has no interest in the camera. On the contrary, he's looking very hard at a document in Heydrich's hands. Plotting comes with the territory at that level, but this is definitely a man with a sense of *destination*.'

As Moncrieff knew, Reinhard Heydrich was another of Himmler's protégés. Despatched to Prague to sort out the unruly Czechs, he'd been ambushed and badly wounded by partisans. Days later, he'd died, and word of the savage reprisals exacted by the SS had reached every corner of the British intelligence community. By then, as the appointed liaison officer between SS headquarters and the Reich Chancellery, Wolff had become Himmler's eyes and ears in the upper reaches of the regime.

This, according to Maskelyne, was a position with immense potential but the passing of Heydrich had triggered a power struggle at the very top of Himmler's sprawling empire, and Wolff had found himself facing serious opposition.

'Like?'

'Walter Schellenberg for one. Wolff had a dalliance with the Jew programme a couple of years back. He was in Poland at the time and he despatched hordes of the Chosen People east after cleaning out the Warsaw ghetto. This comes back to paperwork, *mon brave*. Wolff made the trains run on time. He'll have issued diktats, kept records, maybe even written a letter or two of thanks afterwards. We still have no proper confirmation of what happened to these people but I'd hazard a guess that they're never coming back. Schellenberg knew that. Schellenberg knew everything. Which puts Wolff in a somewhat sticky position.'

Moncrieff nodded. Walter Schellenberg was a spy catcher of genius who liked nothing more than laying traps for both his enemies and his friends. In the early months of the war he'd lured two British agents, both of them working for Broadway, to a meeting on the Dutch border. Kidnapped at gunpoint and hauled back to the Fatherland, they'd blown network after network across countless European cities, prompting Ursula Barton's resignation from the embassy in The Hague, and subsequent appearance at MI5 headquarters in St James's Street. Schellenberg's giddy rise through the ranks of Himmler's *Sicherheitsdienst* had followed, and now he controlled the intelligence arm of the SS. Willi Schultz, who worked for the rival *Abwehr*, loathed him.

'So what happened to Wolff?' Moncrieff reached for a bread roll.

'It seems he had a run of bad luck. First his health gave out, waterworks problems, kidney stones, then he was foolish enough to get divorced and marry his mistress, which didn't please Himmler at all. By last summer, he'd been banished to Italy where he passed his days sorting out the partisans. By all accounts he did a good job. He holds the rank of General, which puts him in charge of the *Waffen-SS* down there. After Kesselring, he's the top man on the Italian front. He has credibility, no one questions that, and he also has motive, which in the current context might be more interesting.'

Moncrieff smiled. In Wolff's shoes, anyone with an interest in their own survival would be worried. The war was undoubtedly coming to an end. Not even Hitler could prevent that. And in the aftermath, assuming you got through the final spasms of violence on the battlefield, there would be some kind of reckoning. For months, reports of death camps in the east had been filtering back to listening ears in St James's Street. The sheer numbers of alleged victims defied belief, and with the war over, there would be awkward questions for would-be accomplices in a crime like this to answer.

'You think Wolff's after some kind of deal?'

'Everyone's after some kind of deal. But that's hardly the point. Does Wolff have the authority to negotiate a surrender in Italy? With Kesselring's blessing, yes he probably does. Are there elements in Berlin that might scent the potential for mischief in whatever happens next? Again, yes.'

'Mischief?'

'Our friend in Moscow trusts no one, least of all his erstwhile allies. He took a good look at us at Yalta and drew his own conclusions. He thinks Churchill is a thief and a drunkard and talks far too much. He's pretty sure Roosevelt is dying. He's also stuffed most of Eastern Europe down his trousers and is now eyeing Berlin. It's there for the taking but it will cost him yet more blood. This, believe it or not, upsets him. And what would upset him more would be word that the Allies, in other words us, intend to make some kind of separate peace, slope arms and retire from the field of battle, thus releasing umpteen Nazi armies to kill yet more Russians. That, for Uncle Joe, would be...' he was eyeing the newly arrived bottle of Margaux, '... less than welcome. Are you with me here?' He glanced up, smiling now. 'If so, it might be wise to lay a plan or two.'

5

On the third night of the journey, Nehmann dreamed about the train. Not the train he was sitting on, not exactly. Not even the succession of dirty carriages that had stretched away to the very end of the platform at the Krasnoyarsk station. But a different train, longer, sleeker, serpentine, a train glimpsed one moment between pine trees in a forest, seen the next moment across a vast expanse of steppe, then viewed from above, the mind's eye swooping and wheeling and climbing, an accomplice to this stealthy wriggle towards a faraway destination.

What might await the train at journey's end? Were there passengers aboard? Would high hopes end in disappointment? Tormented by these questions, Nehmann remained asleep for long enough to find an answer of sorts. The station at the end of the line had the girth of a cathedral. And metres beyond the huge buffers tiny figures were manoeuvring a giant saucer into place. The saucer was brimming with *kasha*, grey, steaming, and the little helpers clapped as the engine dipped its head and began to eat.

Nehmann awoke with a jerk. Leon was dozing beside him and around him, in the gloom, were the same faces, the same bodies, some asleep, some not, but all of them swaying in unison with the motion of the train, a chorus line of ill-dressed volunteer performers as the five-year drama of the Great Patriotic War approached its final act.

A couple of nights before, in the station restaurant, Leon had told him about the Red Army pushing west across Poland, deep into Prussia in the north, Romania in the south, pausing to gobble up a stray German army or two, titbits consumed on the Revolution's irresistible march to glory. Hitler, he said, had gambled on Russian weakness, on Russian incompetence, but successive winters, and the iron in the Soviet soul, had proved him wrong and now – like a spendthrift dining way beyond his means – Hitler was faced with a bill he couldn't possibly pay. And so, in these dog days of the war, the Motherland was due a little revenge and within weeks, he promised, the Red Army would be feasting on Berlin.

Berlin. Nehmann's memories were mercifully untainted by the last two years of war. The last time he'd been there, the city had already adjusted itself to night after night of violence at the hands of the British. The big four-engined bombers dumped hundreds of tons of high explosive into the darkness between the searchlights that probed for targets, and it was rare to emerge from the shelters after the all-clear and not smell burning and taste brick dust in the air. Gaps had begun to appear in the streets around the Wilhelmstrasse, and in the factory areas further out, but even then Nehmann had known that there was far, far worse to come. Had the Germans, so obedient, so naïvely trusting, brought this conflagration on themselves? Had they believed the outrageous lies that he – Werner Nehmann – had helped to peddle? He suspected that the answer was yes, but there was another truth, infinitely simpler: that this war, patriotic or otherwise, had affected everyone in some way or another. You didn't need to be German to have suffered. Neither did you need to be rich.

By now, nearly half past eight by Leon's watch, the thin, cold light of dawn was overtaking the train as it plodded west. Nehmann rubbed his eyes, taking stock. The carriage was packed, which was a blessing because bodies meant heat, and his gaze drifted from face to face, avoiding eye contact but noting the little details that always mattered. The tell-tale clues on leather belts that circled waist after waist, tightened and retightened over the years of war. The youngish man across the corridor, his head lolling on his chest, his curly hair prematurely grey. The stand of hoes and rakes, bound with fraying string, lodged in a far corner of the carriage. And the blind beggarwoman, whom the carriage looked after, her tin mug still clasped in one bony hand, the other protecting the stub of a scavenged cigarette.

The seats in the carriage were arranged in squares of four, and Nehmann looked down to find the bent finger of the old woman in the seat opposite stabbing at his knee. She wore a moth-eaten shawl she'd probably knitted herself and a pair of stout trousers she might have inherited from her dead husband. She had a gap-toothed smile and watery eyes, and she always woke up far too early.

'*Bol-she*,' she said. More.

Nehmann pulled a face, nodded at the still-sleeping Leon, murmured an apology. Far too early. Think of others.

The woman shook her head. She wasn't interested in Leon.

'*Bol-she*,' she repeated.

Nehmann did his best to ignore her, but it was hopeless. Her whole hand, this time, giving Nehmann's knee a little squeeze.

'*Bol-she*.'

'Do as she says. Give her what she wants.' Leon was awake after all.

'You're sure?'

Leon nodded, stifled a yawn, checked his watch, and Nehmann shrugged, giving in to the old woman. He'd tucked the book down the side of his seat. That first full day out of Krasnoyarsk, bored with gazing at the interminable pine forests, he'd buried himself in Tolstoy's story, aware of the old woman's eyes on the book. After an hour or so, he'd offered to lend it to her, but she'd shaken her head. She said she couldn't read. She wanted him to do it for her.

'Do what?'

'Read.' The old woman had touched her lips. 'Aloud.'

Leon had been monitoring this conversation and told Nehmann to go ahead. The journey would last for days and days. Anything to distract from the view, anything to bring a little light relief. And so Nehmann had done the old woman's bidding, returning to the opening page of *The Kreutzer Sonata*, bending to the smallness of the print, and using what talents he had to bring light and shade to Tolstoy's prose.

It had helped that the story began on a train, with passengers coming and going, one of them with a story to tell, and before he'd reached the foot of the first page, the old woman was clapping her hands, delighted, asking whether Nehmann was making all this up. He should speak more loudly, she insisted. Everyone should listen. Everyone in the train. Because this young man was a teller of stories, a weaver of yarns, and he's going to have a part for every single one of us.

This little episode brought a smile to Leon's face, largely because the old woman had – whether she knew it or not – summed up Nehmann's entire professional life. The teller of stories and weaver of yarns had fallen into the lap of the regime's evil genius, the Minister of Propaganda, and although Nehmann had later paid a savage price, that talent had brought him many rewards. And so he'd finished the paragraph, and turned the page, and an hour or so later, when he'd paused for a break, there was a soft ripple of applause from the passengers who'd lent an ear.

The Kreutzer Sonata was over a hundred pages long, and it was Leon who'd had the wit to suggest that Nehmann ration his readings to, say, fifteen pages per day. That way he'd spare his voice, while keeping his audience in suspense. This Nehmann had been only too happy to do and as the train rolled ever westwards, word of his performance had spread throughout the carriage. Strangers began to consult each other on missing episodes, on parts of the back story that might be key to whatever happened next, and this morning – based on murmurs he'd heard around him – he was anticipating a number of visitors to vacate their seats and squat or stand in the narrowness of the aisle to better keep up with the cuckolded civil servant and his doomed wife.

This, to the old woman's delight, is exactly what happened and as more and more faces appeared she kept interrupting the flow of the story, telling Nehmann to stop for a moment while listeners found some small token of their appreciation – a heel of stale bread, a mouthful of pepper vodka, a puff or two on a soggy cigarette. These she piled on her ample lap, and once Nehmann had come to the end of the day's instalment, she spent the afternoon and most of the evening sharing these windfalls between them. This, to Nehmann, was a wonderful clue to the real meaning of Mother Russia, a thought he shared with Leon. Tolstoy had penned the story during the reign of the Tsars. No matter how hard Marxism tried to fence off the past, ordinary folk – given the small blessings of capitalism – were still happy to make themselves at home there.

Leon, visibly amused, helped himself to the remains of a bottle of *kvass*, donated by a visitor from the end of the carriage who'd somehow remained fat.

'You'll appreciate Moscow, my friend.' He emptied the bottle and wiped his mouth, still looking at Nehmann. 'It will be my pleasure.'

*

Nearly a week later, after endless stops on loop lines to allow troop trains to hurry westward, they were approaching the suburbs of the capital. *The Kreutzer Sonata*, after briefer and briefer readings to eke the story out, had finally come to an end with the wife knifed to death, and the tearful husband struggling with the consequences of what he'd done. The women in the carriage, almost all of them, sided with the wife. Such a presence in the house would, they agreed, bore any woman to death. In those days, as in these, you took your pleasures where you could. The men, on the other hand, were more cautious. The civil servant had done his duty. He'd fathered five children, earned a decent living, put food on the table, and the least he could expect was a wife who kept her frustrations to herself. This difference of opinion sparked a lively debate as Moscow rolled ever nearer, a compliment – in Nehmann's eyes – to Lev Tolstoy. Even Leon, his keeper and increasingly his companion, enquired whether he might borrow the book and try another story or two.

'And me?' Nehmann asked. 'What do I get to read?'

'We'll find you a bookshop. You'll be glad to know they still exist.'

'We?'

'You and me.' Leon was smiling again. 'And our friend with the handcuffs.'

This was the first time Nehmann realised that he was still under escort. It turned out that the NKVD guard was travelling in the adjoining carriage, getting out at every stop to make sure

that Nehmann had no plans to escape. This struck him as a
very benign form of restraint, a tribute to Leon's judgement
and perhaps the trust he was extending, and as the wooden
trackside houses that signalled the Moscow suburbs began to
thicken, he gazed out of the window, eager for the sight of a
proper city. A fresh carpet of snow had fallen overnight but
already, by mid-morning, people were sweeping paths to their
front doors. Every space between every house showed signs
of cultivation, rows of cabbages, of onions, of something that
looked like beets.

'Victory gardens.' Leon saw them, too. 'The harder you dig,
the longer you live.'

By now, the debates about marital fidelity over, the carriage
was on the move. Passengers who knew Moscow recognised
familiar landmarks and prepared for the approach of the terminus
where the journey would finally come to an end. Hands reached
for carefully stowed bags. The hoes and the rakes were readied
for arrival. The beggarwoman was pocketing the handful of
kopeks she'd collected since dawn.

Once the train had stopped, Nehmann tried to struggle to
his feet, but Leon restrained him.

'We wait,' he said. 'Until everyone has gone.'

'And then?'

'Hot water.'

*

The Hotel Savoy lay within easy walking distance of Red Square.
Nehmann knew this because Leon instructed the NKVD driver
awaiting them at the station to make a detour in order to show
off the jewel in Moscow's crown. Maybe he's decided I don't
believe him, Nehmann thought. Maybe he's trying to prove that
none of this is a figment of my imagination.

They'd come to a halt beside a sizeable building in orange brick, hard against the Kremlin walls. Nehmann recognised it from photographs published in the Berlin *Morgenpost* the day after the signing of the Nazi–Soviet Non-Aggression Pact.

'Lenin's mausoleum,' he murmured. 'Do I get a look?'

'Sadly not. He's still in Siberia. He's been there a while but we're bringing him back at the end of the month. Operation Object Number One. Strange, isn't it? Lenin never believed in the afterlife, yet the truth is he's still with us.'

'And you?' Nehmann couldn't resist the question.

'We?' That same smile, wry, reflective. 'You're right. We broke open the coffins of the Orthodox saints and despoiled the contents. Yet here we are, still preserving a relic of our own. A bath, I think. Is that you smelling, or me?'

*

The Hotel Savoy was a relic from the days of the Tsar, and once again there were two keys awaiting Leon at reception. Nehmann's assigned room was on the top floor. The ancient lift shuddered upwards until the doors opened to the smell of boiled cabbage and the sight of a bear's head mounted high on the wall. Leon led the way down the corridor, opened the door of the room and stood aside. Nehmann, he said, would have a guard at his door day and night. For the rest of the day he might like to take advantage of the facilities supplied. A call to reception would conjure anything from a modest menu. For the time being Leon had business to take care of, but tomorrow morning he would be very happy to show Nehmann a little of his native city.

'You live here?'

'I do.'

'Born here?'

'Yes.'

'And the *Vozhd*?' Stalin?

'We await his pleasure.' He nodded beyond the open door. 'I took the liberty of making a phone call from one of the stops yesterday. Under your pillow, I think.'

He gestured for Nehmann to step into the room. Still in the corridor, Leon closed and locked the door behind him, leaving Nehmann to look around. The room was enormous, high ceiling, walls painted an oppressive shade of the darkest green, the space cluttered with a confusion of couches, double wardrobes and a bed that could have slept a platoon of soldiers. The wallpaper, once ornate, had begun to peel but there was a mural above the picture rail that ran the length of three of the four walls and featured mounted cavalry and the smoke of some long-ago battle.

Nehmann gazed up at it, shaking his head, then crossed the room to the biggest of three windows. From here he had a perfect view of the street many storeys below. There was a scatter of traffic, biggish cars trailing curls of blue exhaust in the freezing air, and he spent a moment or two watching a woman in a stylish fur coat pausing to check each way before crossing the street. From up here there was no telling her age, but Nehmann chose to believe that she was young, and smelled good, and could turn any head in any bar.

Maybe she lurked on the edges of fame, he thought. Maybe she moved in the right circles, attracted attention, won the hearts of the powerful. Maybe, even now, she was en route to some assignation, either her well-placed lover or some new contact, someone with the key to a door she'd never opened. Curiosity, he knew, was only a starting point in anybody's life, but wedded to determination and raw nerve it could take you anywhere.

The woman finally disappeared. Nehmann checked the bathroom. Getting in wasn't easy because the door hit the washstand and the bath itself was another disappointment.

Like the hotel, it smacked of pre-revolutionary days. Perched on four legs, it felt unstable to the touch and, looking down at the water stains on the wooden floor, Nehmann made a mental note not to overfill it. Decades of guests had worn the enamel off the bottom of the bath, and already Nehmann was anticipating the rough sandpaper kiss on his naked arse.

Backing out of the bathroom, he stood motionless for a moment, gazing around at his new home. A studied cough from the corridor outside doubtless signalled the arrival of the promised guard, but he realised he didn't care. This tomb-like room was thousands and thousands of kilometres away from Kolyma, literally another world, and if he was right about Leon, if he was right to detect a core of decency in the man, then the coming days would be ripe with promise. He smiled to himself, pleased if slightly awed by the prospect of meeting the *Vozhd*, then he suddenly remembered to check under the pillow.

Nehmann loved moments like these and always had. He'd long ago mastered his own impulses. He relished the pleasures of waiting. Anticipation, he often told himself, was better that the moment of discovery.

But not in this case. Finally lifting the pillow, he found himself looking at a fat volume, scarlet covers embossed in rich gold-leaf. He lifted the book to his nose. It smelled of new calfskin. Then he opened it, breathing in the scent of printer's ink, his eye alighting on the title. *War and Peace*. Lev Tolstoy.

6

'This is a very serious city. Especially in winter.'

It was next day, early afternoon. The morning's highlight had been a visit to the metro station at the Revolutionary Square, where Nehmann had admired the murals and the extravagant chandeliers, and relished the gusts of hot air that announced the arrival of a train. Leon seemed genuinely proud of a station that looked more like an art gallery than a transport interchange, and prouder still of the provenance of some of the building materials.

'You see this marble?' He'd pointed down at the platform, subtly veined. 'We stole it from the Dom Monastery. It comes from the cemetery. It used to belong to the dead. That's what makes a place like this so special. We're in the company of the departed.'

The comment had sparked a rare smile from the escort, and Nehmann had filed the moment away for the day when he might make it back to Germany. What was Russia really like? Listen to this.

Now, in the pale sunshine, he was standing outside an anonymous five-storey building that served as NKVD headquarters. The locals, he knew, called it the Big House, and Leon had disappeared inside to make a phone call. Also with

77

them on the street was a tall figure in a grey uniform with square shoulder boards. The uniform conferred a certain authority, and Nehmann gathered from Leon – who certainly knew this man well – that he worked in the Foreign Office. Nehmann had no idea whether this was true or not but he was certainly a better conversational proposition than the escort. Glum? Yes. But clever, too. A very serious city? Did he really mean it?

'Serious how?' Nehmann asked.

'Serious in the way we conduct ourselves, serious in the way we see the world, serious even in the jokes we make. Moscow jokes are pickled in vinegar. They're sharp. They leave an after-taste, and that's because we like to wound. You Georgians are different. Tbilisi is different. All that fierceness and gaiety. That's why the women love you.'

Because we like to wound. Nehmann had been watching a succession of women, most of them middle-aged, who'd been queueing to get past the uniformed guards on the main door. Now he asked what they were doing, why they'd come here.

The diplomat studied them for a moment while the escort turned his back to the wind and lit another cigarette.

'They come to find their husbands.' The diplomat was speaking in German now, his accent – like Leon's – near faultless. 'Your man goes missing one day. He's been to work but he doesn't come home and after a while you ask around, and wait a little, but after nothing happens you decide he must have been picked up for some reason and so maybe the next day you come here to the Big House and give them the details and ask them where that man of yours can possibly have gone. Do they know? Of course they do. And do they make life easy for you? I'm afraid not. You must wait ten years, they tell you. Ten years without the possibility of a letter. Ten years without a clue what might have happened to your lovely man. In your heart, like all the other women in the queue, you know that ten years is code for a bullet in the back of his head, but you can never be sure, never be certain, and that's the whole point. We trade in uncertainty. We keep people in the dark. There are people in this city who believe that Communism is some kind of science. They're wrong. If it was, we'd have tested it on dogs.'

Nehmann was startled. This kind of candour, he thought, could put a man in serious jeopardy, especially given the presence of a stranger. The diplomat had turned away to accept the escort's offer of a brief drag on the cigarette. Now he was back with Nehmann. Earlier, over endless glasses of scalding tea in Leon's room at the hotel, he'd put a series of questions about the years Nehmann had spent in Berlin feeding Goebbels' propaganda machine. The thrust of these questions suggested an intimate knowledge of the workings of various ministries at the heart of the Reich, but when Nehmann asked whether he'd been attached to the Soviet Embassy he'd refused to answer.

'Just convince me you really know Herr Goebbels,' he'd said. 'That's all I need from you.'

Nehmann had done his best. He described how he'd submitted a couple of stories to a secretary in the Promi who he knew had the ear of Goebbels. The Minister had liked what he was reading. Within days, he'd invited Nehmann for a light early evening snack. They'd started with one bottle of Gewürztraminer and ended the evening by emptying three. Goebbels, he'd told the diplomat, seemed to have recognised a kindred soul. Both men had little regard for the truth. Both were fascinated by the dark arts of manipulation. And both loved the rewards that journalism of a certain kind could confer. After a courtship like that, no more than a couple of months, Nehmann was allotted his little corner in the Promi, with absolute freedom to dream up any fiction that took his fancy.

The diplomat, Nehmann knew, had enjoyed his account of the Berlin years. More importantly, he'd made a series of notes – dates, specific stories, individual headlines – and seemed to have taken them at face value, which was important from Nehmann's point of view because for once in his life he'd resisted the temptation to lie. Just where all these notes were headed was a mystery but now the diplomat put a gloved hand on Nehmann's arm and drew his attention to the bulky figure of Leon who'd just emerged from the Big House.

'This may be your last day in Moscow.' He gave Nehmann's arm the briefest squeeze. 'Ever.'

Leon rejoined them. He muttered something to the diplomat that Nehmann didn't catch, then tapped his watch. The hotel was five minutes away. In a sudden flurry of movement, the diplomat extended a hand, wished Nehmann *gute Reise* and departed. Upstairs, once they'd got to the hotel, Leon stood by the biggest of the windows while Nehmann gathered his few possessions. Stalin, Leon said, was out at his dacha at Kuntsevo. An NKVD car was due any moment. Stalin, like time itself, waited for no man.

'It's been a pleasure.' Leon extended a hand. 'And I mean that.'

'You're not coming?'

'No.'

Nehmann gazed at him a moment. Leon was uncomfortable. He could see it in his eyes, in the way he seemed to be urging Nehmann towards the door, and the lift at the end of the corridor, and the waiting car. Finally, Nehmann shook his hand.

'Thanks for the book,' he said.

*

Downstairs, Nehmann left the hotel without a glance from the woman behind the reception desk. The rear door of the black

ZiL was already open, a tall, suited escort in attendance, but Nehmann's eye was taken by the long column of men shuffling up the cobbled street. There must have been hundreds of them, moving in untidy ranks four abreast. In their worn fatigues, they looked thin, weary, beaten. Some of them had a binding of filthy rags around their feet, Kolyma-style, and their heads were down, avoiding eye contact with the uniformed guards. A handful of the guards were on horseback, and a couple kept urging their mounts into the rear of the column, trying to hurry the men up, and when prisoners tripped and fell other guards beat them with batons and rifle butts, hauling them upright again, pushing them back into the column.

Nehmann paused at the kerbside, waiting for the last of the column to pass. When he asked his own escort what was going on, who these men might be, he shrugged.

'Germans,' he grunted.

He gestured for Nehmann to raise his hands. Under the circumstances, it felt uncomfortably like a gesture of surrender, but Nehmann recognised the touch of an expert and the search for a weapon was over within seconds. Nehmann got into the car. The windows at the back were curtained but the shuffle of receding footsteps told him that the street was clear again. The guard in the suit got into the passenger seat beside the driver. The rear doors were locked, he said tersely. Enjoy the ride.

They headed out of Moscow on a big road, parts of which looked newly surfaced. The driver was evidently in a hurry, clocking up more than 120 kph on the speedometer, and uniformed militia, recognising the car, waved them through one intersection after another. After a while – ten minutes? Fifteen? – they were out in the country, thick stands of silver birch on either side of the road, and the promise of more snow from a looming bank of clouds. Then, without warning, the driver dabbed at the brakes and hauled the big car into an abrupt turn. If you didn't know already, thought Nehmann, you'd never spot a hidden entry like this.

The ZiL followed the road deep into the trees. No signs of life. Then, around another corner, a red and white pole, waist-high, forced the car to a stop. Two NKVD guards in capes and caps emerged from a sentry box. One of them bent to the driver's open window, registered Nehmann's presence in the back, and then slapped his gloved hand on the sill of the door. The driver engaged gear again and drove on. Ahead was a long curve, the verges on either side heavy with shrubs, then came a second barrier, a wall this time, five metres at least. There were gun slits between the blocks of concrete and as the driver began to slow, unseen hands opened one of a pair of iron gates.

'This is it?'

Nehmann was looking at a sizeable two-storey house. It was easy on the eye, big timber-framed windows, the walls painted a pale shade of green. The ZiL finally came to a halt and Nehmann caught a glimpse of a patio at the back of the property. In early spring there was still snow on the ground and bulbs in the flowerbeds were still pushing up through the frozen soil but in summer, he thought, this space would be perfect for entertaining, or simply idling in a deckchair with a book.

The guard in the suit was already out of the car. He seemed impervious to the savage bite of the wind and he opened the rear passenger door, gesturing impatiently for Nehmann to join him. Once again, the sense of urgency, of a deadline to be met, was palpable. These men, this entire army of security militia, only existed because of the *Vozhd*. They were there to serve at his pleasure, to meet his many demands, to make sure that no particle of the Soviet hour went unfilled. All the stranger, therefore, to hear a voice Nehmann had least expected.

'Magalashvili?' Heavy Georgian accent.

He spun round and found himself looking at an old man. He was short, broad, swarthy. His eyes were baggy from lack of sleep, his hair was turning grey and his face was pockmarked with tiny scars. His complexion, an earthy brown reddened with blotches, would have troubled any doctor, and when he circled the car his movements were slow and stiff. Nehmann had heard somewhere that a childhood accident in Tbilisi had nearly robbed him of a leg, and when he stopped, his left arm hung down, useless, until his right hand tracked across and tidied it into the pocket of his ancient coat. The coat had fur on both sides, inside and out, and when he shifted his weight on the cold gravel, Nehmann noticed holes in the decrepit old boots. This might have been the dacha's gardener, he thought. Not the most powerful man in the world east of Berlin.

The suited escort, after a dismissive gesture from Stalin, had melted back into the car. The *Vozhd* nodded towards the house. The rest of the afternoon was his own. He'd be happy to offer his visitor a little Georgian hospitality.

The route to the big dining room where Stalin liked to entertain lay down a passage beyond the entrance hall. He paused for a moment beside an upright piano at the end of the corridor and the fingers of his right hand picked out the opening notes of a tune that Nehmann didn't immediately recognise.

'René Clair? 'Sous les toits de Paris'? They told me you were a cultured man, Magalashvili.'

Nehmann caught the hint of mild reproof and asked him to play it again. Stalin offered the faintest smile and let his fingers rest on the keyboard for a second before picking out the tune again. This time, Nehmann got it. He'd first seen the film in Paris in 1931. Three men fall in love with a beautiful Romanian girl, and suffer the consequences, most of them unexpected. It was a comedy with very dark edges and thanks partly to Maurice Chevalier, it had taken France by storm.

Nehmann half closed his eyes and concentrated very hard, knowing that he had to meet this test, that he had at least to offer the refrain's opening lines.

'*Sous les toits de Paris...*' He had a good voice for a song. '*Tu vois ma p'tite Nini...*'

'Excellent. You know the rest?' Stalin stepped away from the piano.

'Of course. What should I call you, sir?'

'Me?' His eyes briefly met Nehmann's, then flicked away. 'My friends call me *Koba*. My enemies, too. You're a Georgian, Magalashvili. Georgians understand each other. *Koba* should be safe. At least for the rest of the afternoon.'

Nehmann nodded and followed him into the dining room. The long table had chairs for eight. There was a fan of paperwork at the far end of the table, and a rack of pipes beside it. A wind-up gramophone stood in one corner and Nehmann's eye was drawn to a black and white framed photograph hanging above the mantlepiece. A younger Stalin was sitting in bright sunshine with an older man, thinner, domed forehead, and a pair of burning eyes sunk deep in his face.

'You recognise this man?' Stalin missed nothing.

'Lenin,' Nehmann said. 'Vladimir Ulyanov.'

Stalin nodded. He took off his fur coat and folded it carefully over the back of one of the chairs, before inviting Nehmann to sit down.

Nehmann took the seat next to the pipe rack. Stalin settled beside him at the head of the table. Under the coat, he'd been wearing a simple military tunic, olive-green, adorned with nothing but a single golden star. Nehmann couldn't take his eyes off the star. Kolyma, he thought. The twelve-hour days at the mine, tormented by mosquitos, the icy bite of the water from the mountains, even in high summer. Had Kolyma gold made this man a Hero of the Soviet Union? He suspected the answer was yes.

'They tell me Svaneti.' Stalin had produced a packet of cigarettes and was using the tobacco from one of them to stuff his pipe.

'That's right.'

'Svaneti produced the best bank robbers. A man needs courage, but he needs brains as well. Quick with the fists, fastest to the draw, you expect that. But he has to be able to *think*. Grow up in Svaneti, in the mountains there, and you'll find a way out of any corner. Am I right, Magalashvili? Or is this just bar talk?'

'You're right, sir.'

'*Koba*.'

'*Koba*.'

'So why did you ever leave?'

'Because I had to. Because I didn't want to become my father.'

'He beat you?'

'No.'

'That makes you lucky, Magalashvili. Maybe you were a saintly child. Somehow, I doubt it. Tell me about Joseph Goebbels, one Georgian to another. Is the man crazy?'

'No.'

'What, then?'

'He's like all of us. He's a prisoner.'

'Of what?'

'His own nature.'

'Very pretty. What does that mean?'

'It means he loves power.'

'For himself?'

'Of course. Power for Goebbels is everything. It gives him control. It means being boss in his own shit hole. It also means he worships Hitler, because Hitler *is* power. He'll do anything for the man, *anything*, tell any lie, take any risk. He also loves fucking women, starlets mainly. From the Promi he has the pick of them from the studios, Czech, German, Italian, it never mattered until he fell in love with one of them.'

'Baarova.'

'You know about Lida?' Stalin didn't answer, merely gestured for Nehmann to continue. 'She was Czech, this woman. Goebbels tried to move her into his own marriage, but his wife went running to Hitler and that was a problem because Hitler's a choirboy when it comes to sex and he rather approved of Frau Goebbels and her lovely children. So Goebbels had to take a good look at himself and make a choice. His mistress or his wife, his family, his kids, and most important of all his beloved Führer. Need I go on?'

'This was years ago.'

'Of course. I've been a bit out of touch for a couple of years. Not my doing, nor my fault, really.'

'No? I understand we picked you up at Stalingrad. Whose fault was that?'

'Hitler's. Goebbels'.'

'And you? In Berlin? What was your role? Why were you *useful*?"

'I was the court jester. I made Goebbels laugh. I also made him look good, smell good. He liked that.'

'Until it all went wrong.'

'Yes.'

'With Baarova.'

'Yes.'

'Because you carried his love letter to Rome and had the nerve to read it en route.'

'Yes.'

'Very Georgian.' Stalin slapped his knee and laughed. He had terrible teeth, stained, broken, uneven. 'So what happens when you meet Goebbels again? Is this a man who forgives easily? Does the word betrayal matter to him? Will you be welcome back in court? Will he give you the time of day? Will he even *recognise* you?'

Nehmann held his gaze, but once again the yellow eyes slid away. This man's knowledge of the circumstances that had sent him to Stalingrad was startling but in a way he'd been expecting it. You didn't put listening ears in every corner of the known world and not reap the benefits. Maybe he'd been listening to the diplomat. Or maybe Nehmann had his own file at the Big House. But that was hardly the point. What mattered now was getting back to Germany.

'I haven't seen Goebbels for nearly three years,' Nehmann said softly. 'For all I know, he might be dead.'

'He isn't.'

'Then how can I help? What do you want me to do?'

Stalin drew on his pipe, and the space between them was suddenly clouded in smoke. When he appeared again, his hand seemed to have found a button beneath the table. A woman appeared at the door. She was carrying a tray. On the tray was a bottle of vodka and two glasses. Also a bowl of what looked like caviar and a pile of blinis.

'Eat,' Stalin nodded at the food. 'And a little of this, I think.'

He poured two measures of vodka and proposed a toast.

'To Svaneti.'

'To home.'

Nehmann tossed back the vodka, aware of Stalin's gaze. At first sight, outside in the garden, he'd formed exactly the impression that the *Vozhd* had wanted to convey. An old man, scarred in every respect: by disease, by a Georgian childhood, and more recently by war. But now, perhaps too late for his own good, he was sensing someone very different. The *Vozhd* listened. The *Vozhd* watched. The *Vozhd* was doubtless in the business of digging little conversational traps, of quietly turning people inside out until they betrayed who they really were. Why? Because trusting anyone simply wasn't in this man's nature.

Power, as Nehmann knew only too well, touched a certain kind of nerve. It bred a merciless blurring of means and ends. It justified the most extreme measures. Surrounded by enemies, real or imagined, you simply dispensed with them all. Hence the years of the Great Terror. Hence the stories he'd heard in Kolyma about the state show trials and the vans marked 'Vegetables' and 'Meat' that left the Lubyanka every night, laden with men heading for the killing fields outside the capital. *Zeks* in Kolyma, political prisoners who'd tasted the murderous regime first hand, ascribed to the *Vozhd* the powers of the Devil. And Nehmann was beginning to suspect they were right.

Stalin had poured more vodka. He wanted to propose another toast.

'To Kureika,' he murmured.

'Where?'

'Kureika.' They touched glasses and tossed the vodka down. Kureika, Stalin said, was at the top of the world, at the very edge of the Arctic Circle. He'd been exiled there the year the Great War started. He'd lived in a wooden hut with a peasant family. He'd worn reindeer fur. The men, he said, worshipped a primitive god and believed in shamans and he'd loved the rawness of their lives. They had a kinship with the spirits of the frozen tundra, and they gave the young Bolshevik a rifle, and ammunition, and sent him out for weeks on end to shoot Arctic foxes, and partridge, and duck. Those days, he said, and especially those nights, were the best times of his life. He'd throw up a shelter, and put on an extra layer of clothes, and he'd lie in the darkness listening to the howling of the wolves beyond the treeline. Then, when all his bullets were gone, he'd return to Kureika with his trophies for the pot, and the men would drink and dance and sing, and a couple of days later, at his own insistence, he'd leave the township and shoulder his rifle, and head back to the chill and silence of the wilderness where he was happiest.

'You want to know what these men were really like? You want me to tell you? One day a man went missing. He'd been out by himself in his kayak, never came back. When I asked them what they'd done about it, they just shrugged, and said that the man was still out there. That was the phrase they used. *Out there*. What it really meant was that the man was dead, probably drowned, but the point was this: that it didn't matter. We can always make another man, they told me. But we can never make a horse.'

He stared at Nehmann for a moment, as if he'd revealed a deep truth, something almost sacred, then he barked with laughter again, and slapped his knee, and reached for the bottle.

'Life is cheap, Magalashvili. Just bear that in mind.'

Cheap. Nehmann was thinking of the women queuing outside the Big House. Their husbands, like the lone kayaker, were out there, in the darkness of this pitiless regime, discarded, never to return. For an insane moment or two, he wondered about putting this point to the mighty *Vozhd* but mercifully he never had the chance because they were on the move again. Evidently needing somewhere more intimate to continue their conversation, Stalin led him through to the warmth of a study next door. It was a plain man's room with a desk, a small icon of Lenin, and a sofa almost as battered as Stalin himself. The sofa doubled as a bed and a worn army blanket was heaped at one end. Here, Stalin capped the bottle of vodka and told Nehmann exactly what he wanted from him.

Arrangements were in place, he said, to fly him west from Moscow to a town in Poland just behind the River Oder. There he would be joining a Red Army unit waiting to push into Germany. It would be Nehmann's responsibility to cross the front line and melt into the flood of refugees the Red Army was driving before them. Berlin, he said, was only a hundred and fifty kilometres away. Within days, he could be back in the Wilhelmstrasse, back in the world he knew so well, back with the likes of Joseph Goebbels.

'And then?'

'Then you make friends again.'

'Why?'

'Because the Germans have gone behind our backs. And so have the Americans. And so have the English. They're devious, Magalashvili. They're making a nice little peace of their own and they think we know nothing. Only Georgians can see through shit like this, which is why you're going to find out exactly what they're up to.'

'And you think Goebbels will know about this?'

'I'm sure he will. And when he tells you what's going on, you pass the news back to us.'

'How do I do that?'

'Ask Goebbels. He knows what to do.'

Stalin got to his feet. The conversation was evidently over but Nehmann had a question.

'But what if I just disappear? What if I make it to Germany and just...' he shrugged, '... mind my own business?'

'That won't happen.'

'Why not?'

Stalin said nothing for a moment. Then he opened a drawer in the desk and pulled out an envelope, handing it to Nehmann.

'Take a look,' he said. 'A bit thinner, maybe? Only you would know.'

The envelope was unsealed. Inside was a black and white photograph, the kind of head and shoulders shot they always took on your first day in the Gulag. Willi Schultz, his head newly shaven, looked terrible. Defiant? Yes. Angry? Very. But skinny as hell.

'You know this man?'

'Of course I do. He looked after me at Stalingrad. We were together when we were taken.'

'And he matters to you?'

'I owe him everything.'

'Then, one Georgian to another, I suggest you'll do our bidding.' The yellow eyes narrowed in what might have been a smile. '*Da?*'

7

Wilhelm Schultz barely recognised peace. He stood on the edge of the harbour in the very middle of Stockholm, trying to remember the last time he'd been here. 1940, he thought, the year the *Wehrmacht* brought home victory after victory, scalps taken the length and breadth of Europe, France beaten, the Low Countries cowed, half of Scandinavia occupied, and Britain a lost little offshore island, begging the Americans for a borrowed rifle or two.

Then, back in the winter of that first proper year of war, he'd been tasked with planting a seed that might flower into peace talks between Berlin and London, using Tam Moncrieff, whom he'd known pre-war, as the messenger. Moncrieff, of course, had played the ex-Marine and told him he was wasting his time, and he'd been right, but that wasn't the point. The point, here in Stockholm, was food in the shops, the streets busy and well lit after dark, the swirl of people coming and going without a single glance over their shoulders.

Back then, the capital of the Thousand Year Reich was still celebrating the blessings of conquest but already there were reports of air raids from Essen and Cologne, from Kiel and Hamburg, and the wiser heads were counting the nights before the RAF raised its game and gathered its skirts and headed further east for Berlin. Nights in the Swedish capital, on the other hand, remained blissfully undisturbed and Schultz remembered staying a day or two longer than strictly necessary, exactly the way you lingered in a hot bath, utterly relaxed and briefly at peace with the world.

*

The Café Almhult was a minute's walk away. The blond young guy he remembered from his previous visit was no longer behind the bar, but the place was comfortably full. It was early evening and most of the tables had already been taken, couples deep in conversation, heads bent over plates of soup and pickled fish, two old men in the corner playing what looked like skat. Of the Swede he'd come to meet, a businessman called Dahlerus, there was no sign.

'Willi? Is that you?' Schultz recognised the voice at once. Valentina, he thought, the woman who ran the place. He finished hanging his leather coat on the back of the empty chair and shuffled round to greet her. She was a big woman, in her late fifties, with a tumble of blonde hair.

'You speak German now?' He was trying to muster a smile.

'*Ein bisschen*.' A little. 'What's the matter? What's happened to you?'

Schultz pulled a face, shrugged, didn't answer. The last time he'd been here, this woman had been more than accommodating. She had a suite of tiny rooms upstairs, but space enough for the once-big man in the battered leather jacket who'd plainly seen a bit of life. Yet another reason for extending his stay on neutral territory.

'You've just arrived?' she said. 'You've come from Berlin?'

'Of course. You're busy. He nodded at the loaded plates that nearly hid the burn marks on her plump forearms. 'Maybe we talk later?'

She didn't move, couldn't take her eyes off him. Then, with a start, she seemed to remember something.

'You're here to meet Birger?'

'I am.'

'He phoned. He won't be coming. Not tonight. He says tomorrow, now. Funny, but he never mentioned your name. A German gentleman, he said. Just that.'

Again, Schultz didn't respond. The couple at the nearby table waiting to be served were beginning to fidget. Valentina ignored them.

'You want some of this?' She nodded at the knuckle of pork, swimming in mustard sauce. 'Maybe you need it, *ja*?'

'I want a drink.'

'Beer?'

'Anything.'

She nodded, took a final look at him, shook her head, then delivered the plates to the waiting diners.

Schultz settled at his table, trying to avoid his own image in the mirror on the wall opposite. With everyone else in company, he wished he'd had the foresight to bring a paper or a book.

Valentina returned with a glass of beer.

'You need to eat,' she said. 'Have they run out of food in Berlin?'

'We're at war,' he said. 'You might have heard.'

'Meat? Fish? Something with cheese? Something to build you up?' She might have been his mother.

'Anything. Whatever's best. You choose.'

'And you're staying tonight? To meet Birger in the morning?'

'Yes.'

'Where?'

He looked up at her, holding her gaze. It had been a very long time since any woman had asked him a question like this.

'You're offering?'

'Of course we're offering.'

'We?'

'My Per. Lovely man. We married last year. He has an apartment you can use. I'll give him a call.'

The apartment, she said, was in a neighbouring street. Schultz had a second beer and did his best with a plate of goulash with choucroute but his stomach was no longer able to cope with a full meal, and he saw the disappointment in Valentina's face when she returned to the table to collect the remains on his plate. The café was still busy.

'No good?'

'Delicious. I shouldn't have had lunch.'

'You want another beer? I've given Per a call. He's coming over later. We can talk, all three of us, when it's quieter.'

Schultz shook his head. When he asked whether she had the key to the apartment, she nodded.

'You want to go straight there? Now?'

'Yes. If it's a problem, I'll find a hotel.'

'No need. Save your money. Tomorrow, maybe? Tomorrow we can talk?'

'Of course.'

'Good,' she stepped a little closer. 'Then you can tell me what happened.'

Before he left the café, Schultz used the phone on the bar counter to call Dahlerus. His wife answered the phone. Her name was Michaela and she was German by birth. Schultz had talked to her a number of times and she recognised his voice at once. Birger, she said, had been called away to yet another business meeting. He was free tomorrow morning, so maybe

Schultz would like to come to the house for breakfast. She gave him an address and directions for the cab, and briefly enquired about life back in Berlin.

'You need the right connections and a sense of humour,' Schultz grunted. 'It also helps to be a mole.'

'A what?'

'A mole. After dark, everything happens underground. Goering could learn a thing or two from the RAF, if only he'd get off his fat arse.'

'I've seen some of the photos in the paper. All the damage. It's truly that bad?'

'Worse.'

Schultz left the café and walked for half an hour, his hands thrust deep in the pockets of his cheap jacket, hugging the shadowed side of street after street. Even by mid-evening, the city still felt alive, and he lost count of the number of blonde women – young, handsome, well fed – who'd turn your head in any company. Walking in roughly a square brought him to the street he needed, an indication that he wasn't quite as useless and disorientated as he sometimes felt, and he found the number of the property without difficulty.

The apartment was on the first floor above a hardware store. There were two locks for the side entrance, and he had a key for each. A flight of narrow stairs led to a tiny landing, and there was a lingering smell of paraffin that must have seeped up from the shop below. He couldn't find the light switch, but he felt his way along the wall to a door. Valentina had warned him about a cat inside. The cat was old, and probably asleep, and he waited for a full minute, his ear pressed to the door, before letting himself in.

Mercifully, the apartment was warm. Schultz found the lights and made himself at home. Valentina had told him where to find food for the cat, and he emptied the remains of a bag of biscuits into a bowl. The cat was asleep in the only bedroom. The bed was unmade, and he shooed the cat off before removing his jacket and boots and climbing beneath the eiderdown. In Moscow, especially during the winter months, you went to sleep early and put out the lights. That way, as he'd realised early on, the entire city could feign death, a state of mind that might – if you were lucky – get you through the next day or so.

*

He woke hours later, the cat curled on top of him. When he shifted his weight, it began to purr, nuzzling the boniness of his chest through the thin serge of his shirt, and he fought the temptation to push it away into the darkness. Instead, to his own slight surprise, he began to stroke it. Better a cat, he thought, than a night with a woman who'd once told him he was a tiger in bed.

Really?

He moved his head slightly, so his cheek lay on the softness of the pillow. He could smell a woman's scent on the pillowslip, and earlier he'd noticed a little nest of black and white photos on the table beside the bed. Per, he thought, must be half Valentina's age. He had a sturdy build, broad shoulders and a crop of golden curls. Half-choirboy, half-lumberjack, he'd be irresistible to a certain kind of woman, and the smile on his face told Schultz she took good care of him. What they said about older woman was true, he thought. The arts of patience and delight only come with age.

The cat was kneading him now, as if preparing a nest for itself, and he began to savour this small moment of peace. Schultz was no stranger to life's uglier challenges. You didn't get to the rank of Colonel in the *Abwehr*, the Army's intelligence organisation, without meeting violence head on, and his talents as a street brawler in the Party's early days had been the best apprenticeship for what followed. But the direction the Reich had taken, with coarseness and vanity prime qualifications for high office, had first troubled and then disgusted him. The people with whom he'd had to deal had a raw lust for power they rarely bothered to disguise, and by the time the *Abwehr* was bending the knee to Himmler's rival organisation, he'd given up on the Reich. To defend a regime like that you needed to be able to ignore excess of every kind, no matter how crude. And Schultz couldn't.

His last active posting had been at Stalingrad where he'd led a smallish detachment of *Abwehr* staff, headquartered in the remains of a suburban bus station. Both the *Abwehr* and the city were themselves on the edge of ruin, but as the merciless Soviet winter took its second bite out of the *Wehrmacht*'s flanks, a small compensation had arrived in the shape of the impish Georgian journalist who'd shed and buried his past in favour of a new name and a new persona.

Schultz had first met Werner Nehmann in Berlin and he'd never quite got to the bottom of his relationship with the Reich's Minister of Propaganda, but he knew that a closeness to Goebbels had brought him opportunities of all kinds and even a modest degree of fame. Neither served him at all well in the abattoir that was Stalingrad, but Nehmann had a particular debt to pay, and, as the killing became a way of life, Schultz was very happy to help him despatch a sadistic SS *Standartenführer* called Jürgen Kalb, with whom Schultz had already crossed swords in Kyiv. It had never been Schultz's intention to eat the man afterwards but by this time he and Nehmann, like everyone else, were beginning to starve. In this respect, he thought, seasoned cannibals were right. Even SS flesh, properly prepared and seasoned, tasted recognisably of pork.

Blood brothers by now, the pair of them were captured by the Russians in a draughty church within days of the Sixth Army's surrender. It happened at dusk and they'd been marched separately at gunpoint into the gathering darkness. Schultz hadn't seen Werner Nehmann since but he'd thought about him a great deal, partly because he loved the man's spirit, his sense of mischief, and partly because he recognised the anger that lay beneath his many talents. Nehmann, he'd concluded, was a survivor.

This thought had been a source of comfort over the months to come, not least because Schultz himself had been so sorely tested. The NKVD, it turned out, knew a great deal about *Abwehr Oberst* Wilhelm Schultz, and wanted to put that knowledge to the service of the Revolution. From Stalingrad, under heavy escort, he'd been taken by train to Moscow. There, in a cheerless interrogation room at the Lubyanka Prison, it had been clear within days that Schultz was going to offer them nothing beyond his name, service number, and rank. At nights, between the interminable interrogations, he'd be taken back to his cell to review yet again the wisdom of staying mute, but when the moment came when they transferred him to another prison, he knew that his life was about to change. Lefortovo specialised in torture. At Lefortovo, they had ways of turning you inside out until you couldn't recognise a single centimetre of your old self, physically or in any other respect. The specialists at Lefortovo, he'd been promised, would take you beyond pain.

They kept a resident wolf in a cage without a lock on the door. They spent hours working on your back and thighs and the soles of your feet, two of them in turn with rubber truncheons. They had a neat little trick that involved sudden blows with the flat of a hand on your neck, which then swells up and locks the jaw. They liked hauling in a woman or two and subjecting her to treatment that only you could stop. They kicked and beat you senseless all day and then flung a crazy, half-dead old man into your cell. His ravings would keep you awake all night and next morning you'd find yourself having coffee in an elegant office with an apparatchik who termed himself 'The Magistrate'. And when even that didn't loosen your tongue, they'd shrug, and drag you down to the basement, and turn you over to the Ukrainians. You knew already about the Ukrainians because they'd warned you about these people. Wild, they'd said. And inventive. And totally in love with pain.

Was this a fairy tale, a fantasy, yet another false promise the People's Revolution couldn't possibly deliver? Alas, no. There were four of them. They were dressed like male nurses: white smocks, rubber galoshes, little white caps that tied neatly at the back. The room where they worked was tiled, both the floor and the walls, more whiteness, and they nodded when you limped in, the mutest of greetings, not a word to suggest what might happen next.

Schultz remembered an old tip, a piece of street wisdom he'd passed on to others during his working career. In circumstances like this, he'd always advised, find something to concentrate on. It could be imagined, some conflated memory or other, or it could be real, either would do, but the trick was to focus on that one remembered face, that one solid object. In this case, Schultz knew he was in trouble because his mind had ceased to function properly and the only thing he could see was a bucket and a mop. The purpose of the bucket was only too obvious. Afterwards, someone would have to clean up.

A big wooden table stood in the middle of the tiled floor. Schultz was made to strip naked and lie full length on his back. Then, from an adjoining room, a long plank was produced.

The plank was thick and bore a series of gouge marks. Two of the Ukrainians laid the plank the length of Schultz's body, its roughness against his bare flesh. The upper end nudged his chin. He could still see. He could still watch the men disappearing again to the room next door, returning with a big axe and an even bigger lump hammer. One on either side of the table, they looked down at him, apparently awaiting a signal of some sort, and then – on a nod from the smallest of the group – they started on him.

Schultz had never forgotten what happened next. Down came the axe, the Ukrainian grunting with the effort, the blade biting into the timber, sending ripples of intense pain into every corner of Schultz's body. Then, from the other Ukrainian, a blunter blow, no less powerful, this time from the face of the lump hammer. Then the axe again. Then the hammer, on and on, over and over, a torrent of blows that sent more pain, white-hot, scalding, liquid, the river from hell, an agony far worse than Schultz had ever conceived possible. Already he could feel the wreckage of his kidneys, of his belly, of the coils of intestine that led to his arse, everything he'd ever taken for granted, all of it shaken loose, ripping apart. No man could survive this, he told himself. Because no sane man would ever want to.

Two minutes? Ten minutes? Half an hour? He'd no idea. But his last memory was the face beside his, the face that belonged to the smallest man in the room. Heavy Ukrainian accent. Very simple message. Have you had enough? Will you talk to us now?

'*Da,*' Schultz had whispered. Yes.

*

Next morning, in Stockholm, Schultz awoke at dawn. He lay still for a moment, the weight of the cat still on his chest, then rolled over until his feet found the bare boards beside the bed. From the living room next door a single window offered a view across the neighbouring rooftops to the cloud of seagulls wheeling and swooping over the harbour. The houses were painted in shades of Scandinavian pastel – light greens and yellows and soft blues – and lifted his spirits after two winters in the grey wastelands of the Moscow suburbs. This was a city, he thought, that didn't deserve a war. More importantly, it had so far managed to turn its back to the slaughter further east and mind its own business.

He found a saucepan and matches for the stove. Also, a painted wooden box containing a thin carpet of tea leaves. Watching the water beginning to stir, feeling that strange tug of freedom a city like this seemed to offer, he thought again of the Ukrainians, of their bucket and mop, of their clinical malevolence, and of the weeks and months that had followed. In some ways the story of that terrible year was all too simple: pre-Plank, and post-Plank. Physical recovery, all too slow, had taken him to an office on the second floor of the Lubyanka. Like every survivor of the torture suites, he had to walk on the tips of his toes to spare his ruined heels, and every morning he'd join this surreal carnival of prisoners negotiating the corridors and stairwells that led to the second floor.

There, he'd spend hours with an official he knew simply as Diski. He was middle-aged, tall, a man of infinite patience who bent over his desk like a librarian, scribbling notes as Schultz talked. He was jug-eared, with thinning grey hair. He always wore the same rumpled grey suit, no tie. His German was perfect, with hints of a Berlin accent, and he spoke with a slight lisp. Over the weeks that followed, he combed the story of Schultz's last two decades, pausing on the smallest details, wanting his view on this personality or that, exploring individual episodes with an economy of effort and a sureness of touch that Schultz – himself an interrogator of immense experience – could only admire.

There was no physical hazard in these visits to Diski's bare little office, but as the weeks went by Schultz felt the essence of his past life, all those memories, all those experiences, being squeezed out and carefully bottled, leaving him a mere husk of a man: brittle, desiccated, empty. It also occurred to him that interrogation was beginning to turn into a kind of job interview, though the precise terms of what might lie in store remained vague.

Then came the moment, late one afternoon, when Diski sat back from the desk, capped his fountain pen and announced that it was over. As a gesture of gratitude for his co-operation, and as a down payment on the services he would render, the state was prepared to make an apartment available to Schultz. It wouldn't be grand, and there'd undoubtedly come times when Schultz would miss the life he'd so meticulously described, but it offered freedom of a sort, and Diski hoped that would be some small recompense for some of the unpleasantness he'd been obliged to undergo.

Diski had never made a speech like this and Schultz sensed that the moment required some kind of response on his part, but all he could managed was a single question: why?

*

Now, Schultz made himself a glass of tea and limped once again to the window. Dawn had truly broken now and there was even a spill of golden light in the east. When the cat appeared, he scooped it up and showed it the view before finding more biscuits for the bowl. On the phone from the café last night, Dahlerus's wife had asked him to come for breakfast around nine. It was already half past eight.

He soaped his face in the tiny bathroom and wondered about a shave but decided against it. Moscow attached much importance to his disguise, to the look he needed to adopt. He was to have come from Berlin. His people there wanted him to be a worker on the move, displaced by the war, a little rough around the edges. A three-day growth of beard would therefore be perfect.

He returned the cat to the bedroom, retrieved the battered German-made suitcase that contained his few belongings and made his way down to the street. He shut the door, made sure it was double-locked, and dropped the keys through the letterbox. Valentina might be disappointed, but she belonged to a life that he could barely remember and he realised that he didn't care.

A passer-by directed him to a taxi rank down by the harbour. A woman in a beaten-up old Volvo read the address Valentina had written on a scrap of paper, took a second look at Schultz, and raised an eyebrow.

'Östermalm?' she said in German. 'Posh.'

She was right. Birger Dahlerus and his wife occupied an enormous corner apartment on the fifth floor of a waterside building barely fifteen minutes away. The concierge on the ground floor watched Schultz limping in from the street, and asked his business, but it turned out that Dahlerus's wife had already left his name and Schultz found himself riding the lift to the fifth floor.

He'd never met Michaela Dahlerus, not in the flesh. He knew that Diski had made careful preparations for this moment, pretending to be phoning from Berlin with news of Schultz's keenness to meet with Birger Dahlerus again, but the moment his wife opened the door he realised that something was wrong. She was nearly as tall as her husband and had kept her looks. She was wearing a soft woollen dress, the lightest shade of grey, cut to showcase her legs. Her complexion was flawless, no trace of make-up, and there was warmth in her smile.

'Herr Schultz?'

'Yes.'

'I'm afraid my husband's already left. He may be back in an hour or so. You're very welcome to come in.'

She stepped aside and let Schultz in. The hall and then the huge living room reminded Schultz of a similar apartment he'd briefly commandeered in occupied Paris: high ceilings, tall windows, polished wood floors with a scatter of interesting rugs. Michaela gestured at an armchair beside the low coffee table. She wanted to know about Berlin, about Germany in general. She was hearing the most terrible things.

'All true, I'm afraid. Certainly in Berlin. And Hamburg. And Cologne. You have somewhere specific in mind?'

'I come from a little place called Neuburg. It's down in Bavaria. On the Donau.'

'And you still have family there?'

'Of course.'

'Then they may be luckier.'

'You really think that?'

'I do, yes. The RAF don't bother with the smaller targets, and neither do the Americans. Here's hoping,' he looked up and mustered a smile. '*Ja?*'

Michaela disappeared to make coffee and a little something for breakfast. In the absence of her husband, she said, it was the least she could do. Schultz sat back, gazing around, enjoying the splashes of sunshine through the big picture windows. It was Diski, back in Moscow, who had briefed him only a week ago on the current state of the Reich. This information, he said, had come from a number of covert sources in Berlin, chiefly embedded Soviet agents, and was rich with the kind of details he needed for conversations like these. Schultz hadn't seen Diski for more than a year, and was surprised how much the man had aged. The Soviets, it was clear, were going to win this war. So how come Diski looked so glum?

Schultz dismissed the thought. His eye had been taken by the pictures hanging on the wall. They were watercolours, landscapes mostly. They were very accomplished, enormously subtle, the wash of greys and greens capturing the melancholy of the pale northern light and looking at them he couldn't help remembering his early attempts to brighten the apartment assigned to him.

It lay in the outskirts of Moscow, in a suburb near the biggest of the city's airports, three bare rooms on the fifth floor of a hideous modern block. One of the rooms, where the previous occupier must have slept, stank of the insecticide used to kill bedbugs, and when Schultz had tried to force open the window, he'd broken the catch, letting in the freezing air day and night. There was a market nearby, and two or three times a week he'd shuffle along the road to buy stunted vegetables and tins of borscht from ageing *babushkas* squatting on dirty blankets on the roadside. One day, he'd noticed a line of tubes of oil paint, only half squeezed. He'd bought half a dozen different colours and managed to lay his hands on a brush and some wood panels from broken boxes and that night he'd made his first stab at a painting of his own.

The result was a mess, a child's muddle of garish blues and reds with no theme or pattern, and he'd lived with it for a day or two before dumping it in the bin. Later, he thought that maybe he should have dreamed up a title, called it 'Migraine' and sold it in the market as his own contribution to socialist realism, but now, looking at the largest of the watercolours hanging on the wall, he realised he'd have been kidding himself. Decent art, like anything else worthwhile in life, demanded a great deal of application.

Michaela returned with a tray of coffee and a plate of warm brioche. Schultz couldn't take his eyes off the brioche. Paris again, he thought. Another life.

'My husband telephoned just now. Meetings, it seems, are like rabbits. They just keep multiplying. He says he won't be back until this evening. Is there any way I might be able to help you?' She settled into a corner of the sofa and crossed her legs.

Schultz helped himself to a brioche. He hadn't heard a phone ringing and suspected she was making this call up. The truth was that Birger Dahlerus had no intention of meeting him, and he wondered why. Back in 1939, on the eve of Hitler's push into Poland, the businessman had done his best to nurture peace talks, and even after war was declared he'd been tireless in his efforts to bring hostilities to an early end, chiefly through his rapport with Hermann Goering. War, Dahlerus had pointed out, could only hurt businesses across the continent, including his own, yet there'd been no possibility of rapprochement.

'He's still close to Goering?' Schultz asked.

'We both are. Is that why you've come?'

'In a way, yes. But the *Reichsmarschall*'s a spent force these days. The Führer blames him for the bombing. Being fat and idle is one thing. Watching Germany burn is quite another.'

This quote came direct from Diski and seemed to touch a nerve in Michaela.

'Are you telling me there's no point in dealing with Hermann?'

'Yes. He counts for nothing any more. Mention his name in front of Hitler and watch what happens. The castles? The banquets? The endless hunts? The trophy kills to be stuffed and mounted? All those limousines? The Führer considers him a glutton and a scoundrel. There's nothing left in that relationship. In fact, Hitler has nothing but contempt for the man.'

'So where would our hopes lie?'

'For what?'

'For peace.'

'With Himmler.' Schultz reached for another brioche. 'As I'm sure you know.'

Diski, again. Himmler, he'd assured Schultz only days ago, knows that the war is lost. Since last year's attempt on Hitler's life, he's found himself more powerful than ever. Hitler doesn't trust his Generals any more, and Himmler has taken their place. Better the head of the SS in charge than a bunch of stiff-necked Prussians with treason in their hearts.

'I know very little about Himmler,' Michaela said carefully. 'But I know Folke Bernadotte.'

'The two of them have been talking, Himmler and Count Bernadotte. Did you know that, too?'

'I do, yes. About the Jews, I think. Herr Himmler is arranging for a lot of them to be released.' She looked suddenly amused. 'My husband tells me you're a spy catcher. Have you come to arrest our friend Folke?'

Schultz laughed, shook his head. Count Bernadotte had royal connections here in Sweden. More importantly, as Head of the Swedish Red Cross, he could also count on a number of important contacts in London and Washington. If you wanted to broker a separate peace with the Western Allies, then Count Bernadotte would be a very good place to start. Especially if you were Himmler and had millions of Jewish prisoners at your disposal.

'Do you think any talks might go well?' Schultz asked.

'You want the truth?'

'Yes, please.'

'Then I get the impression the answer is no. Folke has taken soundings in London. The Allies are still demanding unconditional surrender, and nothing will change that. There's also a problem with Herr Himmler. Folke tells me Hitler gave him important responsibilities on the Eastern Front recently, tried to turn him into a soldier, into a General. I get the feeling it didn't work.'

Schultz nodded. This was true. Himmler had always been an administrator and schemer of genius. Way back before Stalingrad, he'd built the SS into a sprawling empire unchallenged inside the Reich, and Schultz himself had watched his precious *Abwehr* steamrollered by the zealots in black. But more recently, according to Diski, Hitler had handed him control of Army Group Vistula, expecting Himmler to give the Russians a good hiding, and the *Reichsführer-SS* had fallen flat on his face. He had no gift for playing the General, for understanding the ebb and flow of armed conflict, for laying traps and taking risks on the battlefield, and as a result – according to Diski's sources in Berlin – Hitler was fast losing his patience.

'Would your husband welcome an approach from Herr Himmler?' Schultz asked quietly. 'If one was forthcoming?'

'My husband would welcome any initiative that gave us all a lasting peace. It's true when you first met, and it's no less true now.'

'Do I interpret that as a yes?'

Michaela held his gaze for a long moment, then she looked away.

'You've come from Himmler? He sent you?' she asked at last.

'I've come from Berlin. That may be the same thing.'

'And now you go back? Or will the charms of Stockholm detain you for a day or two?'

Schultz didn't answer. Michaela studied him a moment longer, then she got to her feet, smoothing the creases on her dress, and extended a hand. 'It's been a pleasure, Herr Schultz.'

Schultz didn't move. After a while he nodded at one of the pictures on the wall.

'Is that your work?'

'It is, yes.' A sudden smile. 'You approve?'

'I do. Very much.'

Schultz finally got to his feet and extended a hand. She held it a moment longer than strictly necessary, then asked him whether he'd ever had the opportunity of studying one of Hitler's paintings.

'I have, yes.'

'And?'

'They're shit.'

She held his gaze for a long moment, and then smiled.

'My husband always told me you have excellent judgement,' she murmured. 'I'll pass on your thoughts about Herr Himmler.'

8

In London, later that same day, Ursula Barton went missing. Moncrieff had been working on an urgent cable from the OSS office in Bern requesting information on the whereabouts of a German prisoner of war, SS *Obersturmbannführer* Max Wuensche. The much-decorated Wuensche had been captured after D-Day in the Falaise pocket. Moncrieff had accessed his file and was currently trying to find out where he was being held, information to which Barton might have access.

It was Guy Liddell who finally offered a clue to her whereabouts. Liddell, as Director of 'B' Section, was her immediate boss, a languid, slightly rumpled figure whose unfailing courtesy and air of faint detachment hid a sharp intelligence.

'Try the zoo,' he suggested. 'She's got a thing going with a gibbon called Jimmy. She took me to see him recently, did the introductions. Lovely little chap. Real charmer.'

Liddell returned to the file he'd been studying as Moncrieff made for the door, but then he looked up again.

'You've talked to her recently? Ursula? I mean *properly* talked to her?'

'Not really, not for these last few days.'

'But you think she's all right? Nothing bothering her? No particular...' Liddell frowned, '... *problems*?'

Moncrieff gazed down at him, wondering whether to tell him about the V-2 on Farringdon Market, and what they'd discovered later at the Whitechapel Hospital, but decided against it.

'Nothing that I know of, sir,' he smiled. 'I'll give Jimmy your best.'

*

Moncrieff found both Jimmy and Ursula Barton in the Monkey House. He'd paid his shilling at the gate and consulted one of the keepers for directions. It was a bright spring day, the verges beside the paths ablaze with daffodils, and the first real hint of warmth in the sun had brought hundreds of visitors to the Zoological Gardens. Many of them were servicemen in various states of disrepair. Some were on crutches. Others had their plastered arms in slings. One, in the care of a VAD nurse, appeared to have been blinded.

'They get in free,' Barton explained. 'The walking wounded can stay here all day if they want.'

She was squatting beside the heavy mesh wire that shielded the cage from the public. The gibbon was on the other side of the wire. He was smaller than Moncrieff had expected, thick black fur with a collar of white, liquid eyes, slightly mournful expression. He'd exactly copied Barton's crouch, and his long fingers plucked uncertainly at the wire.

'This is Jimmy?'

'This is he. How did you know?'

'Guy told me. He's worried about you. I think I am, too.' Moncrieff gestured at the cage. 'Why here? Why now? Why this little chap?'

'I needed to think.' Barton was peering up at him, her hand shielding her eyes from the glare of the sun. 'And Jimmy, believe

it or not, helps immeasurably. I know it sounds silly, but we talk
sometimes, and I think he understands.'

'Talk about what?'

'This and that. Everything, really.'

'That's not an answer.'

'I know.' She nodded at the gibbon. 'Maybe you should put
the question to Jimmy here. Ask nicely, and you might even
make friends.'

She began to struggle to her feet but when Moncrieff extended
a hand to help her up, she shook her head.

'I can manage perfectly well,' she said. 'But thanks for the
offer.'

Upright now, she dug in the pocket of her coat and produced
a handful of hazel nuts. 'Give him these,' she said. 'It's not
allowed really but he adores them. You'll have a friend for life.'

Moncrieff took the nuts, checked left and right for a patrolling
keeper, and then squatted beside the little gibbon.

'He's young?'

'Ten months. He has no mother.'

'Just you.'

'Just me.'

'Does he bite?'

'Never. If you're lucky, he might blow you a kiss.'

There were three nuts. Moncrieff fed them through the
diamond holes in the mesh, one after another. Jimmy reached
for them absently, nibbled on the first, stored other two in the
drift of straw on the concrete, but his gaze never left Barton's face.

Moncrieff brushed his hands clean, and then stood up.

'I get it now,' he said. 'The bloody animal's in love with you.'

*

They shared a pot of tea at the open-air café at the heart of the zoo. There were more patched-up soldiers at the neighbouring table, and Moncrieff half listened to a couple of privates comparing notes about their least favourite Sergeant-Major while Barton paid a visit. By the time she got back, she seemed to have abandoned her earlier mood. The sense of reverie, of slight wistfulness, had gone.

'Wuensche is in Camp 165.' She'd barely sat down.

Moncrieff scribbled himself a note. Camp 165, at the very top of Scotland, had been built for high-value German officers, a category that would very definitely include SS *Obersturmbannführer* Max Wuensche.

'But why the urgency?' Moncrieff was pouring the tea. 'Why the priority cable from Bern? Am I allowed to ask?'

'Of course. There was a development four days ago. March the 8th to be precise. You'll know about Karl Wolff. He's the top SS man in Italy, second only to Kesselring.'

Moncrieff nodded. Maskelyne had told him about Karl Wolff over lunch at the hotel. An interesting character, he'd said. Not at all your standard-issue psychopath.

'And?'

'He turned up in Zurich to talk to Dulles, I imagine about some kind of peace deal. They met at a ground-floor apartment on the Genferstrasse. We have no knowledge of what happened, which I have to say is troubling, but it seems he stayed the night. The next day he popped back over the border to Italy, where he belongs, and that afternoon is when we got the cable from Dulles at OSS. When the Americans say Urgent they normally mean it.'

'So why does he want us to lay hands on Wuensche?'

'Very good question. You've read the file?'

'I have.'

'Sadly it's incomplete. One of the items it doesn't include is what Wuensche was up to between October 1938 and the end of that next year before he got posted to the LASSAH.' The *Leibstandarte Adolf Hitler* was an elite SS regiment heavily involved in the battle for France.

'And?'

'He was assigned to the *Führerbegleitkommando* at the Chancellery. That meant he was bodyguarding the Führer. They had near-daily contact. The accounts I read during my time at The Hague suggested that Wuensche was Hitler's favourite orderly. That was certainly the view of that fool Payne Best. I remember him telling me that Wuensche was the son Hitler had never had, perfect in every physical detail, blond, handsome, prepared to die for the cause.'

Moncrieff smiled. Captain Payne Best was one of two SIS agents lured into an artful trap laid by Himmler's rising star, Walter Schellenberg. Barton, then working as a translator and secretary at the embassy, had watched them both leaving to drive to a meeting at the German border but never saw either of them again.

'So why are the Americans so eager to lay hands on him?' Moncrieff asked.

'Very good question. It must have something to do with Wolff. The two episodes, the Zurich meeting and then the cable arriving from Dulles, have to be linked. But there's something else, I'm afraid, even more troubling.'

Moncrieff waited. In these situations, he knew better than to press Barton for further details. She liked to think things through, test every link in the chain, take her time.

'Before you traced the man,' she said finally, 'I raised the issue with Guy. It turned out he'd already seen the cable and had conversations elsewhere.'

'With whom?'

'He wouldn't say. I'm assuming Broadway. Those people adore Switzerland. They fight for assignments there. I gather the food is very good, as well as plentiful.'

'And?'

'Guy thinks Dulles has asked for the wretched man to be shipped over, and he says there isn't a chance in hell of that ever happening.'

'But why would Dulles want him?'

'He wouldn't say. Pawn in some game or other? Something to do with Wolff? I haven't the first idea. Broadway have no time for Dulles, especially Claude Dansey. He thinks the OSS people have far too much budget and nothing between their ears. Start buying information for their kind of money, and half the world will be queuing up to sell you rubbish.'

Moncrieff nodded. Claude Dansey was the Deputy Director of MI6. Codenamed 'Z', he was widely hated, even within his own organisation. Liddell himself, rarely given to expletives, had recently described him as 'an utter shit'.

'You think Dansey's trying to queer Dulles's pitch?'

'I do, yes.' Barton was biting her lip now. 'And I must say that isn't helpful. Wolff has a great deal of authority in northern Italy. He commands fifty thousand SS troops. They control the Alpine passes, and he has the ear of Kesselring. Down there beyond the Alps, the German commanders are a law unto themselves. If the pair of them have decided the game's up, if they're offering some kind of local surrender, that could shorten the war. But we simply don't know.'

Ursula Barton, as Moncrieff had long realised, hated any kind of vacuum. One of her favourite words was lacunae, which Moncrieff had been obliged to look up. It meant empty spaces.

By definition, the world of intelligence was riddled with these holes and Barton made it her business to fill them.

'So what do you suggest we do?'

Barton was making another note to herself. At length, she looked up.

'I talked to Broadway this morning. They're denying everything. They tell me they're far too busy to be bothering with the likes of Dulles, or even Wolff, but the sad thing is they've even forgotten how to lie properly. Listen to the space between the words, and they know exactly what's going on. Which might turn out to be a very big problem.'

'For?'

'All of us. The war's coming to an end. Everyone knows that. The question is how, and when, and who controls which bits of our poor bloody continent when it's all over. Yalta, I'm afraid, solved nothing. The Red Army are about to fall on Berlin, and God knows where else. No one seems able to stop them, something that Stalin knows only too well. Look at the map, and you start to wonder about Trieste. As we speak, the Russians are closing on the Adriatic. Yugoslavia belongs to Tito. Head west, occupy the Po Valley, and it's a clear run to the French border. At the moment, that's not possible because there's still fighting in northern Italy, but ask yourself this question: what happens if the Germans surrender? Most of the Italian partisans are Communist. A lot of them belong to the Garibaldi Brigades. Their weapons come in from Yugoslavia, and most of their orders arrive by radio from Moscow, and I have it on good authority that a lot of those weapons have been buried, pending some kind of coup after the war is over. Communism is like water, Tam. It flows downhill until someone has the presence of mind to stop it.'

Barton tapped the table, one carefully trimmed nail making her point. Moncrieff said he understood the geography of the thing, and the insatiable Bolshevik appetite for Western hearts and minds, but enquired, once again, what she wanted to do about it. She studied him for a long moment. She'd lost weight recently, and the slant of afternoon sunshine deepened the hollows of her face. She looked gaunt, Moncrieff realised, and suddenly old. The war, he thought, is taking its toll on all of us.

'I had a very good friend in The Hague.' Barton had brightened. 'She was a Dutch woman, Anneke De Vries. She spoke perfect German and passable French and she was attached to the embassy on the Broadway payroll. She had excellent connections in Holland and across the border in Belgium but like the rest of us she could see that nothing would stop the Germans arriving one morning and taking over. Broadway gave her an agent codename. *Clover.*'

After war was declared, she said, *Clover* sensibly cashed in her chips at the embassy and decamped to Switzerland. She had trouble getting residency but finally found the right people to impress and ended up in a homely little apartment in Locarno. It was still possible to make telephone calls to Switzerland, providing you didn't mind listening ears on the line, and Barton had stayed in touch.

'And she's still there?'

'Very much so. I talked to her only this morning, just before I left to come here. When I suggested that you might be paying her a visit, she sounded delighted.'

'Me?'

'You.'

'When?'

'As soon as possible. One of us needs to get down there to

sort out the misunderstanding about Wuensche, and *Clover* assures me she knows all the people who matter.'

'But why don't you go?'

'Me? I'm afraid I'm a little busy just now.' She edged her chair back from the table, turned her face to the sun, and closed her eyes. 'My Mr Witherby died yesterday morning, which was probably for the best. His funeral will be next week.'

9

On his second day with Marshal Zhukov's 1st Belorussian Front, Nehmann was riding on the back of a T-34 tank. All morning, they'd rolled through a forlorn scattering of Polish villages, most of them half destroyed, some of the ruins still smoking in the wake of the German retreat. The tank bucked and dipped and swayed on the wreckage of the highway, and when another village appeared the young commander standing in the open turret would yell an order above the thunder of the engine, and a thin, grease-stained hand would appear from below with chunks of black bread. These offerings the commander would toss to the skinny kids at the roadside with a cheery wave and a volley of Russian oaths. Fill your bellies, he'd yell. And tell your dad to fuck the Germans if they ever come back.

Nehmann was glad of the engine. The vibration had penetrated deep inside him, a ceaseless clatter that crept up through the soles of his boots, but that didn't matter in the slightest because the hot breath from the engine bay gusted up through the metal vents and kept him warm in the freezing slipstream. He'd been like this since dawn, half standing, half crouching, hanging onto a clamp on the back of the turret, and when they finally juddered to a halt beside a stand of spindly trees in the middle of nowhere to brew tea and *kasha*, his sheer endurance won the admiration of the four-man crew.

Already, he loved these men. He'd been flown from Moscow to join the advance west of a town called Pila, and the last forty-eight hours had revived the reporter in Werner Nehmann. The tank crew had accepted his presence as they appeared to accept everything else. Three and a half years of war had blown many things their way and none of them thought to question this little scrap of a man with his pad and pencil, and his seeming indifference to any hardship. It helped that Nehmann had arrived with two bottles of vodka and supplies of looted German *Wurst*, gifts from the pilot who'd delivered him from Moscow, but when the sausage ran out on that first night it was second nature for the crew to share their own supplies.

It had been difficult to guess their age, these men. Only the driver, a thin-faced redhead from Minsk, was prepared to answer a direct question, and when his claim to be twenty-one produced roars of laughter, Nehmann suspected he was lying. What was easier to sense was the bond these men shared. They could only muster two enamel mugs between them but as the vodka slipped down, and the mugs passed from hand to hand, they loosened up, peering through the clouds of *makhorka* smoke, and embroidering extravagant accounts of all the Germans they'd had the pleasure of killing.

Later, drunk, they'd ended the evening sprawled beside a modest fire on the freezing turf, passing round creased sepia photos of loved ones, and crooning love songs from the Motherland. One of them had described in great detail the last wedding he'd attended, not because of the bride and groom, but because of the *food* on offer, and way past midnight, under a newish moon, one of them had produced a mouth organ. They all knew Konstantin Simonov's ballad, 'Wait For Me', by heart, but the alternative lyrics Nehmann had picked up in the Gulag won him a round of applause.

'Where did you learn that, *tovarish*?'

'Kolyma.'

'You're a fucking *Vory*?'

'A journalist.' Nehmann had lifted his mug in salute. 'Is there a difference?'

Now, next day, they were eating again. Half a dozen tanks had stopped on the edge of a village, waiting for the refuelling bowser, and crews in their heavy padded suits were milling around in the thin sunshine, stamping warmth into their boots and nursing mugs of black tea. One of Nehmann's crew had laid his hands on the heel of a cake, booty from one of the houses in the village, and had used a bayonet to carve it into thin slices. Nehmann, meanwhile, was washing his hands with wet moss and studying one of the other tanks. The enormous tracks were thick with mud from the overnight rain but what caught his attention was the slogan daubed in red paint across the side of the turret.

'*Berlog*?' he queried.

'*Berlog*. The Belly of the Beast, *tovarish*. It means Berlin. Think of it as a warning. We're on our way.' He gestured towards the straggle of nearby houses. 'These people need to know that.'

Another tanker had joined them. He shared the cramped turret with the commander and saw to the loading of the cannon.

'But they're so *old*, these Germans. And so rich, too. You should see some of these places. Why did they ever bother with Russia when they've got so much? What did we have that they didn't? You should take a look. We'll find somewhere nice for you this afternoon. Carpets, *tovarish*. Cattle in the fields. Wood for the fire. Wine in the cellar and a wife in bed. They're on the road now, the ones who can still walk, but it fucking serves them right, that's what I think.'

Nehmann didn't blame them. On the road west, the refugees were everywhere, heads down, hauling little handcarts piled high with the pick of a lifetime's possessions, some of the men wearing two coats. The women, especially, were visibly nervous, refusing to meet the gaze of strangers. At Nehmann's request, the commander had stopped to let him talk to some of these people, impressed by his command of German. He'd taken one youngish woman aside, and managed to win her confidence, and it was quickly obvious that stories of rape and plunder were everywhere, word of mouth that went before these invading hordes. Whether or not his own crew had helped themselves along the way Nehmann didn't know, and didn't ask, but when they fired up the big engine again, and churned across the rain-soft tussock to get back on the road, the crew were like kids, driving madly around clusters of refugees, the commander blowing them kisses, oblivious to the older folk, muttering curses in their wake.

A little further down the road they'd caught sight of a long file of infantrymen in open-top trucks, the shock troops at the heart of this enormous army, and the commander had ordered the driver to slow right down as they growled past. Few of the men spared the tank even a glance. They must have come hundreds – maybe thousands – of kilometres, thought Nehmann, and it certainly showed. Greatcoats mended with shreds of old tarpaulin, boots re-soled with leather ripped from the seats of abandoned German tanks, grubby kids adopted as mascots. The kids, some absurdly young, danced on the back of the truck among the soldiers, their skinny chests criss-crossed with bandoliers of ammunition.

This patched-together People's Army had been a joke in Berlin three years ago as the *Wehrmacht* swept east, but at Stalingrad – as Nehmann knew only too well – it had turned, and fought and brought hundreds of thousands of the Reich's finest to their knees, and now, two long years later, the time had arrived for a settling of accounts. To be German, Nehmann thought, was already a misfortune. To be Prussian, invaded by this Mongol rabble, was often a death sentence.

Later, around noon, the tank stopped again, waved to a halt by an officer with four stars on his grey shoulder boards. A battered staff car was parked on the side of the road, and the young commander hauled himself out of the turret and dismounted for a brief conference. There were more staff officers beside the car. One of them had unfolded a map on the bonnet and the tank commander nodded as a gloved finger stabbed at a cluster of features ringed in red. Back aboard, the commander told Nehmann that they were heading for a place called Altdamm, up near Stettin. There, they would reinforce units already laying siege to the Germans. According to the staff officer, progress in the battle was exceeding expectations. Their efforts, if successful, would shield Marshal Zhukov's right flank and Zhukov, he said with a grin, held the keys to Berlin.

On the road again, the tank dipping and rolling beneath him, Nehmann clung on. He was beginning to tire of the journey, the constant tacking left and right to avoid abandoned vehicles and columns of refugees, and now the added curse of a freezing rain that came sheeting out of a towering bank of clouds to the north. The commander thought they'd make the outskirts of Altdamm by nightfall, and Nehmann, his face turned away from the icy needles blowing across the sodden fields, hoped he was right, but then the engine began to cough beneath his feet, and they were slowing to pull off the road.

The loader, who doubled as the tank's mechanic, struggled out of the turret and gestured for Nehmann to get off the engine casing. He lifted a panel, peered inside, glanced up at the commander and pulled a face, but the commander was already staring down the road behind them. Nehmann half turned to follow his pointing finger and found himself looking at a long column of assorted vehicles that must, he thought, be the main body of this force: big much-dented Studebaker cars and hefty Dodge trucks hauling enormous howitzers, both gifted by the Americans, farm tractors towing light field guns, and then a second echelon of huddled troops in horse-drawn carts and panje wagons. This, to Nehmann, was the carnival of his dreams, proof that nothing would stand in the way of the Red Army's wrath, but then, minutes later at the very end of the column, came a detachment of Cossack cavalrymen on their shaggy little ponies.

They were dressed like pirates, enveloped in their sheepskins and big fur hats. They wore heavy moustaches, and sat erect on their pygmy mounts, ignoring the rain, and every man had loot strapped to his saddle. As they clattered past, Nehmann lost count of the carefully rolled carpets, the plundered clocks and vases, the precious keepsakes looted from estate after enemy estate. One man had even managed to lay hands on a sizeable chicken. Attached to the saddle by a length of cord around its feet, it was still alive, its weary little wings flapping against the piebald flanks of the pony. Watching them disappear up the road, Nehmann could only think of the *Vory* he'd got to know in the Kolyma camps. It was the Soviet genius to enlist people like this – their fierceness, their inbred criminality – and unleash them on the hated enemy. For the Germans, he concluded, the war was nearly over.

*

Dusk found Nehmann on the banks of the River Oder. The loader had fixed the engine and now his new comrades, along with dozens of other crews, were crowded around a tall, intense-looking figure who reminded Nehmann of a priest he'd known back in the Caucasus. This, he'd just been told, was a *politruki*, one of the political commissars who accompanied the front-line troops and made sure they marched in step with the implacable demands of the Revolution. The *politruki* had planted a small red flag on the edge of the river's embankment, and now he was listing the crimes these men had come to avenge. The list went on and on, a dizzying tally of abuse from theft to rape, dozens of casual or deliberate acts of cruelty that demanded retribution, and he used his big hands to conjure visions of deflowered daughters and bereaved mothers back in the wreckage of the homeland.

Nehmann was a connoisseur when it came to oratory like this. At Berlin venues big and small, he'd watched Goebbels do something similar much earlier in the war, lighting a fire in the hearts of his watching audience until the speech ended in the thunder of stamping boots and a forest of extended arms and the roar of *Heil Hitler* repeated again and again. The *politruki* had a similar talent for arousing anger, and provoking revenge. It was an accomplished performance, and Nehmann watched the faces in the half-darkness, the men nodding, occasionally whispering to each other, shifting their weight from foot to foot, ever more eager to move on and tear the enemy limb from limb. At the end of his little speech, the *politruki* asked for men who'd so far neglected to join the Communist Party to step forward. A handful did so, visibly ashamed, and Nehmann watched as the *politruki* produced a pen and a sheaf of membership forms. Every man signed up.

Nehmann's tank crew, as it turned out, were too late to the battle. Next morning, the show was over, and Nehmann

watched column after column of beaten Germans filing past
the wet riverside meadows where dozens of vehicles – tanks,
trucks, panje wagons – had spent the night. According to the
tank commander, these prisoners would be shipped east on
cattle trucks already laden with the loot parcels allotted to each
Soviet trooper. The prisoners, like the loot, would be processed
through the huge railway junction at Kursk, and Nehmann
wondered how many of them would survive the long journey
east to appear in ragged marching order on Moscow streets,
themselves the booty of war.

*

At mid-morning, in what Nehmann sensed was a Red Army
ritual, the tank crews were taken by truck to view the battlefield.
Days of artillery bombardment had levelled many of the town's
buildings, yet the spire of a church still penetrated the blanket of
dusty, acrid smoke that hung over everything like a grey wash on
a canvas that had never quite worked. Corpses lay everywhere,
some human, some animal, mainly horses. Many had been
hideously disfigured by bursting shells or falling masonry, and
Nehmann watched the tankmen as they drifted from body to
body with a curiously detached interest in what they were seeing.

Whether this was indifference, Nehmann didn't know. Sights
like these, he told himself, must be all too familiar after years of
ceaseless combat. He himself, at Stalingrad, had become immune
to the flesh-and-blood consequences of high explosive. But then
one man had paused and crouched briefly beside the body of an
officer before removing a watch from his wrist, and after that
many others took a livelier interest in what might be on offer.

Back beside the tank, Nehmann was saying his goodbyes to
the men who'd so briefly become his comrades-in-arms. He'd
made contact with the NKVD Major who was to ease his passage

over the river and into Germany. Already, he'd changed into the serge trousers and rough flannel shirt liberated from one of the houses in the ruined city. With a heavy greatcoat on top and a pair of worn galoshes, he could melt into the flood of refugees fleeing west. With his fluent German and his quick wit, he knew he could survive any of the roadside checks the next few days might have in store for him. He even had money, a handful of soiled Reichsmark notes that might, if the trains were still running, buy him a rail ticket.

One after another, he pumped the extended hands of the crew. In their very different ways, they were all curious to know what he was up to but every question sparked nothing but a shrug, and a slow smile, and the promise that he'd be the first to Berlin. There, God willing, they'd all meet again and it would be Nehmann's pleasure to lay hands on something decent to drink. The war was on its deathbed, he said. With luck, they'd all survive it.

At this point, the commander announced that he'd a small present he'd like to give to his crew's favourite Georgian. He dug in the pocket of his padded suit and produced a small twist of the cotton waste the crew used to keep their weapons clean.

Nehmann looked at it, perplexed. In the palm of his hand, it weighed nothing.

'Inside,' the commander nodded at the little parcel.

Nehmann unwrapped it and found himself looking at a five-pointed star. It must have been cut from a flattened tin. The scissorwork was faultless, with a hole fashioned at the top, but he could see a smear of what might have been borscht on one side.

Nehmann looked up at the commander. He was genuinely moved and said so.

'Wear it.' The commander produced a thin length of cord. 'It will keep you safe.'

Nehmann nodded, threading the cord through the hole and securing it with a knot before slipping it over his head. Inside his shirt, nestled against his skinny chest, it already felt familiar.

One of the watching crew, the youngest, was nursing another present.

'It's German,' he said, 'from *Wehrmacht* headquarters in the town. I got five of them, one each.' It was a one-piece undergarment in thick cotton. It looked brand new, and when he held it out against Nehmann's slight frame it looked a perfect fit. 'Wear it,' he was grinning. 'Keep yourself warm.'

Nehmann said he was grateful. Christmas, he thought. A little late but more than welcome. Looking at the faces, grinning, expectant, he knew he owed them a present in return. He dug in his bag, not knowing what might come to hand, then his fingers closed around the book. The kilometres they'd travelled together had taken a little of the lustre off the scarlet leather cover but it still weighed heavy in his hand. Nehmann offered it to the commander.

'For when you run out of vodka,' he said. 'On cold nights.'

The commander stared at the title, then his fingers explored the embossed gold title.

'*War and Peace?*' He showed the book to the rest of the crew. Then came a stir of movement as the loader clambered down from the tank. He'd been working on the engine again and his palms were filthy with grime and oil. He spared Nehmann a farewell handshake, but then winked at his mates and pulled up his sleeve to reveal his bare arm.

Five watches. All of them German.

10

That same day, late in the afternoon, Wilhelm Schultz took the tram to Stockholm's Central Station. Diski, his NKVD contact, was waiting on the concourse just metres away from the gated entry to Platform Seven. He was carrying a black leather briefcase of a kind Schultz had seen in offices in the Lubyanka, and he looked tense. In the grey dusk, Schultz could see the long snake of unlit carriages that would take him south to Malmö. Instructions for the rendezvous had been delivered by a voice he didn't recognise on a Stockholm telephone number Diski had given him in Moscow.

Now, the Russian led him to the nearby kiosk where two women were dispensing hot drinks to a thin line of waiting passengers. Diski bought two glasses of *Gloog*, a hot, spiced mulled wine that Schultz had first sampled only the day before, peering at the unfamiliar banknote before he handed it over. Then he motioned Schultz across to an empty space away from a flood of travellers getting off a train that had just arrived.

Schultz asked him how long he'd been in Stockholm, but the answer was already obvious. Diski couldn't take his eyes off the swirl of passengers on the concourse. These people, thought Schultz, had zoo appeal if you'd just survived another Russian winter. They were foreign, exotic, well fed, nicely turned out. Strangers acknowledged strangers, even exchanged smiles. Couples made physical contact, held hands, kissed hello. No one stole a glance over their shoulders, and the street outside was bright with lights. Moscow belonged on a very different planet.

'You came today?' Schultz asked.

'This afternoon. The boat from Riga.' He tapped his watch. 'It leaves again at midnight.'

'You're not coming to Malmö?'

'No.'

Schultz was confused. Back in Moscow, the plan had been for Diski to accompany him south, perhaps even into Germany itself. From the Baltic coast, it was barely four hundred kilometres to Berlin. There, Schultz was under instructions to revive his intelligence contacts in the *Abwehr* and test rumours that the Nazi leadership was beginning to fragment in the scramble to fend off a catastrophic defeat. Diski spoke perfect German and could validate whatever conversations Schultz might be part of. The Kremlin trusted no one.

'You're telling me I'm on my own?'

'Yes.'

'To do what?'

Diski was frowning. When he was especially nervous, he always had a cigarette between his fingers. Now, grinding the remains of the old one into the concourse, he was already lighting another.

'Tell me about Dahlerus,' he said.

Schultz did his best. There was no point lying because the Big House had a presence everywhere, especially in neutral capitals like this, and he was near certain that his every move had been monitored.

'I talked to his wife,' Schultz said. 'That's the best I could do. Dahlerus wants the fighting to stop. He's a businessman.

Peace means profits. Of course he'll talk to Himmler, if that might be useful.'

'And Bernadotte?'

'He's having conversations already. Schellenberg will grease the way. That's how Himmler works. There's another thing. Himmler runs the concentration camps, always has. Back in '42, when I was still in the Reich, the SS had already locked up hundreds of thousands, millions if you're counting the Jews. That gives him something to put on the negotiating table, which is why he's talking to Bernadotte. He runs the Red Cross here. He has a stake in this game, and he has contacts in London and Washington. He wants to see those camps empty, and only Himmler can make that happen.'

'You know that? You've talked to Bernadotte?'

'No. But that's the way it is. People like Himmler are desperate. You Russians are kicking the door in and they're shitting themselves.'

'You think he'd talk to us?'

'I think he'd talk to anyone. It's human nature. You don't have to be a spy to understand any of this.'

Diski raised an eyebrow, and then checked his watch before extracting a biggish envelope from the briefcase.

'Your train leaves in half an hour.' He nodded towards the platform. 'You'll be met at the station in Malmö. Our people there will drive you to an airfield. Things are changing fast in Berlin. Himmler was summoned to the Chancellery several days ago. Hitler is furious about the mess he's making on the front line. It was his idea to give Himmler command of an Army Group and he's turned out to be hopeless. This reflects badly on that Führer of yours, which is something that must never happen, and we gather that Himmler has gone to pieces. He's left Berlin for the SS sanatorium in Hohenlychen. You may know of it.'

Schultz nodded. He'd opened the envelope. Inside he'd found a single train ticket for Malmö, plus a sizeable wad of Reichsmarks and a fully stamped ID card. The photo showed a face that Schultz could barely remember: well fed, confident, with just a hint of a smile.

'Where did you get this?'

'We made it. We had your old ID from Stalingrad and did the rest ourselves. Everything's up to date, except the photo. We've kept you in the *Abwehr*, same rank. You answer to Himmler now but he allows the *Abwehr* crest.' He nodded at the ID card. 'It'll get you through any check, I guarantee it.'

'And this?' A smaller envelope had Himmler's name on it. The name was typed in German characters, not Cyrillic, and the envelope – unlike the paperwork Schultz had come across in Moscow – was excellent quality, with a weight that suggested something important inside.

'You want me to give him this? Himmler?'

'I do, yes. He knows you're coming.'

'So what's inside?'

'That's of no importance, not to you. Simply give him the envelope. You may think it wise to explain your own circumstances. That's up to you. Either way, it's imperative it gets into the hands of Himmler. You have to *know* that. That's your task.'

'And afterwards?'

'Afterwards you go to Berlin, as planned. How you get there is your decision, your choice. Hohenlychen, as I'm sure you know, is only a couple of hours away. In Berlin, you first make contact with this man,' Diski produced a folded sheet of paper from the inside pocket of his greatcoat.

Schultz gazed at it. Careful capital letters. Nothing Cyrillic. Plus two eight-digit numbers.

'Rainer Gehlhausen?' he looked up.

'*Dr* Gehlhausen. He's a surgeon. The first number is the Charité hospital where he works. The other one is his apartment.'

'And he's German?'

'Yes. Normally I'd give you a codename but these aren't normal times. Gehlhausen has been with us since the thirties.'

'And you have contact with him?'

'Of course. And we trust him implicitly. When you meet, extend my greetings and tell him to be patient, though patience is something I doubt he'll need. Doing what this man does, you'd have no doubts that the war is nearly over.'

Schultz glanced at the name again and then looked up.

'And Nehmann?' he enquired. 'Werner?'

'Still in Kolyma, where we can keep an eye on him.' He nodded at the smaller envelope. 'Just make sure that gets to Himmler.'

*

The Malmö train left on time. Schultz's last experience of travelling by rail had taken him from Stalingrad to Moscow two whole years ago, half crushed to death in a third-class carriage. They'd stopped at station after station en route for no good purpose, every door guarded by armed soldiers, nobody on, nobody off, and he remembered gazing out at the peasant faces on the platforms, the chaos of war writ small in their knotted bundles, their dirty children, their outstretched hands, their lowered heads, their muttered prayers.

Now, to his delight and surprise, the Revolution had paid for a first-class ticket and he had an entire compartment, all six seats, to himself. This was a world of plump upholstery, of a carefully swept floor, of armrests, of a curtain that would give him a little privacy from the corridor outside, and even of a menu, slipped into an embossed leather folder. He'd been allocated a seat in the compartment at the very front of the train, and as the big engine cleared its throat and the train juddered and began to move, he sat beside the window, his case stored on the overhead rack, the envelope from Diski on his lap, staring out as the locomotive rumbled over the blackness of water, heading south.

This, according to Diski, was his return to a life he'd thought he'd never see again. As long as he did their bidding and delivered the letter, and made his way to Berlin, he'd be a free man, a German in the land of his birth. Was this why he'd been so carefully processed back in Moscow? First tamed by the Ukrainians? Then preserved and shelved like a jar of pickles in a draughty, falling-apart suburban apartment with a bunch of elderly alcoholics for neighbours? Was his real fate always at the mercy of events in Berlin? With Diski and his masters awaiting the moment when they needed someone like Schultz, someone with the right pedigree, the right connections, to deliver a message, one tiny fragment of the jigsaw, and thus – in some mysterious way – hasten the war to its end? Was his role, in short, to make a brief appearance at the drama's final act? Before the curtain came down and the audience rose to its feet?

Schultz, in his heart, knew the answer was no. The last couple of days in Stockholm had restored a little of his old confidence, his old bravado. In his shed of an apartment in Moscow, he'd been living, as they'd always intended, like a non-person, neither Russian nor properly German, neither dead nor properly alive. Readied beneath his bed was an ancient pair of boots. With the aid of a thin chisel and a borrowed hammer, he'd spent days fashioning a slot where the heel met the sole of the right boot, and when he'd finished he'd slipped a razor blade inside. The slot, virtually invisible, would pass most inspections, while the razor blade meant that never again would he have to face the

Ukrainians. Arrested, he'd simply save the NKVD the chore of killing him.

This single act, he now recognised, had kept him at least half-sane. It meant that they hadn't quite eliminated all of him. It meant that he could still take the initiative, still decide the course of events. The fact that he'd be taking his own life was irrelevant. Because it would be his choice, not theirs.

Now, as the last of the Stockholm suburbs slipped away, he knew he had to build on the sweetness of that one little victory. His years in the *Abwehr*, first on the front line, latterly in a senior position, had taught him many things, but the most important by far was the cardinal rule that applied to everything in the intelligence world. Trust no one. Ever.

Diski's employers had built an entire empire on that single principle, hundreds of thousands of agents across the vastness of the Soviet Union, and however beguiling was this offer of freedom, back there on the station concourse, Schultz knew that it couldn't possibly be so simple. The NKVD gave nothing away. What seemed plausible wasn't, and in the ceaseless struggle to protect the Revolution, everything – including *Oberst* Wilhelm Schultz – was expendable. He could do his best to make sure that this letter got to Himmler. But what would happen afterwards?

Staring into the blackness of the Swedish night, he became aware of another noise over the rumble of the train. Then, in the window, he watched the reflection of a waiter with a trolly pausing outside the compartment. The door slid open. Schultz knew no Swedish. The waiter spoke passable German and asked whether Schultz had made a choice from the menu. When Schultz shook his head, he gestured towards the trolly outside.

'Cold meat or cold fish. Cold potatoes. A little salad.'

Schultz chose meat. A minute or so later, he was looking at a plate of grey-looking beef, thinly sliced, overcooked. The waiter returned with the vegetables, and a basket of rolls.

'You want wine?'

'Red.'

'A half-bottle comes with the ticket. You pay if you want more.'

'A half-bottle is fine.' Schultz gestured down at the tray. 'I need a glass of water, and another knife. The smaller the better.'

'You have two knives already, sir. The second is for the rolls.'

'I need a third.'

The waiter shot him a look and then shrugged. The extra knife was exactly the same size as the second. He gave it a wipe, handed Schultz the water and another glass for the wine, and then left the compartment. Schultz waited for the clatter of the trolly to recede down the corridor before getting to his feet and drawing the curtain across the sliding door. Privacy, he thought. At all costs.

Back in his seat by the window, the tray stored on the seat opposite, Schultz lowered the blind, examining the letter for Himmler, lifting it to the individual light above his shoulder. Turning it over, he knew he was in luck. Whoever had sealed the flap had expended the minimum of effort. The triangle of flap was secured only by its tip. Schultz studied it, and then dipped his forefinger into the glass of water, wiped it nearly dry, and then applied the residue to the tip of the flap. There were heating vents beneath the seats and Schultz bent to expose the back of the envelope to the trickle of hot air. Moments later, he knew he wouldn't need the extra knife.

There was a single sheet of heavy-gauge paper inside, double-folded. Putting the envelope to one side, he wiped his hands on his trousers and then flattened the letter on his lap. The embossed heading was in Cyrillic but he'd been in Russia long enough to recognise key elements. This letter had come from the Kremlin.

The text itself, mercifully, was in German and as he absorbed the three brief paragraphs, he sensed the hand of Diski behind the cautious shuffle of the prose. The sender of the letter presented his compliments to the *Reichsführer-SS*. He regretted the abandonment of the Non-Aggression Pact that had launched this war, and everything that had followed. In the pursuit of what he termed 'a just and sensible outcome', he suggested that the time had come for a pooling of mutual interests. Should the *Reichsführer-SS* be minded to explore this possibility further, then the Soviet Union would happily entertain the notion of bilateral talks at the highest level. These would naturally have, in the first place, to be conducted in the deepest secrecy, and preceded with a public gesture that established – beyond reasonable doubt – the *Reichsführer-SS*'s continuing authority in running the business of the state.

This last condition brought the letter to an end, no expression of good wishes, or even the best of health, but that was hardly the point because what took Schultz's gaze was the signature scrawled across the bottom of the page. The signature itself was terse, forceful, difficult to decipher. Beneath, carefully typed, was a helping hand. 'MK Stalin.'

Schultz looked up a moment. His *Abwehr* days had brought him a number of windfalls but never anything on this scale. His first instinct was to lock the door, which he did, but the moment he tested it to make sure, it slid back on its runners. He locked it again. Same result. This compartment had been pre-allocated, his seat and carriage numbers on the ticket. Did this account for the absence of other passengers? Would the thunder of the adjoining locomotive drown his protests as he fought off any attack? Had he, even this early in the journey, been lured into a trap? Methodically, he discounted the possibilities one by one. He read the letter a second time, and then a third, before returning it to the envelope and sealing the flap properly. Even a minute examination, he thought, would show no signs of interference.

With the letter tucked inside the pocket of his jacket, he raised the blind on the window and poured himself a glass of wine. I'm Stalin, he told himself. I'm the mighty *Vozhd*. Assuming the latter is authentic, accepting the authorship at face value, why would I ever launch a bid like this? Schultz had been studying foreign newspapers in Stockholm. Some of them were English, others American, and he'd even found copies of *Pravda* on the city's newsstands. They were all at least three days old, and he could read neither English nor Russian, but that hardly mattered because the photos and maps, with their helpful little arrows, all told the same story: that millions of Soviet troops were poised on the banks of the River Oder, ready to consign the Thousand Year Reich to an early grave.

In these funeral rites, the city that really mattered was Berlin. Already half destroyed by British and American bombers, she was still the beating heart of the Hitler regime, and whichever army seized her first would have the loudest voice in post-war negotiations. Millions of Red Army troops waiting just two hours' drive from the capital told Stalin that victory was his. The war to date had taken numberless Soviet lives. Schultz himself had seen the evidence in the cripples and widows who peopled the streets around his apartment block. So why waste yet more Russian blood when an early German surrender might be on offer?

This, he knew, was more than a possibility. No one in Russia doubted for a moment that Stalin was sworn to defend the Motherland and to spare her needless suffering. There'd been a big get-together down in the Crimea, Roosevelt and Churchill and the *Vozhd* posing for the cameras at Yalta, but since then the Kremlin had reassured the people that Stalin had successfully put millions of Poles between themselves and any future invader who cared to chance his luck, and the nation seemed to breathe more easily as a result. The *Vozhd* is promising victory, went word on the street. He won't make widows of us all.

And yet. And yet...

Schultz studied his own image in the window. His face was in deep shadow but he fancied he could just detect the tiny bulge in his jacket where he'd stored the letter. His hand tracked upwards, confirming it was still there, then he realised that any further speculation – at least for now – was pointless. All that mattered, as Diski and his masters obviously knew, was getting this letter to its addressee.

He smiled to himself, cupping the wine glass, then he raised his big hand to the image in the window.

'*Prosit*,' he murmured. '*Weidmannsheil!*'

*

'Good hunting?' Schultz woke up seven hours later to find the door of his carriage open and the face of the guard peering in around the curtain. The remains of the meal and the empty wine bottle lay on the tray on the seat opposite.

'Ten minutes to Malmö, sir,' the guard grunted.

The face disappeared. Schultz had been sleeping full-length across three seats, his head pillowed on his carefully folded jacket. He checked that the letter was still there, and then bent to put his boots back on. Already the darkness outside the window was pricked by the lights of the city's suburbs, and when they got a little closer he watched the smoke from the locomotive coiling away in the throw of light from the trackside streets.

The moment he stepped off the train, he realised how cold it was. The sole figure waiting beyond the ticket barrier half lifted an arm in acknowledgement. He was small, even smaller than Werner Nehmann. He was wearing a heavy fur-trimmed coat, not cheap, and he spoke German with a heavy Russian accent.

'Is that all you've got?' He nodded at Schultz's jacket.

Schultz nodded, said nothing. He was watching the handful of other passengers who had got off. Faces. The way they walked. Those little tell-tale clues that all wasn't quite the way it should have been. Satisfied, he turned back.

'What now?'

'I take you to a hotel. It's two in the morning. At seven I collect you again. And then we drive out to the airfield.'

'I don't need a hotel,' Schultz grunted. 'I've slept already.'

'Wrong, my friend. Moscow is paying. How was the journey? The meal? Everything else?' He nodded towards the train. 'Enjoy, *tovarish*. This doesn't happen to many of us.'

Schultz shrugged and followed him out of the station. The hotel was a hundred metres away. Schultz came to a halt at the foot of the steps. He had a favour to ask.

'Anything, *tovarish*.'

'I need a gun. An automatic. German if possible. Also four clips of ammunition.'

The Russian looked at him. If the request took him by surprise, it didn't show. Schultz half expected a nod, a smile of compliance, something faintly deferential, but given the manners of the Revolution he knew it wouldn't happen.

'Seven o'clock,' the Russian said. 'Meet me here.'

*

To his surprise, having double-locked the door and left a crack between the curtains in the window, Schultz was asleep the moment his head hit the pillow. He'd asked the woman at the reception desk for a call at half past six, but he was already awake when the phone rang. He'd slept fully dressed but now he decided to take a shower. With the room still in darkness, he peered through the crack in the curtains. With the exception of a uniformed worker with an enormous broom, the plaza outside was empty.

Schultz dumped his clothes on the bed, checked the door, and then stepped into the shower. The water was hotter than he'd expected and he spent a moment fiddling with the two taps on the wall but then he got the balance just right. A choice of soaps was a luxury he'd ceased to believe in, and he spent long minutes lathering himself from head to toe with a little tablet of something indescribably wonderful before turning off the hot tap and bracing himself for the shock of the icy water. This was a habit he'd long ago adopted in pre-war days, a guaranteed cure for any hangover, and towelling himself dry in front of the full-length mirror he realised what a difference leaving Russia had made. The two-year hangover was gone. He felt whole again. Bits of himself he'd left with the fucking Ukrainians were, after all, slipping back into place. He felt alert, and ready, and somehow *wanted*. His exact role in this puzzling new script remained a mystery but even that he accepted as a kind of blessing. The very best bits of life, he'd always maintained, often showed up as a complete surprise.

*

The Russian was waiting, as promised, at the foot of the steps. He had a sizeable overcoat folded over one skinny arm.

'Here.' He handed it over. 'Before you freeze to fucking death.'

'What about the gun?' The overcoat felt heavy as Schultz put it on.

'It's in the right-hand pocket. A Beretta is the best I can do. It's Italian but I know comrades who swear by it. Be careful once the clip's empty because it no longer holds the slide back. 9mm Parabellum. Four clips, seven in each. *Kommen Sie mit.*'

Schultz was impressed. He'd already found the little automatic in the coat's right-hand pocket and it felt snug in his hand. Another tiny act of restitution, he thought. *Oberst* Schultz. Reporting for duty.

The Russian had a cab waiting on the other side of the plaza. He gestured Schultz into the rear seat and sat beside him.

'The airfield's ten minutes' away,' he said. 'The pilot's name is Jürgen. We use him a lot. He's been through a bit, this boy. You should ask him about the shitshow in the Ardennes. Without us fucking Russians, half the world would be speaking German by now.'

'You said *we*.' Schultz spared him a sideways glance. '*We* use him a lot.'

'That's right.'

'And he's German? This Jürgen?'

'He is,' the Russian was smiling now. '*Luftwaffe* trained. A list of medals he won't even talk about. Don't believe me, ask him yourself.'

*

Jürgen Frenzell was waiting beside a small, single-engine aircraft Schultz recognised at once. He was wearing a thick flying suit with folds of scarf around his neck that might have been silk. The moment Schultz emerged from the taxi, he flicked a lit cigar into the clear dawn light and extended a gloved hand.

'You ever been in one of these?' he nodded at the aircraft.

'Yes.'

'Noisy. You want to talk en route?'

'Yes.'

'Excellent. You'll need phones.'

Schultz stepped away to say goodbye to the Russian as Frenzell opened the pilot's door, but the taxi had already gone. Back beside the plane, Schultz watched the pilot untangling the wires from a spare pair of headphones. He'd never much liked flying, resenting the surrender of control to someone else, but he knew he had no choice. Last time he'd ridden in a Fieseler Storch, the pilot had taken off from the Tiergarten in the middle of Berlin, airborne in less than the length of a football pitch, lifting the nose of the little plane to clear the line of trees beyond the children's play zone. Jürgen Frenzell wouldn't need a proper runway at the end of this morning's journey. Any field would do.

Schultz climbed into the tiny cockpit, still in his coat, and made himself comfortable. Frenzell handed him the headphones and adjusted the volume on the circuit until Schultz was happy. The engine coughed and then fired, and the little plane shivered on the tall spindly legs of the undercarriage, eager – thought Schultz – to be in the air. Moments later, a map descended onto Schultz's lap and he followed Frenzell's gloved finger as he traced their flight path south over the Baltic Sea. An hour and a half to the German coast, he said. Then maybe another ninety minutes over Western Pomerania to Hohenlychen.

'High pressure just now.' He gestured up at the cloudless sky. 'Great visibility. Lots to see. You keep the map. Tell me when I'm going wrong.'

He reached for the throttle, threw a precautionary look in both directions, and then gunned the engine. The little plane gathered speed over the bumpy turf before Frenzell lifted the tail and coaxed it into the air. Minutes later, at barely a thousand feet, Schultz was peering down as the last of Sweden slid beneath the nose.

'You've been to this place before? The sanatorium?'

'Yes,' Schultz nodded. 'I have.'

'So what's it like?'

'It's shit. SS only. When I was last home, they sent the wounded *Waffen* boys there to be repaired. The facilities are fantastic. They've spent lots of money on it but the SS attracts a certain type, as I'm sure you know, and it doesn't take much to dress up in a white coat and become a doctor. You try very hard to ignore rumours, but in war that isn't always easy. Getting better shouldn't put you in the hands of fakes and psychopaths.'

In most company this would be dangerous talk but already Schultz sensed a kinship with this pilot. For one thing, he had the face of a child, but he moved with an awkwardness that suggested physical injuries, and when Schultz took a closer look at that face, he knew that Jürgen Frenzell, like Schultz himself, had played fast and loose in life's tighter corners.

Frenzell wanted to know more about the sanatorium. On the Eastern Front, he said, he'd flown with a pilot who'd once served on *die Fliegelstaffel des Führers*, Hitler's personal squadron. According to him, Hohenlychen was a madhouse, with whole floors reserved for top Nazis who lost their battles with sanity and started frothing at the mouth.

'He told you that? This friend of yours?'

'He did. You want the truth, it made me laugh. Us *Luftwaffe* guys tend not to get involved. But Georg knew. He was a serious man. He didn't make stuff up.'

'This is Georg Messner?' Schultz asked.

'You know him?'

'Tall? Face that had been through a windscreen? Worked for Wolfram von Richthofen? One of the few pilots the great man ever trusted?'

'The same,' Frenzell nodded, glancing across at the map. 'Georg got himself killed on an airstrip in Russia when the Ivans turned up.'

'Tatsinskaya,' Schultz grunted. 'A tank shell blew his tent to pieces. He was inside.'

'You were there?' Frenzell was staring at him now. 'You saw it happen?'

'Not me, a good friend. He tried to get Messner out of that tent but it was too late.'

'But you were there, too?'

'No, I was at the end of the supply line.'

'You mean Stalingrad?'

'I do. I was taken prisoner there. Me and my good friend.'

'And since then?'

'Don't ask.'

Frenzell nodded, said nothing. Then Schultz felt a tiny pressure at waist level. It was Frenzell. He wanted to shake his hand.

They crossed the coast shortly after nine o'clock. Schultz, trying to marry an island below the left wing to the map on his lap, concluded that he was looking at Rugen.

'Wonderful place,' Frenzell was smiling. 'We went there as kids in the summer. If all this shit ever stops I'll have a family of my own one day and take them back. The beaches go on forever and you're spoiled for walks in the forest. I can't think of a better reason for having kids.'

If all this shit ever stops.

They were lower now, and Schultz could see an oncoming town through the dark blur of the propeller. The fierce slant of spring sunshine burnished the red tiled roofs clustered around the town square. A big brick church sported a dome the colour of copper and, as they flew over, Schultz glimpsed a gaggle of figures on the church steps, white faces peering upwards, following the progress of this tiny plane as it droned south.

'Stralsund,' Frenzell grunted. 'Fantastic fish. You'll never taste anything fresher.'

Schultz could only nod. They were over the harbour now, and he could see a couple of work boats moored at the quayside. This was a tidy world of waterside benches, of couples walking tiny dogs on leads, of woodsmoke curling upward from chimneys in the still air, and so far the town seemed to have been physically spared by the war. Schultz was even able to make out a stall or two in what must once have been a busy market, and he fought a briefly choking gust of pride and thanksgiving.

After all the miseries of the last two years, for him and for millions of others, here it still was, *das alte Deutschland*, the old Germany, intact, whole, quietly beautiful. He might have turned the clock back. This might have been a snapshot of a prosperous Pomeranian market town long before anyone thought of Hitler, or the Brownshirts, or the hated Communists, or the annual circus at Nuremberg. So tempting, he thought, to believe there might soon be peace again.

'*Fantastisch*,' he murmured, shaking his head before returning to the map.

They saw the first columns of refugees half an hour later. By now, they were flying a little higher, just under seven hundred metres, and it was Frenzell who pointed forward through the windscreen. It looked, at first glance, like a contour line, long, dark, sinuous, following the path of the road as it wove through the flatness of the countryside.

Franzell pushed the control stick forward, offering Schultz a closer look, and as they lost height the collective shuffle westwards began to resolve itself, first into families, bunched together under the weight of what they could haul or carry, and then into individual figures, hugging the side of the road, stealing nervous glances skywards as the cackle of the approaching plane grew louder and louder.

They were low now, the fields beneath them a green blur, and Schultz watched the column scattering, the old and the lame on sticks, young mothers gathering up their children, a priest crossing himself as he headed for the nearby ditch. Then, seconds later, they'd left the tableau behind them, and Frenzell was climbing again over the sudden emptiness of the landscape.

'They should be heading for Stralsund,' Schultz grunted.

'Wrong, my friend.' Frenzell shook his head. 'The Russians will be there within days.'

*

A little later, Schultz asked when Frenzell had last seen action. The word itself brought a smile to his face.

'I'm guessing you've definitely been away,' he said.

'You're guessing right.'

'Do the Ardennes mean anything to you?'

'Plenty.'

Schultz knew that the Ardennes was an area of Belgium, thickly wooded hills that rolled down towards the French frontier. They were meant to be impassable to heavy armour until Guderian rewrote the rules in 1940 and took the thin French defence line by surprise. Mere weeks later, he was on the Picardy coast, moving north, trapping the British at Dunkirk, and Schultz remembered the euphoria of those July days when Hitler returned to Berlin with the bleeding scalp of France hanging from his belt.

'So what happened this time round?' Schultz asked.

'Same thing. It was back in December. Hitler wanted to smash the Americans and the British while he still could. The weather was on his side, low cloud base, snow, wind, blizzards, no chance of getting airborne. Then we got what looked like a break and some lunatic decided on a para drop. You never even take off if the wind speed over the drop zone exceeds twenty kilometres an hour. They told us it was on the limit, and they were wrong. I was flying a *Tante-Ju*, really ancient, because that's all we had left, and by the time we'd found the DZ the wind had to be three times over the limit. I had the experience to say no and abort but there were young pilots around me, children really, who were still dropping.' He shot Schultz a look. 'Can you imagine parachutists blown into the props of the aircraft behind? You see it first, then you feel it here' – his gloved hand closed around the control stick – 'as the engine takes the hit. Madness. And I said so. Utter fucking madness. But you know something? No one thanks you for the truth in a war like this, especially when you're losing, which is maybe why they've turned me into a taxi driver.'

Schultz nodded. *Tante-Ju* was what the pilots called the big, three-engined transports that had kept Stalingrad resupplied. He was still thinking about parachutists chopped to pieces in the howling slipstream.

'And the attack?'

'The weather lifted, and then the Americans were all over us. Ground-attack Thunderbolts and hundreds of Mustangs if we dared to join the party. Some of our younger guys were on their first missions. The Americans ate them alive, though the Fat One will tell you a different story.'

Schultz nodded. The Fat One was *Reichsmarschall* Hermann Goering, to whom the *Luftwaffe* owed its very existence. He'd built a glittering career on courage and gluttony, but by the time the German advance had ground to a halt on the Eastern Front, the fighting troops had lost all faith in the man. One of the reasons the Sixth Army half starved to death was the Fat One's failure to keep the air bridge open.

'At Stalingrad, the men ended up hating him,' Schultz said. 'If he'd turned up in person, they'd have stuffed him in the pot.'

This made Frenzell laugh.

'I'm not surprised,' he said. 'Whoever wins the air wins the war. Every child in every city bunker knows that. Even Hitler probably knows that. But the mighty Hermann? You tell me ...' His finger strayed to the map on Schultz's lap. To his shame, the navigator had lost track of where they were. 'Here.' Frenzell was tapping an area of lakes well north of Berlin. 'You've heard of Ravensbrück?'

Schultz nodded. Ravensbrück was yet another growth on the body of Himmler's SS empire, the only concentration camp built exclusively for women. He'd never been there in person, never wanted to, but he knew that the very mention of the place would deter most women from stepping out of line.

'You want to take a look?'

Without waiting for an answer, Frenzell pushed the stick sideways, stamped on a rudder pedal and hauled the little plane into a tightish wingover. Schultz felt the suck of the turn deep in his bones, then they were level again and dropping towards a distant rectangle of buildings, surrounded by trees. At two hundred metres, Frenzell levelled out. Schultz, who knew how keen the SS were to keep their secrets to themselves, enquired whether flying this close didn't invite trouble, but Frenzell shook his head.

'The guards will think you're *Onkel Heine* paying a visit,' he chuckled. 'The sanatorium is five minutes away. From what I hear, he's in and out of that place all the time.'

Schultz nodded. *Onkel Heine* was another favourite nickname, this time for Himmler. It was far from kind, but it caught the weirdness of the *Reichsführer-SS*, part-family man, part-psychopath, and the *Abwehr* had used it all the time.

They were flying low over the camp itself now, and Schultz stared down as the aircraft's shadow raced across the parade ground framed by the low white barrack buildings. The camp was surrounded by two barbed wire fences and there were a handful of inmates bent with the effort of hauling a big stone roller across an area of grass, and then they were gone and Schultz glimpsed a quartet of uniformed guards at what he assumed was the main entrance to the camp. They, too, appeared to be women. One of them sprang to attention when a fifth figure stepped out of the guard house and Schultz had time to register the Hitler salute before the camp disappeared beneath them.

Schultz sat back, aware of Frenzell watching him.

'A long way from Stralsund,' he murmured, as he retrimmed the aircraft ahead of a landing at the nearby sanatorium. 'God help those poor bloody women.'

11

Nehmann didn't believe in God, never had. At home, in the shadow of the mountains, he'd never understood the chokehold of the Orthodox church. Some lies were plausible, deserved a willing audience, took place in markets and on doorsteps, earned the tellers a coin or two. Others, especially on Sunday, were frankly a joke. Dress a man in a silly costume, add chanting and clouds of incense, hang icons on the wall and you were suddenly in the business of belief. The richest man in Svaneti was always a priest. Everyone said so.

God was on his mind just now, chiefly because a pastor was ahead of him as the column of refugees stumbled ever westwards. Aside from the cross around his neck, nothing he was wearing identified him as a man of God. Like the thousands of others on the highway, he was wearing as many clothes as he could, partly in deference to the icy wind and partly because the more clothes you wore, thc less you had to carry. Entire wardrobes had taken to the roads of Pomerania, men and women alike, but what gave the pastor away was his habit of moving from group to group, families mainly, urging them to remember their duties to their neighbours, and to the Good Lord.

After two years in Kolyma, Nehmann had his difficulties with the latter concept, and from the scraps of conversation he'd picked up on the road he knew that he wasn't alone. A village called Nemmersdorf came up time and again. Some of the refugees evidently had friends and relatives there. One old man who seemed to have disappeared over the last kilometre or two even claimed to have had a house in the village. Finally, unable to contain his curiosity, Nehmann put a question to the youngster beside him.

'Nemmersdorf?' he enquired casually.

The youth must have been in his late teens. His face was scarlet with acne, and he rarely lifted his head as he plodded along in the footsteps of the older man ahead.

'You've never heard of it?' He didn't look up.

'No.'

'Seriously?'

'Yes.'

'You've been away, or something?'

'Yes.' Nehmann was losing patience. 'So where the fuck is it?'

'East Prussia. The Russians took it. Shot a load of people. Nailed women to the church door. Horrible.'

'But how do we know this?

'Our boys took it back next day. There are photos. Everyone knows about Nemmersdorf. That's what these *Untermenschen* do. Never trust a Russian. Why else would we be on the road?'

Untermenschen. Sub-humans. Nehmann could hear the voice of Goebbels in the youth's righteousness. He had no idea when this atrocity might have happened, and he had no intention of fuelling this boy's curiosity any further, but he recognised the master's hand at work. Settle on a real event. Magnify it out of all proportion. Find – or create – some evidence, ideally bodies. And make sure there's a photographer around. Prejudice, word-of-mouth and fear would do the rest. Easy, he thought, watching the pastor falling into step with yet another luckless refugee.

153

A couple of kilometres back, a little plane had appeared from nowhere. Anything with wings that took an interest in the column was automatically suspect – another triumph for word-of-mouth – and the refugees had scattered as the beat of the engine grew louder and louder. Nehmann, alone it seemed, had recognised the aircraft. It was a Fieseler Storch, and he'd seen dozens of them on the Eastern Front before he was taken prisoner at Stalingrad. It was a German plane, German design, German pilot, and senior commanders often used it as a kind of taxi. As the column melted around him, whole families heading for the nearest ditch, he'd done his best to tell people not to panic but his advice had been ignored. The Storch, it was true, had swooped very low but the image that stayed with him was the sight of the pastor. Not helping people. Not protecting women and babies. But down on his knees, attending to some private confession of his sins. God, he thought. Who only looks after His own.

*

By now, it was mid-afternoon. Nehmann had been walking since dawn, joining the column as it slowly thickened west of the River Oder. Whole families appeared from nowhere with what little they could carry on their backs, or by hand, or on carts if their good fortune ran to a horse or a bullock. No one looked back. Conversations were rare. Only the kids showed the slightest interest in their fellow refugees, making friends with strangers as the morning wore on, treating this surreal episode as a surprise day out from school, but by now even the kids were weary. Where were they headed? Where would they sleep? And what would happen if the Russians crossed the river and caught up?

Nehmann had no answer to any of these questions, but two

years in Kolyma had taught him the art of patience, or perhaps resignation, and he knew better than to fret about outcomes he couldn't possibly anticipate. Then, quite suddenly, the column began to slow, then concertina, and word came back of a problem ahead. Uniforms, muttered the man in front. *Feldgendarmerie*, whispered another.

It was cold already in the wind, but Nehmann felt a deeper chill ice his blood. The *Feldgendarmerie* were the military police. The troops on the Eastern Front called them *Kettenhunde*, or 'Chain Dogs', and hated them. These were the guys who wore a metal gorget around their necks and showed no mercy with men in uniform who'd decided not to die. Lurking behind the front line, they feasted on deserters.

Shit.

Nehmann brought himself to a halt and glanced round. This, he knew, could be the end for him. At Stalingrad, in the depths of winter, he'd killed a senior SS officer called Jürgen Kalb. He'd done it with a spade, at the height of a blizzard, an act of revenge that had brought him great satisfaction. Because at Stalingrad you let nothing go to waste, he'd then butchered, cooked and later eaten the best bits of Kalb, a double crime that had come to the attention of the *Feldgendarmerie*. Willi Schultz had been complicit in all this madness, and they'd both been arrested. By then, the battle had taken hundreds of thousands of lives. Death was everywhere, a living presence, and Nehmann had found a rich irony in the time and energy the Chain Dogs had expended on the disappearance of this notorious SS psychopath. Both men knew they'd probably be shot out of hand within days, but the Sixth Army was on the point of surrender and they'd managed to escape the firing squad before the Russians arrived to take them both prisoner.

Now, if the rumours about the Chain Dogs were true, he was

in real trouble. These people kept records. On file for murder and cannibalism, he'd have some explaining to do.

The column was on the move again, the refugees shuffling forward. The bend ahead offered a view of uniformed figures on both sides of the road, scanning face after face. Nehmann recognised the grey-green jacket and collar tabs of a *Feldgendarmerie* Lieutenant. He knew they were looking for deserters, for single men Nehmann's age and younger who'd turned their backs on the Russians and vanished into refugee columns like this. Head down, he started to limp, trying to make himself look older, more weary, more resigned, a peasant figure who'd lost everything. It didn't work.

It was the Lieutenant who spotted him. He was pointing at Nehmann, addressing himself to a nearby NCO. The Sergeant plunged into the column and seized Nehmann by the arm. Aware of the column melting away around him, Nehmann left the road and limped towards the waiting officer. The look, he thought. The carefully pressed uniform. The dead eyes. The thin mouth. Not a trace of emotion.

'Papers?'

'I don't have any.'

'Name?'

'Wiedermann. Hans.'

'You've come from where?'

'East Prussia.' Nehmann lied with an easy fluency. He'd been doing it for most of his life.

'*Wehrmacht?*'

'I'm a butcher. I worked in an abattoir in Königsberg. Pigs, mainly. Sometimes beef cattle.' He slid his forefinger across his throat and then made a sawing motion with one hand, hoping it might help. 'This war steals everything. Even a man's living.'

'Age?'

'Forty-two.'

'So why aren't you in the Army? Like everyone else?'

Nehmann held the Lieutenant's gaze. Then his hand strayed to his chest.

'I was hospitalised at Kyiv. Killing pigs is easy. Russians are harder.'

'Where? Where were you injured.'

'Kyiv. I just said.'

'But where? Your chest? You have a scar to show me?'

'Inside. Inside the heart. It's congenital, a weakness. My father, my uncles, a brother, we're all the same. We make fine butchers. *Scheiss* soldiers.' He shrugged. 'No scar.'

'Unit?'

'Panzer Group Kleist. We gave the Russians a good hiding.' Nehmann hoped his grin signalled the appropriate helping of loyalty and pride. As it happened, he'd penned several pieces on Kleist's Panzers and still remembered the faces he'd met. Goebbels loved battle-warm despatches like these and had featured both in successive editions of *Das Reich*.

'But no papers?' The Lieutenant was looking thoughtful.

'None. I had to leave in a hurry,' Nehmann nodded back towards the column, 'just like everyone else.'

The Lieutenant nodded, said nothing, then muttered something to the NCO. Nehmann felt the big hand close around his upper arm again. The *Feldgendarmerie* truck was parked nearby. Nehmann asked for help to scramble up into the back. The NCO got in behind him.

'Strip.' He gestured at Nehmann's coat.

'Everything?'

'Everything.'

'But the damage is to the heart itself. There's nothing for you to see.'

'Strip,' the NCO said again.

Nehmann shrugged. Before he'd left the tank crew to cross the river at Altdamm, he'd taken the opportunity to put on the undergarment looted from the *Wehrmacht* quartermaster stores. It was a decision that had kept him warm all night, and throughout the long two days that had followed, but now he realised how reckless he'd been. Kolyma had robbed him of his wits. He should have anticipated these roadside jackals.

'Take it off.' He was down to his shirt.

Nehmann did the NCO's bidding, undoing the shirt buttons one by one, very slowly, desperate to defer the moment the NCO recognised what lay beneath, but the Chain Dog was getting impatient now. He reached for the lower half of the shirt, meaning to rip it open, but then he paused, seeing the undergarment for the first time. He pulled Nehmann towards the daylight flooding into the back of the truck, then Nehmann felt his fingers exploring the newness of the heavy-duty cotton. Finally, he turned Nehmann round and pulled down the collar of his shirt, examining the garment's label.

'A butcher?' he said softly. 'I think not.'

*

They took him to a farmhouse the Chain Dogs had commandeered. It was a longish walk across wet fields beginning to freeze and Nehmann didn't bother to limp any more. The door to the farmhouse opened straight into the kitchen, and the smell of fresh coffee did nothing for Nehmann's peace of mind. Shackled in handcuffs, he sat in a chair in the corner of the room, awaiting the arrival of the Lieutenant. A woman, probably the farmer's wife, was preparing a stew of some kind and from time to time she stole a look at this new addition to her world, but the moment Nehmann smiled at her, she'd turn away, stirring her pot. Fresh meat for the Chain Dogs, thought Nehmann. And a bone or two for the bastards to chew on afterwards.

It was dark by the time the Lieutenant turned up. He pulled a chair to the table and told Nehmann to join him. The NCO, unbidden, fetched a pad and two sharpened pencils before producing a bottle of what looked like schnapps. One glass only. And this for the Lieutenant.

Nehmann was staring at the pad. It was standard issue, headed with the *Feldgendarmerie* crest. He'd last seen one of these in the schoolhouse at Stalingrad where he and Schultz had been interrogated, and he was only too aware how the next couple of hours would decide his fate. The Chain Dogs, like journalists, were gatherers of evidence. Live by the pen, he thought. And die by the pen.

The Lieutenant poured himself a small glass of schnapps and tossed it back. Then he reached for the pen.

'When did you desert?'

'I didn't.'

'You're lying. This is the easy part.' He gestured at the pad. 'If you want to make life tough for yourself, by all means go ahead, but never complain that you weren't warned. Let me put the question a different way. *Why* did you desert?'

'I didn't.'

'So how come you're wearing *Wehrmacht*-issue clothing?'

Nehmann, who'd spent the last hour anticipating this question, hoisted his shackled wrists onto the battered table and nudged the chair closer. Years of working for Goebbels and his minions at the Promi had bred a healthy disregard for the truth but now, he told himself, he'd run out of options. The Chain Dogs always shot their suspects at dawn. No cover story would save him from that.

'I'm a journalist by trade,' he said softly. 'I was taken prisoner at Stalingrad. I've spent the last two years in the Gulag digging gold for the Russians. Any further east and I'd have fallen off the edge of the world. I crossed the Oder a couple of days ago. I'm a friend of Minister Goebbels and my mission is to get to see him after all this time.'

'Mission? Whose mission?'

'Stalin's.'

'*Stalin*?' Nehmann judged the smile to be derisory. 'You mean *Joseph* Stalin?'

'Yes. We talked in his dacha at Kuntsevo. He has a piano in his hallway and a small bust of Lenin in the study he uses as a bedroom. These are facts, Lieutenant. You must have access to senior Russian prisoners. You've also captured Stalin's son, Yakov. You can check what I'm telling you.' Nehmann paused a moment, wondering how far to ride his luck, then nodded at the still-empty pad. 'Write it down, Lieutenant. Kuntsevo. Piano. Lenin bust. Yakov. Something else, as well. Ask around about Stalin's favourite movie. René Clair. *Sous les toits de Paris*. He knows the lyrics by heart. Not a bad voice, either.'

Nehmann sat back. At length, the Lieutenant reached for a pencil and made a couple of notes. Then his head came up again.

'And Goebbels?' he asked.

'Goebbels has a number of houses. The one he shared with his family when I last spent Christmas Day with him is in Bogensee. He has a piano, too. And a wife called Magda who frightens him a little. Ask either of them about me.' He paused again. 'Werner Nehmann.'

'That's your real name?'

'No. My real name is Mikhail Magalashvili, but that's another story. Goebbels knows about that, too. We Georgians are outsiders, just like Goebbels himself, but he prefers to know me as Werner Nehmann. This is a man without friends, Lieutenant. That's something I shouldn't be telling you but under the circumstances, I imagine it might help.' Nehmann nodded at the pad. 'You want me to spell my real name?'

The Lieutenant ignored the question, but Nehmann sensed that this story of his had caught his interest. No one in uniform could doubt that the war was coming to an end, and everyone was going to need friends with a little influence.

'Do you live in Berlin, Lieutenant, by any chance?'

'That's no business of yours.'

'No? The city will be in Soviet hands within weeks. That, at the very least, is something I can guarantee.'

'How?'

'Because I know.'

'Then tell me.'

'I can't. Not until I've told Herr Goebbels first.'

For the first time, the ghost of a smile brightened the Lieutenant's face. Watching him, Nehmann couldn't work out whether it was surprise, or curiosity, or even admiration. Men like these, he told himself, spend their working lives having to deal with rubbish washed up by a war that was clearly out of control. Now, perhaps for the first time, he was confronted by something rather different. Could he afford to discount a story like this? Could he simply dismiss it as a wild fantasy concocted by a man in fear for his life? Or might he make further enquiries?

The silence in the kitchen stretched and stretched. The woman at the stove still had her back turned but Nehmann knew she must have heard every word. The NCO, too, was staring at Nehmann.

Finally, the Lieutenant abandoned his pencil and filled his glass to the top. For a long moment he stared down at it before moistening his lips, raising it in a silent toast, and then emptying it in a single gulp.

Another silence followed, broken by Nehmann.

'One more thing, Lieutenant, if you don't mind. Tomorrow, you'll either shoot me or keep me on ice. That's your choice, your privilege. If it happens to be the latter, if you make your enquiries, contact the Ministry, and discover I'm telling the truth, then I have a favour to ask.'

'Which is?'

'You can get me to Berlin? Under escort? That would make things even easier.'

12

Frenzell was demanding Schultz's gun. The pilot had felt its outline in his pocket early in the flight, and now – safely on the ground at Hohenlychen – he insisted he'd look after it.

'They'll search you twice.' Frenzell nodded towards the sanatorium. 'The first time at the main gate. The second, a more thorough job, at the foot of the steps that lead to the entrance hall.'

'What are they frightened of?' Schultz grunted. 'Some crazy Ivan?'

'Worse than that. Maybe a German with a conscience. Either way, you'll lose the gun.'

About to get out of the aircraft, Schultz had the passenger door open. Now he turned back to Frenzell.

'Is that what you think I am? A German with a conscience?'

'I think you're an *Abwehr* man in enemy territory.' He was eyeing the sanatorium again. 'That may be the same thing.'

'What makes you think I used to work for the *Abwehr*?'

'Georg Messner told me. And that man never lied. Give me the gun and the ammunition.' Frenzell extended a hand. 'If these people offer to take you to Berlin, say no. I'll be here, refuelled.' He paused, waiting for the gun. Schultz didn't move.

'Berlin?' he said.

'Berlin.'

'So what else do you want to tell me?'

'Nothing. The gun. Just give me the gun.'

Schultz was gazing at him, aware of a figure in a black SS uniform hurrying towards them.

'You know the difference between you and Messner?' Frenzell had seen the SS guard, too. 'Georg trusted me. You should, too. Before these bastards do their worst.'

Schultz hesitated a moment longer, then handed over the gun and the clips of ammunition. A final check confirmed he still had the letter for Himmler.

'Wait for me,' Schultz grunted. 'I'll be back.'

The SS guard came to an abrupt halt beside the little aircraft and threw out his right arm in the Hitler salute. Schultz offered a nod in response, aware of the man's surprise, and then disdain. I'm dressed like a gardener, Schultz told himself. I've been away too long. I need to learn my manners.

Schultz explained that he was carrying a letter for the *Reichsführer*. The guard nodded and enquired whether he had an appointment. When Schultz said he hadn't, he hesitated a moment and then escorted him towards the sanatorium. With its steeply pitched roofs and spired turret, it might have been a hotel or even a church, but Schultz knew it had been expressly built for the SS. Through the perimeter fence he could see little groups of convalescents taking advantage of the afternoon sun. Some of them were still heavily bandaged. Others, learning to walk again, had artificial legs, thin shafts of gleaming metal, protruding from their grey SS-issue shorts. From a distance, they looked like half-formed creatures from some laboratory experiment, doubtless a tribute to SS science and SS resilience, but Schultz knew that the patients here were the lucky ones. At Stalingrad, once injured, your hours were numbered.

At the main gate, Schultz paused for a moment, surrendering to a thorough pat-down from another SS guard, grateful that he'd finally listened to Frenzell. A dismissive nod took him through the gate. A path led towards the sanatorium. The last time Schultz had seen Himmler in the flesh was at a conference in Prague three years ago, organised by Reinhard Heydrich, an SS high-flyer who also happened to be a close friend of Schultz's boss, Wilhelm Canaris.

The conference had been called to broker a peace between the two organisations, and Schultz had watched Himmler addressing the three hundred delegates as proceedings began. *Abwehr* colleagues called him *der treue Heine*, faithful Heinrich, because he was halfway up Hitler's arse, and Schultz remembered the way he'd stood at the dais, peering at his typed speech through his thick glasses. With his little pot belly and the pastiness of a man who spent far too long at his desk, he had none of the Führer's fire. The speech he gave, barely bothering to look up, had been perfunctory but even then, before he'd been posted to the east, Schultz had sensed that Hitler's favourite bureaucrat, the man who kept him safe, was elbowing Canaris and his organisation aside. Even the *Abwehr* were helpless in the face of Hitler's private army.

They were at the main door now. Schultz stood back as another pair of amputees stumped past, and then submitted himself to a second search. This happened in a side office dominated by a framed black and white photograph on the wall. Himmler was wearing the uniform of a *Reichsführer-SS*, peering sternly down as one man examined Schultz's coat in detail, while the other gestured for him to remove his jacket. The letter for Himmler was in one of the pockets.

'This is for who?'

'The *Reichsführer*.'

'Why can't you just leave it with us?'

'Because it has to be delivered personally.'

'Do you know what's inside?'

'No.'

The guard nodded. He was feeling the letter now, between his fingers, then he held it up to the light.

'He's really here to see the *Reichsführer*?' He was looking at Schultz's escort.

'So he says.'

The guard nodded, then turned back to Schultz.

'Off,' he gestured at his boots. 'Trousers, too. Everything.'

*

Minutes later, dressed again, Schultz was in the main body of the building. His escort had made a phone call from the office, and now he led Schultz to a sizeable lounge with views over the surrounding lawn. The *Reichsführer*, he said, wouldn't be ready to receive Schultz for an hour or so. In the meantime, he was welcome to join the other men in the lounge. There were copies of *Völkischer Beobachter* and *Das Reich* if he wanted something to read, and there was coffee, too, the real thing.

The lounge was thick with cigarette smoke, and most of the armchairs were occupied. More stained bandages, Schultz thought. More broken bodies. Conversations faltered and heads turned as he made his way towards one of the few unoccupied chairs, and he wondered what these young fanatics made of the ageing tramp who'd so suddenly appeared among them. Canaris, he thought, would make a lot of a scene like this. If you were looking for the story of the last few years then here it was: the SS battered, bruised, but still fighting; the *Abwehr* cast-off, old, semi-derelict.

A copy of *Völkischer Beobachter* lay on a nearby table. Schultz picked it up. Nehmann, he knew, had fed this rag with clever lies from Stalingrad. His talent, which Schultz greatly admired, had turned a pile of shit into some kind of victory. Surrender was inevitable, everyone knew it, but Nehmann was bold and artful enough to insist that German soldiers were hungry for more fighting, more conquest, more glory. The *Wehrmacht* was a machine. It was a thing of wonder and limitless appetite. It fell on other countries and devoured them, sometimes whole, sometimes piecemeal. Nothing could stand in its way, not the Russians, not the winter temperatures plunging to unimaginable depths, not Goering's promised supply flights that never got through. Why? Because Hitler had it right. Because Germany, and Germans, were the *Supermenschen*, irresistible, born and bred to conquer the world. Glancing up at the ruined men around him, remembering the sight of the refugees trudging west, Schultz knew that this was the biggest lie of all, but the moment he returned to the paper, he knew as well that nothing had changed.

The Führer, he read, had taken personal charge of the imminent defence of Berlin. Trenches were being dug in the outer suburbs, roads blocked, traps laid. A new army, the *Volkssturm*, men pledged to fight to the death, had answered the Führer's call to the colours and were under intensive training. And all the while, the promised wonder weapons, the jewels in the crown of Nazi science and Nazi endeavour, were almost ready to be unleashed on the enemy, and thus change the course of the war.

In a personal appeal, accompanying the main story, Goebbels, as Reich Plenipotentiary for Total War, admitted the existence of a handful of faint-hearts, but praised Berliners at large for their courage and resilience, and added a fulsome paragraph about the heroic efforts of *Generaloberst* Schörner in retaking the town of Lauben from the Red Army. 'Schörner's men have shown us the way,' he thundered. 'We, the people, must now follow.'

'They've sent you here for a rest, *Kamerad*?'

Schultz looked up. His nearest neighbour looked young enough to be his son. Unlike so many others in this room, he seemed physically intact, even relaxed, sitting back in the armchair, one long leg crossed over the other. Only his eyes, constantly on the move, and his long fingers, plucking at the crease in his trousers, suggested that all was far from well.

'I'm on an errand.' Schultz folded the paper. 'Just visiting.'

'Then eat.' The young man nodded at a plate of pastries that had appeared beside the coffee pot. 'My name's Harald.' He extended a hand. 'The strudel is especially good.'

'Schultz.' He got to his feet and fetched two slices of the strudel. The young man was right. It was delicious.

'You've been here long?' Schultz was licking his fingers.

'Since December. We got caught in the open outside Bastogne. Those American Thunderbolts are on you in seconds. When you end up praying for bloody Goering, you know you're in trouble.'

'You were in the Ardennes?'

'Yes.'

'And?'

'It was fine to begin with. Before that we were in the Hurtgen Forest. That was hell. Passchendaele with airbursts. You know what the guys say? The ones who came out alive? The first five days you're talking to the trees. The sixth day, the trees answer back. Are all wars like this? Do they always make you crazy?'

Crazy. Taking a closer look, Schultz began to understand. Young Harald's wounds were hidden. The SS, it turned out, attended to the soul as well as the body.

'They've been good to you here?' Schultz gestured round.

'*Fantastisch.* We're a family. We look after each other. When you leave, the cooks in the kitchen bake a special cake. Tomorrow,' he offered a shy smile, 'I get that cake.'

'They're discharging you?'

'12th SS Panzer Division, *Hitlerjugend.* New friends, new faces.' The prospect appeared to delight him.

'Front line?'

'Of course.' The young man nodded down at the paper. 'Is there anything else on offer?'

Schultz's escort had appeared at the door and was beckoning him over. Schultz got to his feet and extended a hand to the young warrior.

'Good luck, eh? And watch those trees.'

Schultz followed his escort along the corridor to the foot of a staircase that led ever upwards. The lift, it seemed, was broken, a malfunction, muttered the escort darkly, that would serve many convalescents as extra physiotherapy. And so they climbed from floor to floor until they'd reached the top of the building. Schultz, catching his breath, paused beside the wrought iron bannisters to peer over. The staircase receded below him, an ever-tightening spiral that offered just a glimpse of the tiny black and white tiles on the ground floor.

'*Schnell.*' The escort was tapping his watch. The message was all too clear. The *Reichsführer*'s time was precious.

The room that Himmler was using as an office was much smaller than Schultz had expected. It had none of the space and swagger that Nazi chieftains used to intimidate visitors, and a second door in the room, Schultz suspected, probably led to Himmler's bedroom. So it was from here, until he was safely discharged from the sanatorium, that the Minister in charge of the Reich's millions of spies, policemen, security agents, and

Waffen-SS fighting troops, would have to control his sprawling empire.

Himmler had been stirring a glass of what looked like herbal tea when Schultz stepped in. His desk was bare – another surprise – and he'd managed to position his chair to catch the fall of spring sunshine through the nearby window. Since the conference in Prague Castle, the *Reichsführer* had visibly aged. He'd also developed something close to languor, a studied calm totally at odds with the nervous, eternally busy autocrat Schultz remembered at the podium three years earlier.

Himmler dismissed the escort with a wave of a hand and nodded at the empty chair. Schultz sat down, watching the raised glass of tea clouding the thick round lenses of his spectacles.

'You have a letter for me?'

Schultz nodded. He placed the envelope carefully on the desk.

'You know who this is from?'

'I have no idea.'

'But you think it may be important?'

'I do, yes.'

'Who told you so?'

Schultz began to explain about his years of virtual house arrest in an apartment in the Moscow suburbs, about marking time until the day arrived – just a week or so ago – when he was despatched to Stockholm.

'Why you, *Oberst* Schultz? And why Sweden?'

'I have contacts there. Had contacts there.'

'Dahlerus?'

'Yes.'

'And what did Birger have to say for himself?'

'Nothing. He refused to meet me.'

'Then why go? Why did they send you?'

'They want to know what's going on between you and

Bernadotte. They thought Dahlerus would have the details. I managed to spend a little time with Birger's wife. She's German, of course.'

'And?'

'She confirmed that you and Count Bernadotte are in touch.'

'She's right. My masseur, Kersten, effected the introduction.' He put the glass of tea carefully to one side. 'You're aware of my work with the Red Cross? Michaela may have mentioned it.'

'Only in general terms.'

'Then let me tell you. I met Count Bernadotte in Berlin last month. Given the state of affairs, he's naturally keen to repatriate as many prisoners from our custody as possible. I made that happen, Schultz. That was me. The Scandinavians are children at heart. They love stories with happy endings. They've painted lots of buses white. More than a hundred to be precise. We've invited them to bring trucks, too. With these they journey from camp to camp. We've set aside facilities at Neuengamme. You know the place?' Schultz shook his head. 'It's near Hamburg. Bernadotte gathers his prisoners in a section of the camp and soon his people will be returned. First to Denmark, and then to Sweden. Those white buses are a gesture, Schultz. We mean to set a different tone before the war comes to an end.' One hand crabbed towards the envelope, then stopped. 'When did you leave Moscow?'

'Ten days ago.'

'So the years since Stalingrad? Here in the homeland?'

'A mystery.'

'As I thought. The last time we met was in Prague, am I right? You were with Canaris. Canaris was staying with Heydrich. Heydrich looked after our interests and performed magnificently. Which made what followed all the more regrettable.'

Schultz nodded, said nothing. Barely weeks after the conference, Reinhard Heydrich had been ambushed by Czech patriots, dying from his injuries shortly afterwards. Himmler had ordered reprisals and an entire village had been wiped out. No one would bother visiting Lidice any more.

'And now?' Schultz enquired.

'The Führer abolished the *Abwehr* more than a year ago, Schultz. That desk of yours, that office, no longer exists. Canaris was arrested and spent a little time cooling his heels. We released him last June and found something meaningless for him to do in Berlin. He was arrested again after that fool Stauffenberg tried to kill the Führer.'

'Really?' This was news to Schultz. Stauffenberg, to his knowledge, was a staff officer with the ear of the top Generals. Like many in the *Wehrmacht*, he held his nose when it came to the Nazis, but disdain was very different from treason.

'He tried to blow the Führer up, Schultz.' Himmler shrugged. 'And failed. Naturally, there were enquiries to be made. One of them led to your old boss.'

'And?'

'He has a top bunk at Flossenbürg. That's where you'll find him if you want to talk about old times.'

Schultz looked away for a moment. Flossenbürg was an SS concentration camp east of Nuremberg. Among other things, the inmates sweated twelve-hour days to produce granite from a nearby quarry to build the Führer's fantasy Berlin. Himmler was watching him carefully.

'You think I want to humiliate your old *Kapo*, Schultz? If so, you'd be wrong. If there's anyone I'd like to humiliate, it would be you.'

'Might I ask why?'

'Because of Kalb. You remember our Jürgen? I have the file

in Berlin but I suspect we won't need it. Your friend Nehmann did the deed but I understand you were there, too. The older man, Schultz. The wiser man, Schultz. You should have stopped him. What Nehmann did was outrageous.'

Schultz couldn't deny it, and in any case he didn't see the point. All he could think of was the view of those bannisters, the clear fall to the ground floor, the best possible way of sparing this man the expense of a bullet or two. Would he still be conscious when he hit those tiles? And did a question like that even matter?

Himmler finished the tea and produced a handkerchief to wipe his mouth. Then, at last, he reached for the envelope. He studied it for a long moment, then extracted a paper knife from the desk drawer and carefully lifted the flap.

'And you got this from where? Remind me.'

'A Russian at Stockholm station.'

'His name?'

'I've no idea.'

'His instructions?'

'To make sure you got it.' Schultz paused for a moment. 'He told me it wouldn't come as a surprise.'

Himmler nodded, appearing to agree, but said nothing. With the same fastidious care, he extracted the single sheet and laid it flat on the desk. He scanned it first, then read it a second time, his eyes lingering on the signature at the bottom. At length he lifted his head.

'We need to be frank with each other, Schultz. My assumption is that you know exactly who this letter comes from. The signature looks authentic. Would I be right in thinking that a reply might be in order?'

Schultz held his gaze. Some of his ex-colleagues in the *Abwehr* referred to this man as the Grand Inquisitor but just now, in Schultz's view, he had the eyes of a sick child: weak, moist, needy.

'You would, *Reichsführer*,' Schultz said at last, 'and I'm afraid it has, once again, to be hand-delivered.'

'By you?'

'Indeed.' Schultz tapped his watch. 'And the *Vozhd* has only days to spare before he launches Operation Kirov.'

'*Kirov?*'

'The final assault, *Reichsführer*.' Schultz offered a thin smile. 'On Berlin.'

Himmler nodded. He was toying with the paper knife while he read the letter for the third time. Then he abandoned the knife and lifted the phone. Moments later came a polite knock on the door, and the escort reappeared.

'Herr Schultz needs a decent meal.' He'd returned the letter to its envelope. 'See to it that he's properly fed.'

The escort saluted and accompanied Schultz to the door. On the landing at the head of the stairs, Schultz paused to take a brief glance over the bannisters. Kirov, he knew, might prove terminal. He had no idea what the Red Army were calling their imminent offensive, and he'd conjured the codename from nowhere. The SS were spoiled for intelligence assets and all Himmler had to do was make a precautionary phone call or two while he mused on the letter from Stalin. After that, Schultz was a dead man.

The sanatorium's canteen lay at the back of the building. At this time of day, mid-afternoon, it was virtually empty. The escort led Schultz to the counter and asked him what he'd like.

'Wiener schnitzel,' Schultz said at once. 'With potatoes.'

The woman behind the counter shook her head. Wrong time of day. Maybe later. The escort glanced at Schultz.

'Wiener schnitzel,' Schultz insisted, 'like the *Reichsführer* promised.'

Mention of Himmler sent the woman back into the kitchen. Moments later, she returned with the news that the meal would be ready as soon as she laid hands on the cook. The escort told Schultz to choose a table while he organised some cutlery. Schultz settled beside the window, gazing out. A gardener was on his knees, bent over a nearby flowerbed, attending to a stand of forsythia and bright clusters of cyclamen. The escort returned with the knives and forks, and a basket of black bread.

'You mind?' He nodded at the bread. His respect for Schultz appeared to have grown.

'Help yourself. You're hungry?'

'Always.'

Schultz nodded. He wanted to know how long this man had been posted to the sanatorium.

'Seven months.'

'And before that?'

'Crete. I was a paratrooper. Dropped in May '41, broke an ankle, and never left for two whole years.'

'And before that?'

'France. Paris, mainly. You think all that makes me a lucky man? You'd be right.'

Schultz had served in Paris, too. They began to swap stories, memories of certain bars, gossip about an officers' brothel in Montmartre that the SS had allegedly wired with microphones.

'It's true,' Schultz nodded. 'I heard some of the tapes. The girls worked in threes. One SS General insisted three wasn't enough.'

The escort laughed. Schultz was still watching the gardener. He'd finished with the flowerbed and now he'd gathered up his tools and was making for a gate in the fence. Beyond the gate was a horse and cart.

The woman behind the counter was approaching with the schnitzel. She laid it carefully in front of Schultz, and for a moment he wondered whether she was going to salute.

'*Guten Appetit*,' she said. Enjoy.

The escort was staring at the schnitzel. It was huge, overlapping one side of the plate, and there was a light dusting of paprika on the raft of buttered potatoes. If the smell of the dish was any guide, the cook had excelled himself.

Schultz gazed at the plate, then shook his head.

'Help me out here?' He was looking at the escort. 'Where do I find the lavatory?'

'Help me out?' The escort hesitated. 'You mean with the schnitzel?'

'Yes,' Schultz was on his feet already. 'I need a shit. Badly.'

The escort looked up at him, suddenly uncertain. Then he reached for Schultz's knife and fork and slid the plate across the table towards himself.

'Go out of the door.' He bent to the schnitzel. 'Second on the right.'

Schultz left his coat on the chair and made for the door. Out in the hallway, he kept to the left, trying to find an exit that would take him into the garden at the rear of the building. Finally, at the very end of the hall, after a gallery of photos from a decade of Nuremberg rallies, he found the door he needed. It was late afternoon now, and the sun – veiled in thin cloud – had lost its warmth.

For a moment, still hugging the shelter of the main building, he was lost. Then, beyond the fence, he glimpsed the breath of the horse clouding on the cold air. Head down, he began to walk towards the fence, praying that his escort was too busy with the schnitzel to bother with the view. The gardener was standing beside his cart, scraping the soil from his spade. Mercifully, the gate was still open.

Schultz slipped through, sparing the gardener a nod and a muttered greeting as he hurried towards the path that led out to the airfield. Everything, he knew, now depended on Frenzell.

Was he still waiting? Had he refuelled? And might he be prepared to risk his own life for a man he barely knew?

The path bent to the right beyond a hedge of carefully trimmed yew, and the moment Schultz rounded the hedge, he saw the little plane. Frenzell was standing beside it, a cigarette in his hand. Schultz broke into a run, windmilling both arms in a bid to attract Frenzell's attention. Get the fucking thing started, he was trying to say. Fire up the engine. We need to be gone.

With Schultz barely a hundred metres away, Frenzell finally looked up. Moments later, he was clambering back into the cockpit, and as Schultz came to a halt, gasping for breath, the propeller began to turn. Frenzell leaned across and pushed the passenger door wide open. Schultz did his best to get in but needed Frenzell's help. Finally, with both doors closed, the Storch began to roll, bumping over the turf.

Prompted by Frenzell, Schultz looked over his shoulder. Two SS guards had appeared from nowhere. Both had drawn pistols, and they stopped to take aim but the little aircraft was already out of range. Schultz thought he heard the bark of handguns over the clatter of the engine but couldn't be sure. Seconds later, they were airborne.

Schultz sat back, aware of a vast sheet of water receding beneath him, and then closed his eyes.

'Can we make it to Berlin?' he shouted. He felt physically sick.

'Just.' Frenzell nodded out towards the setting sun. 'As long as you don't mind landing in the dark.'

The dark. Schultz shook his head, only too aware that luck, or fate, or some act of divine intervention, had spared him the wrath of the SS. At least for now.

'Why did you wait?' he asked at last. 'And why are you taking a risk like this?'

Frenzell shook his head. Over the roar of the engine, he hadn't caught the question. His spare hand found the headphones. Schultz put them on.

'This isn't something you have to do,' he said again. 'So why take the risk?'

Frenzell shrugged. There was a rear-view mirror bolted to the top frame of the windscreen, and his eyes kept drifting up to it.

'Well?' Schultz wanted an answer, not least because the price of survival was never to trust anyone.

'The war's nearly over,' Frenzell said. 'A few more weeks, and we'll all start learning Russian. If I have to disappear, then now might be a good time.'

'Disappear where?'

'West. I'd invite you along but I'm afraid the seat's taken already.'

'Your girlfriend?'

'My wife. We got married a couple of weeks ago. We were going to wait until Easter but these days that's a risk you don't take.'

'Her name?'

'Alina.'

His fingers disappeared into the top pocket of his flying suit, and moments later Schultz found himself looking at a lightly freckled face caught at a moment of absolute candour. Someone, presumably Frenzell, had produced a camera when she'd least expected it. Her shoulders were bare, and her eyes were wide, and her lips were parted in the beginnings of a grin. Schultz could think of a million situations that might have led to a moment like this, but the context didn't matter.

'She's beautiful,' he said. 'You're a lucky man.'

'I know. And that's another reason for getting out.'

'You'll use this plane?'

'I will.' He blew the joystick a kiss. 'What I really needed was a kick up the arse to make it happen. So thank you, my friend.' His eyes were on the mirror again. 'Your gun's under the seat. Don't forget it.'

*

It was dusk by the time they got to Berlin. They were flying low now, hugging the flatness of the landscape, but Schultz could see the dark sprawl of the city to the left.

'Where are we going?'

'Wannsee.'

'Can I ask why?'

'You'll need someone to keep an eye on you. No one gets an easy life by making enemies of the SS. Someone told me you had a date with *Onkel Heine*. Is that true?'

'It is.'

'And?'

'You're right. I need somewhere to keep my head down.'

Frenzell nodded. In the last of the daylight, Schultz recognised the oncoming shape of the Wannsee framed by the darkness of the pine woods. Frenzell dipped a wing and then pulled the aircraft into a tight turn until the windscreen was full of what looked like a playing field. Seconds later, he pulled back the stick, eased the throttle and let the aircraft settle into a perfect three-point landing. Within what seemed like metres, they'd come to a halt.

'Leave the headphones and be careful when you get out.' Frenzell shook Schultz's extended hand. 'Stay away from the prop, too.'

'So where am I going?'

'Follow the road over there. Turn left at the junction at the end. You're looking for number 107. The woman's name is Beata. She's Alina's best friend. They both work at the KWI.'

'Beata?' The name meant nothing to Schultz.

'She used to be Messner's wife. Before he fouled the nest.'

'And is there another man around now?'

'There is.'

'Name?'

'You'll know him.'

'I will?'

'*Ja*.'

Frenzell was already reaching for the throttle. Then he nodded down at the floor beneath the passenger seat.

'The gun,' he said again.

Schultz pocketed the Beretta and the spare clips of ammunition and then stepped away, turning his face from the prop wash as the Storch began to move. Moments later, he was watching the little plane disappear into the darkening sky. Beata? Alina? The Kaiser Wilhelm Institute? Some nameless male who'd evidently taken the place of Georg Messner? Schultz shook his head. The last couple of years had taught him never to surrender to panic, or even anxiety. Life, he'd concluded, was like the weather, impossible to change. Dress for rain. And pray for sunshine.

It was nearly dark now, and he made his way towards the dim shape of a fence. A gate led to a road, and a minute or so later he'd found the promised T-junction. This bigger road was flanked with streetlights but under blackout conditions none of them were lit. Across the road, behind a thick hedge, he sensed a sizeable property. Once again, no lights. For a long moment, Schultz stood motionless, his head cocked like an animal, hunting for clues. A whisper of wind stirred a nearby stand of trees. Then, very faintly, he caught the low cackle of a duck. Water, he thought. Wannsee.

Number 107 was several hundred metres down the road. The houses here were smaller, unhedged. Wooden shutters secured every window, but Schultz could smell the end of winter in the curl of woodsmoke from the single chimney. The pitch of the roof was steep, and a single strand of wire led to the telegraph pole at the kerbside.

Schultz knocked on the door, waited, knocked again. Without the coat he'd left at Hohenlychen, he was freezing. Finally, he heard footsteps and the door inched open. A woman's face, thin, pale. The glasses, and the hint of impatience in the frown, reminded Schultz of a schoolteacher he'd never learned to like.

'Beata?' he enquired.

A brief nod. 'Who are you?'

'My name is Schultz. Frenzell sent me.'

'Jürgen? You're a friend of his?'

'Not really, but he told me about Alina and asked me to say *schön Gruss* to your husband.'

'But it's dark. It's nearly seven. What on earth are you doing here?'

It was a question Schultz should have anticipated but somehow hadn't. The only decision he'd taken was to hint vaguely at trouble in Berlin. He was an ex-*Abwehr* man. Things hadn't been going well. He'd run into Jürgen Frenzell, who'd suggested a trip out into the peace and quiet of Wannsee. Walking up the road, it had seemed a credible proposition but now, confronted by this face at the door, Schultz realised it was anything but.

Beata was about to end the conversation and close the door on this underdressed vagrant but then another face appeared behind her, male, less wary, more curious, and taking a closer look Schultz realised that Jürgen Frenzell had been right. There wasn't a *Hausfrau* in the Reich who didn't know this man. His face on the cover of countless magazines had turned him into a national treasure.

'Dieter Merz.' Schultz started to laugh. 'You flew me down to Lisbon.'

'I did. You were shitting your pants.'

'You're right. That's what flying does to me.'

Merz was small. He was nursing a baby in the crook of one arm. He eased Beata aside and extended his spare hand before standing back and looking Schultz up and down.

'Dieting doesn't suit you,' he sniffed. 'And you smell bad, too. What happened?'

'Long story.'

'Come in.'

Schultz stepped into the house. He caught the tang of resin from newly cut wood, and from the next room came the spit and crackle of a fire.

'I've upset your lady?' Beata had disappeared.

'I doubt it. She's nervous, that's all. Especially around strangers.'

Merz led the way into the room with the fire. The baby had begun to kick and Beata appeared from nowhere to lift it from his arms. She had her back to Schultz. Whatever she was whispering sparked a shake of the head from Merz. He turned back to Schultz. 'Where have you come from?'

'An assignment.'

'Dressed like that?'

'I'm afraid so.'

Merz held his gaze for a moment, then shook his head in wonderment.

'Willi Schultz,' he murmured. 'Still in the spy business? Still beating up strangers?'

Schultz smiled, said nothing. Dieter Merz had been the star of the biggest pre-war flying displays, one of Goebbels' favourites, the little genius who'd stilled the roar at the Zeppelinfeld during the final Nuremberg Rally by appearing from nowhere and pulling a series of outrageous stunts in his trademark Me-109. Schultz had been there that day and a couple of years later, at war now, the Reich's favourite pilot had flown him to Portugal. On the way in from the airfield, they'd been ambushed in a Lisbon suburb, a clumsy interception that Schultz had been only too happy to sort out.

'Beer or schnapps?' Merz was grinning. 'We have both. I make the beer for Beata's father, who can take a joke, so I'd suggest the schnapps.'

'You make that, too?'

'*Ja*. It tastes of nothing but after the second glass that will matter even less. The Russians, if we're lucky, will bring proper vodka. Then real life can start again.'

Beata had disappeared with the baby, and for the first time Schultz caught the scent of cooking. Merz waved him into a chair beside the fire. When Schultz asked about the baby's name, Merz ignored the question. Instead, he wanted to know how the war had been treating him.

'It treats me fine. It's peace with more bangs. You know about people like me. Who wants to die in an armchair?'

'So who do you work for? Now the *Abwehr*'s fucked?'

'*Onkel Heine*. The SS is the only game in town.'

'But you told me he was *ein Arschloch* when we were down in Lisbon.'

'Sure, and he's still an arsehole.'

'And that doesn't matter?'

'Nothing matters. Not these days.'

Merz nodded, catching a new note in Schultz's voice. When he asked where he was living, Schultz shrugged and mentioned an apartment in Moabit. In reality, he'd no idea whether it had survived the bombing but it had once belonged to a woman he knew and years of tradecraft had always told him to build fictions on a raft of remembered fact.

'It's small,' he admitted. 'But it gives me everything a man needs.'

'Ground floor? Top floor? In between?'

'Top floor.'

'Christ. So what did you make of last night's raid? Did it catch you out?'

'It was fine. I have my little corner in the air-raid bunker down the street. Civilians are nice to me. Some of them I even talk to.'

Merz smiled, nodded, said nothing. Moments later, Beata reappeared with the baby, a bottle of home-brewed schnapps and two glasses. She gave the bottle and the glasses to Merz. The label on the bottle was handwritten in blue ink. The ink had run but Schultz could still make out the drift of the question: *Hast du ein Testament gemacht?* Have you made a will?

Merz splashed two fingers of the cloudy schnapps into each glass while Beata muttered something about supper. It was, she said, ready to serve. There was reproach, as well as irritation, in her voice.

Merz hadn't taken his eyes off Schultz. Supper, it seemed, could wait. For a long moment, there was silence. Then Merz smiled again.

'There was no raid last night, Willi. Stay, and eat, and tell us why you're really here.' That same smile as he lifted his glass. '*Prosit ...*'

Beata served borscht with sour cream and thick roundels of homemade bread. They ate in the kitchen, mostly – Merz admitted – because the stove made it warmer than the sitting room. A proper fire was a great idea but the pine logs were far too green to offer anything but token heat. The kitchen was cluttered with wooden toys and stuffed animals in various states of disrepair which made for a domestic intimacy Schultz realised he'd missed.

Beata sat closest to the stove. Her first husband, another flier called Georg Messner, Schultz had also known. He'd been a pilot on the Führer Squadron, an assignment that had led him into the arms of a starlet who'd taken the eye of Goebbels. Messner and Merz had been close friends, flying as a double act at air displays, and after the marriage collapsed Messner had been despatched to ferry supplies into beleaguered Stalingrad before a Russian tank shell killed him. Messner was a hard man to like but Schultz was glad he'd made the effort. Seldom had he met anyone so driven, so solitary, so reclusive. He very rarely talked about the wreckage of his private life but Schultz knew how badly he missed his infant daughter.

Now, at the table, Beata had propped the baby in a wooden highchair. Another daughter, older, had a seat of her own. This, thought Schultz, would be Lottie. He could see Messner in the cast of her face, her eyes especially, and when he asked her directly, she said she was four. The baby, Schultz assumed, belonged to Merz. Her name was Krista.

'So what's been happening in that life of yours?' This from Merz.

Schultz, attending to his bowl of borscht, didn't answer. He savoured spoonful after spoonful, oblivious of the silence. Finally, he mopped the last of the sour cream with a curl of bread and asked what they wanted from him.

'The truth?' This from Merz.

Schultz studied him for a moment. Maybe Lottie, he said, might be ready for bed. Beata shot Merz a look, then led her daughter out of the room. Schultz heard footsteps up a flight of stairs, then the fall of water into a basin. Merz had found another bottle of schnapps.

'You're not living in Berlin?'

'No.'

'Then where?'

Schultz was eyeing the baby.

'I've been away for a while,' he said at last.

'Anywhere nice? Crete? North Africa? Paris again?'

'Stalingrad, to begin with.'

'Shit.' Merz was staring at him. 'That explains everything.'

'About what?'

'The look of you. The sound of you. I'm sure you've told me dozens of lies but you used to be good at it.'

'And now?'

'You're shit at it.' He paused. 'Georg was at Stalingrad. Along with a million others.'

'You mean Messner?'

'Yes.'

'I met him. I got to know him a little.'

'How was he?'

'Hard to be with. Hard to get to know. He'd fucked up...' Schultz gestured round at the kitchen, the toys, the warmth, '... and he knew it.'

'He's dead. I expect you knew that.'

'I did, yes. I'm not sure that would have bothered him much. In some ways he was half-dead already.'

'I know what you mean. There was a guy who paid us a visit a couple of years ago, just turned up from nowhere, a bit like you.'

'Nehmann? Little fellow? Your height?'

'Yes. It was Christmas time. He said he was a journalist. He was on the way back to Stalingrad, poor bastard. Wait...'

Merz got to his feet and began to hunt through one drawer after another. Schultz, aware that the baby couldn't take her eyes off this stranger at the table, moved his chair a little closer.

186

He had no children of his own, and had never really wanted any, but there was something in this child's tiny face that was irresistible. With her plump little legs and gummy smile she was so trusting, so open. More to the point, she wanted to grab Schultz's proffered finger.

'Be careful, my friend. Anything that moves, she'll eat it.'

Merz was back at the table. He offered Schultz the object he'd been looking for. A grid of metal wires descended on a depression the size of a soup spoon on the metal base.

'This was Messner's work,' he said. 'According to Nehmann, he dreamed it up, he designed it. You hard-boil an egg, peel it, rest it in the hole, and the wires do the rest. It's never failed us. Not once. We keep a couple of chickens. From two eggs you get ten slices. I never realised it at the time, but Georg was a genius.'

Schultz took the contraption, moved the grid of wires up and down a couple of times, imagined the egg falling neatly apart. So simple, he thought. You could win a war with something like this, and maybe even the peace afterwards.

'Clever,' he grunted.

'He never showed you?'

'Never breathed a word.'

Beata reappeared. She'd put a sweater on. It was a dowdy shade of brown, shapeless after years of use, and she went to the sink to pour herself a glass of water. She was brisk, full of purpose. She cleared the soup bowls from the table and mopped the tabletop with a cloth before settling beside the baby. The baby still wanted Schultz's finger, but Schultz had moved away a little.

'Well?' This from Merz. 'You want to tell us more?'

'About what?'

'Stalingrad.'

'Do you mind?' Schultz was looking at Beata.

'Of course not,' Beata shrugged. 'You're a guest. You must do as you see fit.'

'Stalingrad,' Merz said again.

Schultz nodded, reached for his glass, took his time. Then he did his best to describe the way it had been over the end of that terrible year, both armies trapped in the jaws of winter, nothing to eat unless you had connections, nothing to look forward to except the near certainty that you'd either freeze or starve to death if the Russians didn't kill you first. By the end, he said, typhus had come as a merciful release to many men.

'That bad?'

'Worse. For two whole summers, no one had got in our way. Victories like those make you fat and happy. We never saw what was coming, never picked up the clues. The Ivans taught us many lessons. Most important of all, they showed us how stupid we'd been.'

'Stupid?'

'Arrogant. Blind. Deaf. Believers in our own propaganda. Until you're on your knees in someone else's country, you have no idea where all those lies will take you.'

Schultz paused for a moment, aware that – at last – he'd manage to catch Beata's attention. There was something new in her eyes. Once or twice, she'd even nodded. Sympathy? Agreement? He'd no idea.

Merz wanted to know how he'd got away from Stalingrad.

'I didn't. Nehmann and I were like brothers by the end. We got caught up in all kinds of madness. You're right. Nehmann was a journalist. Some of those lies were his but he was a good man, here, where it matters.' Schultz's big hand closed briefly over his heart. 'The Russians found us in an empty church. Nehmann had come up with some music and the priest was banging away on the organ.'

'So they took you?'

'We surrendered.'

'And then what?'

'They put me on a train to Moscow. Nehmann I never saw again. Christ knows, he may be dead but somehow I doubt it. You want the details? About Moscow? About the Russians? About the many blessings of their Revolution? My pleasure.'

For much longer than he'd intended, Schultz gave them a candid account of the last two years of his life. He talked about the Lubyanka, and the many ways the NKVD had tried to prise open the bits of him where he kept his *Abwehr* secrets. He asked them to imagine a life led under the glare of lights that never went out, under the gaze of unseen eyes when your only way of measuring time was the daily tick-tock of beating after beating. He introduced them to the Ukrainians in their white smocks, to the world of the plank, and the axe, and the lump hammer, and the hours of supplementary interrogation that followed when he abandoned any trace of self-respect and opened his entire life for their inspection. No secrets left worth protecting. No question he wouldn't answer. Just the knowledge that he'd become a husk of a man, emptied of everything except a growing sense of dread.

Throughout this account, Schultz was aware of the baby beside her mother, and the longer Schultz talked, the more beguiled the baby seemed by his presence at the table. She was far too young to understand what he was saying, but as he plunged deeper into the numbing void that had followed his months at the Lubyanka – the draughty apartment, the consolations of black-market vodka – she kicked her legs and gurgled and reached out to try and seize that thick finger again. Finally, Schultz realised he'd nothing left to say.

'So that was me,' he said, 'my war. It took three years until

I realised what they had in store for me. They wanted me to deliver a letter. The price of a postage stamp might have saved me a great deal of grief.'

'A letter to whom?'

'Himmler. *Onkel Heine.* They believed I knew him, which in a way was true.'

'And who wrote this letter?'

'Stalin. The great *Vozhd.*'

'So what happened?'

'I did their bidding. Himmler is under treatment in the SS sanatorium at Hohenlychen. I gave him the letter this afternoon and refused an invitation to stay. The rest of the story you can blame on Frenzell.'

'He flew you down here?'

'He flew me first from Stockholm, and then to a field down the road. He was also kind enough to give me your address. Your friend's a modest man but I suspect I owe him my life. Himmler hates untidiness, especially when it comes to a postman like me.'

Merz nodded, then exchanged a glance with his wife before reaching for the bottle and recharging Schultz's glass.

'We have an old shed in the garden,' he said. 'Lottie uses it as a den in the summer. It gets cold at night but there's a mattress in there and a pile of blankets, and if you get bored Lottie's very good about sharing her toys.' He paused, waiting for an answer, but Beata had something to add.

'We call it *das Puppenhaus*, Herr Schultz,' she murmured. 'And you're very welcome.'

Das Puppenhaus. The doll's house. Schultz rubbed his big face, and then extended a hand to Beata.

'I was christened Wilhelm,' he said. 'But Merz used to call me Willi.'

13

Tam Moncrieff was no fan of the little Lysander aircraft. They were, he thought, creatures of the night, perfectly equipped to drop into French fields under cover of darkness, deliver an agent and then disappear again before the nearest German caught wind of what might be happening. Back in the glory days of SOE, when the whole of France lay under occupation, Lysanders were invaluable but now the Germans had gone, pushed back towards the borders of their own country, and it wasn't at all clear to Moncrieff why he couldn't get a flight on one of the bigger twin-engined Dakotas that regularly ferried personnel and equipment across the Channel and into France. That way, at the very least, he might have an hour or two of relative comfort to grasp what the next week or so might have in store for him.

Ursula Barton, alas, wouldn't hear of it. Thanks to contacts in SOE, she'd laid hands on a Lysander and had struck a deal that gave MI5 the flight for virtually nothing. With a budget that was shrinking by the day, she pointed out, she couldn't possibly afford the outrageous sums charged by a War Ministry desperate to claw back the money to pay for all those timeservers behind all those Whitehall desks. No, she insisted that Moncrieff present himself at the airfield near Chichester where the Lysanders were hangared. She also gave him a thickish brief outlining known developments to date, plus a handful of books she wanted him to present to her good friend, ex-agent *Clover*.

In a rather touching aside, saying goodbye in her office, she'd revealed her worries about what kind of present she could possibly afford. Sending food or drink was out of the question because the Swiss were spoiled for both. No woman could possibly afford perfume these days, and to lay hands on nylon stockings you had to be on good terms with a Yank. So, in the end, it had to be books.

The books were bundled with binder twine, and before he left the office Moncrieff had taken a cursory look. Two of them were collections of poetry. Gerard Manley Hopkins he admired. Of Henry Vaughan, he knew nothing. One of the remaining volumes was an exploration of faith by a Scottish explorer who'd lived among Buddhist monks, while the other was a thickish history of the Protestant Reformation. Barton, looking up from the litter of paperwork on her desk, had caught his bewilderment at once.

'*Clover*'s joined the Salvation Army,' she said. 'She's in the process of becoming an Officer. I thought I'd mentioned it.'

'But she's still...' Moncrieff shrugged, '... in the game?'

'Christ, yes,' She smiled absently up at him. 'Forgive my French.'

Now, with the snowcapped peaks of the French Alps at last in sight, Moncrieff was reading Barton's brief for the second time. The pilot, a taciturn Scot, was mercifully uninterested in conversation and to Moncrieff's surprise the little plane had more room for his leggy frame than he'd expected. With the sun over his right shoulder, he was doing his best to master the known order of events to date.

The operation, whatever shape it finally took, appeared to have attracted not one but two codenames. The Americans, who were clearly in charge, were calling it *Sunrise*. Churchill, it seemed, preferred *Crossword*. To Moncrieff, long schooled to hunt for the tiniest hint of daylight through the usual thicket of complications, this was itself significant.

Those with the keenest antennae in London had begun to remark on a slippage of power to the Americans that appeared to be irreversible. President Roosevelt had bailed out a near-bankrupt Britain in the early days of the war, while General Dwight D. Eisenhower had masterminded the successful assault on D-Day. There were rumours of a falling out between Eisenhower and the bumptious Montgomery, but no one seemed to doubt for a moment that the Americans were well and truly in charge. It was, after all, their money, their matériel and their huge machine grinding slowly towards a crossing of the River Rhine, and when it came to a settlement at the war's end, Moncrieff sensed that the Americans, under the inscrutable gaze of Stalin, would be calling the shots.

So where did this leave Operation *Sunrise*? Moncrieff, from his desk in St James's Street, had started with the urgent request to ship SS *Sturmhannführer* Max Wuensche to Switzerland. A call to the officer in charge of Camp 165, way up in the wilds of Caithness, had confirmed his presence among the other high-value inmates, but when Moncrieff had steered the conversation round to other fingers in this pie, he'd hit a brick wall. Yes, Herr Wuensche had – to date – a blameless record as a prisoner of war. No, he'd never volunteered anything beyond his rank and service number. And, no, he very definitely would not be leaving under escort on the next train south. When Moncrieff had pressed for more details – expressions of interest, perhaps, from other intelligence agencies – the Lieutenant Colonel in charge, a Scotsman like Moncrieff, had regretfully brought the conversation to an end. Max Wuensche, he murmured, was an active and willing participant in many aspects of camp life.

He was also a painter of some talent and doubtless, after the war, he could look forward to a life of opportunity in the *neue Deutschland*.

Moncrieff had loved this phrase, 'the new Germany', not least because it revealed yet another aspect of the jockeying currently taking place in every corner of the Alliance. He spoke regularly to American contacts in Washington. He bought drinks for some of the wary Free French expatriates who haunted certain pubs in Knightsbridge and Belgravia. He even had links to sources in the Russian Embassy. These conversations, some official, most not, told him that the players around the board were preparing their last throws of the dice, and all of them – without exception – acknowledged that Germany, and therefore Germans, would be a major force as post-war Europe tried to come to terms with what might turn out to be a messy peace.

So who was making sure that Wuensche, the much-decorated SS hero and Hitler's favourite adjutant, would never form part of wherever Operation *Sunrise* was headed next? And was Ursula Barton right in thinking that a Yugoslav partisan advance across the plains of northern Italy, in the wake of a local German surrender, might serve Soviet interests very nicely?

The latter possibility had weighed heavily with Moncrieff. Three years ago, he'd got rather too close to a trail of coincidences and questionable contacts left by a fast-rising MI6 agent called Kim Philby. He and Ursula Barton had begun to have doubts about exactly where this plausible, effective, though endearingly shy operator's loyalties really lay. Their enquiries had given rise to a number of key questions, none of them ever properly addressed, but Moncrieff's involvement had come to a sorry end. He'd been beaten, injected and kidnapped in the middle of the night, and thanks to a drug called Scopolamine the next week or so of his life had become a mystery. This experience had shaken his faith in almost everything, and it had taken the years that followed to restore something of his former self. Tam Moncrieff had started his adult life as a Royal Marine but only recently had he felt the return of that sense of raw physical self-confidence.

Now, as the Lysander sideslipped into an airstrip the size of a pocket handkerchief in the French frontier town of Annemasse, he folded Barton's notes and slid them back into his suitcase. Moments later, the little plane bumped to a halt. The pilot was already signalling to a uniformed attendant in charge of the refuelling bowser. He had to be in Paris before nightfall.

'It's gone four already,' he tapped his watch. 'Good luck wherever you're off to next.'

Getting into Switzerland, Barton had warned, might offer a challenge or two. Travelling as a fully accredited member of the Security Service, complete with MI5 ID, would raise all kinds of difficulties. The Swiss were punctilious when it came to protecting their cherished neutrality, and although it was common knowledge that spies were thick on the ground, officials on the frontier did their best to turn away yet more trouble. And so, after some thought, Ursula Barton had decided to appoint Moncrieff to an administrative role in the Salvation Army.

In the Swiss branch of the organisation, Anneke De Vries – aka ex-agent *Clover* – had recently been appointed an Officer in the organisation, the Salvation Army's equivalent of an ordained minister of religion. Moncrieff was bringing her literature that she would be translating into German and French. These were first-hand attestations to the power of prayer, the reach of gospel, and – above all – the blessings of dedicated work among the poor. This was authentic material, freely available to callers at the Army's impressive headquarters in Queen Victoria Street, and although Barton hadn't troubled the Army's management with this small subterfuge, she could see no reason why it wouldn't ease Moncrieff's path into Switzerland. She'd also furnished him with a Salvation Army ID card, hastily mocked up by a gifted counterfeiter who nested in a tiny office on the top floor of MI5 headquarters.

'When you try, you can look very stern,' she told Moncrieff. 'Self-denial and good works? Never fails. Trust in the Lord and all will be well.'

As easy as that? Moncrieff somehow doubted it, but he'd spent a great deal of time in Europe before the war and he knew how porous borders could be if you knew the language and had a story to tell. The queue on the French side of the frontier was long. It happened to be a Saturday, and he imagined that most of these people must be taking their hard-earned francs into shops in nearby Geneva, where goods unimaginable in France were still for sale. At last, he found himself looking at the uniformed official who appeared to be in charge. Only two flimsy looking wooden barriers stood between him and Switzerland. Moncrieff's passport listed his occupation as 'Army officer'. The official glanced up at him. His German had an inflection that was new to Moncrieff.

'You're here on official business?'

'I am.'

'With a fellow Officer?'

'Indeed.'

'In Bern, perhaps? The embassy? The military attaché?'

'In Locarno.'

'*Locarno*? You have papers? A name? An address?'

'I have these.'

Moncrieff extracted a thickish envelope from his suitcase and handed it over. The official extracted the sheaf of printed witness Barton had acquired from Queen Victoria Street. The official peered at the first page but didn't speak English. He wanted Moncrieff to translate.

Moncrieff, who'd anticipated this moment, selected an account from a woman in London's East End who'd been bombed out early in the war and lost everything, including her house, her second husband, her ancient dad and a much-loved tom cat called Gary. The Salvation Army had come to her rescue and now she was a Soldier for the cause in neighbouring Plaistow.

'That's also in the East End,' Moncrieff said helpfully. 'And I gather the cat's named after Gary Cooper.' He smiled. '*Meet John Doe*? Playing opposite Barbara Stanwyck?'

The official was looking baffled.

'What's this got to do with the Army?'

Moncrief feigned bewilderment for a moment or two. Then his fingers found Barton's precious ID in the pocket of his jacket, and he handed it across.

'Wrong Army. My mistake. I should have mentioned it. This is the *Salvation* Army. Not the other sort.'

'You work for these people?' The official was studying the ID.

'I work for God.'

He explained about William Booth, the Army's founder, about branches of the movement worldwide, and about Anneke De Vries.

'She helps run the Army in Locarno. I have her phone number, if it helps. We have all kinds of issues to address but she'll be translating this material and distributing it throughout Switzerland.'

'But why don't you do that? Your German is excellent.'

'Too busy, I'm afraid.' Moncrieff risked a smile. 'God's work never ends.'

The official's gaze returned to the envelope. Moncrieff sensed that his luck was about to run out but then the official looked up. He wanted to know how bad things were in England.

'Very bad, alas. Peace is something you take for granted until it's not there any more.'

'But you think there's a place for your Army here? In Switzerland?'

'We know there is. Poverty and need start in the human heart.' His hand briefly closed over his chest. 'We're called to rescue the lost, as well as the afflicted. Even here in your country.'

The official was frowning now. Then he glanced at the lengthening queue and reached for Moncrieff's passport.

'One month.' The big stamp descended on the empty page, and he scribbled a date.

'More than enough, I hope.' Moncrieff was pocketing his passport. 'God willing.'

*

Getting to Locarno from Geneva was never going to be easy, Barton had warned, but it was on the second of the two train changes that Moncrieff began to suspect that he was being followed. His new friend was tallish, with cropped hair, a lean, bony face, and deep-set eyes behind a pair of steel-rimmed glasses. His long black leather coat was unbuttoned in the warmth of the train and he'd selected a nearby window seat. It was dark outside after the first change of train and Moncrieff was aware of the man lifting his head from his newspaper to briefly study Moncrieff's reflection in the window. He must have read his edition of the *Journal de Genève* twice by the time they got to Bellinzona.

From here, according to the porter on the station, it was a bare ten minutes to Locarno. The local train would be arriving in minutes. By now, the platform had emptied except for Moncrieff and, a discreet ten metres away, his shadow, the folded newspaper now tucked beneath his arm. Moncrieff was wondering whether to effect a formal introduction when an engine and a single carriage steamed fussily in to take them both to Locarno. Agent *Clover*, Barton had assured him, would be waiting at the station but Moncrieff, checking his watch, was beginning to have his doubts. Switzerland, he suspected, went to bed early. Who would venture out at four minutes to midnight?

He needn't have worried. Half expecting to meet someone in a black uniform with a fetching bonnet, he found himself exchanging a rather formal handshake with a tall woman he would later describe to Ursula Barton as 'handsome'. She was wearing skiing trousers and a pair of rugged boots. A heavy pullover that looked hand-knitted reached down to her knees, and Moncrieff counted the line of scarlet reindeer that stretched across her chest. There were seven. A tangle of blonde curls escaped the woolly cap, and her breath clouded on the cold night air when she asked about the journey.

'It was fine, Fraulein De Vries,' Moncrieff murmured. 'Might I ask you a favour?'

'Of course. Ursula still calls me *Clover*. You can, too.' Her English was flawless, just a tiny shiver of Dutch vowels.

'Thank you,' Moncrieff stepped a little closer. 'There's a man coming towards us. Black leather coat. Glasses. Nothing obvious, please, but might you know him?'

De Vries returned his smile, then covered her nose, confected a sneeze and turned her head away in time to catch a glimpse of the stranger from the train before he hurried towards the ticket barrier.

'Well?'

De Vries held his gaze for a moment, then linked her arm through his. 'I have a little car outside,' she said. 'He'll never keep up.'

It was a Fiat Topolino, tiny, black. Moncrieff squeezed himself into the front, still looking for any sign of his shadow, but the street in front of the station was empty. A five-minute drive took them down to the edge of a lake. The streetlights along the promenade danced on the blackness of the water but, once again, there was no sign of life.

Moncrieff had been here once before, in high summer, twenty years ago. Then, as a young university student eager to put his French and German to the test, he'd spent a very happy five days swimming in the lake and hiking in the nearby mountains until his precious stock of Swiss francs ran out. Barely six months earlier, the town had been full of diplomats putting the finishing touches to the treaty that would cement the gains of the last great war, and it had been easy to believe in the promise of an enduring peace, but now mere decades later, this tidy little Swiss lakeside resort was sheltering itself from a very different world.

'This is your car?'

'It belongs to the Army. I call it the Tank.' De Vries was slowing to a halt in front of a biggish building beside the water. 'This is home. *Chez moi.*' She touched him lightly on the arm. 'You're very welcome.'

A plaque beside the door announced the premises as the *Club d'Aviron de Locarno.*

'You live in a rowing club?'

'Sort of. Don't be frightened. It's not as bad as it sounds.'

She produced a key to open the door, and then stood back as Moncrieff stepped inside. Every rowing club, he thought, must smell the same: a damp bouquet of sweat and effort spiced with the smell of oil and the tang of white spirit used to thin the varnish for the hulls. He stood for a moment in the darkness, then De Vries found the light switch and he was looking at a modest fleet of singles, doubles and quads, all of them nested on wooden launch trollies. Blades were stored on racks on the walls, and in the silence he could hear the soft lap-lap of water beyond the wide double doors at the end.

Moncrieff stepped towards the nearest of the boats, ran his fingers down the curve of the hull, tested the swivel in the rigger.

'You know about rowing?'

'I do, yes. I rowed at university, Edinburgh. Bloody cold this time of year.'

De Vries laughed. She said she had the run of the place. The right word in the right ear, and he could borrow one of the singles any time.

'Stay for ever,' she said. 'Forget this wretched war.'

She led him upstairs. Beyond an area the club used for social events was another locked door. On the other side lay a roomy apartment, two bedrooms, with a lounge at the front that looked onto the water. De Vries wanted to know whether Moncrieff had eaten. He shook his head, telling her he'd had something at Lucerne between trains, and she studied him for a moment before taking off her woolly hat and shaking out her blonde curls.

'You lie badly,' she told him. 'Which surprises me.'

She disappeared into the kitchen and Moncrieff caught the pop of a gas flame and the clatter of crockery as he toured the lounge, sampling the bookshelves and inspecting the art on the wall. The framed photographs were all black and white, mainly close-up shots of birds against landscapes that Moncrieff judged to be Dutch, but there was one oil painting tidied into a corner of the room. It was abstract, a mad, jagged collage of blacks and scarlets and a vivid burned ochre that seemed to speak of a deep anger. To Moncrieff, it had no place in this room. It was an intruder with rough manners and the loudest of voices who'd somehow barged in through the door and insisted on catching the eye. He was still studying it, still wondering, when De Vries returned with a bowl of soup and thick slices of buttered bread.

'Here, please.' She was nodding at the biggest of the three armchairs.

'Where did this come from?' Moncrieff nodded at the painting.

'Me.' She was waiting for him to take a seat. 'It's crude, I know, but it felt important at the time.'

Moncrieff nodded, settling in the armchair.

'And Nevil Shute? Upton Sinclair? Robert Tressell? Don't the Dutch write books? The Germans? The *Swiss*? I've brought you some more. They're presents from Ursula but I suspect your tastes might have moved on.'

'Ursula was a wonderful friend.' De Vries was laughing now. 'But she never quite got me right.'

'How? Do you mind me asking?'

'Not at all. Ursula was my boss. In fact, she was everyone's boss. And I wanted her to think I was a lot more serious than I really am.'

'The Salvation Army sounds serious. Are you telling me she was wrong?'

'The Army was a gift from God.' Her gaze had strayed back to the oil painting. 'I wasn't very well at the time.'

'And the Army helped?'

'It did. It does. And so did that canvas. One way or another I had a lot to get off my chest, and a good friend told me what to do with the paints. Does that make any sense? I'm not sure I care.'

Moncrieff nodded, not knowing quite what to say, and then tasted the soup.

'Potato?' he looked up. 'Barley? Onion?'

'And paprika. It's OK?'

'It's marvellous. So how come you live here?'

'That's the Army, again. They support the club, they helped get it built in the first place. There are kids in this country, believe it or not, who have real problems. We send them here and the club looks after them, which is nice for me because I get to live with a wonderful view.'

'You row, too?'

'I ski. And swim. And ask the nosiest questions. That man on the station, by the way, the one you pointed out.'

'Yes?'

'He's a Slav. His uses the codename *Crusader*, and he works for anyone who'll pay the fees he demands.'

'You know this? You're sure?'

'Absolutely certain, I'm afraid.' There was a hint of mischief in the smile. 'Old habits die hard.'

*

Moncrieff woke late, gone nine in the morning, disturbed by voices from below. Rowers, he thought. Preparing to launch. He got out of bed. De Vries had left an ancient dressing gown on the back of the door, and he put it on. The faintest scent of perfume told him it must be hers, and he was surprised by how well it fitted.

The little kitchen next door was empty but there was a scribbled note telling him to help himself to coffee and the bag of fresh *pains aux raisins* she'd acquired from the bakery across the street. She'd be out until late morning, leading a service in the local citadel. Any of the rowers would supply directions if he was interested in taking a look. 'No obligation,' she'd written at the end. 'Why would you need God?'

Good question. Moncrieff retired to the bathroom, realising it was Sunday. He soaped himself all over with water from the handbasin, then returned to the kitchen to brew coffee. With a plate of *pains aux raisins* on his lap, he settled in an armchair and watched the rowers slipping their hulls into the water. The conditions were perfect, not a breath of wind. The lake was ringed with mountains, and the snow glistened in the sunshine against a near-cloudless sky.

Moncrieff watched one of the rowers. He was older than the rest, and the way he sat the single scull, his body bent while he fiddled with adjustments on the footplate before he came vertical again, spoke of a great deal of experience. His back straight, the sun on his face, his blades extended, his legs began to flex as he slid forward to take the first stroke. This movement, which Moncrieff so well remembered, could have a singular grace, and in the hands of this rower the shell slipped effortlessly forward, scarcely troubling the mirrored surface of the lake.

He took another stroke, and then a third, the scull picking up speed, and Moncrieff followed his progress, aware that he'd been right about the man's pedigree, and aware as well of the truth of a metaphor like this. On assignment, as on the water, you had to rely on yourself, on your own talents, on your own artfulness. You had to leave no trace, you had to balance your little craft against every eventuality, and you had – above all – to understand the importance of stealth. Take the enemy by surprise. Always.

Agent *Crusader*? He sat back in the armchair, the plate empty, his eyes closed in the warmth of the sunshine through the big window. He knew he had to take De Vries's intelligence, her warning, on trust. Quite how she stayed in the game while saving souls was beyond him but what little he'd seen of her so far had been deeply beguiling. She had a confidence, a sense of her own presence, that was – in his experience – very rare. She'd teased out life's tougher knots, lifted her head, cocked a listening ear, accepted a calling, and was happy with the results. Not her life, not any more, but God's.

Moncrieff found himself nodding. Not because he was envious, or wanted something similar for himself, but because he thought he understood. There was nothing otherworldly or semi-divine about his own trade, far from it, but he'd suffered a great deal from time to time and recognised the door you'd try and open if you were in real trouble. De Vries had done exactly that, and he guessed it was serving her extremely well. *Gut gemacht*. Well done. God bless.

Of De Vries, at least, Moncrieff thought he had the measure. But Agent *Crusader*? As a freelance agent, if he was to believe his new hostess, this man would be working for anyone who'd put money in his pocket, but his tradecraft, on the evidence of a single journey, was hopeless. Moncrieff's first instinct was to suspect the hand of Broadway in the very fact that he'd been followed at all, but somehow he doubted that even MI6 would hire someone so hapless. Unless, of course, they simply wanted to mark his card. This is abroad, they were telling him. This is our territory. Please repack your bags and go home.

The link with Broadway, if true, was troubling. He never doubted for a moment that coming to Switzerland like this was an act of trespass, that he had ventured onto their turf, but his encounters with the likes of Kim Philby had taught him that MI6 were in the business of survival in a rough old world, and that they could be ruthless as well as clever in defending their precious turf. Nonetheless, he was still a servant of the Crown, employed by King and Country, and he had legitimate business of his own to transact.

In the file he was carrying was a list of other senior Nazis housed in Camp 165, and now he needed to talk to the Americans to offer a substitute for *Sturmbahnnführer* Wuensche, someone St

James's Street could pledge to deliver, but first he needed a much longer conversation with De Vries. Last night, she'd promised to share what she knew about Operation *Sunrise*, but she was meeting a contact at the citadel before the service began and preferred to parcel this latest intelligence with everything else.

Moncrieff at last opened his eyes. There were half a dozen boats out on the water, jockeying for position on some kind of start line, but away in the distance he could barely make out the single sculler he'd been watching earlier. Alone, he thought. Dependent on no one but himself.

*

The Salvation Army citadel turned out to be a slightly shabby looking building, several hundred metres away from the town centre. There was a school across the road, with a caretaker sweeping the playground, and Moncrieff paused for a moment or two, watching a couple of pigeons inspecting the sweepings he'd left in his wake. According to Moncrieff's calculations, Officer De Vries's service should have come to an end by now, and a thin trickle of worshippers emerging into the sunshine told him he was right.

He found her inside the hall that served as the body of the citadel. Last night, she'd looked like a refugee from the ski slopes. Now, in her dark uniform, sensible shoes and fetching bonnet, she was definitely on active service.

'You found the coffee? The *pains aux raisins*? Made yourself at home?'

'Yes to all three. You should be running a hotel.'

They were alone in the hall. Rows of wooden seats stretched back from a raised stage. An open bible lay on the lectern at the front of the stage, and the entire hall was dominated by an enormous wooden cross, hanging on the rear wall.

They were sitting in the front row. Moncrieff gestured at the seats behind.

'Good turnout? Big congregation?'

'Meagre, I'm afraid. Locarno has always had a clean conscience. Either that, or most of the town's still in bed. We must talk about *Sunrise*.'

Moncrieff nodded. He loved conversations that immediately settled on the matter in hand. Few of his colleagues could manage it, but Ursula Barton had exactly the same talent. Small talk to business in a matter of seconds.

'I understand you know about the first meeting with Wolff?' she said.

'March the 8th? Ten days ago? Am I right?'

'Yes. That took place in Zurich. An American called Allen Dulles seems to be in charge. He heads the Swiss branch of OSS and lives in Bern. He met Wolff that night and they talked in the OSS apartment in Zurich for an hour before Dulles took the train back to Bern. Wolff stayed the night in Zurich and had further discussions with a man called Gaevernitz next morning.' She paused. 'How much do you know about this man?'

'Gaevernitz? Assume nothing.'

'Fine. His first name's Gero. His father was a celebrated professor in Germany. The family are liberal, one reason why Gero decided to sit the war out here in Switzerland. He has his father's looks, and his father's convictions, too. I've met him a number of times. He's a lovely man. He's sincere, and he's principled, and he's clever, and in this country he can speak his mind. He thinks all the Nazi nonsense goes only skin deep in Germany and wants to lend a hand when the time comes to bring this whole thing to an end.'

'You mean Hitler?'

'I mean the war, though it may turn out to be the same thing.

Dulles and Gaevernitz see a great deal of each other. A source of mine is a very close confidant of Gaevernitz and knows more or less what happened after Dulles left him with Karl Wolff in Zurich. Wolff, it seems, believes the war is lost. He's always had faith in Hitler but now he must persuade him to sue for peace. Hitler, of course, won't hear of it. The Allies are still insisting on unconditional surrender and Hitler knows that will be the end of Germany. Gaevernitz says he's leading the country to its grave, and he's probably right.'

'And Wolff?'

'Wolff is a patriot. This is Gaevernitz again, not me. Wolff leads the SS in northern Italy but General Kesselring is in charge. Kesselring is old school. He's taken the soldier's oath, total allegiance to the Führer, and that kind of loyalty has got into his bones. Gaevernitz has an undertaking from Wolff that he will talk to Kesselring about a local surrender south of the Alps – that's hundreds of thousands of troops – but there are no guarantees that Kesselring will agree. He's the only undefeated senior General left in the Reich. He has a reputation to protect.'

Moncrieff nodded. He'd read a great deal about Kesselring, mainly thanks to interview transcriptions with senior Nazi commanders taken prisoner, and he knew that De Vries was right. Even a commander of Kesselring's standing had a great deal to lose in any offstage dealings with the Allies including, in the current mayhem, his head.

'So these talks will go nowhere, surely? Kesselring is the only one who can sign a proper surrender, and that's the last thing he'll ever do.'

'Gaevernitz thinks otherwise. Believe me, he reads these situations well. The word he uses is "fluid". Things change all the time, and he thinks that could be to our advantage.'

'Our?'

'Yours. Dulles has been in touch with Allied headquarters in Caserta. You know about the setup there?'

Moncrieff nodded. The Allied advance into northern Italy was under the control of a British General, Sir Harold Alexander. The Field Marshal held court in some splendour at the Palace of the Bourbons, at Caserta, north of Naples. In intelligence circles, Alexander had a reputation as a reserved man, difficult to read, but he appeared to have fallen out with Montgomery. This was an easy thing to do, thought Moncrieff, but was greatly to Alexander's credit.

'So what does Caserta think?'

'It appears that Alexander's interested. He's sending two aides, one American, one British, to meet Wolff the next time he turns up.'

'Here, you mean?'

'Yes.' She leaned forward. 'But I understand there's a problem. Wolff was never supposed to come to Switzerland in the first place. For whatever reason, he was happy to take the risk, but he told none of his SS bosses in Berlin. If you think that was reckless, you'd be right. Alas, he was caught out. While he was here talking to Dulles, his immediate boss phoned wanting to meet him in Italy but obviously couldn't. His name's Kaltenbrunner. Only Himmler outranks him. Kaltenbrunner made enquiries and in the end he found out about Wolff spending the night in Zurich. Naturally he's demanding a face-to-face interview and an explanation. So far Wolff's managed to avoid the first, but he's had to explain what on earth he was doing on the wrong side of the border.'

'And?

'He said he was arranging a little present for the Führer. It's Hitler's birthday next month. He wants to make the whole thing a surprise.'

Moncrieff was staring at her. At last he understood. 'Wuensche,' he said softly. 'Hitler's favourite adjutant.' 'Exactly.'

'The one we can't release.'

'No?' De Vries's eyes had widened. 'You can't deliver him?'

'It seems not.'

Moncrieff sat back a moment. At least, he thought, I now understand where *Sturmbahnnführer* Wuensche fits in the jigsaw. Would any of the names on the list he was carrying be an acceptable substitute? And, in any event, after more than a week wasn't it a bit late to save Wolff from a summons to Berlin, and to everything that would inevitably follow? Moncrieff knew a great deal about the murderous games played at the highest level of Himmler's SS empire and had no doubts about what the outcome would be.

'Wolff's a dead man.' He was looking at De Vries again. 'Isn't he?'

'You'd think so. I'd think so. Gaevernitz doesn't.'

'No?'

'No, absolutely not. In fact, he's expecting him back tomorrow morning.'

'Who?'

'Wolff.'

'*Wolff?*'

'Indeed. Alexander's two aides turned up yesterday. They came in through the checkpoint at Annemasse a couple of days ago. These are senior military, both Generals, and they're travelling under assumed names. According to another source of mine, a woman I met this morning, they're both wearing American dog tags. She cleans the villa they're staying in. The tags have to come from Dulles. Have to.'

Moncrieff sat back again. If he was sure of anything, he was certain that the Salvation Army had acquired a prime asset in the shape of ex-agent *Clover*. Were MI6 aware of the loss they'd suffered, back in 1939, when Anneke De Vries had watched events at Venlo and walked away? She must have been as angry as Ursula Barton, Moncrieff thought, about the kidnapping on the frontier. A very good reason to buy a handful of oil paints and take it out on the canvas.

Moncrieff turned to De Vries again.

'You mentioned a villa,' he said carefully.

'I did.'

'Where is it?'

'Ascona. The next town on the lake. Gaevernitz has two villas there, one down by the water, very private, the other up on the hill behind. The Americans are on the hill. The talks will take place beside the lake. Wolff and his party are expected tomorrow morning. They'll be crossing the frontier at Chiasso. Swiss intelligence will smooth the way.'

'The villa,' Moncrieff said again. 'How far?'

'From the boathouse? Maybe four kilometres. Half an hour if you're as fit as you look.' She studied Moncrieff a moment, then nodded down at a long wooden bench at the foot of the stage. 'Do you know what we call that in the Army?'

'Tell me.'

'The Mercy Seat.' She was smiling. 'That's where God changes everything.'

14

Moncrieff was up and dressed before dawn. Yesterday afternoon, with the blessing of De Vries, he'd rigged and launched a single scull from the rowing club. Borrowed club colours had given him cover, and he'd stroked slowly away down the lake, curious to see the venue for tomorrow's meeting between the Allied Generals and the head of the SS in northern Italy. Look for a stone-built single-storey villa down at the water's edge, De Vries had told him. A terrace at the front falls sheer into the lake, matched by a circular structure beside it. Two chimneys. Small windows. Maybe an umbrella against the sun if the weather's still fine. Four kilometres, she'd said again. Nothing for a man like you.

Half an hour's sculling had taken him clear of the town's waterfront. The conditions were perfect, the water mirror-calm, the narrow hull cleaving through the water, leaving barely a ripple behind. The last time he'd rowed properly had been in a lake outside Berlin, back in 1938, the summer he'd met Bella Menzies, and he was astonished at how quickly his body settled back into the remembered sweetness of the rhythm. An instructor he'd known in the Royal Marines had once told him that every muscle in the body has a memory, and this abrupt expedition – wholly unexpected – seemed to prove him right.

Beyond the edge of the town, nature was back in charge, the landscape heavily wooded, and he put together a sequence of pieces at full pressure, driving himself hard, sucking the air deep into his lungs, his thighs on fire as he pressed down against the footplate, feeling the sweat beginning to darken his borrowed singlet. Then, as he pulled closer to the bank, he saw the villa. This had to be Gaevernitz's place. It seemed to emerge from nowhere, a rich man's conjuring trick, much like tomorrow's meeting he'd helped to broker, and it answered De Vries's description perfectly. To the left of the villa was a tiny beach, sand and pebbles, and Moncrieff edged the little scull into the shallows until he could step out. He'd always rowed barefoot, and the pebbles felt warm when he eased himself onto the beach.

His first instinct was to explore the villa itself. He'd brought with him a list of high-value German prisoners to offer as substitutes for *Sturmbahnnführer* Wuensche, a calling card that might take him a little closer to the heart of these negotiations, but there was no sign of life in the property so he decided instead to relax. Slipping into the old rhythms afloat was one thing, but the last couple of kilometres had reminded him how unfit he was. There was still heat in the sun. The beach was beautifully secluded. And so he settled on the pebbles, his knees drawn up, hearing nothing but an occasional scuffling in the undergrowth and the distant call of a lone curlew.

A silence like this, in the very middle of a tormented continent, was a rare blessing. Beyond these lakes and mountains, six years of war had extracted a murderous price from nation after nation. Sudden death had become a fact of life and gazing across the water at the distant ring of peaks, Moncrieff couldn't help remembering the piles of rubble and charred timber after the V-2 strike on Farringdon Market. Not just that. Not just the dazed relatives inspecting the body parts still awaiting collection. But the foul grittiness of ash and brick dust that had lingered deep in the back of his throat for hours afterwards.

That taste, he thought, was a curse that had settled like a shroud on Europe. It was a reminder that the killing was far from over. It was the promise of yet more ruin to come. All this was bad enough but, perhaps most important of all, it spoke of the terrifying price of political miscalculation. One man had embarked on a gigantic gamble, and now his country was on its knees.

Would tomorrow's meeting help bring Germany back to its senses? Moncrieff had his doubts. Karl Wolff, by every account, was a sane man. The Nazis had built the finest army in living memory yet his very presence here would be an acknowledgement that the game was up. Wherever you looked on the map, the Thousand Year Reich was physically shrinking by the day, and even Goebbels had run out of lies to sweeten the reckoning to come. The Germans, Moncrieff knew, had a word for it. *Katastrophe.*

At Yalta, after all the drafting and redrafting, the Allies had confirmed only one possible end to the war: unconditional surrender. Germany, pinned to the mat, must be forced to concede, something the Führer would never do. And so even now, after millions of deaths, the killing went on, night after night, at Aachen, at Cologne, on the outskirts of Stettin, savage bites torn out of the bleeding carcass that was the Fatherland. Could one man, one voice at the table, hurry the war to an end? Might that, in some small way, happen tomorrow? Just metres away from where Moncrieff was sitting? Or would this encounter be just another sideshow, another wasted episode as the grotesque carnival of slaughter partied on?

Moncrieff shook his head. He didn't know, and the more he saw of this war, the more he realised that no one else did either. Violence on this scale, formerly unimaginable, developed a momentum of its own. No single country, with the possible exception of Germany itself, seemed able to stop it. And so peace became the most elusive of quarries. In the language of Moncrieff's native Cairngorms, it had to be painstakingly pursued and cornered. You had to be clever. You had to be patient. You had to stay downwind. You had to be invisible. And at the moment of maximum opportunity, you had to steady your nerves, take a shallow breath, close one eye, tighten your finger on the trigger and pray for the cleanest of kills. That, of course, was impossible. Which was why any decent war quickly developed a life of its own.

Stalking peace? Moncrieff smiled at the rightness of the image. His fingers found a nearby pebble, smooth and flat, and he got to his feet and steadied himself before sending the little stone darting across the water. Technique again, he thought. A remembered flick of the wrist, and then the trail of little dimples that followed the stone as it skittered away. Ten jumps? Ten playful little bounces? More than acceptable.

Moncrieff turned back to the villa. By now he was convinced that the place was empty, and he was deciding whether to scale the wall and peer in through a window or two when he heard the low rumble of a diesel engine out on the lake. The noise grew louder, then louder still, and suddenly Moncrieff was looking at a patrol boat, close inshore. It was flying the Swiss ensign at the stern. A uniformed figure in a peaked cap was standing on the raised bridge, and the sweep of his binoculars came to rest on Moncrieff.

The beat of the engine slowed, and the boat lost way. When it finally came to a halt, it was barely ten metres from the beach.

The figure on the bridge wanted to know what Moncrieff was up to. He was speaking German.

Moncrieff nodded down at the boat, and then cupped his hands.

'Having a rest,' he shouted.

'You know this is private? The beach? The house? Everything?'

'I didn't, no.'

'You live here?'

'No.'

'You're Swiss?'

'English. I have a friend at the rowing club.'

Another figure had appeared on the bridge. News that Moncrieff was a foreigner sparked a brief debate. Then the Captain cupped his hands again.

'You have papers? A passport?'

'At the club.'

'Follow us.'

Moncrieff shrugged and got back in the scull. Two more sailors had appeared on the stern of the patrol boat, and one of them was carrying a carbine. The patrol boat began to move, and the curl of dark exhaust caught in Moncrieff's throat. He pulled the scull to one side and quickened his rate until he was abreast of the patrol boat. The two sailors followed him round. Thirty minutes later, rowing much faster than he'd planned, Moncrieff grounded the scull on the concrete apron that served as the club's launch ramp. Exhausted, he led the Captain and one of the sailors up to De Vries's apartment. She met them at the door.

'Hans!' She and the Captain exchanged courtly bows. She seemed to know everyone.

Moncrieff fetched his passport. The Captain glanced at the one-month visa and then returned it. Herr Moncrieff, he said, had been technically guilty of trespass but in the circumstances the Swiss Navy was prepared to overlook the offence. From midnight tonight, he said, these upper reaches of the lake were closed to all private boating until further notice.

'Your German is excellent, Herr Moncrieff. I assume you understand.'

'Perfectly. My apologies. Next time I'll ask.'

'I suspect not, Herr Moncrieff.' The Captain offered a thin smile. 'Because there won't be a next time. Private property means just that. At least here in Switzerland.'

*

Now, in the first faint hints of dawn, De Vries and Moncrieff were driving west, into the neighbouring town of Ascona. Twice he'd tried to insist that he could handle the next few hours on his own, and twice she'd refused to listen. She understood the importance of trying to get a photo of the Allied Generals out on the terrace with Wolff, and she was happy to lend Moncrieff the camera she used for birding shots, but it would be crazy to embark on an assignment like this without local knowledge, especially since Moncrieff's encounter with the Swiss Navy.

De Vries knew the terrain around the Gaevernitz villa well, chiefly because the bulrushes nearby were home to a shy family of coots and she often paid them a visit. Paths, she said, led down the hill from the main road. She had in mind a couple of places, well hidden, that offered a perfect view of the waterside villa. Wolff, according to one of her sources, was expected to arrive from Lugano mid-morning. It would be logical to anticipate a smallish party of SS aides travelling with him and perhaps someone from the Swiss secret service. The two Allied envoys were spending the night at Gaevernitz's other house, much further up the hill. She and Moncrieff, therefore, needed to be in position before full daylight.

Beyond Ascona, she pulled off the main road and parked on a forest track, overhung with stands of pine. She was wearing a camouflage smock she used for her location work, with a pair of dark trousers beneath. She'd recently bought a new lens for her best camera, an Exakta she normally used for capturing wildlife. The lens, she said, was 180mm, enough to fill the viewfinder with a family of young coots from the safety of a hide, but a lens that powerful demanded a stable base. Hence the big wooden tripod she hauled out of the back of the Topolino.

They set off downhill, walking out of the forest, De Vries nursing her camera, Moncrieff shouldering the tripod. He could feel the cold breath of the surrounding mountains, and he stamped warmth into his boots before they crossed the main road and headed once again into the trees.

The slope of the hill was beginning to steepen downwards. The ground was soft underfoot with a bed of last year's pine needles and from time to time he caught glimpses of the lake through the trees below. The water was steel-grey under the canopy of cloud, and he was trying to orientate himself from the ridge of peaks on the far side of the lake when De Vries tugged him to a halt.

'There.' She was pointing off to the left.

Once again, the villa had taken Moncrieff by surprise. From this angle, looking down from above, it seemed much bigger and with a slight shock he realised that there were lights on inside, throwing little rectangles of soft yellow onto the surrounds of the terrace through the unshuttered windows. As he watched, a shadow paused at one of the windows, and Moncrieff froze, motionless, before it moved on. This is where the war may end, he told himself. Amen to that.

They were edging forward very slowly now, Moncrieff in De Vries's footsteps. To his surprise, they seemed to be moving away from the house, crabbing across the face of the slope, until she motioned him once again to stop. A clump of chest-high shrubs among the tall stands of pine offered plenty of cover, and the view of the terrace in front of the villa, when he turned to check, was perfect. De Vries had made a space for herself among the shrubs and told Moncrieff where she wanted the tripod. The face of the hill was steep here and Moncrieff had to fully extend one of the legs. De Vries made final adjustments before bolting the camera onto the plate of the tripod. Then she checked the viewfinder and beckoned Moncrieff to join her.

'See what you think,' she murmured.

Moncrieff bent to the camera. The terrace was perfectly framed and in the quickening light it felt close enough to touch. The villa was a hundred metres away, at least, but every detail in the viewfinder was pin-sharp. Wooden tables had been arranged in a loose semi-circle, and Moncrieff watched as a woman appeared with a tray, spreading a neat pattern of mats over the tablecloths and offloading a pile of plates before returning with a handful of glasses. She wiped each glass carefully. Moncrieff counted seven, somehow heartened that an encounter of such consequence could rest in the hands of so few. Three of these people would be the two Allied Generals from the villa further up the hill, plus Karl Wolff. To capture all three of them in a single photograph – sworn enemies enjoying a conspiratorial glass or two in a setting like this – would, he suspected, be the making of Ursula Barton.

'Well?' De Vries wanted a verdict.

'*Perfekt*,' he said.

*

For the next three hours, not much happened. De Vries's family of coots, to her delight, emerged from their roost and took to the water. A squirrel, attracted by the little cakes De Vries had brought, waited patiently for crumbs. Then, towards ten o'clock, the Swiss Navy patrol boat returned and anchored three hundred metres offshore. By now, the terrace had been swept twice and the tables laid. There were baskets of pastries, and bowls heavy with fruit. Moncrieff, who hadn't seen a fresh banana for years, could only marvel at the sheer reach of the Swiss. The blessings of neutrality, he concluded, were numberless.

Two men in late middle age appeared shortly afterwards. One wore a grey jacket over black trousers, the other – taller – a well-cut suit in a dark blue stripe. They carried themselves with an air of easy command, strolling the length and breadth of the terrace, pausing to pluck a grape or two from the fruit bowl before standing at the low front wall, hands clasped behind their backs, to enjoy the view over the lake. These, Moncrieff concluded, had to be the Allied envoys from Caserta, the Generals despatched from Alexander's headquarters to meet Wolff and weigh whatever proposition he had in mind. They'd have made their way down from the villa further up the hill, and now they were waiting for the most powerful SS commander in northern Italy to appear.

According to De Vries, they'd been here in Ascona for days in anticipation of this meeting, and, watching them deep in conversation beside the wall, Moncrieff wondered what you'd talk about when the first real stirrings of peace were beginning to appear. Would you be cautious? Would you believe a word this man might have to say? And in any event, did you have the authority to move these talks along, to offer encouragement, to make commitments, to demand proof of sincere intent? To none of these questions did he have a sensible answer, partly because an encounter like this was rich with complications, and partly because – to be frank – he was a little out of his depth, but when he stole a glance at De Vries, barely visible among the shrubs, he realised that she, too, must have sensed how this morning might one day feature in the history books. Every war had, finally, to run out of steam. And maybe that long process was about to begin.

Minutes later, there was a stir of movement on the terrace. The Allied Generals turned their backs on the view, and advanced cautiously towards another figure who'd just emerged from the villa. He was tall, handsome, erect. Like the men he'd come to meet, he was wearing a suit, and like them, he radiated a natural authority. Moncrieff had seen photos of Wolff, back in London, and he recognised the set of his face, the high dome of his head, the sweep of thinning silver-grey hair.

'Wolff,' he whispered, as De Vries slowly panned the camera.

The three men were introducing themselves, the taller of the two Allied Generals taking the lead. A couple of aides had appeared with Wolff, and they, too, got a handshake. From where Moncrieff was standing, the grouping was perfect, every face visible, and there was even a hint of sunshine as the clouds began to part. If Anneke De Vries could do justice to a family of tiny coots then Moncrieff had absolutely no doubt that her wildlife talents would capture the scene below.

The woman who'd appeared earlier had returned to the terrace and was pouring what looked like coffee into proffered cups. The taller of the two Allied Generals had evidently asked for tea, and another woman appeared with a china pot. This had to be the Brit, Moncrieff concluded, General Airey. He spooned sugar into his tea and gave it a stir as the American – General Lemnitzer – clapped his hands and delivered a short speech. The villa was too far away for Moncrieff to catch the details, but

Wolff was looking pleased and delivered a brief reply. By now, the three of them had formed a little circle of their own, Wolff full-face, the Allied envoys in profile, and Moncrieff was aware of De Vries awaiting the moment that would tell the whole story. The roll of film she was using offered only eight exposures. It was obvious that she needed nerve as well as patience, and watching her bending to the camera, her forefinger motionless above the shutter button, Moncrieff realised again how wildlife photography must have been the perfect training for a challenge like this. Finally, after a sequence of shots, she leaned back from the tripod and shot him a glance over her shoulder.

'Done,' she said.

*

They climbed the hill as carefully as they'd made the descent, De Vries in front, following a path that led diagonally across the face of the hill, away from the villa. At the main road, they stayed in the shelter of the trees until there was no traffic, and then headed for the cover of the forest on the other side. Back beside the Topolino, De Vries stowed her equipment, and then drove back to Locarno. Instead of returning to her apartment above the rowing club, Moncrieff found himself in a maze of streets behind the town's centre.

'Come.'

They were parked beside a modern-looking apartment block with exterior stairs to a basement. De Vries was nursing her camera and Moncrieff followed her down. The door at the bottom of the steps was already slightly ajar, and De Vries stepped inside.

'Hannalore?' she called.

A woman's voice answered from the depths of the basement, and moments later Moncrieff was looking at a tiny woman with barely any hair. She must have been De Vries's age, maybe a year or two older. She was wearing an artist's smock and a pair of gipsy earrings, and her feet were bare on the parquet floor. The smock, on closer inspection, was scabbed with paint and she'd pinned an enamel butterfly to one shoulder.

She extended a hand for De Vries's camera and led the way down the hall. Moncrieff could already smell the developing chemicals the forgers used on the top floor at St James's Street, and was last into the darkroom at the end of the hall. With the door shut, it was pitch-black inside and Moncrieff listened to Hannalore loading the exposed film into the developing tank. Then came a click as she closed the lid on the tank, and the room was suddenly bathed in a deep red glow from a single bulb high on the wall.

'Lock it, please.' De Vries nodded at the door.

Moncrieff did her bidding and settled down for what he knew would be a longish wait, content to settle in a chair in the corner and listen to the two women talking. They were obviously friends. Most of the chatter was gossip. Not once did De Vries mention the villa by the lake.

Finally, after half an hour to dry, the roll of negatives was ready for inspection. De Vries peered at the film through a magnifying lens, moving slowly from shot to shot until she settled on the one she wanted.

'There,' she murmured. 'That one.'

Heidi had already prepared another bath of developer for the print.

'Size?'

'15 x 10.'

Hannalore nodded and slipped a sheet of photographic paper onto the work bench. Within minutes, his seat abandoned, Moncrieff was watching three faces swim up through the soup of chemicals, first ghostly, then bolder, then in perfect resolution General Lyman L. Lemnitzer, General Terence S. Airey, and SS *Obergruppenführer* Karl Wolff, all three of them smiling. Moncrieff had asked De Vries to record a moment that might alter the course of the war. And there it was: one of the regime's top SS Generals, a man with the Warsaw ghetto on his conscience, busily plotting an end to the madness of these years.

*

At Moncrieff's insistence, they celebrated at a restaurant two streets away. By now it was lunchtime. Moncrieff insisted on a table at the very back of the room, away from prying eyes, and after he'd ordered a beer for himself and a glass of blueberry juice for De Vries, he slipped the print from the thickness of the cardboard envelope and examined it for the first time in full daylight. If you were looking for evidence that Operation *Sunrise* had produced a truly remarkable moment, then here it was. These were men, Moncrieff thought, who plied the same trade. They spoke the language of modern warfare. They knew how to muster large bodies of men, how to move them around, how to deploy them to maximum advantage. They understood the lethal potential of artillery, of close ground support, and they applied the dark arts of modern warfare to battlefield after battlefield. They dealt in the currency of men's lives, thousands of lives, feeding the bonfires that had scorched an entire continent, but they were human, too, and it showed in their faces, in the seeming warmth of their smiles, in the small courtesies that had already marked this morning's meeting. Moncrieff had no idea what next awaited these men, but he knew that kind of speculation was beyond his pay grade. What he had to do now was to get this single image, plus supplementary shots, back to London.

Moncrieff and De Vries lingered over pasta with a marinara sauce. It would be at least an hour before Hannalore printed the rest of the roll, and De Vries didn't want to hurry her. She had also sensed the importance of what was happening down beside the lake, and she was delighted by what she called her own small role in the unfolding drama. Moncrieff, whose eyes kept returning to the envelope, told her not to be so modest. Without a photographic record, especially images of this quality, the meeting at the villa might never have happened. It could be erased from the record, like so much else in the intelligence world.

'To this morning.' Moncrieff raised his glass. 'You did better than well.'

They were back outside the apartment block minutes later. This time, the door was wide open. At Hannalore's request, De Vries had picked up a huge slice of cheesecake from the restaurant, and now she carried it, carefully wrapped, into the gloom of the basement.

She called Hannalore's name, said they were back. No response. De Vries hesitated, tried again. Nothing. She took another step down the hall towards the darkroom at the end, but Moncrieff pulled her back.

'Leave this to me,' he said.

'Leave what?' De Vries was frowning now.

Moncrieff didn't answer. At the end of the hall, as he'd half expected, was another open door. The darkroom, still bathed in red light, lay beyond it. He balled a fist, lacking a weapon of any kind, then stepped inside. In the murky light, at first glance, it was hard to be sure, but then his eyes adjusted, and he knew he'd been right to fear the worst. The shape on the floor beside Hannalore's head was unmistakeable. It had to be an ice pick.

He felt a movement behind him. De Vries, he thought. He turned towards her, blocking her path as she tried to push past him.

'Don't,' he said, pulling the door closed behind him.

15

That same afternoon, Werner Nehmann arrived in Berlin, handcuffed to a *Feldgendarmerie* Sergeant in the back of a mud-encrusted *Kübelwagen*. This was the first time Nehmann had seen the capital of the Reich since the Christmas of 1942, and three years of increasingly heavy bombing had transformed a city he'd grown to love.

This could be a film set, Nehmann thought, staring out at yet another ruined street: windows without glass, balconies hanging over mountains of rubble, addresses chalked on pitted walls for the redirection of mail, spindly kerbside trees stripped bare by blast damage. The last time Nehmann had seen anything like this was at Stalingrad, and years before that in one of the basement editing rooms at the Promi where Goebbels would arrive in a gust of new leather and *eau de cologne*, his brisk attention drawn to raw footage from Warsaw, and Rotterdam, and countless other enemy cities gutted by the *Luftwaffe*, images that would be edited within the hour and despatched to cinemas nationwide.

The *Kübelwagen*, under its sagging canvas roof, was draughty as hell, and Nehmann could smell the sour breath of these familiar Berlin streets – ashes, brick dust, poorly repaired sewers – lingering evidence of months of bombing. It was from here, back in 1940, that the regime had exported violence on the grandest scale. Those early campaigns had gifted the Fatherland with a Greater Reich, thanks to undreamed-of conquests across an entire continent, but it might have been wise – Nehmann thought – to have pondered the consequences just a little bit harder because the enemy had obviously learned the lessons that mattered. Berlin, five long years later, had become a nightly punchbag for RAF bombers, and a city of ghosts in the cold light of day. Even the pigeons, pecking listlessly at the spill of contents from a paper bag, seemed skinnier.

At Nehmann's request, they were driving to the Wilhelmplatz in the city centre. Last night, the Lieutenant who was riding up front in the passenger seat had finally made contact with superiors who had connections to Herr Goebbels. It appeared that the Minister of Propaganda now bore additional responsibility as Reich Defence Commissar for Berlin, and to the Lieutenant's surprise Nehmann's story turned out to be true. Yes, he knew the little Georgian. Yes, he'd put his considerable talents to the service of the Promi. And, yes, the Minister would be very happy to meet him again.

The *Kübelwagen* swept under the Brandenburger Tor, and then turned onto the Wilhelmstrasse, the heart of the Reich.

'The Führer's in residence.' The Lieutenant gestured at the Chancellery. 'Do you know him, too, by any chance?'

Nehmann followed the pointing finger. The Lieutenant was right. Guards outside the doors to the Chancellery, he remembered, were always doubled when Hitler was in town. Then, as the *Kübelwagen* slowed beside the Wilhelmplatz, Nehmann stiffened. The Ministry of Propaganda, with its tall windows and pillared portico, had always been one of the regime's more elegant buildings, well-mannered, a happy compromise between classical proportion and raw power. Some of Goebbels' staff referred to it as the White Palace, a term that Nehmann himself had always regarded as quaint given the blackness of the lies it generated, but even he – especially in the early days – had succumbed to its enchantments.

The *Kübelwagen* came to a halt and Nehmann found himself tugged out of the open door and into the fitful late afternoon sunshine.

'Release him.'

The Sergeant did the Lieutenant's bidding, and Nehmann muttered his appreciation, massaging the blood back into his wrist as he gazed at the ruins of Goebbels' pride and joy.

'When did this happen?'

'Last week. Nine days ago, to be precise. Those fucking Mosquitos is what I heard.'

Mosquitos, it seemed, were plaguing Berlin night after night: fast, twin-engined English bombers that stole in from the darkness, weaving between the searchlight beams, and laid their eggs on targets like these.

'And Goebbels?'

'Elsewhere. The way I hear it, he wants a rocket up Goering's arse. We used to have an air force but those days have gone. That man should be careful. Goebbels still matters, especially in this city.'

'That man?'

'Goering.' The Lieutenant nodded towards the remains of the Ministry. 'If Goebbels wanted a firing squad to teach the Fat One some manners, he'd be spoiled for volunteers.'

Nehmann was looking at a little kiosk in the middle of the plaza. Like the Brandenburg Gate, it had so far been spared by the bombs, and he watched a youngish woman fumbling for change under the gaze of the proprietor. It was here, three years ago, that eager visitors could buy postcards featuring cosy *gemütlich* shots of the Nazi chieftains. Of Goering, with his daughter Edda on his shoulders; of Ribbentrop, relaxing beside his swimming pool; of Goebbels and his wife, with their proud muster of six children. Nehmann shook his head and turned away. In bed, as everywhere else, the Minister was never less than busy.

'There used to be a traffic policeman here,' Nehmann told the Lieutenant. 'He wore a cap and a belted white jacket. He knew everyone, and he had all the time in the world for a conversation. He said his name was Siegfried but that had to be a lie. Goebbels loved him.'

'You want to take a look?' The Lieutenant nodded towards the Ministry.

Nehmann fell into step beside him. Uniformed police were guarding the steps that had once led to the front door. The Lieutenant returned a salute. He and his colleague were welcome to explore a little further but only at their own risk.

'Well?' The Lieutenant had turned to Nehmann.

'Nothing changes,' Nehmann was looking at a sheaf of Promi forms among the rubble, streaked with soot and brick dust. 'Working here was always life or death.'

The Lieutenant held his gaze for a moment, uncertain quite how to react, then shrugged and headed up the steps. A path of sorts had been cleared where the main door had once been, and Nehmann – gestured onwards by the Lieutenant – picked his way carefully inside. Steel beams had been scorched and twisted in the heat of the explosions, and he recognised the charred remains of wooden panelling among the tumble of brick and shattered marble.

'So what happened here?' The Lieutenant had suddenly become a tourist, gazing round at the devastation, then upwards towards a glimpse of sky through the blackened rafters.

'Here was the switchboard.' Nehmann was making it up. 'The women were magicians. They could take you anywhere in the world.'

'How many lines?'

'Hundreds. The Minister loved a conversation.'

'You were really close to him?'

'I was, for a while.'

It was true. From the moment they'd met, Nehmann had sensed a kinship with the Reich's master puppeteer, a joint fascination about the sheer numbers of strings you could pull, responses you could trigger, directions you could flag for the millions of Germans already in love with blood and treasure.

Here, in the White Palace, Goebbels ran a tight ship. He'd appear, promptly, at nine o'clock, ascend to his study, the glad prisoner of his unvarying schedule. There'd be an immediate round of meetings with key courtiers, triggered by the sheer pace of events, followed by an hour or so of calls to check on overnight events. Then, at eleven o'clock, would come the morning conference, always held around the long table beneath the hanging thirties chandelier – important faces from the military, from the world of film production and news-gathering and live theatre. Debate around the table was perfunctory, compliance signalled by nods and murmured agreement, and much later in the day, with the Ministry already half-empty, Goebbels would summon Nehmann to his study, take a break from the pile of film scripts awaiting ministerial approval and share a bottle of Gewürztraminer and perhaps a fat slice or two of white Bavarian sausage.

Goebbels, Nehmann had known from the start, was a solitary, a loner, a man without the burdens of friendship, but his fierce intelligence brooked neither opposition nor incompetence, and he'd built an empire and a power base which gave him immense reach. This spider's web extended to every corner of the Reich. To be in the very middle of it was an experience that Nehmann would never forget, regardless of where it had finally taken him, and when the Lieutenant stooped to retrieve an object in black Bakelite from the pile of rubble at their feet, Nehmann held it in his hand for a moment, happy to give it a name.

'It's a microphone,' he said. 'We had a system that allowed the Minister to interrupt any broadcast, at any time, to address the nation. He could do it from here, in the Promi. Sometimes it was scheduled. Other times, it wasn't. Imagine having that kind of power. Get the right words in the right order...' he glanced down at the microphone, '... and we could do anything.'

'We?'

'We. Did it last? Sadly not. Did his role in my life save me from a bullet after you arrested me? I suspect the answer is yes.' Nehmann broke off to peer more deeply into the wrecked belly of the building, then he shook his head. Of the Theatre Hall, the Throne Room and the Blue Gallery – all the period gems so precious to Goebbels – there were no remains. Neither, at first glance, had any of the antique furniture survived.

Nehmann turned back to the Lieutenant. 'Enough,' he said. 'So where next?'

*

The Chain Dogs took him to a *Feldgendarmerie* barracks beyond the Anhalt station. There, barefoot after the turnkey had taken his boots and socks, Nehmann found himself locked in a cell that stank of bleach. There was a coil of fresh shit in the bucket in the corner, and in the dim light though the high window Nehmann peered at the graffiti on the neighbouring wall. One hand had transcribed three lines he recognised from Rilke. They addressed solitude, beauty and terror. Another warned against any contact with the *Kartoffelsuppe*. A third, in a crabbed hand, had managed a single word: *Heil!*

Was this ironic? And if so, would the brighter recruits among the Chain Dogs have the wit, or even the patience, to understand this sharp little dig in the Reich's bony ribs? On the evidence of this single word, which seemed to have been incised with something sharp, Nehmann couldn't even hazard a guess, but Kolyma had taught him the benefits of concentrating on a single thought, one intense little flicker of speculation, and within minutes – stretched full-length on the concrete plinth – he was asleep.

*

He awoke in darkness, hearing voices outside the door. Then came the turn of a key in the lock and the beam of a torch settled on his face. Instinctively, he shielded his eyes. Goebbels would never set foot in a hole like this. Had he fallen into a trap? Was all the talk about a meeting with the Minister yet another lie? Was he en route to some pitted brick wall and a line of waiting Chain Dogs with a bullet apiece?

'*Kommen Sie.*'

'Where to?'

Hands pulled him roughly to his feet. His boots and socks were returned, and silence fell as he struggled to put them on. Then he was out of the cell and shuffling down the corridor which led to the stairs out of the basement. A courtyard, he knew, lay beyond the building's main door. Was this where his luck would finally run out? The push in the back? The untidy sprawl at the feet of these men? The cold muzzle on the nape of his neck as a Chain Dog stooped briefly to finish the job?

He paused at the top of the steps that led down to the courtyard, sucking the cold air deep into his lungs, steadying himself for whatever might happen next. Then he became aware that a vehicle, a Mercedes this time, was waiting in the darkness. Nehmann recognised the face of the Lieutenant in the back, moving over to give him room on the rear seat as unseen hands pushed him down the steps and into the car.

'Where are we going?' he asked again, his pulse beginning to settle.

'Bogensee,' the Lieutenant grunted. 'Where else?'

'And he's there? Waiting?'

'He is.'

Nehmann nodded. Bogensee was one of Goebbels' three properties. Bogensee was where the Minister had mourned the ruins of his affair with Lida Baarova. Christmas at Bogensee, three years ago, had been Nehmann's last glimpse of his protector. He closed his eyes, settling back against the plump leather, flooded with relief.

The Mercedes left the city centre and headed north, the familiar frieze of pine trees a blur in the dim blue throw of the headlights. Half an hour later, Nehmann recognised the turn that took them through the tall iron gates and into the property itself. The house was low, single-storey, built around a paved area, and as the Mercedes came to a halt in front of the imposing entrance, Nehmann remembered the little contemporary touches, tiny points of detail that had made Goebbels so proud of this ministerial bolthole. The subtle pattern of coloured bricks that formed the columns of the building, the carefully sited planters in Bauhaus concrete, the entwined Aryan couple in mottled grey stone, visible from every front window. Back when Nehmann had helped sprinkle the gladdest tidings over a grateful nation, the occasional summer afternoon out at Bogensee was when he and Goebbels had hatched their best ideas, but now the house was in darkness, the windows shuttered, no signs of life.

'You told me he'd be here.' Nehmann was standing beside the car.

'He is.' A grunt from the Lieutenant. 'The power must be out.'

He escorted Nehmann towards the broad spread of the porch. A polite tap on the door produced nothing. He rapped again, forceful this time, and through the tiny glass panes Nehmann caught a flicker of light at what he remembered as the far end of the hall. It was a candle, the light spilling onto a knitted blue sleeve. Goebbels liked working in his cardigan, Nehmann remembered. This had to be him.

The door opened, and Nehmann took a tiny involuntary step backwards. Goebbels was holding the candle higher, inspecting his visitor at close quarters, his teeth white in what might have been a smile. Nehmann knew about candlelight, knew about the tricks it could play, the shadows it cast, but he knew at once that time and events had been unkind to the *Reichsminister*. He was thinner, paler, more distraught. His face, as deeply seamed as ever, was a mask. The blackness of his eyes spoke of sleepless nights and constant pressure and when his hand briefly settled on Nehmann's arm, it was blotched and angry with eczema. This was a face, Nehmann thought, that he might have glimpsed from the *Kübelwagen* in Berlin's ruined suburbs. He looked, in a word, beaten.

'Not what you expected, Nehmann?' Goebbels could still read him like a book. He held the door open, ordered him inside, dismissed the Lieutenant.

'You don't want us to wait, Herr *Reichsminister*?'

'No.'

Goebbels shut the door, still nursing the candle, and Nehmann suddenly realised that this man had become the Reich's caretaker. In its dying days, he would nurse it to the end, whisper in its

ear, stroke the back of its hand, and switch off the lights once
it was gone.

Wrong again.

'The hour of our calling, Nehmann.' Goebbels was leading
the way deeper into the house. 'You couldn't have arrived at a
better moment. Perfect timing. As always.'

Nehmann thought he caught a chuckle as the Minister rounded
the corner at the end of the long hall. They were walking in file,
one behind the other, and Nehmann was briefly entranced by the
spill of light onto the polished marble floor. Everything else was
in deep shadow but Nehmann recognised a picture or two on
the wall. His favourite had been a Corot looted from a château
in the Loire, chalky cliffs rising from the untidy greens and
greys of the *Englisch-Kanal*, but it seemed to have disappeared.
Goebbels' study used to be at the back of the house, and nothing
had changed.

'You're here alone?' Nehmann asked.

'Magda and the children have gone to the Obersalzberg. The
cook has a headache. The guards Himmler lent me are probably
asleep. So, yes, Nehmann. You find me, once again, alone.'

Magda, Goebbels' wife, was a stern presence in his life who
seemed to have won Hitler's undying admiration. There'd been
some in the ministries along the Wilhelmstrasse who'd suspected
something even closer between Frau Goebbels and the Führer.
Before Stalingrad, when he knew he was in trouble with Goebbels,
Nehmann had looked hard but spotted nothing conclusive.

'Something to drink, Nehmann?' Goebbels had settled behind
his desk. He kept his drinks on a small trolley but Nehmann
could see only schnapps. He topped up the glass at Goebbels'
elbow and then helped himself. Goebbels had stationed the
candle beside a pile of film scripts. One of them was open on
the desk at what looked like the final scene and very little of

the dialogue had survived the attentions of the green ink from the ministerial pen. Was this what you did while the Reich was in flames, Nehmann wondered? Make meaningless changes to a script that would never see the light of day?

'So you became a *Stalinpferd*, Nehmann.' Goebbels was still looking at the script. 'And I'm guessing he worked you half to death.' *Stalinpferd* meant Stalin's donkey, German for 'camp dust'.

'You know about what happened?' Nehmann swallowed a mouthful of schnapps.

'Of course. Those Chain Dogs of yours sent me a full account. The gold mines? In Kolyma? Is that true? Or did you make it up?'

'True, I'm afraid.'

'And Stalingrad?' Goebbels at last abandoned the pen.

'Stalingrad no one will ever talk about. Not for generations. Unless you were there, no one could possibly understand.'

'Because?'

'Because it was beyond description. No words can do it justice.'

'Not even yours?'

'Not even mine.'

'I find that hard to believe, Nehmann.'

'You shouldn't. Ask anyone, anyone who was there.'

'I meant you, Nehmann, not the battle. When it came to words, language, lies, wit, bravado, sheer – dare I say it – *chutzpah*, you never let me down. I sometimes wondered whether you were a Jew. *Ja...*' he reached for his glass, '... *that* clever.'

Nehmann shrugged, said nothing. Goebbels' compliments were always barbed, but he'd never gone quite this far. Jewish? Was Goebbels serious?

'The Chain Dogs tell me you met Stalin,' Goebbels murmured. 'Is that also true?'

'Yes.'

'And?'

'He wants to know how you might feel about a conversation.'

'To what end?'

'I got the impression he wants to go back to 1939.'

'The August pact? Non-aggression? All quiet on the Eastern Front? Quaint, I must say, but not without logic.' Goebbels looked away into the darkness. In candlelight, thought Nehmann, this was a face that might have belonged on a Caravaggio canvas: deep shadows, a face hollowed by something fiercer and more menacing than simple exhaustion. At length, his gaze returned to Nehmann. 'You've been away a while. Things have changed. Back last year I composed a long memorandum for the Führer's attention. Our Allied friends are united in a number of ways but unconditional surrender is the most important. They mean to bring us to our knees. They mean to send us back to the Stone Age. That must not happen, Nehmann, and to that end I composed my thoughts and sent them to the Chancellery.'

'And?'

'The Führer never got to read the memo. Bormann is a primitive but cunning as a fox. He put it at the very bottom of his in-tray and kept it there. I have it on good authority that, in the end, it went into the fire.'

When Nehmann left Berlin, Martin Bormann had been serving as Hitler's personal secretary, controlling every aspect of his working day, a post he evidently still occupied. Nehmann shook his head. For the first time, he began to wonder whether Goebbels was drunk. The Minister was famed for his iron self-control. Only the wilder reaches of his imagination would ever betray him.

'So Stalin?' Nehmann enquired. 'What did you say in the memo?'

'The thrust was simple. I pointed out that Stalin was the only enemy worthy of our respect. Roosevelt is a Jew lover. Churchill is a drunk. Only Stalin has the patience and the courage to bide his time. There's no amount of blood he won't spill for victory.'

'Ours?'

'Of course, but his as well. You have to admire that, Nehmann. You have to applaud the man's unbending will. That's what happened at Yalta, by the way. Read the accounts. Stalin kept his counsel while Churchill blathered on and Roosevelt devoted what time he has left to dying. If you don't believe me just look at the results. Stalin got his way on every issue. He has millions of men under arms. Everything east of the Oder belongs to him. These are facts on the ground, Nehmann. No court of law, no priest, and no army can take that away from him. Thanks to Bormann, the moment for negotiations – him and us – has probably gone.'

'Stalin thinks the Anglos are going behind his back.'

'He's right,' Goebbels nodded. 'They are.'

'Where?'

'Firstly in the Italian theatre. There's an SS General down there who wants to make peace. That's because he's got his back to the Alps and he thinks it's over. Then Stalin has another problem. *Barbarossa* put him in bed with the Anglos, but this time it's Himmler who seems determined to screw him. Our chicken farmer friend is sniffing around the Swedes. He thinks there may be a separate peace on offer with the Anglos but he's wrong. When they say unconditional surrender, they mean it, but that man has always had problems with the real world.'

'That man?'

'Himmler. You weren't around when Hitler gave him an Army Group to play with. A whole Army Group, Nehmann, just imagine that, half a million men. And you know what happened?

Himmler settled down in that nice train of his and made sure his every need was properly attended to. A doctor on call day and night? A chef who understood Bavarian food? Decent French wines? From what I heard, the *Reichsführer-SS* liked to sleep in the afternoon, hated being disturbed. In the meantime, the front was folding and the Russians were helping themselves. I understand the Chain Dogs picked you up in Pomerania, Nehmann, so you don't need me to tell you that we're well and truly in the shit. The only sane question is what happens next.'

'And?'

'We fight. We carry on fighting. Will the Russians make it to Berlin? Of course they will. But we'll fight until there's no Berlin left. Because that, Nehmann, is what it means to be a true German. We followed the Führer into this adventure and we were glad enough when he delivered us a country or two. More than that, he made us feel good about ourselves. He made us forget the last war and the Jew-peace that followed, and it would be very bad manners to forget the obligation we owe him. He was always our leader, Nehmann, our Führer, and he still is. People here, Germans everywhere, would be well advised to remember that. Because otherwise, believe me, there will be consequences.'

Consequences?

Nehmann could only nod. Listening to this tormented ghost of a man, with his ever-lengthening list of responsibilities, it was impossible not to realise where the tides of defeat had left him. He'd always worshipped power. That kind of power, raw, indivisible, was vested in only one figure. Joseph Goebbels had worshipped Adolf Hitler since the day he'd first signed up with the Brownshirts and found himself listening to the man in a Munich beer hall. He'd described that evening to Nehmann early on in their relationship, and nothing appeared to have changed.

Except. Except.

'The Russians will be here in weeks.' Nehmann gestured towards the shuttered window. 'And what then?'

'We fight. I've just told you.'

'But what with? The way I hear it, you're running out of everything. Including bodies.'

'Never. German breath? German blood? As long as our hearts are still pumping, no matter how old, no matter how young, we can still defend ourselves. Better to die on your feet than submit on your knees, Nehmann. You know who said that?'

'Stalin. That's how the Gulag got built.'

'Exactly. But consider the possibilities. We still have men to spare. You've been away, Nehmann. You don't understand our resilience, our determination, the lengths we're prepared to go to. We've created a new army. We've called it the *Volkssturm*. Can we even afford to supply uniforms? In many cases, no. Docs that matter? Not at all. Because these people, these lions, represent the *will* of the people, and that's all that matters. With a *Panzerfaust* and a bicycle you can take on the world, no matter what age you may be. And the world, my friend, will be watching.'

Nehmann nodded, letting the storm across the desk blow itself out. In the *Kübelwagen*, en route to Berlin, the Chain Dogs had been happy to tell him about the *Volkssturm*. They called it *der Eintopf*, the casserole, a despairing mix of old meat and green vegetables, sitting ducks for Soviet tanks. His mates in the T-34, Nehmann thought, would eat this new army alive, a mere snack between proper meals.

Goebbels had at last paused for breath. Nehmann remembered another bone the Reich had tossed to the Chain Dogs.

'People are talking about secret weapons,' he murmured.

'Of course.' Goebbels was leaning forward again, his long fingers steepled on the desk. 'Our rockets are falling every day on London, on Antwerp, on wherever we choose to send them. These are terror weapons, Nehmann. The fastest, the V-2, is the wrath of God, it arrives unannounced, you never even hear it coming. Just a huge bang as your world blows apart. That's science, Nehmann. That's what we're good at. German science. German genius. We have chemical weapons, too, nerve gas, Tabun, Sarin, a thousand times better than anything we used in the last war. Something else, too. You know the KWI?'

Nehmann nodded. The Kaiser Wilhelm Institute was out at Dahlem, the home for hundreds of physicists.

'They're working with uranium, Nehmann. Uranium is a killer. If you get the science right, I'm told you're looking at the biggest bang ever, but even if you grind it fine and drop it over a city you seed radioactivity everywhere. Just think about it. Generations condemned to endless mutations. Every living thing poisoned forever. This is total war, Nehmann. *Totalerkrieg*. We die on our feet while the enemy perish in their own good time.'

'And the Führer has agreed this?'

'He will. Because he'll have no choice.' He paused, then emptied his glass. 'Be honest, my friend. Has any of this come as a surprise?'

Nehmann shook his head, partly because the schnapps was beginning to fog his brain, but mainly because he was starting to wilt under the sheer weight of Goebbels' mania. *Sturm und Drang*. Raw emotion at boiling point. Coupled with a murderous pledge to go down fighting.

'You have ways of getting in touch with the Russians, Nehmann? With Stalin?'

'No. He gave me the impression that wouldn't be necessary.'

'Because?'

'Because you had access to channels of your own.'

'Meaning that I've been talking to them already?'

'Meaning that you know how to, should the opportunity present itself.'

Goebbels held Nehmann's gaze. Then, very softly, he began to laugh.

'You should be a diplomat, Nehmann. That was a perfect answer. Is it true that we have spies working for us? Of course it is. Do we tolerate these people because one day they may prove useful? I'm afraid the answer is yes. Tomorrow, Nehmann, I will arrange for you to be introduced to a man called Erich. He's a film editor of genius. You'll love him. He can take rushes from a battlefield where we've had our arses kicked and turn the bloodbath into the sweetest of victories. You'll recognise his gifts, his talents. You did something similar in print at Stalingrad. I want you to work with him. I want you to write commentary. The Russians have yet to make their final push, but our cameramen are shooting what they can. Make friends with Erich. Enjoy the man. Because he can talk to Moscow and one day soon we may need him.'

'We?'

'You.'

'Meaning?'

Goebbels shook his head. Then he pushed the remains of the bottle of schnapps across the desk and nodded towards the door.

'The night is still young, Nehmann, and I have much work to do. Turn left in the corridor and you're looking for the third door on the right-hand side. My housekeeper has laid out everything you may need. Hot water, I'm afraid, is in short supply but that needn't concern a *Stalinpferd*.'

The evening had evidently come to an end. Nehmann picked up the bottle and was about to make for the door when Goebbels called him back. Then came the scrape of a drawer as he produced a candle and lit it from the flame on his desk.

'You'll need this,' he said. '*Schlafen Sie gut*. And be careful of the hot wax.'

Nehmann left the office, clutching the candle in one hand and the bottle in the other. Already he'd forgotten Goebbels' careful directions. Third door? Fourth? Left-hand side? Right? He tried the second of the doors on the right. The bedroom, he sensed at once, was far too big for a guest of his standing, and in any case he could smell perfume in the air, something heavy, and doubtless expensive.

He stepped deeper into the room, looking round. The bed was enormous and unmade, the sheets rumpled, folds of duvet and counterpane spilling onto the polished wood floor. Nehmann bent to the pillow and sniffed it. Definitely perfume. Still holding the candle, he explored the rest of the room. A line of built-in wardrobes opened to reveal rack after rack of dresses, and when he closed on the dressing table, he stole a long look at the framed infant faces in photograph after photograph. This was where Magda slept, he thought, with or without her husband.

About to leave the room, his eye was suddenly caught by a line of suitcases lying on the floor on the other side of the bed. Most of them were full of clothes, both Magda's and garments belonging to the children, each item carefully folded and stowed, but the suitcase at the end had been reserved for a collection of toys, probably hand-picked.

Nehmann stood motionless for a moment, gazing down. In the soft yellow light of the candle, he could make out the smile on the face of a stuffed doll, paint peeling from the wings of a toy Me-109, a die-cast Tiger Tank missing one of its caterpillar tracks, and a collection of new-looking wooden skittles in the brightest of colours. This is a family on the move, he thought. But where?

The door to the bedroom was still open. Nehmann caught

the lightest footfall. Then came the spill of light from another candle, and he found himself looking at Goebbels.

'Wrong room,' Nehmann muttered. 'My mistake.'

Goebbels said nothing but stepped into the room and paused beside the bed.

'You're looking at the cases?'

'I am.'

'And?'

'I'm guessing you all need a place of safety.' Nehmann grimaced as hot wax dripped onto his hand. 'Might I be right?'

'You are, my friend. And where might that place be?'

'I've no idea.' He paused, remembering something one of the Chain Dogs had mentioned. *'Die Alpenfestung,* maybe?'

'Our little burrow under the mountains, you mean?' Goebbels was smiling. 'Caves with air conditioning? A year's supply of water and food? Impregnable lines of approach? Enough ammunition to keep any army at bay? *Götterdämmerung?* Nicely scored for full orchestra?'

'That's it. I'm told you gave a speech.'

'And you believed it? *You,* Nehmann? Of all people?'

'It's not true?'

'Of course it's not true. Nothing's changed, Nehmann. I still toss our people fresh meat, and they still gobble it up. *Die Alpenfestung* is a fantasy. In the real world, the Führer has a bunker. It's deep under the Chancellery. He's been generous enough to offer us five rooms, which should be enough.' He put his hand on Nehmann's arm, nodding down at the toys. 'When the time comes, it will be a privilege to join him there.'

16

After the third day, Moncrieff began to wonder whether he was half in love with the tortoise. It appeared every morning, a scaly head poking through the rude tangle of spring growth in the tiny garden at the back of the cottage. Moncrieff had cherished a tortoise as a child. He knew they grew to a great age – his father had hinted at a hundred and fifty years – and even now he remembered that they loved fresh vegetables like kale, and dandelions, and mustard leaves.

This tortoise he judged to be old. Moncrieff had spotted it the first afternoon he'd sat in the sunshine, wedged against the wall beneath the kitchen window, enjoying the spring warmth on his face and the bareness of his legs below the borrowed shorts. Perfectly camouflaged, its shell the colour of the local stone, the tortoise would have been watching Moncrieff for a while before he registered its presence. He christened it Angus, in memory of the gamekeeper who'd first taught him how to stalk deer on the bareness of the Cairngorm mountains, and the longer he and the tortoise locked eyes, the more he began to wonder about the times this leathery old creature must have lived through.

He gave it water from a nearby spring, decanted into a saucer. He plucked tender young leaves of chard, carefully shredded and then stiffened with stems of wild grasses. He searched beneath a blackthorn tree and recovered a handful of rotting sloes, casualties of a recent storm. And on the third morning, when De Vries arrived with bread and eggs and a jug of milk from a farmer further up the mountain, he was telling Angus about the wars the tortoise had lived through but never seen, about the fierceness of industrial progress in Europe's smokier corners, and about the diplomats gathering at the nearby lakeside just two decades ago to agree a treaty that would bring a peace that was supposed to last for generations.

'In one way, it happened,' he said. 'But in another it didn't. So why do we keep fighting? Any ideas?'

A polite cough announced the arrival of De Vries. She must be on foot, Moncrieff thought. Otherwise, he'd have heard the throaty bounce and cackle of her Topolino.

'You're talking to the flowers now?'

'Angus.' Moncrieff nodded at the tortoise. 'My new friend.'

'Have we been introduced?'

'I don't think so. Unless you make the effort, they tend to be shy.'

The cottage belonged to one of the rowers down by the lake. A two-hour walk from Locarno took you along the lake shore and then north, into the mountains, where a tiny hamlet nestled among the stands of pine and hornbeam. Invisible from the track, the cottage lay beside a brook that bubbled from a spring somewhere higher up. The fall of water on the mossy rocks softened the silence and the isolation, and Moncrieff had loved the place at first sight. Here, De Vries had assured him, he'd be safe while an investigation was launched into Hannalore's death. The last thing he needed to attract was the attention of the local police.

Now, he made space for her in the splash of sunshine beneath the kitchen window. The sight of the borrowed shorts amused her.

'I should have brought my camera,' she said. 'They're a perfect fit. Hans wouldn't believe it.'

Hans, it turned out, was the lone sculler Moncrieff had watched the first morning he'd woken up beside the lake and found De Vries's big picture window full of rowers. Hans had a business in town. He dealt in antique furniture and after three days in his pied-à-terre, thanks to a series of clues, Moncrieff was beginning to suspect that he and De Vries were more than friends.

'Hannalore?' he asked.

'The police think it was a burglary. Her purse was missing, and there was more money she kept in a drawer, and they couldn't find that, either. Robberies go wrong sometimes. That's their belief, not mine.'

Moncrieff glanced sideways at her. Before De Vries had raised the alarm that afternoon, they'd searched for the roll of negatives from De Vries's camera, and for whatever prints Hannalore had managed to develop, but of both there was no trace.

'So what's the real story?'

'It has to be Wolff and the meeting down by the lake. My guess is that Swiss intelligence wants everything tidied away, no drama, no headlines. Publicity would be an embarrassment. Discretion matters in this country. Everything is supposed to happen in the shadows, discreetly, off-camera.'

'You think we were followed that morning?'

'I'm sure we were. Did I see anyone? No. Does that prove anything? Again, no. Locarno is a small town. In some ways, Switzerland is even smaller. What I can't explain is the ice pick.'

Moncrieff nodded. Since Stalin had Trotsky killed in Mexico five years ago, the ice pick had become a calling card when the NKVD chose to settle their debts.

'So who killed her?' Moncrieff was watching the tortoise backing carefully into the wall of green.

'Good question. Why might be easier. It pains me to say it but those photos of mine probably killed her. We should never have gone for lunch.'

'But who?' Moncrieff insisted. 'Who would have gone to lengths like that?'

'Take your choice. The SS? The Americans? Swiss intelligence? Maybe even your Broadway friends? A conversation like that was never supposed to happen. The fact that it did could upset some important people.' She paused. 'You've still got that print we took to the restaurant?'

'Of course.'

'Well hidden?'

'I suspect so.'

'What does that mean?'

Moncrieff gazed at her for a moment, then got to his feet and extended a hand to help her up. After the brightness of the sunshine, the interior of the cottage was dark. According to De Vries, Hans had done very little to the place since he'd bought it. She said he'd loved its bareness and simplicity, not a stick of antique furniture anywhere, and after three days in residence, Moncrieff knew exactly what he meant. Two smallish rooms downstairs, with a primitive kitchen at the back. A poorly repaired sofa, and a couple of shelves brimming with books, most of them on the subject of mountaineering. With a tortoise for company, Moncrieff thought, what else could a man possibly need?

He led the way upstairs. A cupboard had been wedged into one corner of the smaller bedroom, and, under the pile of assorted boots and shoes inside, Moncrieff had discovered a false floor. He lined the shoes up on the bare floorboards and used his penknife once again to access the hidden compartment.

'There.' Moncrieff stepped back, allowing the light from the window to fall onto the white envelope containing the photo from the Gaevernitz villa. Beneath it, a similar size, was another envelope, manila this time, with a place and a date scrawled in black ink. *Den Haag. April, 1940.*

De Vries was staring at it. Moncrieff extracted the Gaevernitz photo but she scarcely spared it a glance. What mattered was the other envelope.

'You've looked inside?' she asked at last.

'Does it matter if I have?'

'Yes, it does.'

'Then the answer, I'm afraid, is yes.'

'And?'

'They're lovely shots. It's a crass thing to say but Hans is a lucky man.'

De Vries nodded, bit her lip, said nothing. Finally, she reached for the envelope and stepped towards the window.

'I should never have parted with them,' she said quietly. 'I knew at the time it was a mistake.'

'On the contrary. You should be proud of yourself. Literally.'

'You really think so?'

'I do.'

'And you're in a position to make that kind of judgement?' She looked up at him a moment.

'That's a silly question. Daft. I'm offering you a compliment. If you're telling me I should never have looked, then I'm sure you're right. Let's just forget it. Let's pretend I never opened the bloody envelope, never even laid hands on the thing.'

She glanced up at him again, then shook her head. Moments later, Moncrieff was looking once again at a sheaf of photos. They were black and white. All of them featured a younger De Vries sitting in a wooden recess dominated by a tall window. The light from the window fell obliquely on her naked body.

In most of the shots she had one leg crossed over the other but what drew Moncrieff's attention were her breasts. They were full, perfectly shaped, beautiful, and in most of the shots she was paying them a particular attention. Her forefinger circling a nipple. One hand cupping the weight of the breast. Her chin on her chest, nestled in the cleft between her breasts, the barest hint of a smile.

'Who took these?' Moncrieff asked.

'Me. I lined the shot up and exposed for maximum contrast. With the Leicas you can set for a huge range of delay. If you're interested, I settled for ten seconds. I was pleased at the time. It's easier than you might think to get shots like these wrong.'

'They were for publication?'

'God, no.'

'A friend?'

'Only later. A present for Hans. It was his birthday.'

'So why did you take them? Do you mind me asking?'

She shook her head, her gaze returning to the photos, and then one hand strayed to her blouse.

'I was saying goodbye,' she said quietly. 'I'd had three consultations plus a second opinion and there was nowhere left for me to hide. Tumours in both breasts. A double mastectomy.' She looked up at him for a moment, and then blinked. 'I thought at the time I owed myself these shots. Now, I'm not so sure.'

'And Hans?'

'Hans is a wonderful man but sometimes I think he's fallen in love with half a woman.'

'The best half?'

'That's what he says, oddly enough.' She was frowning. 'Put them back, please. He'd be upset if he thought we'd had a conversation like this.'

Moncrieff did her bidding while she turned away, staring out at the spring greenness of the mountainside. With the boots and shoes back in the cupboard, Moncrieff closed the door.

'One last question,' he said. 'That painting of yours in the apartment.'

'The ugly one?'

'The angry one.'

'You thought I was getting something off my chest?' She looked suddenly weary. 'You were right.'

Back downstairs, she took a proper look at the photo from the lakeside villa, and then returned it to the white envelope.

'I have to take you to Bern,' she murmured.

'Who says?'

'Ursula. She phoned. She's staying in a hotel there.'

'All this was *en clair*?' Moncrieff shook his head in disbelief. Swiss intelligence monitored all foreign calls.

'*Pas du tout*. In The Hague, we always talked about goods and markets. For some reason, high-grade intelligence was always carrots. I told her we've never had a better crop. Seeing is believing. That made her laugh. Prove it, she said. As codes go, it's primitive but I know she got the point.'

'Which is?'

'You give her the photo. She'll probably send it home via the diplomatic bag. Or maybe she'll take the risk and hand-carry it.'

Moncrieff nodded.

'You'll drive me to Bern?'

'Yes.'

'So when do we leave?'

'Tonight. It's safer in darkness, as long as the bloody car holds up.'

*

De Vries left shortly afterwards, promising to be back after dusk, this time in her little Fiat. Moncrieff killed what was left of the day as best he could. A proper goodbye to the tortoise would, in some strange way, have been comforting but – unusually – there was no sign of it. Maybe he knows, Moncrieff thought. Maybe, over his long life, he's become indifferent to serial desertions, to the comings and goings of these giants who would appear for a day, or a year, or even a generation. Or maybe, after his hours in the sun, he just wanted to take a nap. Either way, Moncrieff prepared a little bowl of shredded leaves plucked from a stand of watercress beside the stream. Three days of watching the little creature eat told Moncrieff that cress leaves were his favourite, and he wanted Angus to know that his company had been appreciated.

Hours later, when he told De Vries about the bittersweetness of this adieu, she shook her head and told him he was crazy.

'It's a bloody tortoise,' she said. 'It'll outlive us all.'

'I know,' Moncrieff murmured. 'And that's rather the point.'

She was wearing her Salvation Army uniform, the black jacket loosened at the throat, her bonnet stowed on Moncrieff's lap. The tiny Fiat hadn't been designed for a woman her height, and she looked awkward at the wheel, bullying the car through bend after bend as they wound through the mountains. It was a windy night with scudding clouds and a fullish moon, and from time to time Moncrieff glimpsed the whiteness of snow on the higher peaks. He, too, was cramped but the blast of hot air from the car's heater was a blessing and he rather liked the intimacy that the journey had imposed.

His discovery of her photos had sparked a change in De Vries. She was less sure of herself, less commanding. At first, she told Moncrieff, she'd assumed that chance, or blind fate, had put the photos in his path but the more she thought about it, the more she began to suspect that this had always been God's intention. Nothing in this world happened by accident. Everything served a larger purpose.

'Which is?'

'Acceptance.'

'Of what?'

'Loss.'

Moncrieff pondered the word, sensing how important it was.

'Of your womanhood?' he asked at last. 'Of the person you were?'

'Of my vanity. If you want the truth, I loved my breasts. There had been photos before. Not mine. Someone else's. We were young before the war, even Ursula. We enjoyed ourselves. We took risks. Dutch men are great lovers. They know how to treat women, how to appreciate them, how to please.'

'Anyone in particular?'

'Not really. They didn't call me Agent *Clover* for nothing. You know the Dutch saying? A woman well bedded is a gift for life? I was in the giving business. Agent *Clover*. An apartment of her own. Preferences of her own. Very little she wouldn't do if you knew how to ask properly. Clover for the taking. Clover for the enjoying. Another thing, too. I knew how to make men laugh.'

'And that was important?'

'Always. Men are their own worst enemies. On the outside they can be noisy and brash and brave but on the inside they're shy as hell, still in their nappies. Most of them have never grown up. A woman who can make them laugh, a woman with generosity, a woman with proper breasts, big breasts, real breasts, is the mother of their dreams. It's all a fantasy of course, a performance, but I spent the happiest years of my life playing that role. I loved it. I loved the performance. I loved the intimacy and I loved the conversations afterwards. Then...' she shrugged, her fingers tapping impatiently on the wheel, '... one day you feel a lump and then another, and you try very hard to put the uglier thoughts away, and then you have a conversation with your best friend and she tells you there's a war coming and that maybe it's best to have a doctor take a look before things get tricky, and so off you go, whistling your little tune, telling yourself it's all in your head, and guess what? It's not.'

'This was Ursula? Your best friend?'

'Yes. She was married by then and we both knew it had been a terrible decision but that husband of hers had been her one real indulgence in life. The man turned out to be a fool, which is still a cardinal sin for Ursula, but he knew how to steal up and take a woman by surprise and Ursula seemed to admire him for that. He proposed within days and she simply shut her eyes and jumped. I told her she was crazy, but she had no interest in listening. Strange, really. In every other respect she'd always been my older sister, wiser, calmer, a great deal more sane, and nothing's really changed ever since.'

'Really? You mean that? Doing what you do now?'

'Doing what I do now is penance. A girl can have just so much happiness. Then it's time for the bended knee and the Mercy Seat. Am I bitter? Resentful? Not in the least. The Mercy Seat has been a revelation. And that makes me glad.'

Revelation?

Moncrieff knew he should be careful not to take advantage of this sudden outbreak of candour but the car, or perhaps the journey, had suddenly acquired a very different feel. They were locked together in a certain space. If ever there was a time to confess, to reach out, then here it was.

'Glad how?' he asked.

'Glad to have stepped away. Glad to feel free.'

'Of what?'

'Myself.'

'You really think that?'

'I do. I asked for help. In fact I begged for help. And help came.'

'From God?'

'Of course. Who else might there be?'

'I've no idea. Tell me. Give me a clue. Call me naïve. Call me shy. Call me stupid, a fool, just another lost soul, whatever you will, but I just don't get it.'

'Get what?'

'God. Your God. The one you kneel to on the Mercy Seat. I've seen some truly terrible things in my life, and I've listened to accounts that have been far, far worse. We're fighting a war that has taken millions of lives. We're surrounded by the broken and the maimed. Most of these wounds are all too visible. Many others aren't. Ask Ursula about Mr Witherby and see what happens.'

'And this has to do with God?'

'Your God, yes.'

'And yours?'

'Sadly, He doesn't exist.'

'But He can, and He will, if you let him.'

'You really think He's there? On the other side of the door? Do I listen for a rustle of movement? For a polite knock? Do I let Him in? Introduce myself? Beg forgiveness for all the bad things I've done in my life? Is that how it works? Just tell me. That's all I ask.'

De Vries was concentrating hard on an approaching bend in the road. They were high up in the mountains now. Despite the blast of the heater, Moncrieff could feel a definite drop in temperature and there were flurries of snow against the blackness of the night. The little car fought the steepening gradient and shuddered as De Vries dropped a gear and hauled it into the apex of the hairpin bend. Then they were through, and the road was levelling out beyond the dim throw of the headlights, and Moncrieff felt a hand on his thigh.

'God doesn't belong in a cartoon, I'm afraid,' De Vries murmured. 'Understand that, and you'll understand everything. Trust the Mercy Seat. Believe me, God never lies.'

*

A little while later, they began to descend through a zigzag of bends. The snow was falling more heavily, but through the curtain of white Moncrieff glimpsed a tiny nest of lights in the valley below. It looked far too small to be a major city, and when he asked whether these might be the outskirts of Bern, De Vries shook her head.

'This is where the Rhône starts,' she said. 'The village is called Obergoms.'

'And Bern?'

'Two hours away. At least.'

De Vries negotiated the final bend and Moncrieff felt the little car shiver as she corrected the beginnings of a skid. Then they were on the valley floor, the road stretching out before them, a scatter of hotels and houses lying ahead. On the far side of the village, De Vries slowed, her face close to the windscreen. She seemed to be looking for something and, moments later, she found it.

'Here,' she muttered, leaving the main road and making the turn on to virgin snow. She brought the car to a halt and turned off the engine. For the first time, Moncrieff felt a prickle of anxiety. He trusted this woman, largely because he had no choice. What if the promise of Bern was a trap? What if the real journey ended here?

'Where are we?' he asked.

'Obergoms. I just told you.'

'But why stop?'

She looked at him for a moment, and Moncrieff detected just a flicker of pity in her smile. Then she retrieved her bonnet from his lap and put it on.

'We're getting out?' Moncrieff asked.

'We are.'

'Why?'

She didn't answer. Instead she made a final adjustment to the bonnet and turned her head towards him.

'Does it look OK?' She smiled. 'Trust yourself, Tam. Just say yes.'

She got out of the car and waited for him in the snow. For a second, Moncrieff was tempted to take charge. The car's key was still hanging from the ignition. The last time he'd looked at the petrol gauge the tank was still half-full. Bern, according to De Vries, was down the road. Should he obey his baser instincts? Should he assume the worst, that he'd been betrayed, and leave her here? He entertained the thought for a moment longer, then his hand found the handle on the door and he joined her beside the car, ashamed of himself.

A path led to a building barely metres away. Their footsteps crunched in the snow. Flakes were melting on Moncrieff's face and he wiped his eyes as the building resolved itself into a church. Thick stone walls. Crumbling mortar. Tall windows, shorn of any adornment. And a sturdy cross on the cupola at the eastern end.

'We've come to say our prayers?'

Moncrieff had stopped. Adjacent to the church was another building, modest, two storeys, steeply pitched roof. It must have been built on a bluff, or perhaps a cliff, because Moncrieff could see the blackness of what had to be water beyond.

De Vries had ignored the church. She'd paused beside the house, stamping warmth back into her boots, and looking up she beckoned him to join her.

Moncrieff approached warily. He liked De Vries. He trusted her. And he suspected the Mercy Seat was a fine idea if you were in the mood. But a decent automatic and a full clip of ammunition was the least of precautions you'd take in a situation like this, and he was aware – once again – of a feeling of nakedness. Faith was a worthy concept. But it was hopeless at stopping bullets.

They were at the front door now. It was the middle of the night. It was a foreign country. In Moncrieff's jacket pocket was a photograph that had already got a woman killed. What next?

De Vries was knocking softly on the door. At length, it inched open. A hint of a male face, white, bearded.

'Pastor Ulrich?' This from De Vries.

The door opened properly. The two of them embraced. Pastor Ulrich was wearing a dressing gown over a long nightshirt, and he shut the door the moment Moncrieff had followed De Vries inside. The house was warm enough for the pastor to have nothing but slippers on his bare feet. He led the way down the hall. The walls were white. On a bookcase, a single wooden cross. The door at the end opened to reveal a kitchen. The light was already on, a lampshade in green glass suspended by a length of flex over a long kitchen table. Sitting at the end, nursing a glass of something red, was a middle-aged woman who, thought Moncrieff, deserved a proper night's sleep.

'Ursula,' he murmured. 'What a surprise.'

Barton got to her feet and surrendered to a hug from De Vries. The pastor was already at the range. He could offer coffee, cocoa, or *Rottwein*. Moncrieff found himself a chair at the table and sat down, watching De Vries sharing their last four days with Barton. How Moncrieff, clever man, had found his way to Locarno. What a fine rower he'd turned out to be. How they'd crept into the woods above the villa beside the lake and witnessed what followed. And how that episode had cost a good friend her life.

Barton followed this account without betraying a flicker of emotion. Moncrieff had seldom seen her so exhausted, so physically drained. Her face was a mask, pale and drawn, and when De Vries's account came to an end, and she finally took her bonnet off, Barton had only one question.

'You've got a photograph?'

Moncrieff slipped the single print out of its envelope and laid it carefully in front of her. De Vries, at her elbow, identified the faces one by one. SS General Karl Wolff. Major General Terence Airey. Major General Lyman Lemnitzer. Sworn enemies for six long years. Now enjoying the Swiss sunshine.

'Airey's old-school,' Barton murmured. 'Nice man. Perfect manners. We had him round to St James's for drinks a couple of years back.' She tapped the photo. 'What strange things wars are.' She looked up at De Vries, then gave her hand a little squeeze. 'This is exactly what we need.' She nodded at the three faces. 'You're a clever girl.'

Moncrieff wanted to know what happened next. Would Barton be taking the photo back to England? And if so, how?

'We'll be taking it to Bern.'

'We?'

'You and me. I'll make arrangements to get it rephotographed, then we'll ship the original back in the diplomatic bag. In the meantime, we need to talk to Allen Dulles. He has an apartment in Bern, and I understand he's in residence at the moment.'

Moncrieff nodded. It was Dulles, playing the midwife, who had brought these negotiations to term. He headed OSS in

Europe and Moncrieff owed him a personal apology for failing to produce SS *Obersturmbannführer* Wuensche.

'He's here, on the terrace.' De Vries had found Dulles on the photo, a trim figure in a tweed jacket with grey flannel trousers. His face was turned away from the camera, but Moncrieff remembered a ruddy complexion, a small grey moustache, and a pair of rimless glasses.

'He's the Americans' sentry at the gate.' Barton was looking at Moncrieff again. 'This is their show, their turf. We understand he's found common ground in the conversations to date. Wolff was never one of the bitter-enders, far from it, and Dulles wants to build on that. The final decision, of course, will be way above his pay grade and that, I'm afraid, is where the real problems lie.'

The Western Allies, she said, had informed Moscow of Wolff's initial approach more than a week ago. The notification had been deliberately vague, containing few details. Churchill, eager to claim a seat at the table, had followed up with a message of his own to the Kremlin, provoking a demand from Molotov for full Soviet participation in any talks. This, in return, had sparked a furious response from the US Ambassador to Russia, Averell Harriman, who'd pointed out that Russia's Foreign Minister would never, for a second, entertain a Western presence at any Soviet talks. Since then, said Barton, positions had hardened on both sides and only yesterday Molotov had accused the English and the Americans of negotiating behind the Russians' backs.

'The PM's at his wits' end,' she murmured. 'He can't understand how Yalta can possibly have come to this.'

Moncrieff nodded, and his mind went back to the morning he'd answered the summons to Downing Street. Churchill, like any decent politician, was a realist. Yet Stalin had somehow bluffed him into believing that all would be well as the Allies swept to victory.

'So what's our role now?' Moncrieff was looking at Barton.
'*Our* role?'

'Me. My role. What do you want me to do?'

Barton held his gaze for a moment, then stifled a yawn.

'We go to Bern tomorrow. I'm assigning Dulles to you, Tam. I want you to charm him. I nccd you to melt that famous Yankee suspicion. I want you to convince him that we're no threat to his precious turf. And I want you to come back with a lively idea of how much faith they really place in this little dalliance.' She offered him a weary smile, and then tapped her watch. 'Does that sound plausible? On three hours' sleep?'

17

Wilhelm Schultz, after an age in the dismal belly of the Revolution, found himself in a world he could have barely imagined. Gone were the endless mornings patrolling the draughty margins of his Moscow apartment, of lunchtimes trudging through the filthy winter slush to what was left of the local market, of evenings back home under a single bare bulb, trying to coax enough warmth from the broken stove to reheat half a saucepan of yesterday's soup. This morning, in a borrowed hut in a stranger's garden, he was warm, and recently fed, and maybe even safe. The breakfast eggs, delivered several hours ago by Dieter Merz, had come from his hosts' own chickens. The sourdough bread was home baked. And now came the moment when he could attend to his precious gun.

The hut appeared to serve a number of functions. A litter of toys, many of them homemade, gave the space the bright chaos of a nursery. Racks of tools and shelves of jam jars filled with nails and screws went with the armoury of gardening tools carefully tidied into one corner, while the cupboard opposite opened to reveal tins of paint and a metal can of oil.

Schultz sat in the hut's only chair, his back to the open door and the window that looked out on the garden and the rear of the house. He'd spread a discarded copy of *Völkischer*

Beobachter on his lap and now he was using a length of old towelling to clean and grease the little Beretta. The gun was in good condition, and he worked the oil into the slider before sighting along the exposed barrel and tearing off a strip of towelling to serve as a pull-through. He'd no idea whether or not he'd ever have to use the gun but his years in uniform had taught him the importance of being properly armed. Weapons failed when you needed them most. Preparing for the worst, he'd always told himself, is the least a wise man owes himself.

'What's that?' A child's voice, curious, inquisitive.

Schultz glanced round. It was Lottie, the elder daughter. She'd stolen into the hut unannounced, and now she was staring at the line of bullets Schultz had marshalled on a tray beside his foot.

'Soldiers,' Schultz grunted. 'Reporting for duty.'

'Do they have names?'

'Only if you want them to,' he smiled. 'Girls' names? Boys' names? What do you think?'

She didn't answer, not at once. Instead, she dropped to one knee beside the tray.

'Can I touch?' she asked.

Schultz hesitated a moment, then shrugged. A bullet on its own would hurt nobody.

'Be careful,' he said. 'I've just oiled them. You'll need to wipe your fingers afterwards.'

The child nodded, solemn now, acknowledging the responsibility. Very delicately, she pinched a bullet between two fingers and held it up for closer inspection. Her lips were moving but the faintness of her voice eluded Schultz.

'What do you think?' he asked.

'He's called Dieter,' she said. 'Like my daddy.'

'He's a soldier?'

'He flies aeroplanes,' she giggled. 'Like my daddy. He shouldn't be here. He should be at work.'

'Where's work?'

'I don't know. It's where daddy goes.'

'Every day?'

'Nearly every day.' She held the bullet at arm's length, and then pretended to fly it, up and down, round and round, until suddenly she came to a halt, aghast.

'*Mutti*,' she whispered. Mummy.

Schultz spun round again, taken by surprise for the second time. Beata was standing at the open door, staring at her daughter.

'What on earth's going on?

'It's a bullet, Frau Merz. And your daughter will come to no harm.'

'But what is she doing with it? And why do you have a gun? Isn't our house safe enough for you? Would you feel safer elsewhere?' The question was pointed, the implications all too obvious. Moments later, she'd returned the bullet to Schultz, wiped her fingers on her apron, and departed with her daughter. Schultz watched her disappear inside the house, slamming the door shut behind her.

Auf Wiedersehen, he thought with some regret, starting to reassemble the little gun.

*

She was back within the hour, and to Schultz's astonishment she was carrying a kitchen chair in one hand and a steaming mug in the other. She stepped into the hut and gave him the mug.

'Nettle tea,' she said. 'My father's recipe. We're very lucky. He lives just up the road.'

'This is for me?' Schultz was astonished.

'It is. You deserve to be punished for the bullet.' She nodded at the mug. 'Let's see how brave you really are.'

Schultz took a cautious sip at the tea, watching her face over the rim of the mug.

'Bitter,' he said, wiping his mouth with the back of his hand. 'You have any sugar?'

'Sugar?' She shook her head. 'This is Germany. No one has any sugar.'

'Your husband doesn't have connections?'

'Dieter knows everyone. Normally he can lay hands on anything, but sugar is impossible. They call it white gold. He's not my husband, by the way. It's still Frau Messner, if that matters.'

'And does it?'

'Not at all. I keep the name for Lottie's sake.'

'And Merz? Does he mind?'

'No. They were very close, he and Georg, as you know. I talked to Dieter on the phone just now.'

'About the gun?'

'Of course.'

'And?'

'He told me to trust you. He said you'd been around guns all your life. Is that true?'

'Yes.'

'Then I apologise for the little scene just now. I've put Lottie to bed. She still sleeps most afternoons.' She arranged the chair and sat down. She said she had something to ask him. 'It's in the nature of a favour,' she said. 'Or perhaps I need your advice.'

'My pleasure.' Schultz gestured for her to go on.

'You know the KWI? The Kaiser Wilhelm Institute? I happen to work there, have done since before the war.'

'Doing what?'

'Research, mostly. I'm a physicist by trade. I fell in love with logic, just the way good Germans should.'

'It served you well?'

'Better than well. These days, the blessings of work, proper work, work with a future, are hard to find. In that, as in many other respects, I'm a lucky woman. But that's not the point. We scientists talk a great deal. There are few secrets between us. And this is where my job, or perhaps my duty, gets problematic. How much do you know about nuclear science, Herr Schultz?'

'Assume nothing. Maybe you should teach me.'

She stared at him a moment, the briefest smile ghosting across her face, and behind her plainness, and her earnestness, and the way her bony fingers plaited and re-plaited, Schultz began to sense how playful she might be under different circumstances. Not here, not now, not with a stranger who had barged into her life, but much earlier, first with Messner, and then Merz.

'Every atom has a nucleus,' she said. 'Elements are made up of atoms and some elements are less stable than others.'

'Uranium,' Schultz said softly. 'That, at least, I know.'

'Good. You're right. Uranium is very unstable which makes it the perfect element for a regime like this. It's also relatively rare, which can be a problem unless you happen to be a German.'

'We steal it?'

'We help ourselves. Occupying the Sudetenland was a gift. Uranium is there in abundance. You ship it back to the Reich and crush the rock to powder and most of it ended up at the KWI. The scientists who worked in this field built what they called a uranium burner. Basically it's a big concrete pit filled with water with a steel vessel inside. You layer uranium oxide and paraffin wax inside and try to cook up a chain reaction. That's what happens when atoms start dividing and redividing within trillionths of a second. Potentially, without the wax, you're looking at nearly limitless energy, which can mean a very big bang.'

'How big?'

'In theory? Enough to wipe out most of Berlin, or – more to the point – London. People who aren't vaporised will die of radiation poisoning.'

'And our leaders know this?'

'They do, but listen very hard, Herr *Oberst*, because the wonder of this situation is that most of our scientists in the field were Jews. Jewish science carried a yellow star. The regime largely ignored the findings of these rabbinical theorists because it didn't marry with who we really are and that, believe me, has been a blessing. All science needs money, often lots of it, and in this case most of the research Reichsmarks went to Peenemunde, and the rocket programmes.' She paused. 'V-1? V-2?'

Schultz shook his head. He'd never heard of them.

'Really? You mean that?'

'I do.'

'That probably makes you lucky.'

'Why?

'Because they won't be enough to make a difference, but that's not the point because the uranium burner still exists. The development programme, thank God, has taken us nowhere but the burner is still intact, along with three tonnes of uranium oxide stored at the KWI.'

'This stuff can blow up?'

'No. But it's toxic, radioactive. Put it in a bomb, drop it on a city, and let the wind do the rest. This is eugenics gone mad, Herr *Oberst*. Generations of living things – plants, animals, human beings – will be born with hideous mutations. We live in desperate times. Our leaders have no more bullets for their guns. If this will bring the enemy to the negotiating table, then so be it.'

'You're serious?'

'Alas, yes. Someone needs to take the decision – or maybe the temptation – out of German hands.'

'And you're thinking the Russians?'

'I am, yes. They'll be here very soon, that's what everyone's saying.' She smiled at last. 'And given what you told us last night, I'm guessing you probably know when.'

*

Merz returned at dusk. By now, Schultz was back in the house, fully rehabilitated. At some risk, over the past month, Beata had taken a number of photographs of the key locations at the KWI and drawn a detailed map of the site. Schultz sat at the kitchen table, studying the best of the black and white images. A metal-alloy vessel was resting on a wooden floor inside the building that housed the experiment, and half a dozen planks had been lifted to reveal the open mouth of the concrete chamber that served as the burner. A technician was on hand, clad in overalls, goggles and a breathing mask.

Beata tapped the photo.

'They call this place the Virus House,' she said. 'Word on the site suggests they're investigating anthrax, which is clever because it keeps intruders away.'

'And the oxide?' Schultz asked.

'Here... and here... and here...' Her finger strayed to the site map beside the photograph. 'When the Russians arrive they should be talking to our scientists. They'll tell them exactly where to look. Uranium is very heavy, which means that three tonnes are less bulky than you might think. With the right protective equipment, we suspect they could clear the site within a day.'

'We?'

'I and my colleagues. Every last gramme of this stuff should be in safer hands.'

'You mean the Russians?' Merz, standing beside Schultz, was laughing.

'I do.' Beata shot him a look. 'Have you seen the state of our Führer lately?'

*

Merz, as it turned out, had. It was early evening, and Beata was upstairs playing with her daughters before bedtime, leaving Schultz and Merz at the kitchen table.

'Lottie says you're still flying.'

'She's right. Rechlin, mostly, with other trips in between. On a good day, the runway's still intact.'

'This is combat?'

'Test flying, when I'm not on other business. These last few weeks I've been on the *Mistel* programme. I won't bore you with the details but we're talking about an Me-109 strapped on top of a Ju-88. I get to fly the 109 to the target. Five kilometres out, I aim the Ju at the target and hit the release button. Explosive bolts leave me a free man. The Ju is packed with explosives instead of a crew, and with luck – boom – the target is gone. All I then have to do is fly home.' He reached for his glass. More *Weissbier*. 'If you think that's desperate, you'd be right, but it gets worse. This morning's test flight was scrubbed. The plan was to head west but the British crossed the Rhine a couple of days ago and the Americans are already driving towards Frankfurt, and the front is very fluid. Fluid is code for going backwards. It means we're running out of airspace. We'd also, this morning, run out of fuel. Germany is shrinking by the day, Schultz. The way things are going, you'll soon be able to take a Berlin tram across the entire Reich. Think of that,' he laughed. 'The whole country for the price of a tram ticket.'

'And Hitler? You told him this?' Schultz lifted his glass in a salute. '*Prosit.*'

'Hitler is an old man. He's sick in here...' Merz touched his head. 'His left arm doesn't work any more, and I've seen corpses looking healthier than he does. I think I'm there to cheer him up. I've known him since I used to fly on the Führer Squadron with Georg. He hates Goering now because he thinks the Fat One has given up, and that's probably true, but Goebbels keeps feeding him good news and that seems to include me.'

'You told him about the fuel, the lack of airspace?'

'I tell him about the wonders of our test programme. It's a joke, a fiction, but whatever I say doesn't matter. I'm not sure that man ever listens and he's as deaf as a coot now which can't help. There's a vagueness about him. You can see it in his eyes. Sometimes he's just not at home. I put it down to the rubbish he eats, all those pills he takes. Our Führer's chosen to go permanent leave, Schultz, and I'm not sure he's ever coming back.'

'You mean that?'

'I do, yes. He's become a mumbler. He belongs in a shop doorway, or on a bombsite under a rain cape. The old Hitler would have put himself down in the state he's in now, but I don't think that's ever going to happen. For the greater good of the Reich? You remember all that drivel? Between you and me, the *Luftwaffe* attaché at the Chancellery thinks he's going to take us all down with him. The abyss, Schultz. The fiery furnace. Everything in flames. The attaché's blaming Wagner. He's calling it *Führerdämmerung*, and I suspect he might be right.'

Schultz nodded and swallowed another mouthful of beer. The drift of this conversation reminded him powerfully of Stalingrad in the closing days and nights of the battle, everything frozen, nothing to eat, your whole world at the mercy of the Soviet guns. If there was a glorious consolation in the prospect of imminent death, a giddy surrender to the inevitable, it had passed him by. All he'd felt at Stalingrad was hunger, and fear.

'So what happens? To you?'

'We wait. Like everyone else waits. Wannsee could be worse. At least we get a good night's sleep.'

Schultz studied him a moment, and then reached for the pencil Beata had left. On the back of the KWI site map he scribbled two telephone numbers, both of which he'd memorised on the journey out of Stockholm.

'There's a man I need to talk to. He works in the Charité hospital. That's their main number. His name is Rainer Gehlhausen. The other number is private, his apartment. I gather he lives close to the hospital.'

'You want to contact him?

'Yes.'

'Why?'

'Because he knows how to talk to Moscow, and already I should have been in touch.'

'You're telling me he's a spy? This man?' Merz looked briefly shocked.

'He's a medic, Dieter, a surgeon. He saves lives.'

'But a Communist, too?'

'I've no idea, but I imagine the answer might be yes.' He paused. 'Would that make a difference?'

Merz held his gaze for a moment, then shook his head. From upstairs came the sound of a child laughing.

'The phone's by the front door,' he looked at his watch. 'We've got a couple of hours before the RAF arrives. You'll need a change of clothes if he's available tonight.'

'We?'

'We.' Merz was eyeing him up and down. 'Funny thing, Schultz. You're exactly the same build as my father-in-law.'

*

Merz drove a little VW. Judging by the state of the bodywork, it had been lucky to survive the war intact, but Beata's father looked after the engine and it ran – in Merz's phrase – very sweetly. Now, thanks once again to Beata's father, Schultz was wearing a dark green Loden coat with a rather fetching scarlet lining in what had to be silk. The coat, like the grey flannel trousers and polished black shoes, was a perfect fit and smelled faintly of cigars. Beata's father was a widower. He lived three houses away in a tiny cottage beside the lake, and he'd taken great pleasure in throwing open his wardrobe to Schultz. He'd last worn the coat, he confided, for a staff reunion party at the school where he used to teach. Hence the smell. It was also, he added, the last Christmas present his wife had ever given him before, a number of years earlier, she'd died.

Now, as Merz negotiated the blackout, Schultz gazed out at the dark bulk of buildings on either side of the empty road. The closer they got to the city centre, the more the city disappeared before his eyes, street after ruined street erased by long months of constant bombing. Once, it had been his business to know this place in intimate detail. Now, entire areas were barely recognisable.

'The bomber's changed everything.' He was watching an elderly woman arguing with a *Blockwarten* in the shadows of a half-destroyed apartment block. 'We should have seen this coming.'

'We did.'

'Really?'

Merz nodded, slowing to avoid a chunk of masonry in the middle of the road. This last year, he said, he'd often been airborne among the incoming bomber streams in one of the Me-110s specially adapted for night fighting.

'We put a cannon behind the canopy.' He was smiling. 'The gun is fixed to fire upwards and the trick is to find a target and slide underneath. You have to get really close and those planes are huge but they have a blind spot. Once you're tucked underneath, all you have to do is manoeuvre beneath one of the wings and stay there. The wings are full of fuel. We use special high-explosive rounds and a two-second burst is all you need. The fuel ignites, and after that it's over. The English never see us. *Das Ende* comes from nowhere. Whoosh. Gone.'

Death comes from nowhere, Schultz thought. *Das Ende* steals in from the darkness, implacable, unseen. In Paris, he'd conducted an affair with a well-connected French woman, *une grande dame* with friends on the far right and Fascist talents in bed. Unusually, she spoke German and she'd done her best to teach him a little French. The word she returned to time after time was *le vide*, the emptiness, the nothing, *das Ende*.

At first he'd put this preoccupation of hers down to some adolescent flirtation with the café *philosophes* in her university days but once he'd got to know the woman properly he realised that *le vide* was the empty shape of things to come. She'd watched what had happened to France in the thirties, understood where it led, anticipated the moral vacuum that awaited every player in the war that was bound to arrive. When it finally turned up, a little later than everyone expected, *Wehrmacht* messes across Paris were where the nightly celebrations began, and Schultz himself had often lifted a glass to the next victory, and the one after that. England? The rest of France? The chance to give those bloody Russians a kicking? How wrong he'd been.

Schultz gathered the Loden coat a little more tightly around him, still shocked by the state of a Berlin he'd once loved. Jürgen Frenzell, the pilot who'd saved his life at Hohenlychen, had talked of other cities laid waste, of Hamburg, and Cologne, and Lübeck, but only now did Schultz understand that nothing he'd once taken for granted could survive a war like this.

'We fucked up,' he grunted. 'And now look at us.'

The Charité hospital lay in the city centre above a bend in the Spree. Merz parked the VW in an adjoining street, and they walked the four hundred metres to the main entrance. Over the crunch of broken glass underfoot, Schultz caught the whistle of a steam engine from the nearby *Hauptbahnhof*, and then the ghostly clank-clank of a departing train. To get out of Berlin at this time of night, he thought, was probably a shrewd decision.

The big space inside the hospital entrance was packed, a milling crowd of Berliners, the casualties already bandaged, their haunted relatives doing their best to offer support. On the phone, less than an hour earlier, Gehlhausen had seemed unsurprised by the call. Half past seven, he'd said. Walk down the corridor on the left and look for woman giving out drinks from a trolly. She's at the same place every night. On the wall behind her is a *Kraft durch Freude* poster. I can give you five minutes, no more. When Schultz had asked how he'd recognise him, Gehlhausen had offered a mirthless laugh.

'Black patch over the left eye,' he'd murmured. 'That's why they call me the Pirate.'

Now, beside the trolly, Schultz could see no sign of a black patch. Neither, to his slight surprise, were there many takers for the big urn of ersatz coffee and the thin slices of black bread on offer. The *Kraft durch Freude* poster featured a garish painting of a cruise liner, grateful Party members waving from every deck, a teasing reminder that the regime had once been more than generous. Schultz had found a seat on a bench on the other side of the corridor and stared at the poster for a long moment. A week's holiday for virtually nothing had never had the slightest appeal but he'd known whole families whose lives had been transformed by the Führer's largesse.

'Herr Schultz? Am I right?'

Schultz tore himself away. A tall, cadaverous figure in a stained white coat loomed over him. Untidy curls of grey hair escaped a surgical cap. There were splashes of fresh blood and other fluids on the white rubber boots, and traces of a number scrawled in black ink on the palm of the extended hand.

'Herr Gehlhausen?' Schultz struggled to his feet.

'Me. Nice coat. *Kommen Sie mit.*'

Merz, watching this brief exchange, signalled that he'd wait for Schultz's return. Gehlhausen, meanwhile, had already opened a door down the corridor. This was a man brimming with cheerful impatience. Schultz had been anticipating weariness, maybe even resignation. That's what non-stop surgery, coupled with a little spying, would do to you. Far from it.

'You've worked here long?' he asked after Gehlhausen had closed the door.

'Forever. Once upon a time we made people better. Now we stick the pieces back together again.'

'There's a difference?'

'Alas, yes. Our problem is beds. We've run out. Goebbels, bless the blackness of his soul, has offered ten thousand more. He has an eye for a phrase, that man. *Katastrophe* beds. Is that a diagnosis, one wonders? A promise of delights to come?'

There were no chairs in the room. Gehlhausen had folded his long frame onto the single table, moving a box full of forms to make room for himself. Now, one long finger was adjusting the patch over his right eye.

'Nice coat,' he said again. 'You *Abwehr* people always had taste.'

'You know about me?'

'A little. Enough. You don't look well, Schultz. Eat more. I have tidings. You'll need something to write with. Here...'

Schultz took the proffered fountain pen and peered into the box.

'What are these?' He looked up.

'Death certificates. We've got thousands. Help yourself.'

Schultz took a form. It was blank on the reverse side.

'Well?'

'You need to get yourself to Switzerland. Bern. I have a hotel address for you. Ask for a woman called Ursula Barton.'

'I know of Barton.'

'You've met her already?'

'No. She works for British intelligence. Tam Moncrieff?'

'Never heard of him. Barton has a photograph. There's a face you'll recognise on that shot and she'll be grateful for your help. His name is Karl Wolff. He's an SS General, their top man in Italy. The camera has caught him in compromising circumstances.'

'With a woman? A man?'

'I'm afraid I have no idea. I'm simply the messenger. You know this man Wolff?'

'I've met him, yes, a while ago.'

'So you can recognise him?'

'Yes. Is Barton expecting me?'

'No. And neither does she know you've been in Russia. As far as she's concerned you're now working for Himmler. You have a post with the SD. The *Abwehr* is no more. Her copy of that photo would be more than useful. Bern. The Hotel Felix. Rathausgasse. She booked in yesterday. Ursula Barton. Write it down, Schultz. I'm a busy man.'

Schultz scribbled the name on the back of the death certificate, then looked up.

'How have I found her? How do I explain that?'

'You work for Himmler. You're SD. You know everything.'

'And I give the photo to you? Assuming I lay hands on it?'

'You do.'

'And when? When is this supposed to happen?'

'As soon as possible.'

'But how am I supposed to get there?'

Gehlhausen stared at him a moment, then he abandoned the table, checked his watch and extended a hand.

'I'm told you're a resourceful man, Schultz.' He gestured at the hotel address. 'Make it happen. We have anything else to discuss?' He smiled, then patted Schultz's arm. 'I think not.'

Schultz was back in the VW, aware that he hadn't had time to raise Beata's concerns about the uranium oxide at the KWI, but under the circumstances it was probably just as well. Merz had made a phone call to a colleague and knew that the first wave of the biggest of tonight's incoming raids was currently crossing the Dutch border. Either Hanover, Wolfsburg or Berlin were the likely targets.

'We have less than an hour, Schultz. It could have been much worse. What did your man have to say?'

'I have to get to Bern.'

'Why?' Merz shot him a look.

Schultz shook his head. It was one thing to offer sanctuary for a couple of nights, he muttered, quite another to become involved.

'But we are involved,' Merz insisted. 'The moment we opened our door to you, we got involved. I want to help you, Schultz. You were a good man in Lisbon, and you're a good man now.'

Schultz was flattered but tried hard not to let it show.

'You know Bern?' he asked after a while

'Of course I know Bern. Zurich, too. If you've got the right clearance, know the right people, you're flying to Switzerland all the time, mainly courier missions. Often, it's spares for their air force. Recently, it's been other stuff. Last week I took forty kilos in gold bullion. I was flying an Me-110. I strapped both boxes to the rear gunner's seat and stayed low to avoid the bloody ack-ack. The Swiss aren't the pussycats everyone thinks they are. They're trigger-happy as hell. They'll shoot anything down.' He cursed, swerving to avoid what might have been a dog. Then he steadied the car and checked the rear-view mirror before glancing across at his passenger. 'Bern, Schultz? Are you serious?'

Schultz nodded, and held his gaze. It couldn't possibly be this easy, he thought. Had he been set up? Did Merz, too, work for Moscow?

'Well?' Merz wanted an answer.

'Bern, then.' Schultz's fingers were exploring the pocket of the Loden coat. 'You want a cigar?'

18

Late. And so far, no sign of the expected air raid.

Werner Nehmann had been in the editing suite since dusk. The little room was claustrophobic, no windows, not even a fan to stir the stale air. Erich, who worked here all the time, had done his best to brighten his surroundings, and Nehmann had already expressed a lively interest in the montage of photos pinned to a wall board.

They were all of the same woman. Her name was Karin. She had the body of a starlet and the face that suggested an almost gipsy-like languor. Sometimes she was with Erich, or with another woman who was apparently her girlfriend, but mostly she was alone. Some of the poses were domestic – Karin absorbed in a magazine, Karin nuzzling a young-looking German Shepherd dog – but others had been shot outdoors, and the one that had taken Nehmann's immediate interest was a study of a naked Karin on a blanket, propped on her elbows, surrounded by trees and fallen leaves.

Her face was tanned in the slant of late sunshine, and the tangle of black curls softened the hardness in her eyes. The rich curves of her body, to Nehmann, seemed to stretch forever, the deep hollow of her back, the pert swell of her bum, her legs spread wide on the warmth of the blanket, and the camera had caught the moment she was chewing on a blade of grass. Autumn last year, Erich had murmured, and she let me fuck her all afternoon.

Now, Erich rewound the newsreel rough cut for the third time while Nehmann bent to his borrowed pad, checking the cues he'd need for each segment of commentary. For the facts – names, dates, locations, unit designations – he'd had to rely on his new friend, but it had been obvious at once that Erich was a master at the editing table. Back in the days when he'd been working for Goebbels full-time, Nehmann had spent hundreds of hours in rooms like this, fielding raw footage from advance units as the *Wehrmacht* pushed first into Poland, and later into France. Then, the torrent of victories had needed none of Nehmann's sorcery on the soundtrack because the pictures had spoken for themselves: downed Polish fighters, wrecked French armour, long lines of prisoners trudging past the camera. Now, though, the fortunes of war had made for very different pictures and Nehmann had to coax whatever warmth he could from the embers of a dying Reich.

'Ready?' Erich had frozen the first frame of the report on the screen that dominated the editing table.

Nehmann glanced up. When he'd talked to the *Reichsminister* this morning, still out at Bogensee, Goebbels had been as clear as ever about the precise thrust of this newsreel. It was to start at an old manor house near Wriezen. The property had once belonged to Marshal Blücher, Goebbels explained. It lay ten kilometres west of the Oder, and he'd managed to coax Hitler into making a visit for the benefit of the cameras. An assortment of officers had been summoned back from front-line units to greet their leader and dress the set, but the Führer had been assured that he'd be spared introductions to ordinary working soldiers. On that basis, coupled with the knowledge that the roads to and from Berlin would be monitored by heavily armed SS patrols,

Hitler had agreed to make himself available. In the present circumstances, Goebbels had told Nehmann this morning, this would in all probability be Hitler's last excursion out of Berlin. Essential, therefore, for cinema audiences to see their Führer at his best.

Intrigued by this glimpse of decay at the very top of the Reich, Nehmann had asked Erich to show him the rushes from Wriezen. The very existence of the Reich depended, above all, on the figure in the long leather coat. Any hint of weakness, of infirmity, even of indecision, and the faith of the *Volk* might begin to waver. Without Hitler, without the man immortalised in a thousand spotlights, the Reich was nothing. It would be Hamlet without the prince, the darkest of voids at the heart of the blackest of regimes. Even the Germans, beguiled and lied to for more than a decade, would spot the trick that history had played, and that was an outcome Goebbels was determined to avoid.

'We need you, Nehmann,' he'd murmured as he'd walked his overnight guest to the waiting Mercedes. 'Erich works miracles with the pictures. What's missing is your touch on the soundtrack. Make the Führer the giant that he used to be.'

This, Nehmann and Erich agreed, was a major challenge. The cameraman at Wriezen was a good friend of Erich's and he'd gone to some lengths to describe what Hitler had looked like when he'd struggled out of the car on his arrival from Berlin. The chalk-white face. The glittering eyes. The constant tremor in his left hand. The exhausted stoop when he paused to mutter a word to officers drawn up to await his inspection. This, said the cameraman, was bad enough but he'd stayed behind afterwards to pick up some extra shots and he'd watched those same officers talking among themselves, their eyes on the Führer convoy as it drove away. Was this what had really happened to Germany? Was that the man for whom most of them were about to die?

The edited sequence at Wriezen lasted two minutes fifty-seven seconds. Erich had wrung every drop of optimism out of the footage, showcased Hitler in those brief moments when he seemed normal and erect, milked the rushes for a nod from one officer, a smile from another, an upward tilt of the chin from a third, and then intercut training sequences with tanks and artillery from a different time and place, suggesting that the might of the Red Army had taken one too many liberties with their blind drive westwards, and were about to pay a terrible price.

In keeping with Goebbels' instructions, there followed a heartening series of interlinked sequences from Berlin itself: Russian and French prisoners digging trenches in the eastern suburbs, supervised by *Wehrmacht* engineers; Berlin *Hausfrauen* exchanging ration cards for food at implausibly well-stocked shops; a squad of keen but ageing volunteers learning how to take out a Russian tank with a *Panzerfaust*; kids swimming in the Spree under the benign eye of a *Wehrmacht* NCO. The sheer visual logic was clear: spring is nearly here, soon the flowers will bloom again, and never lose heart because all will be well.

'Happy to try?'

Nehmann nodded, and Erich started to run the rough cut. It was a tribute to his editing skills that Nehmann had been able to keep his commentary so bare, so neutral, just the odd factual prompt from time to time, and then a warm note of applause for our brave front-line warriors as the focus shifted to Berlin. We're ready, went the message. And all our futures couldn't be resting in better hands.

With a total running time of just under seven minutes, the rough cut ended on a perfectly framed shot of a young mother lifting her baby from a pram. Then came a close-up nuzzle, a hug, and a big smile for the camera before the picture faded to black. Erich had yet to lay the sound effects and the music, but

Nehmann had no doubts about the brief flicker of warmth this would kindle in the only heart that mattered. Not the audience of Berliners, long resigned to being lied to, not the tens of millions of Germans nationwide, many of them bombed out of their houses, not the residents of East Prussia, by now refugees, but Goebbels, truly the Prince of Darkness.

'*Scheisse, nein?*' Erich yawned, his eyes drifting to his precious gipsy, still on her belly among the fallen leaves. Nehmann nodded in agreement, wondering idly whether Erich really had contacts in Moscow as Goebbels had claimed. More shit? Or maybe, in this crazy war, the truth?

Goebbels himself arrived shortly afterwards. As usual, he insisted on approving the rough cut before Erich set to work on the final product. He offered Nehmann a perfunctory nod of greeting and settled in Erich's chair at the editing table. As pictures began to roll, Nehmann added commentary from his scribbled notes. The newsreel over, Goebbels was still staring at the empty screen.

'Perfect,' he murmured at last.

Nehmann had been watching the pale hands on the lap of Goebbels' leather coat, the way he kept scratching at the angry, inflamed patches of eczema. Was this what years of propaganda did to you? Did all those lies begin to devour your very flesh?

'Next we need a radio speech.' Goebbels was still gazing at the screen. 'The Führer is naturally reluctant. He claims he has nothing to say. It's our job, Nehmann, to *give* him something to say. The people need to hear his voice. They need reassurance. They need to feel his presence. A drop or two of *Führerklebstoff*, my little Georgian friend. It keeps us all in one piece. No more than twenty minutes, Nehmann. Something truly inspirational. See what you can do.'

Führerklebstoff. Hitler glue. Something to stick his fractured *Volk* back together again. Goebbels was suddenly on his feet, his business done. Even with the special heels, he was a small, slight man.

'Half an hour, Nehmann.'

'Half an hour what?'

'In half an hour my driver will be back to pick you up.' A brief, mirthless smile. 'Enjoy, *ja*?'

Enjoy? Goebbels had gone. Nehmann had been about to ask Erich about getting a bed for the night, or even a corner of this tiny room. Now it occurred to him that Goebbels might have hatched other plans. Did this mean another evening out at Bogensee? He rather hoped not.

'*Führerklebstoff?*' Erich was preparing to make a start on the fine cut. 'What kind of nonsense is that?'

*

Nehmann was at the kerbside when the Mercedes returned. There was still no sign of an air raid warning, the howl of the neighbourhood siren, or the three repeated notes on the radio that every Berliner had learned to dread, but still the streets were empty. Fear has become a habit, Nehmann thought, watching the big limousine glide to a halt.

'Where are we going?' With Nehmann inside, the Mercedes was already on the move.

'Eichwalde.' The driver was studying Nehmann in the rear-view mirror. 'Nice.'

'You have an address?' Nehmann knew nothing about Eichwalde.

'Of course.'

'This is some kind of hotel? A *pension*, maybe?'

'A *pension*?' The driver was laughing. 'You'd prefer that? Relax, my friend. I don't know what you've done for the Minister, but one day you might let me know the secret, eh?'

As far as Nehmann could judge, they were heading south-west, away from the city centre, following the course of the river. District by district, the brutal consequences of the bombing began to soften and by the time the Mercedes slowed to make a turn off the main road, the fingerprints of the RAF had vanished. In the darkness, Nehmann could make out hints of early blossom in the trees lining the streets, not a trace of rubble on the carefully swept pavements, even a face of an elderly man at an open upstairs window, the glow of a cigarette between his fingers. This must have been one of the city's more desirable pre-war suburbs, Nehmann thought: orderly, well-mannered, looked after.

'Here, my friend.' The laughter was softer this time. '*Schlafen Sie gut, ja?*'

Sleep well? The car had come to a halt outside a neat two-storey house. Nehmann stared at it through the thick bullet-proof glass. There were stands of daffodils in the tiny front garden, more flowers in a vase in the downstairs window, and as he watched he saw a cat appear from nowhere and settle beside the front door. He's used to late-night visitors, Nehmann thought. He knows the door is about to be opened.

Nehmann got out and stooped to the driver's window. Even here, even now, he was wary of a trap.

'Just one clue? A name, maybe?'

'No need. Just relax. Believe me, you're a lucky man.'

Moments later, the car had gone. Nehmann stared down the empty street, then shrugged and made his way to the front door. The cat peered up at him, extending a languid paw. Nehmann felt the tug of the animal's claws through the thinness of his trousers. A first knock on the door stirred no response, and neither did the second. He stepped across to the window and tried to peer in through the narrow gap in the curtains. The room was dominated by something black, something substantial, but it was too dark to see exactly what. Then he heard a stir of movement and the door opened behind him and he half turned, crouching now, ready to defend himself, a reflex that had twice saved his life in the Kolyma camps.

'Who is it?'

The voice hadn't changed, not by a note, not by a semi-quaver. The same slight huskiness. The same hint of what Nehmann had finally recognised as mystery. It's a piano in that room, he thought. How foolish not to recognise it.

'Maria? Is that you?'

He stepped towards the door. He could see her now. Two years of trying to forget that face, of doing his best to erase every moment of the times they'd spent together, had come to this. Goebbels, once again, had ambushed him. Nehmann's eyes were moist. He could think of nothing to say. Except trying to voice the question he'd been wanting to ask for two long years.

'Kiss me?'

She stepped back, preserving the space between them. She was wearing a long nightshirt. Her feet were bare. She'd put on a little weight, and it suited her. Sallow complexion, her hair a little longer, the rich promise of those lips as full as ever.

'You were expecting me?' Nehmann asked.

'Yes.'

'He told you I was coming? Goebbels?'

'Yes.'

'And are you glad I'm here?'

For the first time, she smiled and opened the door a little wider, letting him in. Nehmann recognised the perfume at once, the lightest oriental scent hanging in the stillness of the air. He could picture the fluted curves of the bottle she'd kept beside the bed in the apartment they'd shared more than two long years ago.

'He buys it for you? Shalimar by Guerlin?'

'I buy it myself. A bottle can last for years if you've nowhere to go.'

'But tonight?'

'Tonight is different. A celebration? I hope so. But I've learned never to make myself promises. Please. This way.'

Nehmann gazed at her as she disappeared into a room at the rear of the house. She'd never been this formal, this guarded. My territory, she seemed to be saying. My life.

He joined her in the kitchen. Plates of prepared hors d'œuvres lay on the table. A fan of thinly sliced gherkins. Fat olives glistening with olive oil. Fillets of herring soused in peppercorns and onion. A dish of mayonnaise. Even a knuckle of pork. An offering like this had to have come from Goebbels. Had to. Nehmann didn't know whether to be grateful or insulted. It was Goebbels who'd barged into their lives and claimed Maria for himself, who'd listened to her playing at the Moabit nightclub where they'd first met, who'd recognised her talent and her looks and the way she could beguile any audience, and who'd put her on the airwaves nationwide, building a huge audience. Nehmann had listened to her on a shortwave frequency you could pick up in Stalingrad. She'd been playing a Beethoven sonata, the *Pathétique*, on her regular weekly radio show. Autumn 1942, he thought. And the first chill breath of the Russian winter.

She had a bottle of white wine in a bucket. When she fetched it out, Nehmann heard the tell-tale clink of ice cubes.

'Where did you get those?'

'The Adlon. They were delivered this evening.'

'Goebbels again?'

'I'm afraid so. For Shalimar by Guerlin you only need money. Ice cubes demand something extra.'

'You still see him? Goebbels?'

'Yes. Not very often these days, not since Hitler gave him the city to defend, but yes. He comes when he can.'

'And that's a good thing?'

'It's necessary.'

'*Necessary?*'

She nodded, saying nothing, then asked him to pour the wine. Nehmann was staring at a plate of sliced hard-boiled egg, sprinkled with paprika and arranged in the shape of a speech mark.

'You did this yourself? Took a knife to the egg?'

'No.' She stared at him a moment. 'There's another way. I'll show you. Everyone's got them. Twenty pfennigs in the market.'

She fetched the wire slicer from a cupboard in the corner and Nehmann stared at it for a long moment, weighing it in the palm of his hand. Tatsinskaya, he thought. And Russian tanks shelling the airfield moments before the last Ju-52s lumbered into the air.

'A friend of mine invented this,' he said. 'His name was Messner, Georg Messner. He thought it would bring him a pension for life. Sadly, he was wrong.'

'What happened?'

'He got blown up by the Russians.' Nehmann nodded at the slicer. 'That's all that was left of him. I brought the slicer back that last Christmas, gave it to his wife. It wasn't much but it might have helped.'

Maria nodded. She wanted to know more about the Eastern Front, about Stalingrad, and about what had happened afterwards.

'I saved all your pieces from the *Beobachter* and *Das Reich*,' she said. 'Sometimes you made Stalingrad sound like a vacation, and I know that made some people angry, but all the clues were in there if you knew where to look.'

'And?'

'I knew where to look. I could hear your voice sometimes, and that was a comfort. I don't know whether this helps but Goebbels thought you were a genius.'

'His genius? His property? Me, the monkey? Him, the organ grinder?'

'He never said that. He knew he couldn't control you, not properly, and I think he respected that.'

'Knew?'

'Knows.' Nehmann sensed she wanted to change the subject, and he was right. 'They took you prisoner? The Russians?'

'They did. Me and an *Abwehr* man called Willi Schultz. We were like brothers by the end.'

'And he's still alive?'

'I've no idea. He was older than me, and a battle like that takes everything out of you. Then the Russians send you to the Gulag and use what's left, and after that you're lucky to be still alive. So...' he shrugged, '...who knows what happened to Schultz. Cold like that can sometimes be a blessing. Men die without taking much notice.'

'Horrible.'

'You're right. I'm sorry.'

'Don't be. Tell me everything, the whole story.' For the first time, she came close to him and reached for his hand. She looked at it a moment, the way you might examine an object in an antique shop, looking for flaws, testing the provenance, then she curled the fingers and lifted them to her lips and kissed them. Nehmann had shut his eyes. Even he was lost for words.

*

They ate in the kitchen, Maria feeding Nehmann with titbits from the plates on the table while he described his journey east, and the long years that had followed. When a particular memory trespassed into territory he was loath to share, he paused, and frowned, and hunted for the phrases that would spare her the worst, but she shook her head, and insisted on the truth, every last detail. She wanted to know. She wanted to understand. This war, she said, has never been less than ugly. The hunger. The lying. The vicious fight for petty advantage in every market, on every tram, in every air raid shelter. But she imagined that nothing could be more brutal than the war the men had fought in the east, not for glory, not even for gain, but for the savage pleasure of enslaving millions.

'Am I right?'

'You are.'

'And were we ever aware of that?'

'No.'

'So isn't this a debt you owe? If not to everyone, then just to me?'

Her held her gaze, then he began to laugh. The first bottle of Riesling had gone, and they'd nearly emptied the second.

'What's so funny?'

'This.' He gestured at the plates on the table, the last of the wine. 'I spend years writing fairy tales, then someone suddenly demands the truth. I'm happy to oblige but it's not a story you'd ever want to tell your children.'

'No?'

'Never. There's no painkiller that would touch the kind of lives we've been through. Not unless you include alcohol. Willi Schultz would know that. I know that. And so do millions of others. There comes a point in every man's life when you recognise the animal inside. And if you're very lucky, that might see you through.'

'And you. Your animal?'

'We're still good friends. We do each other favours. We agreed a pact.'

'The pact of what?'

'Silence. Not telling. Trying to forget. If you don't take care, the past can kill you. Better to lock it somewhere safe and hide the key. No one ever died of peace of mind.'

She gazed at him. She was very close now, her chair beside his, her face rapt. There was something in her eyes, a frank curiosity coupled with appreciation. She might have been a student at an intimate seminar. She was here to absorb, to digest, to learn. Nothing he could ever say would shock her.

'You still play?' He reached out and touched her face.

'I do, yes.'

'For Goebbels? For broadcast? For the Reich?'

'For me. I've fallen in love with Rachmaninoff. This is *Untermensch musik*. I pull the curtains and close every door and play very softly.'

'And Goebbels?'

'He loves Rachmaninoff, too. This is a state secret.' She nodded, suddenly solemn. 'Tell no one.'

'Love's a big word.'

'I know.'

'Does Goebbels love you?'

'Goebbels loves himself. It's the only emotion he really trusts and even that gets him into trouble.'

'And you?'

'Me?'

'You and Goebbels…?'

'We have a problem. On a good night, he calls me unfinished business which I suspect he means as a compliment, but he calls the war that as well so I'm left a little lost.'

'And on a bad night?'

'On a bad night he stamps and shouts and gets very angry.'

'At you?'

'At everything. His nerves are shot and he knows the war is beyond him, beyond us all, and that makes things even worse. But none of that is of slightest consequence because that man has kept me safe, and in this regime protection is all that matters.'

Nehmann nodded and reached for her hand. Maria was half Jewish. Without Goebbels, she – like her sisters – would have been one of the disappeared.

'A pact, then? You and him? His animal and yours?'

'Yes.' She pulled him closer, kissed him softly on the lips. She tasted of garlic from the dish of mayonnaise, and Nehmann remembered late summer afternoons when they took the tram home from a picnic beside the Spree, and made love in the apartment when they got home. Maria always left the tall windows open, enjoying the soft billow of the evening breeze in the curtains, and afterwards she'd slip out of bed, and ghost herself through to the big sitting room, and settle at the keyboard, and play passages of Beethoven that she knew he loved.

Nehmann broke off a moment, holding her at arm's length. 'Tell me one thing,' he said. 'How come Goebbels brought me out here?'

'You really want to know?'

'I do.'

She studied him for a moment, and then got to her feet, and led him back to the hall and the staircase. The bedrooms in the house were on the top floor, three doors, all closed.

'That one.' Maria nodded at the middle door. 'But be careful.'

'Why?'

'She's a very light sleeper.'

Nehmann stared at her. Picking through the rubble of the last few years had fogged his brain. For a second or two, he thought he'd misheard her, assumed it must be some kind of joke, but then she shook her head, knowing exactly what was going through his head, and put a finger to her lips.

'Quietly,' she whispered.

Nehmann opened the door. The spill from the single bulb on the landing barely penetrated the gloom. He stood motionless in the open doorway until he made out the cot in the corner, and the chest of drawers, and the hand-painted cardboard parrot suspended from the ceiling. Then came a soft chuckle from the cot, a sound he'd never forget, and a sigh as the child rolled over and fell asleep again. Looking down at the face on the pillow, he tried to detect some faint likeness to the face in the mirror every morning, but he knew it was important, for once, not to fool himself.

Back on the landing, he closed the door.

'Her name?'

'Dominika. Like my mother. It's Polish.'

'And how old is she?'

'Nearly two. She was born on 21 June 1943.'

'Midsummer's Day.'

'Exactly.'

Nehmann was doing the sums. He'd been with Maria in Berlin before he'd shipped out to Stalingrad. That made it just possible. The child's name felt instantly familiar. Dominika. He tried it out again, and again, fighting the question he knew he had to ask.

'Mine, then?' he asked at last.

'I think so, yes.'

'You *think* so?

'Yes.' Maria was leading him to the adjoining door. 'Either yours or my other friend's.'

'Goebbels?'

'I'm afraid so.' She smiled. 'But does that really matter?'

19

Moncrieff was late. Six hours ago, he'd agreed to meet Ursula Barton for breakfast in the hotel dining room at nine o'clock. It had already gone ten but mercifully she was still there, alone at a table beside the window, shrouded in a coat and bent over what appeared to be a letter. The lone waiter had already cleared most of the other tables. If Moncrieff was to eat at all, he had a choice of two madeleines, both of them stale to the touch.

He carried his plate back to the table. The Hotel Felix stood on one of the city's busiest streets and he paused beside the big picture window, gazing out at a line of shoppers, mainly women, queueing outside a department store. Huge advertisements proclaimed the first day of the spring sale, and the mannequins in the windows were dressed for summer. After the gloom of London, with shops of every description ever emptier, the bustle and obvious wealth of Bern came as a reminder of happier times.

Barton felt it, too.

'Hard to credit, isn't it? The fruits of neutrality?' She'd put her fountain pen carefully to one side. 'The coffee's cold. Shall I call for a fresh pot?'

Moncrieff settled at the table and studied her for a moment as she summoned the waiter. Last night, leaving Obergoms in the car Barton had borrowed from the British Embassy, Moncrieff had offered to take the wheel after it became obvious that she couldn't cope with the snow in the mountains. As the journey developed, he'd done his best to bring her up to date with events in Locarno, describing what had happened to Hannalore – the missing negatives, the stolen prints, the ice pick discarded beside her body in the darkroom – and he'd been surprised that she hadn't expressed more interest. Thanks to the snow, the journey had taken far longer than he'd anticipated and after the first hour, whenever he'd spared her a glance, she'd been asleep.

Now, still waiting for the coffee, she seemed shrunken, physically diminished, her face paler and more drawn than ever. With a slight shock, he also realised that she'd started to pick at her nails. The cuticles were reddened, and the nails themselves were bitten to the quick. When he asked if she was all right, if a couple of hours' proper sleep had done her any good, she dismissed his concern.

'Bit of a cold coming on.' She was looking at the letter again. 'Weather like last night's, I suppose that shouldn't be a surprise.'

The coffee arrived. Barton insisted on pouring, and when Moncrieff raised the issue of Hannalore again, she shot him a look.

'I've been thinking about that,' she murmured. 'You say you were followed from the border? That first afternoon?'

'Yes.'

'And De Vries recognised the man?'

'She did. She said he was a Serb. Belgrade. Used the codename *Crusader*. Made his money as a freelance.'

'That would probably be right. The Soviets have a big presence here in Bern, and in Zurich, too, but further out they subcontract. Moscow has deep pockets, which is odd given their circumstances, and a Yugoslav on the books would give them extra peace of mind. Tito is a Communist. The Russians haven't got much time for trust but they'd view Tito partisans, at the very least, as semi-reliable. Your companion on the train, I'm guessing, took his orders from Moscow.'

'And killed Hannalore?'

'More than possible. The clue is the work she'd already done in the darkroom. She'd seen those prints. She knew what had happened down by the lake. A meeting like that, *evidence* like that, would be deeply unwelcome. Already the Soviets have picked up rumours about Wolff. They'll shout and protest and make lots of noise about betrayal but there's darkness in the Russian soul, Tam, and elements in Moscow would like to see the SS at the negotiating table. They want signatures on a piece of paper, the Germans gone, and northern Italy emptied for what happens next. The key, as I think I've mentioned before, is Trieste. The Red Army need to be there first. After that, anything can happen.'

Moncrieff nodded. The coffee was remarkably good, much better than he'd expected, and he was beginning to revive. Trieste was the key, he agreed. Head west across the flatlands of the Po Valley, and the Red Army would find themselves within striking distance of France. The Resistance controlled areas of the south. Many in the leadership were Communists, and the same was true in Italy. The right had let Europe down and six years of spilled blood and wholesale destruction had left a yearning for a better world. Might the Russians be pushing at an open door?

Moncrieff put the question to Barton. For the first time, a smile warmed her face and Moncrieff felt the brief pressure of her hand on his.

'That's very bold, Tam, if I may say so. What happened to Hannalore should serve as a warning. You won't need persuading about the Russians. They have every reason to table evidence of that meeting, and you and Anneke have supplied it.' She nodded, giving his hand a little squeeze, then her gaze drifted back to the letter. As far as Moncrieff could judge, it was uncompleted, a sentence running out of breath halfway down the page. 'I'm writing to Mrs Witherby, Tam. The funeral takes place next week. I've managed to acquire the woman's address but the real problem is knowing what to say. To tell you the truth, I hardly knew the man, and I certainly don't know his widow. A word or two over a purchase at a market stall? A shared joke? A couple of tips on cooking rabbit if it happens to be on the tough side? Does that qualify as a friendship? Or am I being hopelessly maudlin? Be honest, Tam. Tell me the truth.'

Moncrieff took his time in answering. Barton had already been in touch with Allen Dulles. She'd phoned him the previous day, and he'd agreed to meet Moncrieff for a brief discussion. The meeting was scheduled for eleven o'clock but even on foot, Dulles's apartment was barely fifteen minutes away. What extra light this encounter might shed on the possibilities for a German surrender in northern Italy was anyone's guess but what seemed to matter just now was what Barton had to say to a widow she'd never met.

'You admired the man,' Moncrieff was gazing at the letter. 'For some reason, he touched a nerve. That should be enough.'

*

Herrengasse was a cobbled street on the ridge that overlooked the River Aare. An arcade offered a number of small galleries, as well as a shop selling antique French furniture, and below the promenade on the other side of the street a vineyard tumbled down the slope towards the water. Moncrieff, who was a couple of minutes early, took the opportunity to pause and savour the view. From here, the vast frieze of the Bernese Alps filled the horizon, and he recognised the twin peaks of the Eiger and the Jungfrau. If you were an American spymaster charged with keeping an eye on Europe, he thought, there might be worse places to pitch your tent.

Number 23 was last in the row of townhouses that adjoined the arcade. Moncrieff rang the doorbell and waited. At length, the door opened.

'Dulles.' He was checking up and down the street. 'You must be Moncrieff.'

'I am.'

'Come in.' The handshake was firm.

Moncrieff followed him through to a sitting room. Red drapes framed the tall windows and a small table was almost invisible beneath a nest of bottles. Logs were piled on either side of the open fireplace, and among the stand of framed photographs on the nearby piano Moncrieff recognised Franklin D. Roosevelt and Harry Truman standing in front of a sizeable crowd, hand in hand, their arms aloft.

'Chicago.' Dulles was filling his pipe. 'Democratic conventions can be fun but that one was special. A fourth term? Could he pull it off? No one in that stadium had the slightest doubt. That's the measure of the man. He's a born persuader. Take my word on it, democracy needs more FDRs.'

He rounded on Moncrieff and waved him into an armchair. With his moustache, and rimless glasses, and slightly worn jacket, he might have belonged in a university, maybe a professor of some kind, but there was a briskness in his every movement that spoke of a more worldly calling. He struck a match, used his thumb to give the bowl of the pipe a final tamp, and briefly disappeared behind a cloud of blue smoke. When he emerged, the question couldn't have been briefer.

'Wuensche?' he asked.

Moncrieff explained about Camp 165, up in the wilds of Scotland. The prisoners there were all high-value, experienced officers who'd served with distinction.

'These men think for themselves,' he said. 'My understanding is that the possibility of repatriation was put to Wuensche, and he declined.'

'On what grounds?'

'He regarded it as a form of betrayal.'

'Of the regime?' Dulles looked briefly startled.

'Of his fellow prisoners. The authorities up there have tried to foster an *esprit de corps*, and it appears to have worked. One for all, all for one.'

'Remarkable.' Dulles permitted himself a bark of laughter. 'I almost believe you.'

'Here.' Moncrieff, eager to get beyond SS *Obersturmbannführer* Wuensche, had produced a list of other names.

'And these are...?' Dulles was running his pipe stem down the page.

'German POWs, obviously. Are they of lesser importance? I'm afraid the answer is yes, but in every case the prisoner has indicated a willingness to be sent home.'

Dulles nodded, a gesture of dismissal. Given the circumstances, he said, Wuensche was the only candidate who would pass muster and in any case time and events had moved on.

'Meaning?'

'Meaning we don't need an *amuse-gueule* any more.'

Moncrieff smiled. He liked dialogue like this, give-and-take spiced with a slightly acid wit. The notion of Hitler's favourite adjutant offered as a titbit at the tables of the mighty was a moment he knew Ursula Barton would appreciate.

'So where are we with Wolff?' Moncrieff enquired.

'We?' Dulles voice had hardened.

'We,' Moncrieff confirmed. 'Last time I checked we were fighting this war together. Isn't that still the case? Or do the English always jump to the wrong conclusions?'

The boldness of the question took Dulles by surprise. He sucked at his pipe for a moment, never taking his eyes off his visitor.

'You're MI5,' he said at last. 'Am I right?'

'Yes.'

'I had lunch with one of your guys yesterday. He's attached to the embassy. He's MI6 and he was wondering why on earth you and Mrs Barton have bothered to turn up in this town. He gave me the impression that your colleagues have everything under control, everything taken care of, no need to panic.'

'Colleagues?'

'Broadway. MI6.' The smile was mirthless. 'Are they really colleagues? Maybe you'd prefer some other term...'

'Not at all. King and Country? We all drink from the same trough.'

'That I doubt.'

'Might I ask why?'

'I'm sure you don't have to. In DC, we spend more time fighting our friends than our enemies. Why would life be any less crazy in London?'

Moncrieff nodded, conceding the point. Espionage was a snake pit. Anyone naïve enough to think otherwise rarely survived.

'Tell me about Wolff,' he said again. 'Let's pretend we have a common interest here.'

Dulles pondered the suggestion for a moment or two. He used the pipe like a shield, striking another match, buying himself time. At length he expelled a plume of blue smoke and leaned forward, his elbows on his knees, a gesture – Moncrieff realised – of faux intimacy. Trust me, he was saying. I can help you out here.

'Wolff is in Berlin just now. He's been there for several days. He's trying to cover his butt, which is exactly what Wuensche would have done, but that didn't work out as we all know so now he has to take care of Kaltenbrunner and Kesselring. They won't be easy conversations, believe me. Kesselring is old-school. Every bone in his body belongs to the Army. He's taken the soldier's oath and he has a reputation to protect. Kaltenbrunner is Wolff's boss and wants to open his own channels. Everyone in an SS uniform is running for cover, and that includes Himmler. These guys play hardball. Yesterday they took Wolff's family into protective custody to try and keep him in line. Wolff, since you've asked, can be reckless to the point of insanity. For an SS guy that makes him unusual. Or, on second thoughts, maybe not. Either way, you get that for free, my friend, but now I'm afraid Uncle Sam's pot is empty. Will the Krauts call time out in Italy? Offer some kind of surrender? I suspect the answer is yes, largely because the war, in any event, is coming to an end. Will *Reichsführer-SS* Wolff's advances hasten that process? Maybe. You want my advice? Go home to London and watch this space.'

Moncrieff was smiling again. The implications of this conversation couldn't be more obvious. He and Ursula Barton were interlopers, babes in the Swiss wood, poking around in the undergrowth, interested in issues that shouldn't concern them. Best to beat a retreat and mind their own business.

'And afterwards?' Moncrieff enquired.

'After what?'

'After the war ends? What then? What becomes of us all? You and your buddies? Us amateurs back home? Germany? The Thousand Year Reich?'

Dulles sat back in the chair, then his eyes strayed to the nest of photos on the piano.

'You want my opinion? In confidence? One spy to another? FDR's a sick man. He won't last the course. Truman's cut from plainer cloth. He's Midwest, born and raised. He has none of the Chief's artfulness. He's a regular guy and thinks just the same as all the other regular guys. Europe is a busted flush and the way Truman will figure it, you folks over here have just spent half the war waiting for us to finish the thing. My guess is this. The Germans will surrender because they have no choice and the war will come to an end. We'll spend a bunch of money putting you all on your feet, Germany especially, and then we'll amuse ourselves elsewhere. I might be wrong. We might hang around a while. But if that Prime Minister of yours thinks the days of the British Empire aren't numbered, then he's even more senile than I'm led to believe.'

'And Russia?'

'The Russians have been half bled to death and they won't let that happen again. They own half of Europe already and they won't let go. Every alliance in history has an eat-by date. The Russians are perpetually hungry. That's a fact. Yalta proved it. So I guess we should bolt our doors and keep the wolves at bay.' He got to his feet and extended a hand. 'Good luck, Mr Moncrieff. From where we Yanks are standing, I suspect you'll need it.'

*

Moncrieff took a different route back to the hotel. The clouds over Bern had at last parted and there was a hint of real warmth in the sun. He lingered for a moment on the promenade, gazing down at the blue-green water, watching a rowing eight pushing hard against the current, and then strolled on until he found a restaurant with a view of a fountain depicting an ogre stuffing children into his mouth. It was lunchtime by now, and the restaurant looked full, but a word in the ear of maître d' secured Moncrieff a small table tucked beside the fall of curtain at the window. The ogre, he'd decided, had to be some kind of Swiss joke. After a child or two, more chocolate.

The aromas coming from the open kitchen door made him realise how hungry he was, and when the waitress arrived he ordered half a bottle of Gewürztraminer and a dish of *Älpermagronen*, a creamy gratin he'd first eaten in his student days in Locarno. The waitress nodded at the surrounding tables and warned him that the food might be a while arriving. Unbidden, she went to the nearby rack of newspapers and returned with a copy of that morning's *Neue Zürcher Zeitung*, a gesture that pleased Moncrieff because it meant that she took him for a native Swiss.

He glanced at the front page. General Patton's tanks were within a hundred kilometres of Leipzig. French First Army units had occupied Karlsruhe, while troops from the US 90th Division had liberated gold and a huge collection of art treasures from a salt mine near Bad Hersfeld. Moncrieff looked up, savouring this glimpse of the wider war. Allen Dulles, the face of the OSS in Europe, had been stating the obvious in anticipating the end of hostilities. No country, no regime, could survive an onslaught like this and everyone knew it. The Swiss, as far as Moncrieff could judge, kept their heads down, untroubled by the thunder of Allied armies as they battled to be first to Berlin, and in many ways Moncrieff couldn't blame them. Blessed with the biggest mountain range in Western Europe, they'd sensibly hunkered down in their lush valleys and were now waiting for the storm to blow itself out. War, he thought, was a foreign virus for these people. On no account should it affect the steady pulse of Swiss daily life.

He stared out at the cobbled street. More shoppers. More arcades. More opportunities for well-dressed woman to pause beside a window display of gift-wrapped chocolates, or diamond brooches, or handmade boots, and reach lazily into their leather handbags for a purse bursting with Swiss francs. This, after all, was the whole point of the war. If Dulles was right, and Europe got back on its feet with help from American largesse, then the good times would return. Where that might leave Britain, bereft of empire, was anyone's guess but for Moncrieff the sight of Ursula Barton, alone at her table in the empty hotel restaurant, had made a deep impression. Fretful, exhausted, gnawing at her ruined nails, she seemed to speak for the larger nation that had, by the skin of its teeth, weathered these years of struggle. Soon, thought Moncrieff, the killing and the dying would be over and with luck he'd be back to the silence and solace of the mountains he loved.

He glanced down at the *Zeitung* again, then a movement on the pavement outside caught his eye. Instinctively, he opened the paper and nudged his chair back until the curtain hid him from the street. If he was right, the figure in the long black leather coat would appear any second. And he did. Cropped hair. Bony face. Deep-set eyes behind steel-rimmed glasses. He came to a halt for a moment, half hidden in the swirl of pedestrians, and then the crowd parted to reveal him once again and this time Moncrieff knew that his instincts had served him well. The last time he'd seen this man was outside the railway station at Locarno, the evening he'd first met De Vries. Was he really a Serb? Was this the killer who'd crept into Hannalore's darkroom and put an ice pick through her skull? And if so, what was Agent *Crusader* doing here in Bern?

He was crossing the road now, signalling to someone on the other side, some faceless accomplice in the shadowed arcade. Two of them, Moncrieff thought. He glanced at his watch. There was still no sign of the promised meal, and it wasn't too late to leave the restaurant and melt into the lunchtime crowds, but something told Moncrieff that this would be folly. One of them he could probably evade. Two argued for an uglier outcome.

Crusader was crossing the road again, pointing at the restaurant. His accomplice was behind him, pausing to avoid a woman on a bicycle. He was shorter, well-built, younger, but he had the same sallow complexion, the same deadness in his eyes, and the moment he hit the pavement Moncrieff knew at least one of them would come into the restaurant. It was *Crusader*, the older man. Moncrieff raised the newspaper, hiding his face as he heard the door open, praying that the waitress didn't choose this moment to arrive with his order. The door had closed again but there was no way of knowing whether his tail had gone or not. For how long had he been followed? And how on earth had he known about the visit to Bern?

'*Entschuldigen Sie?*' Excuse me?

It was the waitress. Moncrieff did his best to make room for the food without revealing his face but his very awkwardness stirred the waitress's interest.

'*Geht es Ihnen gut, sir?*' Are you OK?

Moncrieff smiled up at her, said everything was fine, gestured at an article in this morning's *Zeitung*, apologised for his rudeness, asked her to leave the plate and the wine. She gazed down at him, mystified, then did his bidding. Then she was gone.

Moncrieff let another minute or so tick by. The gratin smelled wonderful, and he could already taste that first glass of Gewürztraminer. Then, very slowly, he lowered the paper, checking carefully round. Of the two figures from the street, there was no sign.

*

Back at the hotel, an hour or so later, he knocked on Barton's door. She was in the process of photographing the De Vries print he'd brought from Locarno. The sheets on her bed were rumpled and, judging by her smile, she'd managed to catch up on her sleep. When she asked about Dulles, Moncrieff pulled a face. The Americans, he said, had already decided the course of the war. Patton was racing for Berlin while here in the shadows, the OSS were skirmishing with an equally fierce intensity. Dulles wanted no one on his turf, least of all a couple of trespassers from MI5.

'And Six? Broadway? The so-called attachés at the embassy?'

'I get the impression they compare notes.'

'About us?'

'Very probably.'

He told her about the Watchers outside the restaurant, the face he'd recognised from the train, how close he'd come to being trapped.

'Someone's on to me,' he said. 'Someone knew I was coming here. Maybe they followed me to the Herrengasse. They certainly picked me up on the way out.'

'That would mean they knew about this place.'

'Exactly.'

Barton nodded. She was using one of the tiny specialist cameras supplied by the technicians at St James's Street, and now she put it carefully to one side. At the window she paused for a moment, staring down at the street outside the hotel, and when Moncrieff put the question again, wanting to know how anyone could possibly have been so well briefed about his

307

movements, she waited for a moment or two before turning back to him.

'Our embassy's in Thunstrasse,' she said. 'It's big, bigger than we really need. It has plenty of accommodation.' She forced a smile. 'Haven't you wondered why I prefer us to be here?'

20

It was early afternoon before Dieter Merz took off from the airfield at Rechlin. Schultz was in the rear cockpit, beginning to sweat in the warmth of the sun through the Perspex canopy. He had the Loden coat folded on his lap and he could feel the outline of the Beretta in one of the pockets. That, at least, was a comfort and he sat back and closed his eyes as the aircraft began to roll, his feet on a large wooden box of aircraft spares.

He'd last been in an Me-110 four long years ago, en route to Lisbon with Merz once again at the controls, and nothing appeared to have changed. The same smell of engine oil and unburned exhaust. The same sharp tug of the safety harness when Merz wheeled onto the runway and braked before gunning the engines. The same choking sense of claustrophobia that quickened the thunder of his own pulse. Until he went to Russia, Schultz had a been a stranger to fear but flying he still detested.

They lifted off, and Schultz opened his eyes to watch the shadow of the plane grow smaller as it raced across the fields beyond the airstrip. Rechlin was an hour north of Berlin by road, a couple of sizeable hangars and a nearby production facility where engineers battled to launch new prototypes in a war that everyone agreed was lost. Enemy aircraft, according to Merz, would appear overhead from time to time. Untroubled by the *Luftwaffe*, they'd drop a line of bombs along the runway and then depart, leaving gangs of Polish prisoners to fill the smouldering craters.

These visitations, Merz said, had become a ritual, a gesture largely devoid of any real significance, simply a poke or two at the cooling corpse that was Germany, and everybody at Rechlin knew it. As for Merz himself, he was happy to put the new aircraft through their test programmes, and happier still to fly consignments, and occasionally personnel, into neutral Switzerland. If you knew where to go, Zurich and Basel and Bern could be the treasure house of your dreams. Both Beata and Lottie adored Swiss chocolate.

They flew low, Merz alert for enemy fighters, and when the Alps began to loom ahead he dropped lower still before roaring into Swiss airspace. Schultz, who'd managed to trick his body into sleep, woke up to the blur of a tiny village flashing by beneath the wings. A snatched glimpse of two women in conversation outside a church. A figure with a hoe, surrounded by what looked like cabbages, gazing skywards, shielding his eyes against the glare of the sun. Disturbed cattle running amok on pastureland newly greened by spring.

Finally, minutes later, Merz raised the Bern controller on the radio and sought permission to land. The airfield was smaller than Schultz had imagined and after clearing his path through the immigration checks, Merz led him to a taxi at the front of the terminal building. Schultz gave a driver the address of the hotel and turned back to Merz who was flying on to an air force base near Zurich where engineers were awaiting delivery of the Messerschmitt spares.

'Good luck.' Merz was watching a ground crew refuelling his Me-110. 'I'll be back by noon tomorrow.'

*

Within minutes, Schultz found himself in the middle of the city. After the desolation of Berlin, briefly glimpsed last night, Bern was another world. Stockholm, he thought, gazing out at the busy streets, the couples on park benches enjoying the last of the afternoon warmth, the cake stands in café windows, brimming with numberless gateaux.

At the Hotel Felix, Schultz waited at the table that served as a reception desk. The woman in charge was on the phone. The conversation over, he asked about a Mrs Barton. She stared up at him for a moment, and then checked her watch.

'I'm afraid she's out. Would you care to leave a message Herr...?'

'... Schultz.' It was a male voice this time, someone very close. The receptionist was smiling now, making a note of the name, expressing her thanks.

'*Gern geschehen*,' said the voice. Always happy to help.

Perfect German, Schultz thought, with just a hint of a Scots accent if you knew where to look. Another voice from his past. Not just Dieter Merz, but the tall ex-Marine he'd never quite fathomed out.

'Moncrieff?' At last, he turned round. This, he knew, was no place for a proper conversation. Might there be a bar here?

*

There was. The receptionist directed them to a smallish space at the rear of the hotel and lifted the phone to summon the barmaid. The bar itself was U-shaped with enough stools for half a dozen drinkers. Well-stocked shelves offered a choice of beers and spirits, and there was plenty of wine as long as you bought by the bottle.

'Why are you here, Schultz?' Moncrieff was pleased to see him. 'Nothing happens in your life by accident.'

'You're right.' Schultz had settled for a glass of Flensburger. 'And you?'

'King and Country, as ever. If they tell me to come to Switzerland, what choice does a patriot have?'

'That's not an answer,' Schultz grunted. 'A man needs more clues.'

'*Verboten*, I'm afraid. I'm instructed not to talk to strangers, least of all someone in your line of business. Wonderful coat, by the way. And why are you so thin?'

Schultz studied him. This moment had come rather more quickly than he'd expected, and the presence of Moncrieff was a surprise, but he was well prepared. He nodded at the smallest of the three tables, the one that offered the most privacy.

'You mind, my friend? Old habits die hard.'

Moncrieff followed him to the table, enquired about life in Berlin.

'I work for *Onkel Heine* and those bastards at the SD these days,' Schultz growled. 'You may have heard. Canaris did his best but he's in Flossenbürg now, breaking rocks.'

'So I understand.' The head of the *Abwehr*, never a fan of the Nazi hooligans, was suspected of designs on the Führer's life. 'So how did you know how to find us?'

'Himmler knows everything. That's part of his charm. This country is like their fucking cheese, Moncrieff. It stinks of money and it's full of holes.'

'You're telling me Himmler sent you?'

'Of course.'

'Why would he do that?'

'Because he's losing his grip. Hitler gave him an Army Group to play with. When he fucked up, Hitler started biting the carpet. At that point, *Heine* booked himself into a sanatorium and sulked. Himmler could never work a crowd like his master but he's not without talent when it comes to the paperwork. He knows how to organise and he's got this spooky fucking thing about reading the runes, but his problem just now is that the runes don't need reading. We're all about to be fucked, fucked royally, fucked from every direction, and *Heine* wants that to happen on his own terms. Big problem, Moncrieff. Because it turns out he's not the only one. There's a noise just now in Berlin, a bit of a rustle, a bit of a scamper, and if you listen hard it will tell you everything. Rats. Everywhere. And some of them even have whiskers and a tail. You ask me what I'm doing here? I've been charged with rodent control, Moncrieff. And we understand you have a photograph that might help.'

'We?'

'Me...' he emptied his glass, '... and my lovely boss.'

'You're telling me you're here on Himmler's direct orders?'

'I'm telling you I'm a good little soldier. Berlin was always a madhouse but these days the lunatics are out of control. One mistake, one word in the wrong ear, and it's four o'clock in the morning and the car's waiting outside. If they kill you on the spot, you're a lucky man. Normally, it's Prinz-Albrecht-Strasse.' He nodded. 'And they always take you downstairs.'

Moncrieff nodded. The basement at Gestapo headquarters housed the torture suites. He'd been there himself. Even pre-war, they knew how to strap a man to a see-saw bench and fill his lungs with ice-cold water, an experience he remembered sharing with Schultz a year or so later on a winter's night in a Stockholm bar.

'But you've survived so far?' Moncrieff asked. 'Is that what you're telling me?'

'Not really. Just getting by is exhausting. You're looking out for yourself day and night. Everything you say, everything you might be silly enough to put on paper, could be a death sentence. Look at the state of me. You're right. I'm a wreck, Moncrieff, but at least I'm fucking *alive*.'

Moncrieff sat back and signalled for another round of drinks. He'd never seen Schultz like this. What had happened to the brawler in the battered leather jacket he'd known and respected in Paris? In Nuremberg? In Sweden? In Lisbon? How come an operator who knew and understood the value of reticence could suddenly have so much to say? Where was the iron nerve? The talent for mischief and carefully baited traps? The ceaseless calculation behind those scary eyes? Gone, he thought. But why?

The drinks arrived. Schultz scarcely spared the waitress a glance.

'This photograph...' Moncrieff was toying with his glass. 'What does it concern?'

'An SS General. His name is Wolff, Karl Wolff. He's made a name for himself in certain circles and there was a time when Hitler loved him.'

'And now?'

'Hitler loves nobody. And that puts the shits up *Onkel Heine*. I count you as a friend, Moncrieff, or perhaps a *Kamerad*. Himmler thinks Wolff has ratted, and he wants proof. Can I make it any plainer? Or do you want me on my knees?'

'No need, Willi. But what makes you think we have this photograph?'

'We know you do.'

'Then you've seen it already?'

'Of course not. I wouldn't be here otherwise.'

'But you know this man? Wolff?'

'Yes.'

'How?'

'We had dealings in Berlin a couple of years ago. He's in Italy now, the *Kapo*, the man in charge. But I'm sure you know that already.'

Moncrieff didn't answer, not directly. Instead he reached for his beer and took a long pull.

'Just suppose this photo exists,' he said carefully. 'Would you want to take it away?'

'Yes. In a perfect world, yes. You could call it a favour. You could call it whatever you like. You could do it because we go way back when the war was a pleasure and we both knew it. The state we're in just now, believe me, no photograph will make the slightest difference to anything. Whatever happens, like I just said, we're fucked.'

'And if you couldn't take it away? The photo?'

'Then at least I can say I've seen it, that I know what it's about. Believe it or not, Moncrieff, I still carry a little weight with people who matter.'

Moncrieff nodded, said he didn't doubt that for a moment. Then he paused. One final question, he thought. Then I need to talk to Barton.

'Tell me, Schultz. What do you think about Walter? Why did they kill him?'

'You mean Schellenberg?'

'Yes.'

Schultz held his gaze. His eyes were unblinking, his face totally impassive.

'I can't talk about that,' he murmured. 'And you'll know the reason why.'

*

Ursula Barton returned to the hotel minutes later. The receptionist helpfully directed her to the bar, and Moncrieff made the introductions. Schultz, who once paid at least lip service to the smaller courtesies, didn't get up.

'Give me half an hour.' Moncrieff was looking down at him. 'Don't leave.'

Moncrieff escorted Barton up to her room.

'That's *the* Wilhelm Schultz? The *Abwehr*'s star turn?'

'Yes. I'm afraid he's seen better days but that probably applies to all of us. Just now, he says he's working for Himmler.'

'The SD?'

'Yes.'

'And we believe him?'

'I'm not sure. I laid a trap about Schellenberg at the end of our conversation, but he was clever enough to spot it. Something's happened to him, something he's not admitting, and this evening I'll find out exactly what, but in the meantime he wants a look at De Vries's photo.'

'How does he know it exists?'

'Very good question. What were those two Serbs doing outside my restaurant window?'

'*Touché.*' Barton settled herself on the bed. She looked exhausted again. 'I've been at the embassy most of the afternoon. It wasn't easy but I managed to access the visitor log. Comings and goings, mainly local, of course, but the occasional state visit from Broadway, as well.'

'Like?'

'You're not going to enjoy this, Tam.'

'Really?' he stared at her, already sensing the name that was shaping on her lips. 'You mean Philby?'

'I'm afraid so.'

'He's been here recently?'

'Last week. He arrived the day before you flew down. By that time, I'd negotiated the deal for the Lysander. If you knew where to look, your destination would have been common knowledge. Annemasse? On the Swiss border? Philby would be on to that in seconds. He stayed here for three days. Plenty of time to get everything organised. That's where the Serbs came from. That accounts for De Vries's friend. Even for the ice pick. Philby may be psychopathic but at least he's got a sense of humour.'

Moncrieff nodded. Three years ago, prompted by Barton's belief that Broadway's rising star might be taking his orders from Moscow, the pair of them had done their best to lure Philby into a trap. The consequences had been catastrophic, not least for Moncrieff, and since then Philby's standing at MI6 appeared to have become unassailable. Recently, Moncrieff had even heard rumours that, post-war, he might one day be the favoured candidate to run the entire organisation.

Barton had gone into the bathroom and shut the door. Moncrieff heard the splash of water, and then she was back again, drying her face with a towel.

'So how do we play this?' Moncrieff asked. 'What do you want me to do?'

'Schultz is still with us?'

'He'll be downstairs. He wants De Vries's photo.'

'Why?'

'He says it's for Himmler. Schultz plays the postman, makes the delivery. He says everyone's running for cover in Berlin and I believe him. Laying hands on the photo might buy his own survival. That's the implication.'

Barton – a frail, tormented figure – was looking at her hands. Moncrieff had always been surprised by how suddenly the strongest individuals could cave in under pressure, and here was the living proof. In both peace and war she'd always been resolute, a forbidding presence at Guy Liddell's elbow, unsparing with herself and others, demanding the highest standards of performance and probity, refusing to yield as the country threatened to buckle under the sheer volume of strangers knocking at its door. In her small corner of the organisation, she'd weathered that storm, coaxed order out of chaos, steadied colleagues who were visibly wilting beneath the mad torrent of events, and yet here she was, her head bowed, gnawing at yet another nail, irresolute, overwhelmed.

'I'm leaving it to you, Tam.' She looked up at him. 'Take the photo. Make your own decision. One favour though...' Her hand crabbed across the bed towards the camera. 'Take this, too. I want a shot of Schultz.'

'Might I ask why?'

'Very good question.' She was staring up at him. 'There's a file to be built, Tam, the whole sordid story, and one day, God help me, I'm going to make sure that happens.'

God help me? Moncrieff knew exactly what she meant. This war, in the end, was simply too big, too voracious, too all-consuming for any single individual. Whole armies, tens of thousands of men, fighting on, posting small or less small victories. Bomber fleets destroying entire cities, street by street, raid by raid. Propaganda machines feasting on lies while street gossip offered the uncertain comforts of a homelier truth: that the world had gone mad, that the war had developed a crazy momentum of its own, that nothing you'd ever taken for granted would be spared in this final conflagration. Wars, he thought, are so easy to start. And after that, in numberless ways, they demanded a constant surrender. *Katastrophe* indeed. Writ large, and – in the case of Ursula Barton – writ small.

The feeling of numbness at the sight of a woman he'd learned to respect wouldn't leave him. Like so many others, she'd been barged aside by the pressure of events, something he'd never seen coming and even now didn't quite believe, and a little of this bewilderment he needed to share with Schultz.

The hotel receptionist had recommended a small restaurant in a cul-de-sac five minutes' walk towards the river. It served very good fish and the owner knew his wine. Schultz said he wasn't hungry but Moncrieff insisted. A mere exchange of information, he insisted, wasn't enough. They needed to talk, and if that was too high a price for Schultz then Moncrieff quite understood. Nice to meet you again after such a long time. *Auf Wiedersehen und viel Gluck.* Goodbye and good luck.

*

'So what's this about?' Apart from a lone cleric picking at the remains of a trout, the restaurant was empty.

'Us, Schultz.'

'Us?'

'You and me.'

Schultz stared at him, still evasive, then shook his head. 'Are you drunk, Moncrieff? Is this some kind of proposition? What have you been hiding all these years? Is it true what they say about the English? One hand on your wallet? The other on your cock?'

Schultz, as Moncrieff understood only too well, wanted him to laugh. The prospect of a meal had been unwelcome, of a proper conversation plainly even less so. Better to trade banter, play the fool, have a few drinks, do whatever deal on the photo, and then retire to their separate corners of this contented little city. Safe, Moncrieff thought. That's what he wants. That's what we all want.

'Rules of engagement, Schultz. I have the photo but we have to talk, too.'

319

'About what?'

'About your war, and about mine.'

'Why?'

'Because there comes a time when you have to sit it down, and make it pay attention, and ask it a serious question or two. We let this thing happen, Schultz, all of us, and it might be wise to ask how, and perhaps why.'

Schultz, for the first time, seemed to understand.

'You're serious?'

'I am.'

'And the photo?'

'Forget the bloody photo.'

'But you really have it?'

'I do. The photo is for later. The photo comes after the cheese course, after the dessert. The photo, believe me, will resolve nothing. The photo is dust in the wind. The photo is a footnote to all the madness. We're not in some trench, Schultz. We're not at twenty thousand feet frightened to death of never getting home. We're in Switzerland. This is where peace happens. This is where people get fat and happy and graze their cattle and make their cheeses and found another bank or two and get even fatter and even happier and turn their backs on the rest of the world. If we can't talk now, here, just the two of us, then you're right, we're well and truly fucked.'

Schultz lifted an eyebrow, then reached for the *carte des vins* and slumped back in his chair, silent. There was a glimpse of Ursula Barton in his gesture, Moncrieff thought. He could detect just a hint of despairing resignation but with it came something else. Deeper down, he'd touched a nerve in this man. Maybe he, too, wanted to talk. Maybe the war had been too much even for Wilhelm Schultz.

'Well?' Moncrieff asked.

Schultz was frowning. He seemed to be the prisoner of some unfathomable dilemma. Finally, he tossed the *carte des vins* aside.

'Chateauneuf-du-Pape,' he said. 'To begin with.'

For a while, not very long, they sparred. Then the waiter brought a basket of rolls, and Moncrieff watched Schultz's big hands tearing the warm dough apart, not a crumb on the tablecloth safe from stabs with his moistened finger while he talked about his early days in the *Abwehr* under a new director freshly arrived from the *Reichsmarine*, Wilhelm Canaris. Canaris, he said, was hard to read, a compliment in Schultz's book, and from his shared office in the Bendlerblock overlooking the Landwehr Canal, Schultz had slowly come to realise that the hooligans who'd seized the Weimar Republic by the scruff of the neck and shaken it to death, who'd swept into the ministries along the Wilhelmstrasse, who'd smashed democracy in a matter of months and made a bonfire of the remains, that these murderous lunatics were not – as he'd begun to assume – entirely unchallenged. On the contrary, there were still decent men, patriots, Germans for whom history offered something more than the executioner's axe and the bended knee.

'They tried, Moncrieff. They truly did. Back in '38, they had the ear of the Generals. Hitler always understood the power of the present. Kicking the French out of the Rhineland was a present. Marching into Austria was a present. So far, so fucking good. Every day was Christmas. The Führer would build an *Autobahn* all the way to Vienna. These people were our people. They spoke our language. *Heil Hitler.* Happy New Year. But the Sudetenland? Then the rest of Czecho? Was the man serious? Did he want London and Paris on our backs? Did he want us all in the trenches again? Even that old warhorse Beck thought no fucking way. But then you know all this.'

Moncrieff nodded. It was true. The first time he'd met Wilhelm Schultz was back in 1938, first Paris, then Berlin, and finally Nuremberg. Moncrieff had been the apprentice spy, fresh from service with the Royal Marines, fluent in German, eager to return to a continent he'd loved. Schultz, by then, was already a veteran, an ex-street fighter with Ernst Röhm's *Sturmabteilung*, and a survivor of the murderous Night of the Long Knives. Discretion, and a growing distaste for Nazi manners, had taken him to military intelligence, and to an ever-widening set of responsibilities, because he was sharp, and spoke the language of the streets, and had the wits and the raw nerve to handle the worst that the demented Nazi regime could dream up.

'We let you down, Schultz. Halifax? Chamberlain? We both know the *Wehrmacht* would have marched on Berlin and put paid to Hitler had Munich never happened.'

'*May* have marched. It was a prospect, Moncrieff, a thought to salve the Prussian conscience. Loyalty's bred in these peoples' bones. Like it or not, Hitler was the Chancellor, got himself elected. They'd sworn the Soldier's Oath. The fact that their precious Führer was also a madman was awkward but as long as he kept delivering those presents no one really minded.'

'But how about you? What did you think at the time?'

'I'd seen these people close up when I was with the Brownshirts. I knew the way they operated, what they were capable of. Most of them stayed in the gutter. The ones who didn't ended up running the fucking country, and most of Europe as well. You want to know when I knew we were finished?'

'We?'

'The *Abwehr*. What remained of our conscience. It was '39. Hitler had bluffed his way into the Sudetenland, and then the rest of Czecho, and now it was the Polacks' turn. By now, even you Brits realised just how dangerous this man was but by then it was

far too late. Hitler made a speech in the Reichstag the day before
we jumped on the Poles. A load of us from the Bendlerblock were
ordered to attend. There were maybe a hundred men in uniform
there. The rest of them were politicians, all of them with shiny
knees and half the Wilhelmstrasse up their slimy arses. Hitler
was crap that day, couldn't raise the old magic, didn't bother,
but that wasn't the point. The point was what he was wearing.
Just guess, Moncrieff. Imagine you're there. Imagine you've got
a perfect view. What's the man *wearing?*'

Moncrieff shook his head, said he hadn't the first clue.

'An SS uniform, my friend. Black. He had it specially made
for him a couple of days earlier. Later I met the tailor who'd done
the fitting, made the little alterations. Hitler had started to put
on weight. All those creamed potatoes. All those eggs. All that
Kaffee und Kuchen routine at the Berghof. But even that wasn't
the point. The point was the uniform itself. Hitler had got the
better of the Generals, and that meant he'd got the better of us,
too. No one cared about military intelligence any more because
the only name in town that mattered was Himmler's, and he
was there in the front row in the Reichstag, with that smug little
smile on his face. Why? Because the SS had won. Because to
matter at all you had to wear black. At first, we didn't believe it.
Then we were into Poland, kicking the shit out of the Polacks,
and no one realised what was going on behind the front line. In
the *Wehrmacht* you carry a rifle and take your chances with the
enemy. With the *Einsatzgruppen*, those odds don't apply. You
do exactly as you please, kill whoever you like, make them dig
their own graves first. They call it tidying up. Hitler, it turns
out, hates dirt of any kind. Punctilious, our Leader. Keeps his
nails clean.'

Moncrieff nodded. It was impossible to mistake this vehemence
for anything but disgust.

'And you were helpless? Is that what you're saying?'

'We were. Why? Because nothing wins an argument quicker than success. Within a month, Poland didn't exist. The French Army, by and large, were still in barracks. The British hadn't lifted a finger. No one was ready for Hitler, not because he hadn't warned them what was coming, but because they hadn't listened. That's how this war started, Moncrieff. Because none of you fucking *listened*.'

Moncrieff nodded. Both glasses were empty, and the waiter arrived to refill them. Without sparing him a glance, Schultz ordered another bottle.

'This is on me, my friend.'

'Himmler's paying?'

'I'm paying.' Schultz raised his glass.

'To peace?'

'To Châteauneuf.'

Moncrieff smiled. The wine was delicious.

'We last met in Lisbon, Willi. You were kind enough to deliver a letter from Goering. Hess wanted to end the war but Churchill wouldn't have it. Remember all that?'

'Of course I do. You were fucking a lady who'd fled to Moscow and joined the Revolution.'

'Bella Menzies.'

'That's right. We'd all known her in Berlin before the war. Credit to the woman. Given what we all did for a living, no one had the first clue her interests extended beyond the British Embassy. Did you ever know? As a matter of interest?'

'Never.'

'And it never made a difference? Afterwards?'

'Obviously not.'

'Then credit to you, too, my friend. The spirit is willing but the flesh is weak? Bullshit. The Bible had it wrong. Flesh, every time. Flesh, always. The spirit stands no fucking chance. She was a good-looking woman. She knew how to make people laugh, even Nazis, and in Berlin that took real talent, believe me.' He paused. 'You must miss her.'

'I do.'

'Then I'm sorry. And I mean that.' He reached for his glass. 'Bella.'

'Bella,' Moncrieff said tonelessly. 'You were there, Schultz. You were there in Kyiv. I only got to see that photo you sent very recently. Barton had been keeping it to herself,' a thin smile, 'until she thought I was ready.'

'And were you?'

'No. But then I suspect I'll never be ready.'

Schultz nodded. He wanted, he said, to offer a little advice.

'Don't be too glum, Moncrieff. Life is shit already. Don't make it worse.'

'I'm a Scot. You're right, we brood. It's in the blood. You can hear it in the music we make. The bagpipes didn't happen by accident. A call to arms and a call to prayer. Hopeless. We're Celts. We can't help ourselves.'

'That's what your lady told me.'

'About?'

'You. If it matters, she thought it made you a good man.'

'And that was a compliment?'

'Yes. She also said you couldn't help yourself, which I'm guessing is the same thing. Good by nature is the best it gets. That's her saying it, not me.'

'You were close? The pair of you? In Kyiv?'

'We were. She needed help and I was happy to do whatever I could.'

'So what happened?'

'You don't want to know.'

'I do, Schultz. Otherwise I wouldn't have asked you.'

Schultz nodded, lifting his glass, eycing Moncrieff over the brim. He swallowed a mouthful of wine, then another.

'She upset our friends in black,' he said at last.

'The SS?'

'Yes.'

'And?'

'They made her pay for it.'

'How?'

'It doesn't matter.'

'It does, Willi. Just bloody tell me.'

'OK,' Schultz shrugged. 'First they had her raped. Twice. Then, a while later, they killed her. There.' He sat back. 'Does that make you feel better?'

Moncrieff looked away. None of this was really a surprise. By defecting to Moscow in the first place, Bella had declared her determination to risk the possibility of an ugly ending. Her life in Moscow, according to her own laconic account, hadn't sharpened her appetite for Lenin's brave new world but at least she'd survived. In Kyiv, on the other hand, she plainly hadn't.

'So what took her there?' Moncrieff asked softly. 'Last time I saw her, she was heading for Moscow. What changed?'

'She thought she'd been betrayed.'

'By whom? Someone in Moscow?'

Schultz shook his head but didn't answer.

'Someone closer to home?'

A shrug, this time.

'Someone English? Someone I might know? This is in your gift, Willi. You work for Himmler. Soon I might show you the photo you're after. That's one scalp for your belt. Give me a name, and that's two reasons Himmler might look fondly upon you. Assuming, of course, that you're really here on his behalf.'

'You think I'm not?

'I've no idea. I just want the name, Willi. The name of whoever wanted her dead. Not the SS. Not some psychopath in a black uniform. But whoever it was that needed protection. This is simple logic, Willi. She knew too much for her own good. Whoever betrayed her, in the eyes of Moscow, was more important. Don't tell me you can't follow that. Don't tell me she didn't give you the name herself. You know, Willi. You *know*.'

'Whose war are you fighting? Ours? Or your own?'

'Ours?' Moncrieff blinked. 'You said *ours*?'

'I did, my friend. And that's the only clue you get. Here comes our friend, thank Christ.'

The waiter arrived with the new bottle of Châteauneuf-du-Pape, already uncorked. Schultz told him to leave it on the table. Then he returned to Moncrieff.

'The photo?'

Moncrieff held his gaze, and then shrugged. He slipped the photo from the envelope and slid it across the tablecloth. Schultz studied it a moment, and then his thick finger hovered over the figure in the middle of the group.

'That's Wolff,' he grunted. 'The others I don't know.'

'But you're still in military intelligence.' Moncrieff feigned surprise. 'The other two are senior Allied officers, both of them Generals. You're really telling me you don't know?'

'I am, yes. You were right first time, Moncrieff. This photo is of no consequence. It's decaying food on the wrong shelf. Even if I was starving, I wouldn't give you ten pfennigs for it. We must eat, by the way. If only to do justice to this magnificent wine.'

*

It was midnight before they returned to the hotel. They'd spent hours over the meal, comparing notes, sharing the lighter moments of a war that had taken a while to sour. When pressed, Schultz had admitted to heading the *Abwehr* outpost at Stalingrad but insisted that he and his men had managed to get out on one of the last flights. Since then, he hinted vaguely at a series of other assignments but blamed his lack of recall on the battle Hitler had been careless enough to lose.

'They called it *der Kessel*,' Moncrieff had mused. *Der Kessel* meant 'cauldron'. 'Fair, do you think?'

'Fair? Bollocks. Hot things happen in cauldrons. Stalingrad was the deep freeze. You lost everything, chiefly hope. We were lucky. The other poor bastards weren't.'

It was at this stage, moments before Moncrieff settled the bill, that Schultz consented to have his photo taken. A souvenir, he agreed, would be more than fitting. He'd give Moncrieff a forwarding address for after the war's end.

Now, Moncrieff had a key to the hotel's main door. There were two single beds in his room, he said, and Schultz was welcome to one of them. Schultz nodded. He thought a nightcap might be in order.

'The barmaid's Swiss,' Moncrieff pointed out. 'I expect she's been in bed for hours.'

'Then we help ourselves. I'm German, remember. It's the closest we get to statecraft.'

Moncrieff laughed, leading the way to the bar. To his surprise, the lights were still on. As soon as he'd stepped inside, he froze. Two figures were sitting on stools at the empty bar, both nursing beers. The last time he'd seen them was lunchtime, through the window of the restaurant in the city centre where he'd eaten. The older of the two men produced a handgun and gestured for Moncrieff to raise his hands.

'*Crusader*,' Moncrieff murmured. 'What a pleasant surprise.'

The Serb didn't react. Moncrieff was aware of Schultz's presence behind him.

'Give me that camera,' he muttered.

'In my left pocket.'

Moncrieff, his hands still held high, felt the weight of the little camera leaving his coat pocket. Was Schultz somehow part of this ambush? Was he to lose all De Vries's prints? He prayed that the answer was no.

Schultz pushed past him. When the younger of the two men tried to block his path to the lavatory, Schultz gestured down at his own groin.

'You want me to piss all over you? A pleasure, my friend, but I can think of better ways of ending the evening.'

The Serb looked briefly surprised. Then he followed Schultz into the lavatory.

'Sit.' *Crusader* waved Moncrieff towards the table, taking the seat opposite, the gun steady in his hand. 'You have the photo?'

Moncrieff was beginning to regret the third bottle of Châteauneuf. Should he pretend an ignorance of German? Should he kick the table over and trust his long-ago unarmed combat skills? Or should he simply act the way he felt? Drunk and now suddenly angry.

'Who the fuck are you?' he said in German. 'And why *Crusader*? Have you got something to get off your chest? Or does it look nice on paper?'

'No business of yours.'

'Wrong, my friend. It's every business of mine. You killed a woman in Locarno? Yes?'

'You're talking crap.' A tiny upward tilt of the gun. 'Just give me the photo.'

'I haven't got it.'

'You're lying.'

'You want to take a look? You want to get a bit closer? You want to be rid of this fucking table? Be my guest.'

The Serb's eyes narrowed for a moment.

'So where is it?'

'It's upstairs. It's in my room. Let's go up there together, just you and me, see where it takes us. Would you like that? All you have to say is yes.'

'You're drunk.'

'I am. You know anything about the Scots?'

'The what?'

'The Scots? The ladies from hell? That's me, my friend. Bagpipes and a kilt and no quarter when it comes to the enemy. You know how the English think of Scotland? They think it's Balkan. They think it's wild. They think the rivers run with blood. And you know something else? Something that only you can confirm for real? They're right. The Scots are tribal. They're clan people. They love settling debts. And you know the worst news of all? They're bloody *good* at it.'

Crusader was frowning now, part impatience, part confusion. In theory, thought Moncrieff, he thinks this episode should have been over at the first time of asking. Moncrieff had no doubts that the gun was loaded, and the Serb doubtless presumed that any sane man would have done his bidding. Instead of which he now found himself on the receiving end of a torrent of Gaelic nonsense about blood feuds and retribution. Just another minute or so, thought Moncrieff. Just buy yourself time enough for Schultz to reappear. Two against two would be odds they could cope with.

But Schultz didn't reappear, a delay in proceedings that appeared to disturb the Serb even further. By now, after a couple of minutes on the iniquities of the Highland Clearances,

Moncrieff was describing the bloodier moments of the Battle of Bannockburn.

'Hundreds of bodies,' he nodded, sombre now. 'Many of them headless and all of them English. Is this really what you people want? Or might there be another way?'

There was. The lavatory door opened, and Moncrieff looked across the room to see Schultz emerging. Of the younger Serb, there was no sign. Schultz paused beside the bar and swallowed a mouthful of one of the beers. Then he came across to the table.

'The photo?' He was looking at Moncrieff. There was blood on his knuckles and a small cut above his right eye. When the Serb ordered him to sit down, he told him to shut the fuck up. 'The photo,' he said again. 'Just give it to me.'

Moncrieff shrugged. Did what he was told. The Serb's gun, to his intense satisfaction, was beginning to waver and it was his turn to keep checking the lavatory door.

Schultz shook the photo from its envelope, checked it briefly, then gave it to the Serb.

'Is this what you want?' The Serb glanced at it, then nodded. 'OK. This you get to keep. You need to sort out that friend of yours. He's in the lavatory. He might need a little help. After that, we never want to see you again. Do we understand each other? Or do we have to put it another way?'

The Serb was now looking at a small handgun that had appeared from the pocket of Schultz's Loden coat. Moncrieff saw it, too. It was a Beretta. Remarkable, he thought. Quite the old Schultz.

The Serb struggled to his feet and Schultz stood aside as he made for the lavatory. Then he returned to the bar and finished the beer on the counter.

'Key?' He was looking at Moncrieff. 'You need to let me out.'

Moncrieff accompanied him to the front door. In the chill of the street, Schultz briefly paused. Then he produced Barton's camera.

'*Gern.*' He pressed the camera into Moncrieff's hand. '*Wie immer.*'

A pleasure. As always.

Moncrieff stared at him, nonplussed, then looked down at the camera. Schultz lingered a moment longer. Then he was gone.

21

Nehmann spent two days prowling Berlin. By now it was early April, and on the first morning he left Maria and the child and took one of the few trains still running from Eichwalde, sitting beside the window as the carriage lurched and squealed towards the city centre on the recently repaired track. For some reason, all the glass in the carriage had been painted, and Nehmann stared out at the ruined streets through a mist of cyan blue as the trackside damage thickened. The effect, truly surreal, seemed to hold the city at arm's length. Berlin, he thought, has already become a ghost.

At stations closer to the *Hauptbahnhof*, the carriage began to fill with working men. Many of them were Ukrainian, loosely guarded. They wore the blue badge of the *Ostarbeiter*, and they brought with them the stale barracks smell that Nehmann recognised from the Kolyma camps. The bolder ones, he noticed, were starting to eye the prettier Berlin women, doubtless in anticipation of the moment the Red Army arrived and set them free.

Nehmann had a pad on his knee, scribbling notes as thoughts occurred to him. This, too, attracted disapproving glances from fellow passengers but Nehmann didn't care. Goebbels might want to see the first draft of the Hitler broadcast at any time, and so – like a visiting doctor – he had to take the temperature of the city and gauge the mood of its people. He needed ideas, impressions, points of departure. He needed to be ready.

That first day, he walked from district to district, trying to reimagine the city he'd known and loved from the handful of clues that remained. An advertising column that had once promised *thé dansant* and boxing tournaments was now covered with a jigsaw of more personal messages: the scribbled new addresses of bombed-out families, heartfelt appeals for lost relatives, even the offer of an entire apartment for the price of a pre-war holiday.

A hundred metres along the same street, he paused briefly to watch a stout woman in a dressing gown shovelling rubble out of a third-floor window in an apartment block he'd once visited. Two of the balconies had already gone and the woman retired moments later, leaving a brief silence broken almost at once by the sharp explosion of a falling tile from the building next door. If Berlin was a movie, Nehmann thought, then the soundtrack would tell you everything you needed to know: the gush of water from fractured mains, the squeal of a passing pram piled high with furniture, the squelch of countless boots tramping through mud thickened by brick dust and soot. Everyone, Nehmann noticed, walked in the middle of the street. Not because the view was better, but to avoid being crushed as yet another façade tottered and then noisily collapsed.

Everywhere Nehmann looked, the street corners and the restaurants, and the entrances to the U-Bahn, was thick with uniformed patrols. Some were *Wehrmacht*, others SS or police, and with the demand for papers went searching questions about how, exactly, each individual accounted for his time and his presence. Nehmann was curious about these interrogations but when he finally reached the outer suburbs he realised that thousands of Berliners had been grabbed off the streets to turn the city into a fortress. A gang of office workers was digging anti-tank trenches across a sodden playing field. Women were piling sundry wreckage on a zigzag line of burned-out cars to barricade a cobbled boulevard. Nehmann stopped to talk to one of them. She was young and resentful and made it plain that she couldn't wait for the Red Army to appear. The war had gone on for far too long and everyone knew what would happen next. Better a Russian on your belly, she said, than a house on your head.

By late afternoon that first day, tired of tramping from district to district, Nehmann ducked into a cinema for a rest. A handful of Berliners were staring up at the newsreel Nehmann recognised only too well: an ageing Führer inspecting the line of uniformed officers at Wriezen. For a moment, he was tempted to ask whether any of them believed this nonsense but then he realised that on every empty seat lay a single sheet of paper. He himself was sitting on one, and in the flicker of light from the screen, once he'd smoothed it flat, he realised that he was looking at a summons from the resistance. The message was crude, the spelling woeful, the layout worse. It was time for the *Volk* to reclaim their city. The capitalist warmongers had brought nothing but chaos. Nehmann folded the appeal into his pocket, remembering the woman building the barricade. Peace, he concluded, deserved better propaganda than this.

The early evening, that first day, found him in Grosse Frankfurter Strasse, an area of the city he remembered for its concentration of engineering works. This was where you could once take the pulse of a different Berlin, away from the busy cafés and glittering hotels on the Ku'damm, but both the buildings and the workers had vanished, leaving nothing but mountains of rubble. Nehmann stood in the gathering darkness, tasting the slightest hint of sulphur in the wind, listening to the rattle of a loose window frame in the single façade that had survived the bombing. Then came the clang-clang of a distant tram and he realised that the Berlin he'd known had gone, probably forever, and that he needed to be back in Eichwalde, back with Maria and the baby, back where the wind would be a friend again, laden with the scents of spring.

Maria, when he finally made it home, was frantic. He'd promised to be back before dusk. It was now gone nine o'clock. Everyone knew about the blackout in Berlin, how dangerous it could be, and she'd been worried sick. Nehmann did his best to comfort her, a new role in his life, and after he'd done justice to the meal she'd prepared she broke down again.

This time, mercifully, it wasn't his fault. A friend she'd made locally had a relationship with a man on the edges of the resistance. He'd been betrayed by a neighbour, brutally interrogated and then hauled before the People's Court. Their verdict had come as no surprise, and the week before last he'd been beheaded. Beheading, as Nehmann now knew, was the regime's reflex reaction to the most trivial threat. Only yesterday, according to a housewife he'd talked to in Rahnsdorf, two men had gone to the executioner's block after riots over the local supply of bread.

'Here...' Maria had found a letter she'd been looking for.

Nehmann glanced at the addressee.

'This is your friend?'

'Brigitte, yes. Just read it.' She blew her nose. 'Please.'

Nehmann bent to the letter. It was on headed paper and came from the office of the People's Court. With regard to proceedings against the accused, a Herr Lahm, the secretary of the court, was charged with recovering monies spent in the discharge of the sentence. These included the amount stipulated under Articles 49 and 52 of the Court Fees Act for the commission of the execution itself, costs incurred by the public defender, imprisonment expenses at the rate of RM 1.50 per diem, plus postal costs for the despatch of the bill of charges. In all, Maria's friend was facing a demand for RM 183, an impossible sum.

'She doesn't have it.' Maria nodded at the letter. 'And she's terrified they'll come for her next.'

'On what grounds?'

'Contempt of court. That can be a capital offence, too. In fact, anything can. Put one foot out of line...' she drew a finger across her throat.

'And Lahm? Was he really guilty?'

'Of course not. He must have upset a neighbour. People know how to settle debts these days.'

Nehmann nodded. Very little could surprise him after two years in the Gulag, but the German obsession with paperwork never ceased to amaze him. On the drive into Berlin he'd asked the Chain Dog Lieutenant what faith he'd have in bands of stay-behind partisans making life tough for the Russians. The Lieutenant had laughed. 'I'm sure they'd be happy to storm a railway station or two,' he'd said. 'As long as they bought platform tickets first.'

Now Nehmann asked whether Goebbels might be able to help.

'How?'

'By talking to the Court. By having the bill rescinded.'

'Never.'

'He wouldn't do it?'

'I wouldn't ask.'

'Why not?'

'Goebbels wants me on my knees. The moment that happens, he'll have no more use for me. No...' she shook her head. 'Never.'

Nehmann nodded. For this, as for so much else in Maria, he had the greatest respect.

'I'd pay the bill myself,' he muttered. 'But I haven't got that kind of money.'

*

Next morning, the atmosphere still tense, Nehmann decided to return to the station and take the train once again to Berlin. According to Maria, Goebbels wanted them both to attend a meeting at the Berlin Philharmoniker the following afternoon to discuss the programme for a forthcoming concert. The meeting would be chaired by Goebbels himself, and Maria would be on hand to offer her thoughts on what might be musically appropriate.

'But why me?' Nehmann had asked. 'Why does he need me there?'

'He says you owe him a script.'

'That's true. He's expecting me to bring it?'

The answer was evidently yes, and so now Nehmann knew he had to get to work. The city, as ever, yielded glimpse after glimpse of just how desperate its situation had become. The mutilated veteran beside the *Hauptbahnhof* who raised a stump of an arm in a salute to a passing *Wehrmacht* patrol. The way that even businessmen carried a suitcase or a rucksack or a shoulder bag crammed with a steel helmet, and a gas mask, and eye goggles in case they needed to spend the night elsewhere. And finally, around lunchtime, the sight of a photographer's darkroom, savagely exposed by a near miss.

By now, Nehmann was on the outskirts of Moabit and he clambered over a mountain of rubble to take a closer look. A series of prints had been pegged to a line at the rear of the darkroom to dry out. They all featured the same young faces and they were all wearing the uniform of the *Hitlerjugend*. With their ties, and their shorts, and their leather bandoliers, these toy soldiers were now manning Berlin's defences as Nehmann knew only too well because just this morning he'd seen them with his own eyes.

The shots had been taken in a studio setting, properly lit and formally posed, doubtless at the insistence of proud parents, but what iced Nehmann's blood was the light in these children's eyes. They'd bought into all the Führer crap. They'd listened to Goebbels, and they'd believed him. And now, within weeks, they'd be going to their deaths. Not with resignation, but a fierce pride. Nehmann shook his head, imagining what his Soviet tank crew would do to targets like these. A single shell, he thought. And someone with a shovel turning up afterwards to take care of the mess.

*

Early afternoon found Nehmann at the Silesian station. This, he knew, was where Hitler's most recent expedition out of the city had come to an end. He'd arrived after dark to be greeted by the usual convoy of cars, and his driver, according to Maria, had taken a much longer route back to the Chancellery than usual in order to spare the Führer the evidence of what enemy bombers were doing to his cherished Berlin. Now, though, Nehmann wanted to check rumours that refugee kids were arriving from the east in open cattle wagons, many of them frozen to death.

In an office on the first floor of the station, he found a middle-aged man in a rumpled suit attacking a timetable with a child's crayon. The crayon was red, and one departure after another had been consigned to oblivion. Nehmann offered his Promi pass but the official barely spared it a glance, and when Nehmann added that he was a journalist working directly for the *Reichsminister* himself, he shrugged. He'd never had much time for Goebbels, he admitted, though lately the little man seemed to have tripped over one or two home truths.

'Like?' Nehmann was curious.

'Like we're fucked. That doesn't help, though, does it? When all he's offering is more of the bloody same? Nothing to eat. Water that tastes of shit. And millions of Ivans at the gate. Get it over with, I say. Make a peace, *any* fucking peace, and be done with it. So how can I help you?'

Nehmann mentioned trains shipping kids in from the east. The official said it was true.

'And some of them are dead?'

'Yeah,' he nodded again. 'And they're the lucky ones.'

*

The remark stayed with Nehmann for the rest of the afternoon. Round the corner from the station he found himself a table at the back of a bar that was, for once, warm. The owner, who'd lost an eye, brought him a beer, with the offer of potato soup and a hunk of bread if he was hungry. Nehmann shook his head and watched him limping back to his post behind the counter.

The lucky ones, he thought. Berlin humour had always appealed to him, the frank acceptance that every politician was a born liar, that Hitler himself was probably half-Jewish, and that a *Volk* stupid enough to believe a word the great man said deserved everything that would inevitably follow. The fact that the reckoning had now arrived, that much of the city was a boneyard, was neither here nor there. The official at the station was more right than he knew. The moment Goebbels abandoned lies for the truth was the moment you knew the Reich was in deep trouble.

Nehmann opened his pad and stared at the blankness of

the page. The woman he'd talked to yesterday at the barricade had told him about a city-wide competition for the award of the best anti-tank barrier. She'd had a very sour view of life in general, and he'd no idea whether or not she'd made it up, but the idea had the Promi's fingerprints all over it. Survival of the fittest. Triumph of the will. Plus numberless other Nazi propositions that had weathered the recent series of disasters.

Nehmann picked up his pen and began to scribble down an idea or two. What if he were to structure a Führer broadcast around a whole cluster of citizen events? Not just the Best Anti-Tank Barrier, but the Neatest Pile of Rubble, the Safest Way to Self-Abort and What Best To Do With The Knitting Needle Afterwards? Wouldn't that trigger a flood of volunteering effort? Help people feel better about themselves? Make them fall in love with their Führer once again? Assuming he could get the delivery right? That bittersweet mix of the apocalyptic, the surreal, and the absurd?

Nehmann stared at the list and began to warm to the idea. For all the wrong reasons, it would make Berliners laugh and he liked that proposition very much. He glanced up and caught the eye of the owner at the bar and gestured at his empty glass. Another beer. Definitely.

*

Hours later, the howl of the siren took him by surprise. It was years since Nehmann had last seen the inside of an air raid shelter and he sat back as the bar began to empty, drinkers emptying their glasses, exchanging weary glances, and making for the door. At the bar, Nehmann asked for directions.

'The nearest one's a couple of minutes away. Follow the crowd.'

On the street outside, thanks to the blackout, it took a while for Nehmann's eyes to adjust. Five beers? Six? More? He couldn't remember. Then came a shove in his back as the swelling crowd hurried him down the street, and he simply relaxed, riding the press of bodies until the mouth of the shelter appeared and he found himself plunging downwards, his feet barely touching the concrete stairs.

The heavy steel doors at the bottom were still open. The shelter felt enormous, a vast corridor that seemed to recede forever. Wherever he looked there were chairs of every description, wicker, cane, footrests, even whole couches, but all of them were already occupied, with more people sitting on the floor, their legs drawn up, hugging their knees. The bare concrete of the shelter walls was softened by a huge collection of suitcases, many of them souvenirs from happier times. Nehmann, who folded himself into a tiny space, began to read some of the labels. Hotel Belle Vue, Sorrento. Ritz Hotel, London. A Lufthansa flight to Istanbul. The crowd at the door, by now, had thinned. Then came a barked order from a *Blockwarten* and the big steel doors were pulled shut with a harsh metallic clang.

The woman beside Nehmann crossed herself and closed her eyes. Her companion, a slightly younger man in a uniform Nehmann didn't recognise, struggled to his feet. He took off his cap and began to pick his way among the waiting bodies, a whispered invitation here, a word of explanation there. People nodded, women felt for their purses, and as Nehmann watched, the cap quickly filled with money.

'What's he collecting for?'

The question made the woman jump.

'The men on the barricades,' she said. 'They have twenty bullets each. Some of these bullets are Greek. They're no good. You can buy proper ones if you know where to go.'

Nehmann raised an eyebrow, making room for her companion as he returned, tucking the cap and the money on the floor between them. Then, dimly, people picked up the drone of aircraft overhead, and the bark of anti-aircraft guns much closer, and the murmur of conversation stilled, and whole families stared up at the roof, the women pulling their coats a little tighter around them as their kids began to wail.

By now, a great deal more sober, Nehmann was aware of the smell of mould, the smell you get from an old cellar, and in spite of the press of bodies he could feel the cold rising from the concrete floor. Then, from nowhere, came an enormous explosion, and the entire shelter seemed to physically rise and shiver, and a blast of hot air rattled the gas vents in the steel doors. Nehmann felt a bursting pressure in his ears and chest as the naked light bulbs hanging from the low roof flickered and died. Instinctively, he reached out for support, his hand crabbing across the concrete until he felt the outline of the cap, and softer folds of money inside.

Women were crying now, not just the kids, and the woman beside Nehmann was beginning to hyperventilate. She was clinging to her companion in the darkness, rocking from side to side, marooned in her worst nightmare, begging for the mad chorus in the streets outside to end. Her companion had his arm around her but seemed incapable of offering comfort.

'It'll be over soon,' Nehmann whispered to her. 'Because it always is.'

By now, he'd pocketed as much of the paper money as he could find. Minutes later, the aircraft gone, the lights flickered back on, a harsh overhead brightness that turned heads away, and as the crowd began to stir, and the *Blockwarten* ordered the steel doors to be opened, Nehmann got to his feet, mumbled an apology, and headed for the stairs.

Outside, Berlin was as dark as ever, and it took Nehmann a while to find a taxi. For RM 3, the driver was happy to take him back to Eichwalde.

*

Maria's house, when Nehmann finally found it, was in darkness. He tapped softly on the door and waited for signs of life, but nothing happened. When he tried again, he heard a door open upstairs. Moments later, he was looking at Maria. She said she'd been in bed, and once Nehmann was inside and the light was on he could see she'd been crying.

'It's not late,' he said at once. 'I got caught in a raid.'

She looked at him, said nothing. Then she led the way into the living room. On the bare table lay a typewriter and a sheaf of foolscap paper. Beside it, propped on a saucer, was a candle.

'It's a Triumph,' Nehmann was looking at the typewriter. 'I used one of these at the Promi.'

'They delivered it this afternoon.'

'For me?'

'Of course. The meeting at the Philharmoniker has been changed. It's tomorrow morning now.'

'You talked to him? Goebbels?'

'Yes.'

'And?'

'He's sending a car at ten o'clock.' She was looking at the typewriter. 'And he's expecting the speech.'

Nehmann nodded. Her message was clear. Then his eye drifted to the neat pile of blankets on the floor.

'You want me to sleep down here?'

'Yes. It's for the best.'

'Is that Goebbels I hear? Or you?'

'Me.'

Nehmann shrugged. So be it, he thought. He reached for the typewriter, depressed a couple of keys, gave the roller a twirl. It was stiff from lack of use. Then he remembered the money. He'd counted it in the taxi. Over a hundred Reichsmarks.

'This is for your friend.' He dug the roll of notes out of his pocket. 'It won't be as much as they want but it might help.'

Maria was staring at the money. 'Where did you get that?'

'It doesn't matter. Just take it.' He smiled. 'Please.'

She gazed at it a little longer, then shook her head.

'There's no point.' She was close to tears again. 'She's gone.'

'Gone?'

'She took her own life. It happened this afternoon. A neighbour came round to tell me. You know what happened? Those people frightened her to death. Literally.'

'That's what they do. That's what they're good at. Here, take the money, spend it on the little one, on Dominika, and maybe tell her about us when she's old enough to understand.'

'Us?' Her voice was toneless.

'Us. The way we were. Before we made her. Before I went away. Before they sent me back. Before all this.' He pressed the money into her hand. 'Dominika,' he said again.

Nehmann held her hand a moment longer, then kissed her forehead the way you might put a child to bed and nodded towards the door.

'Please?' he murmured. 'Do you mind?'

*

Maria gone, Nehmann lit the candle and stared at the typewriter. Goebbels, as he knew, had long ago mastered the art of gesture. Often, it was a surprise sentence or two buried in an otherwise routine speech. Other times, when a secretary least expected it, she might find herself looking at an explosion of roses and a line of verse.

Nehmann, too, had been on the receiving end of this largesse. In the early days, after the fall of France, Goebbels had sent him a crate of twice-looted champagne, once from a château on the outskirts of Tours, the second time from the cellar of *Reichsminister* Ribbentrop. This gesture had been rich with delicious complications because everyone knew that Goebbels loathed the Reich's Foreign Minister. 'Toast the fool in his own champagne,' Goebbels had written in the accompanying card. 'And save the rest for the day of his funeral.'

Good advice, Nehmann had thought at the time, but the intervening years had taught him the real price that a closeness to Goebbels could exact, and now, feeding a sheet of foolscap into the roller, he recognised this final gesture for what it was. Live by the typewriter. Or die by the typewriter. Your choice.

He sat at the table for a long moment, enjoying the spill of light from the candle, and his own shadow dancing on the wall as he tightened the ribbon and made a tiny adjustment to the way the paper sat in the machine. These, he realised, were reflex movements, part of his tradecraft, clues to who he really was. In the shape of this typewriter, Goebbels had offered him a final challenge. What happened next would dictate the rest of his life, no matter how brief.

Nehmann closed his eyes a moment. It was September 1942. He was back in Berlin, summoned by Goebbels to add a little of his trademark magic to the final draft of a speech Hitler was due to make at the Sportpalast. Expecting the usual torrent of visionary drivel, Nehmann hadn't been disappointed. Hitler, Goebbels warned, was determined to make a stand, both at Stalingrad itself and here in Berlin where the world – including Moscow – awaited some clue that the leader of the Reich was still in touch with reality. Nehmann had done his best to add a cautionary note or two about the sheer depth of Soviet resources, and about the hazards of the coming winter, but his reservations – no matter how cleverly phrased – had been dismissed, and that afternoon Nehmann had sat uncomfortably among a sea of fanatics as Hitler mounted the podium.

What followed had stayed with him throughout the winter months in Stalingrad, and over the years in the Kolyma Gulag that were to follow. Rommel's Afrika Korps might be facing real opposition at last, and supply lines on the Eastern Front were already dangerously stretched, but the Führer was interested only in good news. Churchill was a buffoon, he roared. Roosevelt sat in the lap of the Jews. The Western Allies were broken in spirit, the Russians were a primitive race from the depths of Asia, and now the city on the Volga, the diamond in Stalin's crown, would soon be in German hands. This monumental feat of arms, he promised, would kick open the door to the Caucasus, and the vast oil fields beyond would fuel the greatest empire the world had ever seen. '*Ein Volk*,' he bellowed. '*Ein Reich. Ein Führer*,' the crowd bellowed back, rising to their feet, a forest of raised arms as Hitler's mad speech came to an end.

Nehmann could see him up on the stage at the Sportpalast, his face beaded with sweat, one arm still clasping the rostrum while the other acknowledged the waves of Führer-worship that rose, and curled, and finally broke around him, and now Nehmann sought to preserve that moment, knowing that it held the key to what he needed to write. The harsh Austrian accent. The implacable will. The guarantee of victory after victory. The raw assurance that nothing, absolutely nothing, could withstand the iron at the heart of the German soul.

Nehmann's fingers settled on the keyboard. My friends, he began. My comrades. My brothers-in-arms. Fate has always been our friend, our ally, our strength on the battlefield, and our guiding light as country after country, people after people, acknowledged our might, our implacable will and the role that awaits us once the fighting is done. That same hand of fate is always with us, a physical presence, impossible to dismiss, and it offers the steady voice of comfort when times are hard and our prospects look bleak. Now, perhaps, is one of those times, but I want to share with you the secret that can turn the bitterness of defeat into the sweetness of victory. It is, in a word, paprika.

Paprika.

From overhead came the cry of the baby, and then the soft patter of footsteps as Maria hurried to her bedside.

Paprika.

Nehmann could hear Maria calming their infant daughter. At moments like these, she'd told him last night, Dominika liked to be read a story. Nehmann had nodded, unsurprised. Because stories were irresistible. Because stories could untangle any knot. Because stories could take you anywhere.

He began to type again. Goebbels was right. Even now, even when the broken heart of Germany lay at the mercy of two converging armies, there still remained a radio audience of millions. These eager souls wanted reassurance. They wanted comfort. They wanted, in short, stories.

Times are hard, he wrote. But times have been worse. Nehmann sat back for a moment, gazing at the lines of type, then his fingers found the only ten letters that really mattered, the ten letters that had taken two million lives, the ten letters that had – two and a half years later – brought the Thousand Year Reich to its knees.

Stalingrad, he wrote. Imagine the snow, the bite of winter. Imagine winter as a wolf, waiting for you to stumble and fall.

Imagine the Russians, whole armies of them, barely an arm's length away. Think of the letters that never arrive, of the faces you'll never see again, of the warmth of your wife's body in the bed you've left behind. Imagine losing most of your fingers to frostbite, and most of your mind to what defeat will bring.

Paprika.

January. The coldest month of all. Your spit freezes in midair. A horse dies in front of you and unless you start eating it within minutes, it will break your teeth. The same truth holds for all flesh, even human flesh. Best to eat your best friend while that body of his is still warm. Because, by now, you may have no teeth at all.

Paprika.

Nehmann had once been an apprentice butcher. He knew how to joint a carcass, how to discard bone and sinew, how to take his knife to the grinder and worry out those choicest cuts that would keep any man alive for a day or two more. He put this precious knowledge at Hitler's disposal, embedded it deep in the speech as it began to develop, offered advice about cooking times, about the possibilities of salting and pickling, and – most important of all – how to disguise the sweet porkiness of human flesh.

Paprika.

A church up the street from Maria's house had a bell that tolled the hours. By four in the morning, after a long tussle with the closing paragraphs, Nehmann knew he at last had the makings of a speech. It wouldn't be anything that either Goebbels or Hitler would be expecting but that didn't matter. Because for once in his life, to his intense satisfaction, Nehmann had made way for the truth.

Upstairs, thanks to Maria, his infant daughter had long been asleep, another cause for celebration. Nehmann stole into the kitchen. He knew where Maria kept her emergency bottle of schnapps, and he poured himself half a tumbler, toasting himself with the final gulp. Back in the sitting room, he arranged cushions on the floor, blew out the candle, and lay beneath a single blanket, daring the darkness to take him. Now, he thought, I must find an envelope for my precious speech. Seconds later, he was asleep.

*

The Mercedes despatched by Goebbels arrived slightly late next morning. Maria and Nehmann sat in the back, the child between them. After enemy air raids had destroyed first one, and then a second of the regular venues at the disposal of the Berlin Philharmoniker, they'd now found a rehearsal home in the Beethoven Halle.

One of Goebbels' aides was waiting outside the main entrance. He recognised Nehmann from his days at the Ministry and raised his arm in the Hitler salute. Nehmann offered an amiable nod and introduced Maria.

'No need.' The aide winked. 'We know the *Reichminister*'s Fraulein very well. *Kommen Sie mit.*'

The building appeared to have suffered a series of near misses in the recent raids. Great chunks of stucco were missing from the façade and the pillars supporting the entrance were pocked by shrapnel, but the moment they stepped inside Nehmann could hear music, something large, plenty of brass.

'Bruckner,' Maria whispered. 'The Fourth Symphony.'

The aide led the way up a long staircase. The carpet was threadbare and one or two of the marble steps felt unsteady underfoot but, as they climbed, the music swelled in volume, and the moment they got to the first floor, and the aide opened a door, the music engulfed them.

'The rehearsal should be over soon,' the aide whispered. 'The Minister will be arriving shortly.'

Nehmann found himself in a spacious box overlooking the body of the hall. The long crescents of seats were empty on the floor below, but a sizeable orchestra had mustered on the big stage. It was cold enough to cloud the breath of the conductor as he paused the orchestra and asked for more attack from the strings section, and many of the players were wearing jackets or heavy sweaters.

Maria had already found a seat at the front of the box. She had the child on her lap but when Nehmann eyed the seat beside her, she shook her head.

'For the Minister,' she said simply.

Goebbels arrived moments later. He was wearing a grey suit and he was accompanied by two younger men Nehmann didn't recognise. Members of his staff? Bodyguards of some sort? He couldn't be sure. Goebbels stooped to Maria and kissed her on both cheeks before cupping the child's face and whispering something that Nehmann didn't catch. So far, he'd spared no one else a glance and Nehmann understood at once what was really going on. This, like every encounter in the upper reaches of the Reich, was about territory. Mine, Goebbels was saying. My woman. My child. Mine to own. Mine by tribal right.

The orchestra began to play again, the strings a little more vivid, and Goebbels watched them for a moment or two before removing his leather gloves and clapping his hands. The conductor peered round, irritated, then recognised the gaunt little figure up in the box.

'A moment of your time, Herr Borchard. Do you mind?'

The conductor put his baton aside and left the stage. A minute of so later, out of breath, he joined them in the box. Once, Nehmann thought, he must have been a handsome man, good face, strong jaw, a mane of greying hair, but the long years of war had left their mark. He looked exhausted, and the presence of Goebbels appeared to disturb him.

The Minister laid a hand on his arm. He wanted to present a very good friend of his. Maria was already on her feet, eager for the introduction, her daughter held tight. Nehmann, once again, was ignored.

'You read those notes of mine?' Goebbels asked Borchard.

'Of course.'

'And your thoughts? *Götterdämmerung* first? Just the final scene, of course. Might that be in order? Then Beethoven? The violin concerto? Before we get to that favourite of yours?' Goebbels nodded towards the auditorium. 'Bruckner?'

'Perfect.'

'*Fraulein?*' Goebbels had turned to Maria.

'I agree.'

'Excellent,' Goebbels was back with Borchard. 'Then I suggest we delay you no longer. The twelfth? Five o'clock in the afternoon? Early, I know, but it would be a shame to have a bomb in our lap.'

Borchard was staring at Goebbels. Then it occurred to him that the ordeal was over, the programme agreed, and with a brief nod to Maria he left the box. Goebbels was smiling to himself, looking down at the orchestra. He waited until the music started again, then exchanged a glance with the aide who had greeted Maria and Nehmann. The aide nodded and left the box.

'Well? You have it?' Goebbels was looking at Nehmann.

Nehmann nodded, said nothing. Goebbels extended a hand. Now, he was saying. I want to read it now.

Nehmann shrugged, extracted the envelope from the pocket of his jacket, handed it across. Goebbels unfolded the three pages of the Führer speech and scanned each in turn. His face was a mask. Finally, he returned the speech to the envelope and slipped it into his own pocket.

'My wife gave you those spices,' he said. 'I suspect you owe her a thank-you.'

It was true. Nehmann had spent a day and a night out at Bogensee before his last departure for Stalingrad. Once again, Goebbels had demanded his advice on an article he'd authored.

'You called it *Totaler Krieg*,' Nehmann said softly. 'And it was total shit.'

The phrase made Maria flinch. Goebbels was still looking at Nehmann.

'But you made it bolder, my little friend. There was a line you came up with. Stalingrad, you had me write, where death never takes time off. Brilliant. Better than brilliant. Perfect. And then Magda wondered about a present because it was Christmas, and you asked for spices.'

'I did.'

'Including paprika.'

'Yes.'

'And that's what she found you. And now you write me this.' He patted the pocket of his jacket. 'Men eating men? *Our* men? *Our* soldiers? Are you serious, Nehmann? You want the Führer to read this rubbish? On the *radio*?'

'It's true,' Nehmann shrugged. 'And one of those men was me.'

The aide had returned to the box. With him was a youth of perhaps fifteen in the uniform of the *Hitlerjugend*. He had a wicker basket hanging from a strap around his neck. In the basket was a loosely knotted handkerchief.

'This is Harald.' Goebbels patted him on the shoulder. 'He and his friends will be stationed at every exit when the concert ends. I'd have asked him to join us earlier but Maestro Borchard, I understand, has a weak stomach.' He glanced at the youth.

'Well, Harald? What will you be offering to the cream of our wonderful city?'

The youth unknotted the handkerchief. Inside were three capsules, one of them brass, the other two made of glass.

'And inside, Harald?'

'Prussic acid, Herr *Reichsminister*.'

'Prussic acid, Nehmann. Cyanide. Each of these baskets will be full. Supplies may be thin on the ground these days, but we have enough of these bonbons for everyone in the audience. People can help themselves. It's their decision. Bite hard enough, and your troubles will be over. So, Nehmann...' He'd stepped very close now. Nehmann could smell the sourness of his breath. '... which one? Your choice. Brass or glass? The car is still waiting downstairs. It will take you to the Prinz-Albrecht-Strasse. Himmler, I know, favours the brass capsule but you may have ideas of your own.' He smiled. 'Never let anyone tell you this regime of ours lacks generosity.'

22

The old Schultz, Merz thought. The transformation had been remarkable. The moment they'd met in Switzerland for the return flight to Berlin, he'd been a different man. The taciturn confidence, the old swagger, had returned. Swap the Loden coat for his trademark leather jacket, Merz thought, and Schultz was back in the role he'd always played best. This was the *Abwehr* enforcer he'd briefly got to know in Lisbon, full of guile and raw appetite, a man who'd spent his entire life refusing to negotiate any kind of pact with violence. Even a sudden pocket of turbulence on the approach to Rechlin, a vicious blast of wind that came from nowhere and nearly flipped the aircraft over, had failed to disturb him.

'Just land the fucking thing,' Schultz had growled from the rear seat. 'And be done with it.'

Now, nearly a week later, Merz was driving him to the KWI. Beata was with them, too, her skinny frame folded into the back of the VW. Rumours were sweeping the city that the final Russian push was imminent, that the thin defensive line on the Oder would buckle within hours, that the Red Army was a couple of days' march away. Major roads had become a tangle of barricades, and street patrols were searching any male under fifty in the hunt for deserters, but Merz was no stranger to the city's short cuts and they arrived at the Institute unchallenged.

Beata showed her pass at the gate, accounted for her colleagues, and then directed Merz to an office block that seemed to form an annexe to the main building. Two *Wehrmacht* trucks were parked outside, and a succession of young soldiers were doing their best to avoid the teeming rain as they hauled boxes of documents and equipment out of the building.

'Walther's team have been heading south all week,' Beata explained. 'This consignment will probably be the last.'

Walther, as Schultz now knew, was Professor Walther Gerlach, head of the physics section at the Reich's Research Council, and a key player in the *Uranverein* project. This, as Beata had been explaining, was a bid to put a working atomic bomb in the hands of the *Luftwaffe*. Experiments conducted here at the KWI had suggested enough explosive yield to level a small city but Berlin had become far too dangerous to risk either the uranium burner, or the precious scientists who understood the dark magic of nuclear fission, and so the entire project had been evacuated to the relative safety of sites in southern Germany.

Beata led the way to an upstairs office at the end of a corridor patterned by muddy boots. The office was bare except for a single table and a broken chair. The wind was howling through a broken windowpane and when Schultz looked for clues to account for all the water on the floor, Beata apologised for the state of the ceiling. The maze of cracks, she said, were the result of the heaviest of last month's air raids. Hence the decision to move the *Uranverein* project south.

Schultz was looking at the blackboard. A long list of items had been tallied in yellow chalk. They included one and a half tonnes of uranium cubes, one and a half tonnes of heavy water, ten tonnes of graphite blocks, plus an undesignated weight of something Schultz couldn't make out.

'What's Cd48?' He was peering hard at the chalk squiggle.

'Cadmium metal,' Beata was at the window, staring down at the trucks. 'You need it in case the chain reaction goes out of control. Inserted in the burner, it stops everything.'

Schultz nodded. Every item on the blackboard had been ticked.

'All this stuff has gone?'

'Yes.'

'Where exactly?'

'In the first place to Stadthilm. That's in Thuringia. Then Walther seems to think it might be safer even further south. Either Hechingen or Haigerloch. There's a cave at Haigerloch where we've built another burner.'

Schultz made a note of all three names. Hechingen and Haigerloch were south of Stuttgart.

'And this chain reaction thing?' He gestured at his pad. 'It's happened? You've done it?'

'No.'

'Soon, though?'

'I doubt it. The physics are complicated. We haven't got enough heavy water. And in any case the war is nearly over. What's happening down south gives Goebbels a chance to keep bragging but everyone knows the trucks are part of the pantomime. Even Walther understands that, poor man.'

'So what will happen to him?'

'I've no idea. I suppose we've all got a value in the right hands. I imagine it depends who gets to Walther first. The Americans? The Russians? No one knows.'

'And you?'

'I'm a Berlin housewife. I have two kids and a father to look after. Merz, too. That's enough to keep any woman busy, believe me.'

'But your name will be all over the documentation, wherever it ends up. That's what happens when wars run out of steam. People like me look at the smallest print, work out the relationships, draw a diagram or two, put a price on every life. You're telling me that hasn't occurred to you?'

'Of course it's occurred to me.'

'And?'

'I belong here, in Berlin. I just told you.'

Schultz nodded. He was looking at Merz.

'And you, my friend? You're not tempted to steal an aeroplane? Put your family in the back and fly away before everything goes quiet round here and everyone starts learning Russian?'

Merz simply smiled, and Schultz had the feeling that he might have been closer to the truth than Beata would ever admit. Too bad, he thought, gazing at the blackboard again.

'So what's left?' he asked Beata. 'What do you want my Russian friends to take care of?'

*

Minutes later, they were out in the rain again, tramping through a drift of rubble towards the building they called the Virus House. The door was secured with a newish padlock and Schultz examined it for a moment or two, testing the clasp before Beata intervened. There was no point, she said, in forcing any kind of entry because the burner had been disabled, leaving nothing but uranium residues which should be handled with great care. What mattered were the steel drums.

She led the way around the building, splashing through the puddles from the incessant rain. At the back of the Virus House was a line of 200-litre drums, some white, some blue. They'd all been stamped with the yellow radiation symbol but exposure to the weather had begun to rust the metal seams and the joint where the flange of the lid seated into the circular rim. Schultz stood in the rain, counting the drums. There were seventeen.

'And this is...?' He was looking at Beata.

'Uranium oxide. We call it yellowcake. There's a lot to do before you get to a bomb but without this stuff you can't even make a start. It's very heavy.'

Schultz gave the nearest drum a shove. It didn't move. He nodded, thoughtful.

'And is there anything else I should be looking at?'

Beata nodded. Two hundred and fifty kilograms of metallic uranium and twenty litres of the precious heavy water, she said, were stored elsewhere.

'And this stuff matters?'

'Enormously.'

Schultz checked his watch and caught Merz's eye.

'Gehlhausen,' he grunted. 'He may be conscious by now.'

*

The surgeon at the Charité hospital had been bombed out of his apartment while Schultz and Merz were in Switzerland. On his return, Schultz had tried to make contact but no one seemed to know the real story. Only on the fourth attempt had Schultz managed to raise the senior nursing officer charged with supervising his recovery. Gehlhausen, she said, had never given much attention to the air raid protocols, preferring the comfort of his bed to the local shelter, and he'd now paid the price. A team of *Trümmerexperten* had dug him out of the remains of the apartment block and taken him back to his place of work. At the Charité, nursing staff were doing their best to rouse him from intermittent bouts of unconsciousness but he still remained on the critical list. *Trümmerexperten* meant 'rubble experts'.

Merz dropped Beata back at home before driving Schultz into the city. The nursing officer he'd talked to on the phone occupied an office on the fourth floor that was no bigger than a cupboard. Merz stayed in the corridor while Schultz squeezed inside and offered his ID to the woman hunched over the tiny desk. She was Schultz's age and, like Schultz himself, she needed a great deal more sleep. The sight of the *Abwehr* crest on the ID sparked a slow smile that Schultz found oddly stirring. She had the build of a diva, broad-chested, generous.

'My brother was in the *Abwehr*, Herr *Oberst*. You carry this as a souvenir?'

'I work for the SD now, like everyone else at the Bendlerblock. Difficult to credit, I know, but the pass still opens every door.'

'Including mine.'

'Indeed.' Schultz was looking round. Not the slightest concession to either comfort or rank. No windows. No pictures on the wall. Nothing to brighten this airless space. 'Claustrophobia doesn't bother you?' he asked.

'My brother who served in the *Abwehr* was the clever one. There were three more of them, plus two sisters. We had a small apartment. We lived on top of each other. A life like that prepares you for anything, Herr *Oberst*, even this.'

'You sound grateful.'

'As it happens, I am. They wanted two of us in here to begin with, and we tried it for a day or two, but in the end I managed to fight him off.'

'Poor man.'

'On the contrary, he'd already declared his intentions, which made the whole negotiation so much simpler. Brothers teach you how to fight, believe me.'

'That bad?'

'Worse. The wretched man never cleaned his teeth. His telephone manners were appalling and he had no taste for paperwork. After two days, I simply locked him out. Physically, he was grotesque. The *Abwehr* wouldn't have given him a second look.' Another smile. 'Why am I telling you all this, Herr *Oberst*?'

'I've no idea.' Schultz held her gaze. 'But don't stop.'

She nodded, thoughtful, then reached for a pen and scribbled something on the back of an envelope.

'My number, Herr *Oberst*. It's rare when the face doesn't disappoint. My name is Gisela. I enjoyed our conversation on the phone, by the way, and you'll be pleased to know that this morning Herr Gehlhausen appears to be more alive than dead. One thing before I take you down to see him. It's been bothering my nurses for a while and I imagine you might be able to shed a little light on the issue. We all thought we knew him but maybe that's not true. Do you mind?'

'Not at all.'

'Then why does this surgeon of ours speak Russian in his dreams?'

*

Gehlhausen occupied a corner bed in a big ward on the floor below. The wreckage of his legs, pinned and splinted, was protected by a cage of stiffened wire tented with a sheet, and layers of bandage around his head were lightly pinked with blood. A broken arm had been plastered and lay beside him on the bed like something he'd decided to discard. Nurses had already been busy on the whiteness of the cast, and Schultz bent to read the biggest of the messages. *To our favourite pirate*, one of the nurses had written, *get well soon*.

The nursing officer was whispering in Gehlhausen's ear. His good eye opened, revolved, settled on Schultz.

'Do I know you?' His voice was weak, barely a whisper.

'Probably not.' Schultz laid a hand on his good arm. 'You've been in a fight?'

'I'm afraid so. The other man died. You've come to arrest me?'

Gisela, amused, found a chair for Schultz and then joined a couple of nurses at the big table in the middle of the ward.

'You remember what happened, Herr Gehlhausen?'

'I remember nothing.'

'You mean the raid? What happened?'

'I mean nothing.'

'Working here? Being a surgeon?'

'Nothing.' He lifted his good arm and his bony hand, still latticed with cuts, managed a brief flutter of resignation. 'Gone,' he whispered. 'All of it.'

Schultz gazed round. The beds were very close together, an indication – he imagined – of the sheer weight of demand on a hospital like this, but the nearest patients were either asleep or unconscious. Nonetheless, just in case, he inched his chair a little closer, his mouth inches from Gehlhausen's ear. Two lonely years in a Moscow suburb had given him a pitiful command of the language but a couple of the local *babushkas* had admired his accent and he sensed that now was the moment to risk a phrase or two. If anything could penetrate the fog in this man's brain, then maybe Russian might do it.

'*Dobriy den?*' he whispered. How are you?

The good eye was still open. It registered a brief moment of confusion, then a smile settled on Gehlhausen's ruined face.

'*Wie bitte?*' Again, please?

'*Dobriy den?*'

Gehlhausen nodded, winced, then mustered an answer.

'*Prekrasno.*' He pulled a face. *Prekrasno* meant wonderful, brilliant, on top of the world.

Schultz sat back for a moment, aware of the nurses watching from their table in the middle of the ward. Already, Schultz loved this man, loved his sense of humour. With most of his body in pieces, the Pirate had never felt better.

'*Mockba?*' Schultz enquired. Moscow?

'*Da?*' Yes?

Schultz felt a prickle of frustration. He was fast running out of his precious store of phrases, and he certainly couldn't manage the next question, so he went back to German. Maybe a sniff or two of Russian had unlocked his memory, Schultz thought. Maybe.

'You talk to Moscow?' he murmured.

'*Da.*'

'How?'

'*Da.*'

'You use the telephone?' He mimed a receiver to his ear and mouth. 'You have a number?'

'*Nyet.*' No.

'No telephone? Or no number?'

'*Da.*'

'Radio, maybe?'

'*Da.*'

'You have a wavelength? A name? A special time?'

The eye was now beginning to lose focus. Schultz had no idea whether Gehlhausen had even heard the question but then came the lightest pressure on his arm as the bony hand settled briefly and then moved on.

'*Rad tebya veedyet,*' the voice was weak now. '*Bol'shoye spasibo.*' Good to see you. Thank you so much.

The eye at last closed, and Schultz recognised that his opportunity had come and gone. Gehlhausen had briefly surfaced but now he needed the comfort of the depths again. A radio, Schultz thought. Probably in his apartment. It made perfect sense.

Feeling a stir of movement behind him, he looked up to find the nursing officer gazing down at Gehlhausen.

'You got what you came for, Herr *Oberst*?'

'Maybe. You've got the address of his apartment?'

'Of course. But it doesn't exist any more.' She nodded down at him. 'That's why he's lying here. That's the whole point.'

'I know.' Schultz was on his feet now. 'But I'd still be obliged. Do you mind, Gisela? Or am I taking advantage here?'

The nursing officer gazed at him a moment, a look of frank appraisal, then she smiled.

'That's very *Abwehr* of you, Herr *Oberst*. I suggest you phone me tonight, after seven o'clock. I think you have the number.'

*

Schultz declined the offer of a lift back to Wannsee with Merz. Instead, he found a bar behind the nearby *Hauptbahnhof*. Rumours of a delivery of *Wurst* had drawn a sizeable crowd and most of the tables were occupied. The place was filthy, the floor muddy from the rain, abandoned copies of the *Beobachter* swept into a corner and the lone barmaid was overwhelmed by dozens of unwashed glasses. Schultz waited for his turn at the counter, but the queue was thickening by the minute and in the end he joined the barmaid, uninvited, and set about the glasses. Giving the last one a final wipe, he helped himself to a bottle of Kindl pils, leaving a scatter of coins on the counter, aware of a figure at a table just metres away, watching his every move.

When Schultz finally emerged from the scrum of drinkers, the bottle tilted to his mouth, the figure at the table mimed applause and nodded at the empty seat beside him. He was Schultz's age, maybe a year or two older. The cheap felt of the overcoat was blotched with rain and his glasses were held together with a twist of once-white tape.

'Karyl,' he grunted. He had a navvy's handshake. 'They get you to cook here as well?'

Schultz laughed, shook his head. He'd dropped in for a beer. Fool that he was, he'd always associated bars with service. Wrong.

'But these days?' Schultz shrugged. 'Who fucking cares?'

They talked for a while as yet more drinkers joined the crush around the bar. Schultz's new companion turned out to be a builder. He was making a tidy living from patching up lightly damaged properties and had a Berliner's eye for an opportunity.

'Bricks,' he said. 'All you need is a horse and cart and some place safe to keep them. The English do the real work every night of the week. Get up early enough, and you can take your pick. Some of them are duds, of course, smashed to pieces but most bricks are tough as fuck. They're also free.'

'You do all the work yourself?' Schultz was looking at the huge hands.

'Once I did but using *Trümmerfrauen* is quicker. I swear those women could eat most buildings alive. They're cheap, too. A handful of Reichsmarks buys half a dozen for as long as I need them.'

Trümmerfrauen. Rubble women.

'You're serious?'

'*Ja*. These women clean up. The building's gone, often the people inside, too. There's pickings everywhere, not just bricks. The women are like me. They get up early. They have an eye for what will sell. Clothes? Furniture? Cooking stuff? They're wise old birds of prey. By lunchtime, they've picked everything clean. And then they give me a hand with the bricks.' He paused. 'You're a Berliner? You live here?'

'Yeah. Of course.'

'So how come any of this is new to you?'

*

Trümmerfrauen. Schultz phoned Gisela from a booth on the station concourse. It was mid-evening now, and the crowds in the darkness making for the waiting trains had begun to thin. As well as gas masks and a helmet, most of these travellers appeared to be carrying an assortment of other items and Schultz wondered how many of these trophies had been harvested from bomb sites. Most nights, he thought, the RAF dumped entire lifetimes onto the street and within hours, next day, they'd been ghosted away.

'Hello?'

Schultz bent to the phone. It was Gisela, the nursing officer.

'Schultz, your *Abwehr* friend. You have an address for me?'

'I do.' She gave him the name of a street off Bernauerstrasse. Number 21. Apartment 3.

'This is where he lived? Gehlhausen?'

'No, Herr *Oberst*.' She had a throaty laugh. 'This is my place. Find yourself a taxi. It'll be quicker.'

For once, there was no queue at the rank outside the station. Schultz sat in the back of a battered Volkswagen that stank, for some reason, of sour milk. The prospect of the next few hours filled him with the kind of anticipatory relish that he could barely remember. No woman worth the name had crossed his path in Russia, and even if she had he wasn't at all sure he'd have trusted his body to rise to the occasion. Now, though, was very different, and he didn't have the slightest doubt that he could meet this woman's very obvious expectations.

366

The last week or so, back in a country he thought he knew well, he'd noticed a degree of abandon that had taken him by surprise. He'd even discussed it at some length with Merz. People are letting go, he'd said. Maybe it's the blackout. Maybe they think their days are numbered. But either way, the result is the same. In whatever shape or form, opportunities are there to be seized. Fuck the consequences. Fuck everything. Just do it.

Merz had agreed. It started after Stalingrad, he said quietly. Take a walk in any park after dark and total strangers want to be your friend. Not forever. Not even for that night. Just for the time it takes to find somewhere dry, and not too bumpy, and get down to it. Just that. Ten minutes. Fifteen, if you're lucky. Then off and into the dark again. No conversation. No curiosity except whatever awaits the ends of your fingers. Just the deed, the release, the letting go.

The trees along Strelitzer Strasse were nearly in full leaf. It was still too early for the air raid siren and the darkened street was empty. Number 21, when the driver found the apartment block, was still intact, no sign of bomb damage on the carefully rendered stucco, not a trace of rubble on the newly swept pavement. The woman who opened the main door to Schultz's knock was wearing a *Reichsmarine* greatcoat and a heavy woollen skirt that reached her ankles and looked far too young for either garment. Aware of Schultz's interest, she said she was dressed for the weather, not the catwalk, and returned to her perch at the foot of the stairs. Then she reached behind her for three items of mail, all addressed to Frau Esslin.

'This is Gisela?'

'Of course.'

'You've been expecting me?'

'We have.'

'We?'

'My mother and I. But don't worry...' she smiled, '... I'm on duty here all night.'

'And your father? Herr Esslin?'

'Gone. You have my mother to yourself, Herr *Oberst*. And don't forget these.'

Schultz took the letters and made for the stairs. Gone, he thought. Yet another tell-tale fingerprint left by this fucking war, a million possibilities compressed to a single syllable. Gone.

Gisela was waiting for him behind her open door. The loose nightgown left very little to Schultz's imagination. She was a handsome woman, generously built where it mattered most, but she confessed at once that she was worried about the possibility of an air raid.

'My fault,' she said. 'I should have got you here earlier. It's gone eight, already. The siren could go any moment and the *Blockwarten* was born to be difficult.'

'Your telephone?' Schultz was amused by her bluntness. 'One call might do it.'

'Really? Is that a promise, Herr *Oberst*?'

The moment she closed the door, Schultz became aware of a smell. It was yeasty, thick, scents of the zoo. The telephone was on a shelf at the end of the hall, and here the smell was overpowering.

'Blame my daughter, Herr *Oberst*.' Aware of Schultz's interest, Gisela nodded at the adjacent door. 'She breeds rabbits.'

'For pets? For company?'

'For the pot. Any extras, we sell. Even the *Blockwarten* is happy to part with a Reichsmark or two but he still chases us into the bloody shelter.' She nodded at the phone. 'You've got a number?'

Schultz rang Dieter Merz and asked about incoming raids. To his knowledge, Merz said, there would be no enemy activity over Germany tonight. The same weather system that had brought all the rain was still backed up over England. No take-offs. No flying. No bombs.

'So where are you?' he asked.

'I think I've made a friend.' Schultz was eyeing Gisela. 'I'll let you know.'

*

What now followed was to stay with Schultz for months to come. The fact that he'd somehow arranged for the English to take the night off seemed to have cemented Gisela's reverence for the *Abwehr*. She led him into her bedroom and hung the Loden coat on the back of her door, running her fingers across the pleats in the silk lining. The essence of any man, she told him, lay in his taste. In his taste for clothes, for all the subtle arts of display, and in a ruder sense, in the physical taste of the man himself. His breath. His tongue. His juices. She kissed him twice. First to say *guten Abend*. And a second time, to offer him a proper welcome. Just to touch her, to have this woman in his arms, was – for Schultz – a moment of profound relief. She was right. Thanks to Dieter Merz they had all night. And he knew already that this thing of theirs, whatever it was, would work.

It did. She was tender, and considerate, and large in her appetites. She had a quick instinct for what pleased him most and was eager to satisfy him in ways that made him wonder whether he'd stepped into the movie of his dreams. This was a different kind of abandon, nothing to do with frenzied couplings in darkened parks, and in the smallest hours, exhausted now, he surrendered to a contentment that both surprised and delighted him. Gisela was very happy to talk about her ex-husband, a senior officer on a U-boat sunk off the Savannah River in the crazy months that followed Pearl Harbor. And Schultz was happier still when she respected his reticence to share his own story.

'Bad things?' she queried.

'Very bad.'

'And now?'

'You mean here?'

'Yes.'

'Here is...' he couldn't help smiling, '... *perfekt*.'

She nodded, pleased with the answer. When she asked him whether he ever lied to women, he nodded.

'Often.'

'Why?'

'Because sometimes it was necessary.'

'Was?'

'Was.'

'So when did you last have a woman?'

The question, so simple, so guileless, made him smile but when she asked him a second time, he shook his head.

'Not telling?' she murmured.

'No.'

'Later, maybe?'

'No.'

'That makes you a hard man, Herr *Oberst*.' Her face was very close. 'I like that.'

'Hard how?'

'Hard on what matters to you. And hard on yourself. I like that, especially, and you know why?'

'Tell me.'

'Because it's so rare.' She kissed him, studied him for a long moment, and then threw back the sheet and straddled him. 'Again?' she murmured. 'Even more slowly?'

Schultz left next morning shortly after dawn. Gisela saw him off at the door. She'd given him two keepsakes, two souvenirs, two reasons not to forget her. One was the address of Gehlhausen's apartment. The other was an object, still warm, briefly cocooned in muslin.

On his way downstairs, Schultz met Gisela's daughter. She was looking at the muslin.

'She gave you a rabbit?'

'She did.'

'Enjoy,' she smiled. 'She does the same for every man.'

Schultz made his way to the edge of the district where Gehlhausen had been living. The news that he was only one of many who had shared Gisela's bed didn't disturb him in the least. His years in the *Abwehr* had given him a near-infallible ability to spot a lie, and he knew that last night neither of them had been faking. Whether this complicity was something she managed to conjure with every man in her life didn't concern him. What mattered was the sudden lull in all the noise, and clamour, and violence. For one whole night he'd been back on terms with something very close to peace, and for that – no matter how brief it might turn out to be – he was inexpressibly grateful.

*

An hour in the pale sunshine took him to the remains of the apartment block that had so nearly killed Gehlhausen. Judging by the adjacent buildings, heavily damaged, the block was much smaller than Schultz had been expecting, and already the *Trümmerfrauen* had restored a little order to the sooty pile of rubble and assorted timber that Gehlhausen had so recently regarded as home. Blocks of stone had been sorted into one area, bricks in another. Two women were squatting among the debris, warming their big hands on a flicker of flame they'd kindled from the damp wood, and Schultz asked them how long they'd been working here.

'You're police? Military?'

'Neither.'

'So why the questions?'

Schultz saw no point in straying far from the truth. He had a friend who'd occupied one of the apartments. He'd been badly injured but he was still alive, over in the Charité hospital. And he'd asked Schultz to take a look for whatever possessions might have survived.

'He's got a name? This friend?'

'Gehlhausen.'

One woman looked at the other and nodded. It was a nod of recognition, and Schultz's pulse began to quicken.

'He was some kind of doctor, this man?'

'He was. Still is.'

'You're after medical stuff? Those things they wear round their necks? Listen to your heart? Find out all your secrets?' She cackled with laughter.

'That would be a start. You've found a stethoscope? Is that what you're telling me?'

Schultz mimed the instrument, his fingers raised to his ears.

'Might have. What else are you after?'

'Whatever you've found. Whatever belongs to him.'

The woman struggled to her feet, then nodded at the knotted bundle of muslin, now pinked with blood.

'What's in there?'

'A rabbit.'

'*Fresh?*' She couldn't believe it. 'Where did you get that?'

Schultz wouldn't answer. Instead he asked again about whatever possessions these women might have scavenged from the rubble. Had they sold them already? Had they gone?

'Some of them, yes.'

'And the rest?'

'We've got a place round the corner.' She was staring at the rabbit again. 'You want to come and have a look?'

An hour and a half later, Schultz's luck finally ran out. He'd left the *Trümmerfrauen* after sifting through the items they'd recovered from the remains of Gehlhausen's apartment building. These objects, most of them barely recognisable, were people's lives laid bare: items of clothing, most of them female, cherished faces in smashed photographic frames, a child's doll with one arm hanging off, a soiled copy of *Mein Kampf*, but of a shortwave transmitter, or even a radio, there was no sign. The only item of any interest to Schultz fitted in the palm of his hand, and it cost him the rabbit to take it away. Maybe I can go back to the Charité, he thought. Maybe – as long as Gehlhausen hasn't died – this might trigger a memory or two.

The three-man patrol were *Volkssturm*. The oldest gestured for the others to form a barrier across the pavement as Schultz approached.

'*Papiere?*'

Schultz produced his ID, handed it over. Two heads bent to inspect it. The other man was gazing at Schultz's Loden coat.

'*Abwehr?*' The oldest *Volkssturm* again. He had a slightly academic air, and an accent to match, and he was looking puzzled.

Schultz hesitated. This was the first time he'd been subject to a proper check and he felt the first prickle of anxiety. What if Diski's faith in this ID had been misplaced? What if any mention of the *Abwehr* had been deleted from Reich paperwork?

'*Hande hoch!*' The *Volkssturm* motioned for Schultz to put his hands in the air, then took a tiny, fastidious step backwards while the youngest of the three began to search Schultz's pockets.

He found the item from the *Trümmerfrauen* at once and gave it to the *Volkssturm*.

'What's this?'

'A Morse key.'

The *Volkssturm* peered at it more closely, felt its weight in the palm of his hand.

'You use this?'

'Yes.'

'For sending messages?'

'Of course.'

'But why carry it around?'

To this question, Schultz had no immediate answer. Instead, he decided to pull rank.

'I'm an *Oberst*,' he pointed out. 'As you can see.'

'But why aren't you in uniform?'

'Because certain assignments require civilian dress. The details, I'm afraid, are delicate. You understand what I'm saying?'

The *Volkssturm* shook his head, resenting Schultz's tone of voice. He'd never seen a piece of ID like this. Neither did he trust a man carrying a Morse key.

'The coat,' he said. 'Take it off.'

'Why?'

'Just do as I say.'

Schultz held his gaze for a moment, aware of the exchange of smiles between the other two men. Then he shrugged and took the coat off.

'It's yours,' he said. 'Keep it.'

'Really? And you think that will take care of it? Herr *Oberst*?' The phrase was heavy with sarcasm.

The *Volkssturm* tossed the Loden coat to the younger man and told him to fetch the *Kübelwagen* before turning back to Schultz.

'You know the Prinz-Albrecht-Strasse, Herr *Oberst*?'

'Of course.'

'And you know what those people get up to?'

'Yes.'

'Excellent. Then I'm sure we can resolve this matter.' He glanced down and tapped the ID. 'A word from your colleagues, and you're a free man again.'

23

Ursula Barton and Tam Moncrieff left Switzerland that same afternoon, taking the train to Geneva and crossing the border into France. Swiss officials checked their visas, expressed little interest in their bags, and waved them through. When Moncrieff raised an eyebrow at their good fortune, Barton simply shrugged. People are losing interest, she muttered, even here.

She'd reserved two seats on a military flight from the airfield at Annecy. The seats were in different parts of the aircraft, which Moncrieff viewed as a blessing. Wedged between a portly Royal Tank Regiment Colonel, and the scratched Perspex of the window, he stared out at the rumpled grey carpet of cloud below as the aircraft droned north, still trying to come to terms with last night's news about Bella. While he'd made a kind of peace with her passing, he'd always resisted trying to imagine how it might have happened. Now, thanks to Schultz, that luxury had gone.

To die in battle, he thought, would be one thing. To be raped, and then tossed away, quite another. He knew that this was the small change of any war, always had been, but that was no consolation. He'd known Bella intimately, every nook, every cranny. He knew how proud she was, and how vivid. Reckless? Occasionally. Brave? Undoubtedly. But canny, too, with a rare talent for sidestepping life's larger disasters. Ask any man whose life she had touched, and the verdict would be the same: that Bella Menzies and rape simply didn't belong in the same sentence. Moncrieff closed his eyes and shook his head. Another lazy peacetime assumption that had proved all too wrong. War was no friend of virtue. Least of all hers.

It was nearly dark by the time they landed at Northolt. Ursula Barton had arranged for a car to be waiting to ferry them into London. The driver was eager for news of the latest Allied advances. How were the Yanks getting on in the Ruhr Valley? When would the Russians be on the move again? Moncrieff coped with the flood of questions as best he could, largely thanks to the *Neue Zürcher Zeitung*, but Barton scarcely said a word. When the driver dropped her outside her semi in Shepherd's Bush, she turned briefly to Moncrieff before getting out of the car.

'Liddell will want to see us tomorrow afternoon,' she muttered. 'Three o'clock if you've nothing better to do.'

She arrived at the meeting a little late with two photographs, both shot in Bern. Liddell had just returned to St James's Street from an extended lunchtime rehearsal, storing his cello in a corner of the office. The string quartet, he'd been explaining to Moncrieff, was readying for an end-of-hostilities concert. Vivaldi mainly. A welcome splash of Italian sunshine after all the gothic gloom.

Now he got to his feet behind the desk, his hand extended, a courtly gesture to welcome Barton back, but she seemed oblivious. By the time Moncrieff had fetched her a chair, she'd laid one of the photos in front of Liddell. Moncrieff recognised the faces on the terrace beside the lake.

Liddell studied the photo for a long moment.

'Remarkable,' he murmured. 'We have the negative?'

'I'm afraid not, sir.' Moncrieff explained about the darkroom in Locarno, and the attack on Hannalore, a little surprised to be the one to break the news.

'Golly.' Liddell's gaze returned to the photo. 'You mean this is all we've got?'

'It's the best of the bunch.' Barton this time. 'I managed to rephotograph the print before that one went missing as well. Tam fell into bad company shortly afterwards, but it seems that Schultz can still play the warrior when the spirit moves him.'

'This is Wilhelm Schultz? Canaris' man?'

'The very same. Tam?'

The explanation, once again, fell to Moncrieff. Willi Schultz, he said, had turned up at the hotel. They'd shared a companionable evening at a Bern fish restaurant, followed by a coda that neither of them had expected. By this time, Liddell was inspecting the other photograph.

'And this is?' He slipped the print across the desk towards Moncrieff, who hadn't seen this photo before. A youngish figure, semi-naked, was sprawled on a lavatory. His trousers were round his ankles. His leather belt had been looped around his neck and then secured to the long pipe that delivered water from the overhead cistern. His hands, too, had been manacled behind him but it was impossible to see how. One eye was already closing and his nose would have to be reset. No wonder Schultz had been so pleased with himself.

'That's *Crusader*'s oppo. The pair of them were waiting for us back at the hotel bar. We're guessing he's a fellow Serb.'

'*Crusader?*'

'A freelance, according to De Vries.'

'Working for whom?'

'Moscow.' Barton this time. 'Otherwise none of this makes sense.'

'And you think he was responsible for the unpleasantness in Locarno?'

'I do, yes.'

'Meaning?' Liddell was looking at Moncrieff.

'Meaning the Soviets have a full record of the meeting by the lake.' He nodded at the other print. 'Schultz gave *Crusader* that, too. Exhibit one. Thank God Ursula had rephotographed it.'

'But why would Schultz give it away?'

'Very good question, sir. Nothing in Willi's life has ever been simple.'

Liddell nodded. His gaze had returned to the figures by the lake, SS *Obergruppenführer* Karl Wolff locked in conversation with two of the Allies' senior Generals.

'This situation has begun to exercise our leaders,' he said quietly. 'Roosevelt and Stalin are exchanging letters by the day, and Winston's doing his best to table our own interests. The Soviets believe we've gone behind their backs to end the war on our terms and this would appear to make their case.' He looked up, tapping the photo. 'I can see no Russians in that little huddle, can you?'

Moncrieff shook his head. He'd been there. He'd watched very carefully. No Russians.

'The Prime Minister's anxious?' This from Moncrieff.

'Exasperated. He's had sight of Moscow's latest. Stalin is very unhappy. He points out that the Germans are fighting like hell for some tiny railway junction in Czecho while we get Osnabrück, and Mannheim, and Kassel, all of them barely defended. Those cities fall into our laps, says Uncle Joe, and we spill no blood. He's definitely smelling conspiracy, which shouldn't surprise any of us, but I must say that a photograph like this doesn't help.'

'You're suggesting we should never have acquired it in the first place?' Barton's tone was icy.

'On the contrary, I'm suggesting it was careless to lose it.'

'That wasn't our fault. Tam walked into a trap. Someone knew he was coming. From the moment he stepped into Switzerland, they were onto him.'

'They?'

'*Crusader.*' She nodded at the figure in the lavatory. 'Latterly with a little help from his friend. Of course the Russians are keen to find out about Wolff, about secret meetings, about what's really going on. That's what took them to *Crusader.* That's what put him on the train to keep an eye on Tam. But the real question is who drew him to Tam in the first place.'

'And?'

'And what, sir?'

'You have any suggestions? Anything helpful that might move this discussion on? This morning, Downing Street appeared to believe that it's in German interests to make mischief. They want to set us at each other's throats. They want the alliance to fall apart, East and West, and on the evidence of the current correspondence, I must say it appears to be working. A separate peace with us would suit Hitler very well. He may even suggest we link hands to fight the Soviets, which would be a glorious irony, would it not? We'd all be back in the thirties, fighting the Red Menace.'

Moncrieff was watching Liddell very carefully, the way the fingers of his right hand were drumming some secret rhythm on the scuffed green leather desktop. So soft, he thought. So intimate. So private. Did every musician take cover like this? Had years of playing in his string quartet removed him from the real world? From the challenge of an alliance under extreme pressure? Would the head of 'B' Section prefer to bring this troubling discussion to an end?

'*Crusader* knew, sir.' Barton wasn't giving up. 'My question is how?'

'And you have some thoughts? You think word leaked ahead of Tam's departure?'

'I do, sir. Yes.'

'To someone close to home?'

'Yes.'

'You have a name, by any chance?'

'Philby.'

'Evidence?'

'He paid the embassy a visit last week. In Bern. He was there for three days.'

'For what reason?'

'I've no idea. But neither did the handful of people I talked to at the embassy, which is rather the point. There was some talk of meetings in town. I gather he paid Zurich a visit. But Broadway's always the ghost at the feast as far as our diplomatic friends are concerned.'

'Too tribal? Poor table manners?' Liddell smiled. 'Too *secret*?'

'That, with respect, sir, is silly.'

'Silly, how? Surely the bloody man might have a multitude of perfectly good reasons for taking himself off to Bern. As I understand it, we despatched Tam to mend fences with Dulles, to apologise for not being able to produce Wuensche, to offer him another *petit cadeau*. What on earth does any of that have to do with Broadway?'

'Not Broadway, sir. Philby.'

'You're telling me there's a difference?'

'I'm suggesting there might be.'

'In what sense, pray?' Liddell was frowning now, an expression of mild reproof. 'We're very close to the end of the war, my dear. The umpire may draw stumps at any moment. The peace, I admit, will be a challenge and I fear that our little corner of the tent may become seriously untidy. There will be lots and lots to do. We have a small army of internees, as we all know. They'll have to be sorted and re-sorted. Some will be duds. They can be sent home. Others may be more promising, may deserve a conversation or two, may be prepared to put themselves at our disposal. That little dance will take months, possibly longer, and our only blessing is that by then this wretched war will be over.' He held Barton's gaze for a moment, and then he nodded once again at the figures on the terrace by the lake. 'This little contretemps will blow over. I guarantee it. Your anxieties about Mr Philby, dare I say it, are theological. This is not the time for family quarrels. I say again, the peace may be more challenging than the war. I suggest...' He broke off, staring at Barton as she got to her feet, smoothed the wrinkles from her skirt and turned on her heel. Moments later she'd gone, leaving nothing but the squeal of a distant tram.

Liddell was still gazing at the door. Then he shook his head. '*Verruckt*,' he murmured. Crazy.

*

The holding cells at Gestapo headquarters on the Prinz-Albrecht-Strasse were in the basement. Each cell measured 1.5 x 2.5 metres. A bed folded down from the wall, and beside a small table was a stool. Morning and evening, prisoners were given a mug of lukewarm ersatz coffee and two slices of bread with marmalade, while lunch appeared at noon. It was always soup. And the thin broth always featured small chunks of soggy potato.

Today, Nehmann counted three of them. Counting, he realised, had become central to his sanity, the barest thread that secured him to what remained of his life. Every morning, when he awoke, he used his spoon to make another tiny mark on the wall beside his bed, a tally of early mornings, any one of which could have been his last. So far, he'd been here for four days. Four days of expecting the footsteps down the corridor, the scrape of a key turning in his cell door, the rough hands pushing him into one of the neighbouring interrogation suites, the brief pantomime of question and faltering answer, followed by the inevitable end. According to Goebbels, the Gestapo were mean when it came to precious ammunition. These days, a single bullet through the back of the head was all you could expect.

And yet, for reasons Nehmann couldn't fathom, it hadn't happened. In one sense this was a blessing. His ankles had been shackled on arrival but at least he was still alive, and so far there'd been no attempts to interrogate him. Yet the very fact that nothing had happened – no visits to the torture suites, no list of charges, not the least indication that anyone, except the elderly warder who delivered his food, even knew he was here – had left him in limbo. Kolyma, in a thousand ways, had been infinitely worse but never in his life had Nehmann had to cope with this strange absence of more or less everything. No official contacts of any kind. No threats. No explanations. No Gulag battle for rations or warmth. And worst of all, no books, no paper, no pen. Nothing to read. And no way of starting a modest conversation, even on paper, even with himself.

Once a day, after the evening bread and marmalade, the warder accompanied him to the washroom at the end of the corridor. Here – still shackled – he could use the lavatory and the cold shower. There was no soap and the scrap of towelling was a tease, absolutely useless, but what was worse was the absence of anyone else. When he asked the warder whether the Reich had run out of prisoners, the old man rolled his sad eyes and muttered something about one of God's jokes, but when Nehmann tried to push him further he simply shrugged and turned his head away.

The neighbouring cells, of course, were still occupied. Nehmann could hear stirrings of movement on both sides, and late in the evening there came animal screams from the interrogation suites, yet these noises off began to resemble the soundtrack for some surreal film, yet another clever ploy on Goebbels' part to drive his once-favourite journalist out of his mind.

Goebbels? Was it really his doing? Nehmann would have loved to believe that the Reich Commissar for the Defence of Berlin, the Reich Minister of Propaganda, still had time to settle this private debt, but the truth – he suspected – was much simpler. In the shape of his drafted speech, Mikhail Magalashvili had insulted both the Führer and his precious Reich. Neither of them could cope with this brief glimpse of the truth, and so Nehmann, after days or maybe weeks adrift, would have to pay the price.

That bothered him. He didn't want to die and thinking about it was no help at all. He feared the sudden appearance of armed guards at the door, the stumble up the staircase to the courtyard, and then – bare seconds later – having to kneel in the cold dawn, listening to the slide of the single bullet into the executioner's Luger. But what was much worse, at least for now, was the penance that went before it. All his life, in ways so subtle he'd sometimes never noticed, he'd been in charge. Now that had gone. Leaving, quite literally, nothing.

Then, on the evening of the fifth day, relief. It came in the shape of tap-tapping on the pipes that ran between the cells, faint at first, then stronger. Nehmann swung himself off the bed and knelt beside the pipe, listening intently. The tapping stopped, and then resumed, faster this time, and letter by letter Nehmann began to coax meaning from the torrent of dots and dashes. The old man in the Kolyma gold mines, the bunkmate who'd taught him Morse code, had done his work well. News, announced the tapper, had come from the concentration camp at Flossenbürg. Admiral Canaris had been put to death. May he rest in peace.

Nehmann waited for silence, and then composed a reply.

'How do you know?'

Silence again. Then, fully a minute later, another message. The old guy who brings the food told me.

'Do you think it's true?'

'*True*?' The repetition was abrupt. His evening classes in Kolyma had never taught Nehmann the Morse for laughter, but he fancied that's what the repetition implied. True? False? Who fucking cares any more?

Good point, Nehmann thought.

'RIP,' he tapped back. 'Us next?'

*

Five days later, Franklin D. Roosevelt died. Moncrieff was at his desk in St James's Street, checking the schedules for the first internees to be released after the war's end. A soft knock on his door revealed Guy Liddell. His shapeless cardigan and worn corduroy trousers, thought Moncrieff, must have been a relic of peacetime.

He handed Moncrieff a telegram. It had arrived only minutes earlier from the British Embassy in Washington. President Roosevelt had died in Warm Springs, Georgia, and arrangements were already in hand to swear in the vice-president at a brief ceremony in the White House.

'This is good news, Tam, believe it or not.' Liddell settled briefly on a corner of Moncrieff's desk. 'Truman will have no truck with *Sunrise*. He's just not made that way.'

Operation *Sunrise* was the bid to lead Wolff to surrender

talks in northern Italy. As far as Moncrieff was aware, relations between Moscow and Washington were more acrimonious than ever.

'Winston wants nothing more to do with Wolff,' Liddell said. 'He thought it was a dangerous idea to begin with and nothing's changed his mind.'

'He's seen the photo we brought back?'

'He has, Tam, and he's asked me to pass on his thanks. After Yalta, Stalin's pique has shaken him. Thin-skinned doesn't begin to cover it. Neither does obduracy. The word he's using is paranoic. He believes Stalin is made of the driest tinder and, more importantly, he thinks that photo of yours set him on fire. He thinks the man's become impossible.'

'He's assuming Stalin has seen the photo, too?'

'He is, yes. And here's something else he apparently said. Best not to sup with the Devil at all, and you know why? Because no spoon in the world is long enough.'

Moncrieff smiled. It was a nice expression.

'And Ursula? Any word?'

'We sent the quacks in yesterday.'

'Quacks? Plural?'

'One's a physician. He can find nothing physically wrong with her. The other man's a psychiatrist.'

'And?'

'Severe depression.' He shook his head, a gesture of regret. 'Much as we suspected.'

*

Goebbels learned the news about the death of the president after midnight. He'd just returned home after celebrating the Berlin Philharmoniker's final concert. To his intense satisfaction, the hall had been full, every seat taken, and afterwards guests had paused beside the *Hitlerjugend* at the exit doors, inspecting the tiny phials of cyanide.

Some helped themselves, taking enough supplies for their entire family. Others declined, shaking their heads, buttoning their coats and heading for the twilit streets outside. One elderly male guest, in a whispered aside that Goebbels had caught, suggested that listening to Wagner in certain moods was quite enough make you suicidal. This apostasy put a brief smile on Goebbels' face and afterwards, at the reception, he made a fierce speech about waiting for God and fate to show their hands.

Back home at Bogensee, the news of Roosevelt's death was awaiting him. Goebbels read the message from the German News Agency twice, just to make sure. Then he sank behind his desk in the room he used as an office, realising just how momentous this development could be. The new president had to be Truman, and Truman – he was certain – would have none of Roosevelt's patience with Stalin. The days of to-and-fro correspondence over the Wolff affair, no matter how barbed, were over. Stalin was a thief, helping himself to country after country in Eastern Europe, and Truman knew exactly how to handle people like that. Personally, Goebbels had some respect for Stalin but his attempts to recruit Hitler to the Soviet cause had failed. Now, therefore, was the moment to hold Berlin, await the collapse of the Allied coalition, and then plot the Reich's survival.

By now, it was the early hours of Friday 13th April.

*

Three days later, in the middle of the night, Maria awoke in her house in Eichwalde. For a moment she couldn't understand what could have woken Dominika. The child had been teething all day, miserable with her aching gums, and Maria had moved the cot into her own bedroom, trying to offer a little comfort. Now, the child was tossing and turning, inconsolable, and Maria bent over the cot, watching her, until she, too, heard the ominous rumble of what she first took to be thunder. She went to the window and pulled back the curtain. It was a cloudy night, but there was no sign of lightning. Then she opened the window a little, and the noise got much louder. It's coming from the east, she thought, beginning to shiver in the cold night air.

Nehmann heard it, too, hours later, not through the walls of his windowless cell, but thanks to his neighbour's command of Morse code. The Russians are on the move, went the message. Nehmann reached for his spoon.

'How do you know?' he tapped back.

'It's the talk of the showers. The Reds are storming the Seelow Heights. Everyone knows.'

The Seelow Heights. Nehmann had a faint recollection of a pre-war visit he'd paid with a young dancer from the Polish Ballet on tour in Berlin. They'd borrowed a car and driven east towards the River Oder. The Heights overlooked the river valley, and it was said there were nice walks over the sandy hills. The rumours had turned out to be true but this morning that was hardly the point. The Seelow Heights were barely a two-hour drive from Berlin.

Nehmann, with nothing but a spoon in place of pen and paper, had already decided to start a news agency. The price of his sanity in whatever time was left to him would be a series of despatches. He was calling it *Paprika Rundfunk*, and in response to an acid enquiry from his neighbour, relayed on the pipes, he pledged to add a little spice to the passage of events.

Already, he'd invented a flotilla of new U-boats, emerging from shipyards along the Elbe, able to surface off the English coast and bombard major cities with death rays. Now, in the wake of the news from the Oder, he announced the successful despatch of a new breed of super-bombers, packed with high explosive and deadly nerve gas, all of them headed for the Russians storming the Seelow Heights.

'Thank God for the *Mistel* project.' He tap-tapped with his spoon. '*Der Führertraum* come true.'

Der Führertraum was the Führer dream and provoked the wrath of Nehmann's new correspondent.

'*Führertraum*, bollocks,' he tapped back. 'You're the fucking dreamer.'

'I am.' Nehmann was delighted. 'And you've no idea where that can take you. My next despatch? Why the Führer is disguising his age in order to join the *Volkssturm*. And how post-war Germany, once again victorious, will be living on fried eggs and mashed potato and those horrible pastries they serve at the fucking Berghof. The Red Army, sensibly, is already planning their retreat. They want nothing to do with us. Who can blame them? More follows.'

That night, Nehmann awaited the summons that would take him to the interrogation suite. He'd insulted the Führer once to Goebbels, and now again on *Paprika Rundfunk*. That, surely, would trigger at least a conversation but – once again – absolutely nothing happened.

*

Four days later, with the Russians already in the suburbs of Berlin, Moncrieff decided to pay Ursula Barton a visit. St James's Street, like the rest of the capital, was gripped by what Guy Liddell was calling *Friedensfieber*, or peace-fever. One of the Watchers had opened a book for when the Germans would chuck in the towel and call it a day. The bulk of the betting settled on the middle of the first week in May but the cannier punters, the ones with a knowledge of Bolshevik history, laid their bets on 1st May. Stalin would never resist the temptation, they insisted. May Day is sacred in the Ivans' calendar, and what Stalin wants, Stalin gets.

Moncrieff wasn't so sure. In the late afternoon, he took the bus to Shepherd's Bush and found a pub that still served malt whisky. For more money than he could really afford he bought an entire bottle of Talisker, partly because he knew Barton liked it a great deal, and partly because the taste would take him back to the mountains he always missed. On her doorstep, he eyed the shabby paintwork and spring growth that was already out of control, waiting for her to let him in. Only after the third knock did the door finally open.

She looked terrible. Her hair, never her best feature, seemed to have gone iron-grey overnight. Dry, unkempt, it framed a face the colour of putty. She was wearing a dress she must have bought for a sturdier body. The shade of cream would have once suited her but there were soup stains down the front and two buttons were missing.

She gazed at him, her eyes blank, one hand still on the door.

'Tam,' Moncrieff said. 'Me. Tam.'

She nodded, none the wiser, then retreated into the semi-darkness of the hall as he stepped inside. The smell hit him at once, a gust of old cooking fat and rotting food. In the kitchen, he found the butler sink piled high with unwashed plates, and a dustbin by the door was brimming with assorted refuse. Tam put the bottle of Talisker carefully to one side and took off his jacket before tackling the mess. Barton watched him for a minute or two, uncomprehending, and then sensibly beat a retreat. Half an hour later, with a pair of carefully washed glasses, he joined her in the front sitting room.

'What's that?' She was looking at the bottle.

'Malt whisky. A little treat.'

'Talisker? Wonderful.' She suddenly clapped her hands. 'I used to drink it with a friend.'

'That was probably me.'

'Tam? Tam Moncrieff?'

'Definitely me.'

'Really?' She was squinting at him now, and Moncrieff – to his delight – sensed an alibi in the making. She'd finally surfaced. She knew who he was. They might even risk a conversation.

Moncrieff moved the spare armchair closer. Everything felt sticky to his touch, and the whole house probably deserved a thorough spring clean, but what mattered just now was coaxing this woman he'd never ceased to respect back to life. She wanted that to happen. He could see it in her eyes, in the way her hand found his. Help me, she was saying. Tell me who I am.

'We miss you,' he said. 'Even Guy misses you. These days he's like a dog without his keeper. We need you back, we really do. So let's drink to that.'

He poured two glasses of the malt, passed one over, watched her hand – clawlike – tighten around it.

'To peace.' He lifted his glass.

'Guy?' She was staring at him now. 'Guy Liddell?'

'Him, too. Cheers.'

Moncrieff took a long swallow of the malt. Barton watched him carefully, the way a child might, then did the same. One hand went to her chest as she began to cough.

'You need water? Let me get it.'

'No.' She shook her head. 'My back. Give it a tap or two.'

Moncrieff got to his feet and circled her armchair, coaxing her upper body forward before patting her back. The coughing stopped and she reached for his spare hand again, gazing up

at him, something close to panic in her eyes, and Moncrieff
dropped to his knees, putting his arms around her. She felt frail,
birdlike. And she was beginning to tremble.

'What's the matter?' he whispered. 'Just tell me.'

She shook her head, told him she was an old fool, forbade
him to pay her any attention, then she seemed to slump in his
arms and a little of the malt slopped onto her lap. She gazed at
it for a long moment, then shook her head.

'I'm frightened, Tam. I really am.'

'Of peace? Of me? Of Liddell?'

'Of everything.'

*

That same day, Friday 20th April, was Hitler's fifty-sixth birthday.
Goebbels roused a troubled nation to offer their collective good
wishes while Nazi tribal chiefs flocked to the Führer bunker
under the Chancellery with their tribute presents. Nazi flags
were raised on ruined buildings across the surviving remains
of the Reich. In Berlin, weary housewives dropped half-rotten
potatoes onto open fires on their sagging balconies and sent
their daughters to join the queues for water from the standpipe
in the street below. At the Hohenlychen Sanatorium, meanwhile,
Himmler toasted his Führer in looted French champagne, and
laid plans to meet Count Bernadotte for exploratory peace
negotiations in Lübeck in just three days' time.

That afternoon, Hitler emerged from his bunker and made
a brief appearance in the ruined gardens of the Chancellery. He
worked his way slowly down a line of *Hitlerjugend*, tweaking a
cheek here, patting a shoulder there, pinning the Iron Cross to a
handful of infant chests, careful to conceal his shaking left hand
behind his back. From the nearby courtyard of the Ministry of
Foreign Affairs came the sharp bark of small arms fire. Some

of the *Hitlerjugend* were nervous and exchanged glances, but Goebbels – who was also present – told them not to worry. It's only the Führer's secretaries, he explained. Putting in a little pistol practice for when the Russians arrive.

Later, remembering this scene in the silence of his darkened house at Bogensee, Goebbels made a rare admission to himself. Not even Nehmann, he thought, could have brightened the Führer's birthday.

*

That night, a little drunk, Moncrieff stayed in Shepherd's Bush. The Talisker malt seemed to have restored just a glimpse of the old Ursula, and she sat up late with him, a sleepy tom cat on her lap, chairs drawn up around the steady hiss of the gas fire while Moncrieff fed coins into the meter and did his best to share what he knew of the fate of Operation *Sunrise*.

Roosevelt's death, he confirmed, had brought negotiations to a halt. Under pressure from the White House, the OSS had instructed Allen Dulles to break off all contact with the Germans in northern Italy. In the meantime, the Russians were pressing hard to be first to occupy Trieste and had instructed the Serb partisans to meet them there.

'Then they've won.' Barton was staring hard at the remains of her fourth glass. There was a little colour back in her face, and she kept fondling the cat. 'If the Germans are still holding out in northern Italy, then we're denied Trieste. And if we're denied Trieste, the Soviets will be nicely poised for what follows.'

Moncrieff nodded, glad that the last couple of weeks had begun to return to her.

'There's something else, though, isn't there…?' he suggested carefully.

'You mean about the Russians?'

'Possibly.'

'I'm afraid I'm not following you. My fault, my dear. Might there be a drop more, do you think?'

She emptied the glass and held it out while Moncrieff poured a generous measure. The next minute or two, he knew, were all-important. There were some secrets that even Talisker couldn't unlock.

'Philby,' he murmured. 'What do we really think?'

She held his gaze, said nothing. The question had kindled something in her eyes. Anger? Apprehension? Despair? He didn't know.

'The man's a traitor,' she said at last. 'He's working for the Russians and I've thought so for a long time. The fact that he's still operational will tell you more about us than them, or even him, but the facts put it beyond doubt.'

She began to tally them on the fingers of her left hand. His pre-war background in Germany and Austria. His marriage to a fervent Communist. His role as a reporter in the civil war in Spain. The testament of defectors like Krivitsky. And, most important of all, his fingerprints all over the missing week in Moncrieff's own life. Assigned to shadow Philby, sending him a message that he'd aroused suspicions in MI5, Moncrieff had been outwitted at every turn before being kidnapped and drugged.

'That had to be Philby showing his hand. I've done my best to flag the wretched man, I truly have, but no one ever listens. And now? This thing in Bern? *Crusader*? That bloody photo? It's all of a piece, Tam. It has to be. We never learn. Ever. And in my book, we'll deserve whatever happens next.'

'Like?'

'The bloody man's clever. That's rare in our game, or rarer than it should be. With his wits, and his nerve, and that charming stutter, he could end up in charge of everything, you, me, everything. As it is, they've just given him a new section of his own, Section Nine, counter-espionage, lifting the drawbridge and getting the boiling oil ready for whatever happens next. Can you believe that? Catching spies used to be our job, Tam. I've wept these last few days, I truly have.' She shook her head, gazing round. 'Look at the state of this place. Look at what I've turned into. Do you think I'm unaware, Tam? Be honest.'

'But earlier, when I knocked on your door...?'

'Earlier I was playing the derelict. Believe me, that's not hard. There are parts of me that have been derelict for years. Do you know what I've been up to since they set the quacks on me? I've been writing to my sister. The one in Germany. The handsome Gretel. The one who got everything that I never got. The looks. The wit. The ability to laugh at herself. She lives in a very different part of the forest, Tam, and I've made it my business to write it all down for her. Where I've been, what I've got up to, what I'm proud of, what I'm not. That bloody awful marriage of mine, for instance. Then ending up in this place, with my discs of Rossini and collection of empty bottles. Everything, Tam. The whole bloody lot. Good riddance, I say. Get it off your chest, woman.'

Moncrieff nodded, startled. He'd never heard her talk like this, never dreamed such a speech was in her.

'And will you send her this...' he shrugged, '... letter? Diary? Memoir? Whatever it is?'

'Of course I will, except there's one problem.' She broke off to reach for the bottle again.

Moncrieff watched her pouring the malt, impressed by the steadiness of her hand.

'So what's the problem?' he asked at last. 'What would ever stop you?'

She eyed him for a moment or two, and then her shoulders slumped, and her head went down, and she began to shake. Moncrieff was on his knees again by her chair, waiting for the storm to pass. Finally her head came up again, her eyes filmy with tears.

'Gretel doesn't exist, Tam.' She produced a soiled handkerchief. 'There's only ever been me.'

*

On 22nd April, Goebbels moved into the Führer bunker. His allotted suite of rooms had space for his wife and their six children. Magda Goebbels unpacked the children's toys and impressed upon them the importance of not getting in the way of the grown-ups. Papa and the Führer were still fighting the war. Defeat was unthinkable, a naughty rumour spread by the Reich's many enemies. The older children looked at each other. The air smelled funny, said Helga, and why was everyone in such a bad mood?

*

Three days later, 25th April, two Gestapo guards appeared at Schultz's cell door. Schultz had been awake for hours, listening to the muffled roar of battle in the world outside. Most of the explosions he recognised as artillery fire, and the building shuddered from time to time as the shells crept ever closer.

The youngest of the guards, who appeared to be in charge, informed him that the time had come for him to face interrogation. Schultz, who'd been expecting this summons from the moment he'd arrived at Prinz-Albrecht-Strasse, said nothing. In Moscow, the NKVD entrusted their high-value prisoners to the Ukrainians. Here, the task of breaking a man fell to a smallish team recruited from the cesspit that was the Budapest underworld. Schultz had

396

read some of the interrogation transcripts while he still had a desk at *Abwehr* headquarters. The contrast between accounts offered before and after torture at the hands of these animals was stark. As the Russians began to throttle the entire city, he had no doubts about what awaited him.

He took a last look at his cell. Keeping it neat and tidy had helped him stay sane. He bent to the floor beside the water pipe and retrieved his spoon. He gave it a wipe on the corner of the blanket, and then laid it carefully on the table.

'*Schnell.*' It was the older guard this time. He was getting impatient.

Schultz shuffled awkwardly into the corridor, cursing the shackles on his ankles. When he asked whether they might be released, the younger guard laughed. For once, instead of turning right, Schultz was pointed towards the staircase that led to the ground floor. At the foot of the steps he came to a halt and between them, the guards half pushed, half carried him upwards. Schultz fell twice, jarring his knees on the grey concrete, and by the time he got to the top, blood was seeping through the thin fabric of his borrowed trousers. The hors d'œuvre before the main course, he thought grimly. Just to get me in the mood.

Mercifully, the office was barely a couple of steps away. A knock from one of the guards opened the door, and Schultz found himself looking at a youngish man in a grey suit. His hair was a little long for a building like this, and there was a hint of amusement in the light blue eyes behind the glasses. For a moment, Schultz thought he recognised the smile but he couldn't be sure.

'Herr *Oberst*? My name is Erwin Neuer. *Brigadeführer* Schellenberg presents his apologies. He wanted to be here to shake your hand but ...' he frowned, aware of the shackles for the first time. 'You have a key?' The question was addressed to the older guard.

Schultz watched the man on his knees, wrestling with the stiffness of the lock. Walter Schellenberg was Himmler's prize asset, the *Reichsführer-SS*'s eyes and ears, the urbane genius who'd masterminded the overthrow of the *Abwehr* and danced to the top of the SD. Schultz had known Schellenberg well, first by reputation, then face to face, and had always had a grudging respect for the man.

The guards had been dismissed. Neuer helped Schultz towards the desk and settled him in one of the two chairs. From here, Schultz had a view of the courtyard at the very centre of Gestapo headquarters. After weeks in his cell, the wash of grey light came as a faint surprise. It was thickened by towering clouds of smoke, and the percussive thump of artillery fire was much louder now. The sash window was open at the top and Schultz caught the sour reek of cordite on the chillness of the breeze.

'So where are they?' he asked. 'The Ivans?'

'Last time I heard...' Neuer had sat down, '... they'd just occupied Dahlem.'

'You mean the KWI?'

'Yes.'

'They've taken a good look at the site there?'

'I'm afraid I have no details.'

'And the Americans?'

'They joined up with the Soviets this morning. Torgau, I think, on the Elbe. I was with Schellenberg yesterday, up in Pomerania. The roads are full of *Wehrmacht*. I know it's forbidden but the word we ought to be using is retreat. Or perhaps *Katastrophe*. The front line is crumbling everywhere. We can't take the punches any more. If this was a boxing match, the referee would have stopped it days ago.' He paused, playing with a pencil. 'We understand you had a meeting with the *Reichsführer-SS*.'

'We?'

'Schellenberg and I. Your departure gave you away, Herr *Oberst*. The *Reichsführer* lacks a sense of humour, as you know. Turning your back like that would have given the old *Abwehr* a bad name.'

'On the contrary, we were the ones with the manners. Schellenberg used to go riding with Canaris every morning in the Grunewald, back in the days when we had time for each other. You remember that?'

'I do, yes. Schellenberg did his best to get me onto a horse but I never really took to it.' Another pause. 'You've heard about Canaris?'

'I have, yes.'

'Deeply regrettable but under the circumstances, I imagine there was no option.'

'You *imagine*?' Schultz was trying hard to keep his temper. 'You work for these people, Herr Neuer. You're SD, *Sicherheitsdienst*. You answer to Himmler, *Onkel Heine*. He runs the camps. He orders the investigations, asks the hard questions. He decides who lives and who dies. You *imagine*?'

'We understand you've been away a while, Herr *Oberst*. The Gulag? Am I right?'

'Moscow. I never had to dig ship canals or mine for gold but the principle's the same. I was there at their pleasure. They could do what they wanted, when they wanted. That concentrates a man's mind, believe me.'

'And you had contacts with the NKVD?'

'Of course. They were my keepers.'

'And these contacts were at a high level?'

'High enough to make my life a little less unpleasant.'

'I don't doubt it. Does the name Stauffenberg mean anything?'

'Claus von Stauffenberg? Panzer man? Served under Rommel in Africa?"

'That was a while back. He tried to blow up the Führer last year and Canaris turned out to be part of that plot. The Führer is unforgiving, as we all know. Which means that *Onkel Heine* must attend to his duties.'

'By hanging Canaris?'

'Of course. Plus thousands of others. The Führer would expect no less.'

'And you? And Schellenberg?'

Neuer wouldn't answer the question, not directly. Instead, he got up and closed the window before settling again behind the desk.

'The game's up, Herr *Oberst*. We know it, Himmler knows it, even Hitler probably senses that all is not well. Under those circumstances, it might pay a man to make certain provisions.'

'For what?'

'For his future. That letter you delivered to the *Reichsführer* appears to be genuine, however misconceived.'

'Meaning?'

'Meaning Himmler will never talk to the Russians. The English? Maybe. The Americans? Yes. These last few days we've been trying to build a bridge through Sweden.'

'Count Bernadotte?'

'Exactly. Himmler and Stauffenberg met him in Lübeck last night. It didn't go well. Himmler is a bag of nerves these days. It doesn't pay to share a car with him at the wheel, but he still believes he's the Führer-in-waiting. The Americans want nothing to do with him, and Hitler will have his head the moment he finds out what's going on. The outlook for *Onkel Heine* is, I'm afraid, poor.'

'And you? And that boss of yours?'

'We're on manoeuvres, Herr *Oberst*. Reconnaissance is our business, as it used to be yours, and we believe the immediate future, at least in this city, will belong to the Soviets. That situation will offer certain possibilities. Both of us, especially *Brigadeführer* Schellenberg, have a great deal of knowledge. We know what's really been going on this last year or two. If I was Zhukov, or even Stalin, I wouldn't hesitate to take advantage of us.'

'You're asking me to negotiate on your behalf?'

'When the time is ripe, yes.'

'With whom?'

'In the first place, with the NKVD. We assume you have the contacts. That would be logical.'

Schultz nodded, sat back, did his best to hide his amusement. He'd left the cell a dead man. Now, barely minutes later, he was being recruited to save someone else's life. War, he thought. Madness in a trim grey suit and a pair of glasses.

*

The next day, 27th April, a Triple Priority cable arrived at OSS headquarters in Bern. After firm instructions from Washington just days ago to break off negotiations with SS *Obergruppenführer* Karl Wolff, Allen Dulles was now ordered to hasten the despatch of German envoys to the Allied HQ at Caserta, where preparations were underway for the official surrender of all German forces south of the Alps.

At three o'clock the following afternoon, Generals Lemnitzer and Airey were at the airfield that served Allied HQ, awaiting the arrival of two German Generals empowered to sign the surrender. The Generals disembarked from their aircraft, and greetings were limited to a stiff exchange of bows. Over the hours that followed there were protracted wrangles over elements in the surrender document, but there were no doubts on either side that the Reich's days in the Italian sunshine were over. One of the witnesses to the signing of the surrender document, at Stalin's insistence, was a Russian Major General, Alexsi Pavlovich Kislenko.

*

Nehmann at first had been puzzled by the sudden silence on the water pipes. No more news from the showers. No more applause for his less guarded comments about a variety of Nazi tribal chiefs. No more gruff reminders that the war was now lapping at the battlements of Hitler's secret army. In his last despatch, Nehmann's neighbour had been all too explicit about the fate that probably awaited them all. These people always settle their debts, he'd tapped. Even at the very end.

The very end. Was this what had happened to *Paprika Rundfunk*'s faithful listener? Had he been dragged out to the courtyard and despatched? Was his dead body worth a gallon or two of precious gasoline? Or did they simply leave him to the dogs? Nehmann mourned his absence for four long days, then came a hesitant tapping that drew Nehmann from his bunk. Shackled, he knelt beside the water pipe, listening intently. Nothing happened. Nehmann reached for his spoon.

'Again?' he tapped.

Nothing.

'Please repeat,' he said, keeping the Morse very slow, very deliberate, tap-tap-tap.

This time, faintly, came a reply. A novice, he thought. Either someone very old who's forgotten most of the groups, or someone much younger, who's only just started to learn.

He lifted his spoon, asked once again for the message, and this time there was no doubt.

'*Der Führer.*' Nehmann was staring at the pipe. '*Todt.*'
Hitler. Dead.

*

The news reached Moncrieff at St James's Street that same
evening, which happened to be a Monday. Even at weekends,
shackled to his desk, he'd been working late. Liddell had assigned
him a punishing schedule of potential internee releases to be
assessed and approved, a task that demanded an unbroken
sequence of twelve-hour days. Now, he looked up to find 'B'
Section's director at the door.

'He's gone, Tam.' Liddell was holding a bottle of champagne
and a clutch of glasses.

'Who?'

'Hitler.'

'Killed?' Moncrieff had put his pen down.

'Suicide. It's on the tapes. Reuters. Have we still got that flag,
by the way? And is it presentable? Tomorrow, Tam. First thing.
Run it up the bloody pole.' He settled the glasses on the desk
and poured the champagne. '*Prosit, mein Kamerad.* Here's to
bloody peace.'

Later that night, still at his desk, Moncrieff took a call from
a voice he recognised.

'Ivor Maskelyne?' Just the name was enough to put a smile
on Moncrieff's face. 'I take it you've heard?'

'I have indeed. Joy and rejoicing. And my Broadway chums
tell me it doesn't stop there, either. Hitler took his dog and
that lovely Elsa Braun with him. She'd apparently married him
only hours before. Can you imagine that? Making wifehood
the condition of your own bloody suicide? *Führerdämmerung.*
Scored for all three of them.'

'Anyone else?'

'The money's on Goebbels next.' Maskelyne chuckled. 'There are eight of them in that family so here's hoping they can lay hands on enough pills. Listen, *mon brave*, there are plans afoot for a modest celebration, and it seems your name's on the list.'

'For what?'

'A get-together. And maybe a glass or two. This is Broadway again, I'm afraid. They want someone from your neck of the woods to show his face and you appear to be the only one with table manners.'

'Very funny. Whose idea was this? Specifically?'

'Can't possibly comment, old son. Most of the time you lot depend on guesswork, so I'd stick with that. Can I assume a yes? He can be very persistent.'

'He?'

Another chuckle. Then the line went dead.

*

Early next morning, Erwin Neuer escorted Schultz to a waiting Mercedes. For the past six days, Schultz had been camping in the air raid shelter in the bowels of Gestapo headquarters with a scatter of other prisoners. Here, in the so-called Himmler bunker, Neuer had assured him that he'd be safe, not simply from air raids and Soviet artillery, but from the attentions of the SS. Thanks to a cable from Schellenberg, with rumoured support from the *Reichsführer* himself, *Oberst* Schultz was to be treated as a guest, rather than a prisoner. In terms of his well-being, this diktat made absolutely no difference. The same bread and marmalade. The same potato soup. But at least, as long as he believed this sudden reverse in his fortunes, Schultz was to be spared a visit to the courtyard.

Now, sharing the back of the Mercedes with Neuer, Schultz stared out at the battlescape that had once been the capital of the

Reich. It was still early, dawn a blush of pink beneath a ledge of cloud away to the east, but the grey light revealed nothing except rubble, and drifting clouds of dust kicked up by the wind, and the gaunt bones of ministries along the Wilhelmstrasse, gutted by point-blank fire.

The driver pulled into what once had been the kerb, and half turned to await instructions. Neuer was watching a group of Russian infantry, their weapons trained on the remains of a building on Vossstrasse. Slowly, one by one, a straggle of senior officers appeared in the dawn light, led by a *Wehrmacht* trooper. He was a big man, and he gazed around for a moment or two, not quite believing what he was seeing, and then he raised his rifle. Attached to the bayonet was a length of dirty white cloth. The Russians took a step or two backwards, and then waved the surrender party towards a waiting armoured car, thick rubber tyres, single cannon.

'*Scheisse.*' Schultz shook his head. This, he knew, was history in the making. After all the bloodshed, all the destruction, all the long years of suffering, four figures were stumbling through the cold Berlin dawn, trying to avoid the rubble.

'So what now?' he asked Neuer.

'We follow.'

The surrender party climbed awkwardly into the back of the armoured car. One of the Russians slammed the door shut and gave it a kick before the vehicle set off, its wheels spinning among the debris. Turning into the Hermann-Goering Strasse and crossing the Potsdamer Platz, it was already moving at speed, bucketing from one pothole to the next, the driver's hand on the horn. Watching from the back of the Mercedes, Schultz could only think of some wounded animal, maddened by victory, howling down the empty streets.

Minutes later, they stopped outside a house on the

Schulenburgring. A fine rain had drifted in from the west, and Schultz watched as the driver opened the rear door of the armoured car and hurried his passengers across the pavement and into the house under the carbines of more Russian troopers crouching in the rain.

'Who's in there? Who's waiting?' Schultz nodded at the house.

'Zhukov. He's taking the surrender.'

'Of Germany?'

'Of Berlin. After this morning, everything else will follow.'

Schultz nodded, said nothing. Then a long file of German prisoners appeared, loosely escorted, shuffling through the thin grey dawn. Their heads were down, and face after face registered nothing but the numbness of defeat.

'So why are we here?' Schultz asked, after the prisoners had gone.

'Zhukov has an NKVD man in his entourage. His German is perfect. He's serving as an interpreter. What's happening in there won't take long because there's nothing to talk about. The terms are settled.' A thin smile. 'Unconditional surrender.'

'And then?'

'And then we talk to the NKVD man.'

*

Nehmann awoke to silence. These last few days, the thunder of battle had engulfed the heart of Berlin, a crescendo without end, body blow after body blow that had crept ever closer, rocking the entire building. By now, Nehmann suspected that other prisoners had been evacuated from their cells, probably to some kind of shelter in the basement, but that invitation had never come his way and so he'd lain mute on his bed, his hands over his ears, resigned to whatever the final curtain of this mad drama had in store for him.

Now, though, it had ended. He struggled out of bed in the darkness. Generators fed the lights in the building but even they appeared not to be working. Had they surrendered? And had their German masters also thrown in the towel? And if so, might this account for the silence? His hands groped for his spoon, and he crouched beside the water pipe, tapping a plaintive message. Is there anyone there? And why is it so quiet?

Nothing happened. He tried again, and then a third time, but finally abandoned the effort. The darkness, it occurred to him, might go on for ever. Even peace, if that's what this was, could be merciless.

*

Moncrieff took the phone call at lunchtime, bent over yet another internee schedule in his office at St James's Street. It was Ivor Maskelyne again, phoning from his rooms in Balliol.

'Marching orders, you lucky man.'

'For what?'

'Tonight's little get-together. I now understand it's Section Five only, all those clever buggers out in the wilds of St Albans, bit of a reunion. They've come up with a few games, too. Have you got a pencil handy? Everyone takes a photograph, and a single object, and will be expected to talk about them. Prepare a decent story, too. I imagine you'll be on your feet half the night, and I anticipate lots of bawdy versifying afterwards. No need to take flowers, though, so that might come as a bit of a relief. Do you happen to know the Tower at all?'

'The Tower?' Moncrieff was lost.

'Of London, *mon brave*. They used to put it on stamps behind the King's head. You're to present yourself at the main entrance for eight o'clock. Ask for Alf. He'll let you in.'

'Tonight's impossible.' Moncrieff was looking at the pile of paperwork on his desk. 'My apologies but I won't be there.'

'Out of the question, I'm afraid.'

'Who says?'

'That boss of yours, Guy Liddell. He thinks it's a thoroughly good wheeze. Nice to give peace a flying start before the proper celebrations and he thinks you're the man to make that happen. Everyone's sick of war, *mon brave*. We all need to be friends again.'

Moncrieff nodded, knowing he'd been outflanked.

'So what happens once I get in?' he asked. 'Where am I going?'

'Broadway have commandeered a room in St Thomas's Tower. I'm assured there's lots of grub, and buckets of bubbly, and maybe even a wench or two.' Maskelyne was laughing now. 'And you'll never guess what lies beneath.'

'Tell me.'

'Traitors' Gate.'

*

Nehmann was asleep when the footsteps came to a halt outside his door. Hearing voices, he jerked awake. It was still dark in the cell, an inky blackness that told him nothing about the time of day, or what might happen next, or whether Berlin even existed any more. Then came the squeal of a key turning in the lock, and a stir of slightly colder air told him that the door had opened. For a long moment, nothing happened. Nehmann was sitting up now, facing the door. It could be anyone, he thought. Solitary confinement, yourself alone, robs you of everything.

'Who is it?' he was trying to mask his anxiety.

'Me, my friend.' The cheerfulness in the voice sounded familiar but Nehmann couldn't quite place it. 'The train? *The Kreutzer Sonata*? That poor bloody man and his whore of a wife? You once told me journalists have long memories. Was I right to believe you?'

'Leon?' Nehmann was frowning now. 'The Leon from Kolyma? The Leon from that fucking railway station in the middle of nowhere? The Leon who gave me *War and Peace?*'

'The same. Don't believe me? Here's another clue. It's a present this time. With the compliments of Moscow.' A torch switched on, sweeping the cell until it found the figure on the bunk. Nehmann shielded his eyes, then peered between the spread of his fingers as the beam settled on another presence, standing beside the NKVD man. The huge hands. The hunch of the shoulders. The breadth of the chest. And the briefest shake of the head. The freezing spaces of the church in Stalingrad, he thought. The priest bent over the organ. The dying chords of the *Pathétique*. And outside, under the eyes of the Soviets, the parting nod he'd thought was for ever.

'*Paprika* fucking *Rundfunk?*' Schultz growled. 'That could only be you.'

24

Moncrieff was late getting to the Tower of London. The last time he'd been here was nearly four years ago. On that occasion, he'd been assigned to probe the circumstances that had drawn Rudolf Hess to fly to Scotland and bail out. He'd discovered the Deputy Führer in a freezing cell-like room accessed by a spiral stone staircase but now he found himself in a very different part of the building. St Thomas's Tower lay beside the Thames. Already, Moncrieff could hear the sound of laughter.

Dress code, Maskelyne had assured him, was emphatically a matter of personal taste and Moncrieff was dressed for the hills: comfortable corduroy trousers, soft cotton shirt, old tweed jacket. A flight of stone steps took him to a modest room dominated by an old oak table. Youngish women dressed as wenches were fussing over dishes of food Moncrieff had last seen in the better organised internment camps: thinly sliced pemmican, portions of Woolton Pie, baskets of sliced bread the colour of death. One of the wenches caught Moncrieff's eye, and he recognised the cool, generations-old beauty that went with pre-war country house weekends. Her efforts at a Cockney accent were unconvincing.

'No cooking facilities, I'm afraid, sir, so it has to be alfresco. The boys next door think they're back at school and that makes them very happy.'

Moncrieff was looking at a mountain of boiled potatoes, brightened with chopped nettles.

'Anything to drink?'

'Spoiled for choice, sir. Most of it's next door already. I dare say you'll be helping yourself.'

Moncrieff had brought the keeper's bag he carried on outings from the Glebe House. He extracted a manila envelope and passed it across.

'One favour? Do you mind?'

'Not at all, sir. As long as it ain't naughty.'

'I'm afraid it's very naughty. There's a Mr Philby in there...' he nodded towards the open door. 'You know him?'

'Of course, sir. It's his do. Head of the table. Senior prefect.' She smiled. 'I expect he'll be saying grace soon.'

'Excellent.' Moncrieff nodded at the envelope. 'When you get the chance, just tuck that beside his chair.'

'He's not to see it?'

'God no.' Moncrieff planted a kiss on her cheek. 'My life is in your hands.'

The woman was feeling the shape of the envelope. Then she looked up, and Moncrieff recognised a flicker of real interest in her eyes.

'You're one of them?' She'd abandoned the Cockney accent. 'I find that hard to believe.'

*

The gathering next door was more intimate than Moncrieff had anticipated. The room was lit by candles, shadows dancing on the ancient timbered walls, and he counted no more than a dozen figures sitting around the long table. Some of them were wearing dinner jackets in various states of disrepair. One had a row of medals pinned to a Leander blazer. Another, small and fussy, had dressed himself as Montgomery. The slouch beret and the Desert Rat combat blouse had caught the essence of the man, and Moncrieff watched him scolding his neighbour for a breach of manners. The thin, reedy voice, the intense concentration, the stabbing forefinger, all were perfect.

'Gentlemen, we are honoured.' The tap of a knife on glass stilled the laughter.

It was Philby. He was wearing a patterned Arab headscarf in faded shades of red, and the baggy Army blouse that Moncrieff had last seen on his long-ago visit to Section Five at their St Albans headquarters. The jacket had once belonged to Philby's father. When it gets wet in the rain, he'd told Moncrieff, I can still smell him.

Now, he got to his feet, a generous sweep of his arm serving as an introduction to the faces at the table. Thanks to the munificence of several City livery companies, he said, the evening had been blessed with some truly remarkable wine. The *banderilleros* of Section Five, that happy band of provocateurs, were also happy to offer a barrel of porter, freshly tapped, plus an assortment of other delights available in bottles of every conceivable shape and provenance. Tonight, they'd decided to dispense with formalities. Grub would be left on the table. Most of it was inedible and best left to die of neglect. The drink, on the other hand, deserved serious attention and the presence of a *novillo* with Tam Moncrieff's reputation was indeed an extra blessing.

'You're very welcome, my friend.' He nodded at the empty chair. 'Let's put this bloody war to bed.'

The little speech sparked a storm of applause, hands banging on the table, heads turning to take a proper look at Moncrieff, a couple of the older figures reaching for bottles to recharge their glasses. Philby, Moncrieff sensed at once, was in rude form. In the parlance of the bull ring, a *novillo* was a mere apprentice.

His assigned place, to Moncrieff's relief, put him beside Ivor Maskelyne.

'I'd recommend the Manzanilla for starters.' Maskelyne was already pouring. 'We should raise a glass to the Worshipful Skinners. The days of thin pickings, thank God, are over.'

Moncrieff swallowed a mouthful of the wine. It was cold and slightly tart, in perfect condition. He could taste sunshine with just a hint of the wild tarragon he remembered from the bony Andalusian hills. Bella and I could have spent the rest of our lives making friends of a wine like this, he thought.

'Wolff?' he asked Maskelyne.

'He's a happy man. For one thing he's managed to keep his head on his shoulders. Given the company he's been keeping, that's some achievement. For another, it's his birthday next week. Forty-five is a decent achievement for someone in his game.'

'And the surrender?'

'Done. Dusted. Date-stamped. Consigned to history. Alexander's also despatched Freyburg's Kiwis to Trieste to take on the Chetniks. They should be arriving as we speak. Good hunting, eh?' He lifted his glass. 'Here's to Uncle Joe's next sulk.'

'He's just taken Berlin,' Moncrieff pointed out.

'A day late, though. The calendar is the handle that winds the Bolshevik clock. May Day counts for everything with our Kremlin chums. It's the feast of the saints in Moscow. Twenty-four hours late in raising the red flag? Marvellous pictures but heads, I fear, will still roll.'

'A happy thought?'

'Far from it.' Maskelyne shot him a look. 'But we've come for the dancing, *mon brave*, have we not?'

The evening was now properly underway. The commandeered wenches arrived with the bowls from next door. One of them was carrying Moncrieff's envelope and she knelt quickly to leave it behind Philby's chair. Philby, deep in conversation with a younger colleague, barely acknowledged her. Then some comment provoked a sudden bark of laughter, and he threw back his head, patting his colleague on the arm, but his eyes kept returning to the man from St James's Street who'd kept them waiting. Perhaps I'm the luckless bull, Moncrieff thought. Awaiting the *estocada*.

Few hands were picking at the food and most at the table were drunk by the time Philby ordered the games to begin. He wanted stories, preferably funny or rude, that would mark the passing of the last few years. Field Marshal Montgomery was on his feet at once, hands on his hips, gazing sternly around. Everyone at the table knew that this prickly little man had driven Eisenhower to distraction but his rant about the crusade he demanded to lead was perfectly judged. Not just to Berlin, he demanded. Not just to Minsk. Not just to Moscow. But to the *Holy Land*. His finger stabbed the air as he rounded on Philby. 'Every man deserves a legacy,' he insisted. 'The smaller people crucify me daily but their efforts will be in vain. I shall park my caravan on the Mount of Olives, and go to bed even earlier than usual because tomorrow, gentlemen, Jerusalem shall be mine.'

His pronunciation of 'tomorrow', with the 'rr's adrift, brought the house down. Even Philby was clapping. Once the applause had died, Philby asked for more volunteers. The man in the Leander blazer began a convoluted story about a trap he'd laid in Istanbul but lost his thread. His near neighbour, who was wearing the top half of an Admiral's dress uniform, recalled the day that Section Five had taken their cricket team to an internment camp near Woking and lost to a bunch of Italian POWs. This sparked a guffaw from Philby, who reminisced briefly about the afternoon Tam Moncrieff had turned out for the same team at Glenalmond and botched a sitter in the outfield.

'No matter, Tam.' He quelled the gales of laughter. 'I'm sure you can cap that.'

Moncrieff got to his feet. He hadn't devoted much thought to what he might say but, looking at the wet eyes and shiny faces around the table, he felt nothing but a sudden gust of deep anger. He wanted to take these people back to 1938. He wanted them to imagine that last Party Rally at Nuremberg. He wanted them to be part of the huge crowd in the Zeppelinfeld, silenced for a moment by the sudden appearance of an Me-109 swooping in from the west.

At the controls, he said, was a young flier who'd become the toast of the Reich. Every housewife, every woman with German blood in her veins, wanted just a second of that young man's undivided attention, and none of them doubted for a moment that he could have fathered an entire nation of his own. His friends called him *der Kleine*, Moncrieff murmured, the Little One, but he was big in every sense that really mattered.

'But that, gentlemen, isn't the point of my story...' he waited for the laughter to die, '... because later that evening I got a summons to pay court to Goering. He had a caravan, too. It was parked beside the Zeppelinfeld in a compound on its own. He'd also laid hands on six bottles of Spanish brandy and unlike Monty he had no qualms about broaching them. That night, for whatever reason, the great man was in the mood to celebrate. He had a thirst on him. He was reckless by nature. In the last war, over the trenches, he'd taken a risk or two and had never seen any reason to stop. He wanted my company, any company, and he was glad to have me there. And so we drank. And drank. And drank. And you know what he told me? Get rid of Hitler, he said, and peace stands a fighting chance. Just that. Put a bullet in the Führer's fat head, and the world may be safe again. Was he the only one to see what was coming?

To *fear* what was coming? Of course he wasn't. You'll know their names. Oster. Canaris. Ludwig Beck. Diplomats. Spies. Generals. So what am I saying, gentlemen? What am I telling you? Simply this. That 1939, and everything that followed, need never have happened. Not if we'd been listening properly. And not if we'd drawn the appropriate conclusions. To peace, my friends. Despite the price.'

Moncrieff's toast was greeted by silence. Only Ivor Maskelyne rose in response.

'My thoughts entirely.' He glanced down at Moncrieff. '*Gut gesagt.*' Well said.

Heads now turned to Philby. Moncrieff, who recognised the playful little smile, knew he'd let the air out of the evening's balloon but he didn't care. He'd spent seven years waiting to share one or two home truths, and now – in this surreal setting – he'd done just that.

War had happened because people like these around the table, for whatever reason, hadn't done their jobs properly. Appeasement had fed Hitler's gigantic appetites, and millions had died as a direct result.

'You have a photo for us, Tam? By any chance?' Philby was toying with his glass.

'I have, yes.'

'And is it as glum as that pretty little speech?'

'I'm afraid that's for you to judge.'

'So may we see it?'

'Of course.'

Moncrieff directed Philby's attention to the envelope behind his chair. Surprised for once, Philby bent to retrieve it.

Heads craned around the table. People were eager to see what was inside. Philby slipped the photo out and studied it a moment.

'Well, sir?' It was Montgomery. 'Do we all get a peek?'

Philby nodded. The sleepy charm and the playful little smile had gone. He held the photo up as Section Five's finest sought to make sense of the image. The broken nose. The trousers heaped around his ankles. His neck belted to the cistern's downpipe. Rough justice administered by Willi Schultz.

'Exhibit one, I assume?' Philby was looking at Moncrieff. 'So what's it really like in that head of yours?'

*

It was Ivor Maskelyne who managed to revive the party. More bottles from the Worshipful Company of Skinners passed from hand to hand, and the entertainment, once it resumed, produced stories and images that made even Moncrieff smile. The last round of the games featured treasured objects, and when Moncrieff's turn came, he rose to offer a flattened pebble.

'This came from Lake Maggiore,' he said. 'And I offer it in the spirit of a challenge. As a kid I loved skimming pebbles. Just now, outside, it's low tide. I checked earlier. 10.43. So why don't we muster downstairs, on that little beach? We keep track of the number of skims I get. If it's an odd number, I go in. If it's evens, you lot get wet. Fair?'

With the roar of approval came the scrape of chairs on the wooden floor as the party got to its feet and made for the door. In the thunder of feet on the wooden stairs that led to the beach, Moncrieff sensed relief that the evening was ending the way it had began, with laughter and a kind of wild glee.

Last out of the room was Philby. He paused at the head of the staircase, gesturing for Moncrieff and Maskelyne to go ahead, as ever the perfect host.

'Very neat,' he murmured. 'Guy would be proud of you.'

The foreshore at the foot of the tower was littered with debris from the falling tide. Beside it, the black mouth of Traitors'

Gate. Moncrieff paused a moment, aware of a barge ghosting downriver towards Tower Bridge and the docks beyond. Section Five had formed a ragged line beside the water. Some were already taking off their shoes and socks. Children, Moncrieff thought, released from the war and given their heads for the evening.

He watched a couple at the end of the line, struggling drunkenly to support each other. Was it a dance? Were they having a fight? He shrugged, clapping his hands to attract attention before recapping the rules. Odds, I lose. Evens, you go in. Then he turned to Philby.

'On your call?' he suggested.

Philby nodded, waiting for Moncrieff to make space for himself, then counted down from three. On zero, Moncrieff sent the little pebble flying into the darkness and the moment it left his hand, with that little flick of the wrist, he knew he'd judged it perfectly. The first splash was visible, the second less so, then nothing remained but a series of tiny plops as the pebble skittered across the water.

In some ways, Moncrieff thought later, this must have come as a disappointment, but nothing could silence Section Five at its most vocal.

'Seventeen,' yelled one voice.

'Thirteen.'

'Nine.'

'Twenty-one.'

'Seven.'

'Twelve.' This last from Philby. 'And I hold the casting vote.'

White faces turned towards him in the darkness. No one could quite believe it. Section Five betrayed by its own leader? Could life get any more unfair?

Then came a wild yelp as the first volunteer, fully clothed, threw himself into the water. More followed, some in various states of undress, churning the brown sludge until only three figures remained on the tiny crescent of beach.

'Christ, just look at them,' Maskelyne had lit a fat cigar. 'How on earth did we ever win that bloody war?'

'Maybe we didn't.' It was Philby, a soft voice in the darkness. 'Ever think about that?'

*

Memories of that first day of freedom in Berlin, for Nehmann, never left him. Leon, with commendable tact, shepherded them from destination to destination, acting as driver as they picked their way round the ruined capital, and translator when they were waved down at the many Soviet checkpoints that had appeared in the wake of the German garrison's surrender. Already road signs in Russian were directing troops to commandeered *Wehrmacht* barracks and roadside feeding stations. The latter were manned by beefy Soviet women, all of them in uniform, and when they stopped for Leon to fetch mugs of tea from a huge samovar propped on a baulk of timber, Nehmann watched the line of waiting infantry melt away at Leon's approach.

'He has clout?' asked Schultz. 'This friend of yours?'

'Lots. He got me in to see Stalin.'

'You *met* him?'

'I did.'

'And?'

'He's a Georgian. That's all you need to know.'

'And that's enough?'

'For what?'

'All this?' Schultz gestured at the wasteland that had once been one of the city's busiest intersections. 'Germany on its fucking knees?'

'More than enough. The man's a rascal. I doubt he has an honest bone in his body, but he scares everyone shitless. It starts with the Russians and it spreads west. One look at his eyes tells you everything. Yellow, Willi. The colour of badness.'

Badness. Nehmann was grinning. Freedom was something he'd given up on and he couldn't quite get used to the feeling. Wreckage everywhere. Untold opportunities if you kept your nerve.

Leon returned with the tea. When he asked where they wanted to go next, Schultz said the KWI.

'The Institute?'

'Yes.'

'Why?'

'I have to show you something.'

'It's important?'

'Important enough to have put me in front of a *Volkssturm* patrol.'

Leon nodded, and watching him sip the tea, Nehmann had the feeling he knew exactly what had prompted this request.

*

The Kaiser Wilhelm Institute was in Dahlem. At the first checkpoint, a senior NKVD officer ordered them all out of the car. Leon took him aside while uniformed guards searched both Nehmann and Schultz. By now, the officer had scrawled something on a scrap of paper, applied a rubber stamp and handed it to Leon. The next checkpoint was within sight of the Institute's main complex, and the NKVD presence was even heavier, but one look at Leon's *laissez-passer* and the Mercedes was waved through.

The site itself was crawling with armed troops. With them, in a variety of uniforms, were other personnel Leon referred to as 'technicians'. They'd been shipped in specially, he said, moving half a day behind the Red Army's front line in anticipation of sealing off this site.

'Why?' Nehmann was looking at Schultz.

Schultz got out of the car. Leon negotiated an escort to accompany them into the grounds. The squat, ugly building Schultz recognised as the Virus House lay ahead, ringed by an inner circle of heavily armed guards. Exhaust fumes were drifting in the wind from a couple of Red Army trucks, and the site stank of cheap gasoline.

Schultz led the way round the side of the building, and then gestured at the work party manhandling drums onto the back of one of the trucks. The men were wearing gas masks and heavy gloves, and it took four of them to lift each drum. They must have dropped one of them because the top had come off and the contents had spilled across the sodden turf. A lone soldier with a spade was doing his best to scrape the stuff up.

'What is it?' Nehmann was trying to make sense of the scene.

'Uranium oxide,' Schultz grunted. 'The scientists call it yellowcake.'

'So what do you do with it?' He was frowning now. 'Why all the security?'

'We take it back home.' This from Leon. 'And try to turn it into a bomb before the Americans blow us all up.'

Nehmann blinked. The soldier with the spade had nearly finished.

'He's serious?' Nehmann was looking at Schultz.

Schultz said nothing for a moment, then checked his watch. 'Lunch?'

At Nehmann's suggestion, they went to a bar favoured by journalists from the Promi. There was no glass in the windows, and the top half of the building seemed to have disappeared, but a word to the barman conjured Nehmann two foaming glasses of Kindl.

'He probably remembers you.' This from Schultz.

'That's what I thought.'

'And?'

'He doesn't. It's this stuff that worked.' Nehmann had a roll of Russian currency from Leon, who'd elected to stay outside in the car.

'I think he's in love with you,' Schultz growled. 'Watch your arse.'

The thought had occurred to Nehmann, too. He'd sensed something close to affection developing on the journey out of the Gulag. He'd never doubted for a moment that Leon's faith in the regime trumped everything else, that he'd put a bullet in Nehmann's head if he had to, but there was another life beyond the Bolshevik brainwash, and Nehmann suspected that Leon had glimpsed it. Just now, a glance through the window revealed the Russian deep in a book. The man has soul, he thought. Books can make life tough where he comes from.

Schultz ordered more beers. When the woman behind the bar offered to cook for them – half an egg each and a spoonful or two of potato mashed with swede – Nehmann said yes. He wanted to know more about the KWI, and about the yellowcake. Schultz obliged with an account of his flight from Sweden, and the events that had finally delivered him to the lakeside house at Wannsee.

'You *met* Himmler?'

'I did.'

'And?'

'The man's finished. He nearly did for me, too.' Schultz described the Wiener schnitzel, the greediness of his escort, and the luck he'd ridden in making his escape. After the last two years, he grunted, God owed him a favour and, thanks to a flier called Jürgen Frenzell, he'd finally made it back to Berlin.

'The letter from Stalin was a death sentence,' he said. 'I should have known that from the start.'

'And the yellowcake?'

'You'll know the woman of the Wannsee house.'

'How come?'

'She said you paid a visit, way back. Messner's egg slicer?'

Nehmann was thinking hard. Then he had it.

'My last trip to Berlin,' he said. 'I was en route back to the airfield. I had a minute on the doorstep to hand it over.' He paused. 'Thin woman? Baby in her arms? Angry?'

'Principled. Her name's Beata. She's a physicist. She still works at the KWI and she wanted that stuff gone. She's a woman who loves tidying up. She's also got a conscience. She told me the regime have been screwing science for years. All they've ever wanted is a bigger bang, and she was determined to remove the temptation.'

'So Leon's serious about a bomb?'

'I'm guessing he is. She explained the chemistry to me, but I'm still in the dark. Either way, it seems to matter so thank Christ for the NKVD.'

Nehmann nodded. Something else had been bothering him.

'That ID pass that got you in trouble with the *Volkssturm*. Who gave it to you?'

'A man called Diski. He was NKVD, too.'

'Didn't he know the *Abwehr* no longer existed?

'That's what I asked Leon. He said it was probably deliberate.'

'To get you arrested?'

'To get me inside the Prinz-Albrecht-Strasse. The NKVD knew I'd cracked under pressure once. That could happen again. The Russians want maximum disruption. They want everyone at each other's throats. Show them a decent room and they'll kick the shit out of everything. That's the way they operate. *Onkel Heine*? Walter Schellenberg? Karl Wolff? All of them going off like fireworks? Crossed lines? Cut throats? The scramble to keep your head in one piece? Our friends in Moscow love it.'

'And you?'

'Me?' Schultz shrugged. 'So far, like I say, I've been lucky. Do I take any of that for granted? Fuck, no. Leon's made me an offer, by the way. Half of this country's going to be Russian from now on. He thinks I might be the perfect fit.'

'As a spy?'

'As a policeman. Which is probably the same thing.'

*

By mid-afternoon they were back in the car. When Nehmann asked to be taken to Eichwalde, Leon closed his book and simply nodded.

'You know where it is?' Nehmann was staring at him.

'Yes.'

'You don't need an address?'

'No.' He reached for the ignition key.

They drove out of the city centre. On every street, gangs of *Trümmerfrauen* were on their knees in the rubble, sorting the broken masonry by size, readying piles of bricks for collection, black ants working at a speed any man would be proud of, dismembering what was left of the city centre. Further south, the Russians appeared to have spared most of the suburbs, and when they finally arrived outside Maria's house, Schultz was shaking his head.

'She lives here?'

'She does.'

'So how come...?' Schultz gestured round at the newly

424

trimmed hedges, the bright stands of daffodils, the cat sprawled in the spring sunshine.

'Goebbels.' Nehmann was reaching for the door handle. 'He was king of the city, and he probably still is.'

Wrong. Leon was already at the front door. Instead of knocking, he was examining a bunch of keys. The second one he selected opened the door.

'Please.' He stood aside.

Nehmann knew at once that the house was empty. The big clock in the hall had stopped at twenty past seven, and the air felt chill.

'There's no one here?' He turned to Leon.

'No.'

'You know where they've gone?'

'We took them east. She was very happy to go. The child, too.'

'Her idea?'

'Ours, but a good one.'

Nehmann nodded, none the wiser, and stepped into the living room. The curtains were closed and for some reason the lights wouldn't work, but he could make out an envelope on the bare table. When he took a closer look, he recognised a name in Cyrillic script. Mikhail Magalashvili.

'This is for me? She left it?'

Leon said nothing. He crossed to the window and pulled the curtains back, suddenly flooding the room in daylight.

Nehmann opened the envelope. Inside he found a black and white photo. It showed a man's body, flat on his back. His left leg was bare, except for an ankle sock, and scorch marks had blackened his torso. His skull, too, showed signs of damage. His mouth lay open in a rictus grin, and his left arm had somehow been frozen, the hand raised and clawlike as if stretching for something not quite within reach.

'This is Goebbels?' Nehmann had taken a closer look at the face, the shape of the skull.

'It is. He committed suicide in the bunker. Once Hitler had shot himself, there was nothing left for him.'

'And Magda? The children?'

'Gone.'

Gone. Nehmann was still staring at the photo. Those happy, dangerous years at this man's beck and call. The risks he'd taken, the battles he'd lost and won, and then the assignment east, to near-certain death. He thought of the candle swimming out of the darkness at the Bogensee house, of the fidgety presence in the editing room, of that giant brain that had helped turn an entire country into a charnel house. Nehmann had been on board for that giddy ride, and for the most part gladly, but now there was nothing left but this half-charred body, mercilessly exposed.

Gone, he thought again.

'Maria left this?' Nehmann was looking at Leon.

'No. I did.'

'But does she know? That he's dead?'

'Yes.'

'You told her?'

'Not me. Someone else.'

'And?'

'She seemed unsurprised.'

'Relieved?'

'Unsurprised. If you're asking whether or not she'd welcome a meeting, I suspect the answer is yes.'

'And can you make that happen?'

'We can. But we have a proposition we should put to you first. Comrade Stalin was impressed, by the way. It might help you to know that.'

25

Tuesday 6th May, nearly a week later, was declared Victory in Europe Day. Guy Liddell, prompted by MI5's Director, had already given 'B' Section leave to join the revels but Moncrieff had no appetite for celebration. Instead, he decided to pay Ursula Barton another visit.

It was a beautiful morning, a foretaste of summer, not a cloud in the sky. Moncrieff took the trolley bus to Shepherd's Bush. The news on the radio had been full of the capital's plans for VE Day, and he sat on the top deck, gazing down at the queues already forming at bus stops into central London. Museums had been thrown open. Parks readied for picnickers. And in Trafalgar Square there were plans for a rally. Patriotism on the grandest scale, he thought, enlivened with a song or two.

There was no answer when he knocked on Barton's front door. He tried again, and then a third time before stepping back and gazing up at her bedroom window. The curtains were pulled tight. Might she be sleeping late? Might she have closed her ears to all the clamour? All the celebration? A path led round the side of the house to the back garden. No one had bothered with the riot of spring growth, and the little rectangle of lawn, especially, needed attention. Briefly he wondered whether she might have a mower. In weather like this, there would be worse ways of saying goodbye to the war.

The back door, to his surprise, was unlocked. He stepped into the kitchen. It was much the way he'd left it, everything tidied away, but there lingered a very bad smell, a sour sweetness thickened by something that seemed to have an almost physical presence. It was the smell of neglect, he thought, and perhaps something darker, and when he opened the door to the hall he could hear a voice on the radio, very low.

'Ursula?' He listened beside the open door to the hall. No reply.

The curtains in the front room were pulled tight but he could still make out an empty glass and a plate on the occasional table beside her armchair. There were crumbs on the plate, dry to his touch, and when he sniffed the glass he caught a faint peaty tang of malt whisky. Talisker, he thought.

The radio was tuned to the Home Service. A BBC voice was reporting from Reims, in France. Yesterday, General Jodl had signed the official surrender document at General Eisenhower's headquarters and fighting everywhere was officially over. There followed a muddle of excited French voices, mainly women, one of whom began to sing a spirited version of the Marseillaise. Standing in the gloom, Moncrieff became aware of a little nest of pencils, secured with an elastic band, tucked into the side of the chair. He stared at them for a moment. Was this where Barton corresponded with her non-existent sister? Was this room, this entire house, haunted by the ghost of Gretel?

He made his way upstairs, aware of the smell getting stronger. He knew that Barton's bedroom lay at the front of the house, and he paused at the door before knocking softly and whispering her name. From downstairs came the muted roar of a crowd and then a song he recognised, the marching ditty that had accompanied thousands of men to France in those long-ago days when the Germans had settled their accounts with the Poles and retired for a nap. We called it the Phoney War, he thought. And we had absolutely no idea what lay in store.

'Ursula? Are you there?' Again, no answer.

Gently, he opened the door. Then came a scuffle and a yowl and he stepped back as the tom cat plunged past him and disappeared down the stairs. The stench, now, was overpowering. The threadbare carpet at his feet had been ripped to pieces, doubtless by the cat, but what drew his attention was the long shape beneath the eiderdown. He stared at it for a moment. Then his fingers found the light switch and he stepped carefully around the dry black curls of shit until he was looking down at the face on the pillow.

The cat had been clawing her cheek, and the side of her neck. Blood had crusted around the deeper wounds, and there were signs that the animal had began to nibble at the softness behind her ear, but her eyes were closed and Moncrieff tried to convince himself that she'd found some kind of peace. Her flesh was cold and waxy to his touch, and when he tried to find a pulse at the base of her neck, he knew he was wasting his time.

The telephone was on a table in the hall downstairs. Moncrieff dialled Liddell's home number but there was no reply. When he tried the main switchboard at St James's Street, the duty clerk told him that Mr Liddell was probably at rehearsals all day. When Moncrieff enquired further, she laughed.

'You haven't heard? St Mary Abbot's Church. Off Kensington High Street. Half past seven. If Vivaldi's your thing, you're in for a treat.'

Moncrieff went back upstairs. There was no way of telling how or why Ursula Barton had died, or even when it may have happened, and he knew that his next call must go to the police, but here and now he knew he owed her, at the very least, a decent search. Already he'd noticed the corner of an envelope protruding from her pillow. He eased it out. Inside was a sheaf of photographs, black and white, carefully lit and posed. They all showed the same woman: middle-aged, strong face, permed blonde hair, snub nose. In many of the poses, she was smoking a cigarette, and one shot in particular caught Moncrieff's eye.

She was sitting on a camp bed, her bare legs crossed. Open sandals suggested summer, and hints of a busy life spilled out of the holdall at her feet. She was holding the cigarette at a certain angle, a hint of the *demi-monde*, and the expression on her face suggested the imminence of some kind of adventure. Judging by the state of the photo, it had been much handled, and when Moncrieff returned the photos to the envelope, he made sure it was at the top. He knew this face. He'd even listened to the woman on the radio. And he began to sense another hand behind this sad little tableau.

Next door, Moncrieff managed to rouse Barton's neighbour. He was an old man, braces over an open shirt, not much hair. He stood in the sunshine, gazing at the property next door, trying to do his best to answer Moncrieff's questions. He'd last seen Mrs Barton a week or so ago. No, she hadn't looked too good but she was a tough old bird and wouldn't listen to offers of help. She'd always kept herself to herself, which suited him and his missus very nicely. Her garden was a bit of a sight but apart from that they had no complaints.

When Moncrieff said she'd passed away, he looked briefly shocked.

'When?'

'I don't know. Days ago, I'm guessing. Did you hear anything, any signs of movement, anything out of the ordinary?'

The old man gave the question some thought. By now, he'd been joined by his wife.

'That Wednesday night,' she said at once. 'When I woke you up.'

'Yeah?' The old man was looking confused.

'Wednesday night?' Moncrieff was looking at the wife.

'Yeah. Either that, or Thursday. No, Wednesday, definitely, because I'd been down the market that morning and spent all my coupons.'

Moncrieff nodded. Wednesday had been the night Philby and Broadway partied at the Tower of London.

'So what happened?'

'There was just a noise. Her bedroom's next to ours. You can hear things through the wall. Someone moving. Someone talking. She lived alone, Mrs Barton. She was quiet as a mouse, not a peep.'

'You heard this voice?'

'Yeah.'

'Male? Female?'

'A bloke. Then he was gone and it was all quiet again and...' she drew her cardigan a little tighter, '... I went back to sleep.'

*

Wednesday. Moncrieff was back next door. A search in every room simply confirmed what he already knew about Ursula Barton: a reclusive figure, few friends, a handful of mementos, largely from Germany and Holland, plus a vast collection of classical music discs, with a heavy emphasis on opera. In this house, thanks to its owner, you'd be spoiled for Verdi and Puccini but of the intimacies she claimed to have shared with Gretel there was no trace.

Wednesday. Towards noon, Moncrieff lifted the phone and

summoned the police. They arrived within the hour, a uniformed Sergeant and a plain clothes detective. They confirmed that Mrs Barton was dead and took details for both the deceased and for Moncrieff. When they asked him about his occupation, he told them he worked for the government. When they pressed him for a contact, someone who'd serve as a reference, he promised to be in touch.

'Is that a problem, sir?'

'It might be.'

'Do you mind me asking why?'

'Yes, I do rather.' He smiled. 'There's a couple next door. You might ask the woman about Wednesday night.'

*

Moncrieff was back home by early afternoon. The Kensington mews where he was camping in a friend's little cottage had been festooned with bunting, and his neighbours had laid out food and drink on trestle tables in the sunshine. Someone had laid hands on a record player, and couples were dancing to Benny Goodman. Moncrieff accepted a glass of stout and promised to return to join the party as soon as he could.

De Vries, when he called her minutes later, was also celebrating. Even sleepy Locarno, she said, was *en fête*. For once she was able to tempt perfect strangers into conversation and she hoped this outbreak of bonhomie would go on for ever. When Moncrieff broke the news about Barton, she went very quiet.

'When?' she said at last.

'I found her this morning. She'd been dead for a while. Probably the best part of a week.'

'How? Why?'

'I don't know. Not yet.'

He explained briefly about the police. He expected they'd mount some kind of investigation. In the meantime, there would be lots to sort out.

'You mean Ursula? Her affairs?'

'Yes.'

'But she's got no one.'

'Exactly.'

'Then I'll come over.' She paused. 'Expect me tomorrow.'

*

Moncrieff rejoined the celebrations in the mews. He drank sparingly, but danced a lot, mainly with a fellow Scot who'd lost her husband at Monte Cassino. Her name was Moira. She had an Aberdonian's reserve but she was handsome, and good company, and unsparing about the madness of the war. When he told her that he was off to a concert that night, she said she was tempted to join him but Moncrieff was glad when mention of Vivaldi string quartets drew a shake of the head.

*

St Mary Abbot's Church was nearly full by the time Moncrieff arrived. It was a big building, oppressively gothic. Seats and music stands had been readied in a loose semi-circle on the space in front of the altar, and the congregation rose in applause when the musicians appeared. Guy Liddell was the last to take his seat, making careful adjustments to the slant of the big cello before tuning up. Then, as the lights in the nave dimmed, he flexed his long fingers and peered out at the audience, tiny nods of recognition for faces he knew.

The music was bright and full of vigour, the perfect antidote to the slow trudge through the years of war, and Moncrieff sat at the back of the church, remembering the couples jitterbugging

433

in the mews outside his window. The final quartet came to an end in a fizzy crescendo, and the audience were once again on their feet. The leader of the quartet, a slightly saturnine figure whom Moncrieff didn't recognise, thanked the rector for the loan of his church, President Truman for the loan of his armies, and the Good Lord for the prospect of a decent night's sleep. This coda to the evening's entertainment sparked another round of applause. The leader of the quartet was smiling now. Drinks and maybe even a slice of cake, he announced, would be on offer in the vestry. Members of the audience who hadn't already suffered enough, were welcome to partake.

Moncrieff found Liddell backed into a corner beside a row of surplices, trapped by a loud woman with views about diminuendo. Moncrieff caught his eye, and Liddell disengaged himself with a murmured apology, taking Moncrieff's elbow and steering him towards the table where drinks were being served.

'The red, I think.' Liddell presented Moncrieff with a glass. 'The white's filthy and they couldn't find enough ice to make it drinkable. Well done for the other night at the Tower, incidentally. I understand you were the life and soul.'

Moncrieff ignored what might have been a compliment. As ever, he thought, nothing was quite the way it sounded.

'Ursula's dead,' he said. 'I tried to phone you earlier.'

'Dead?' Liddell's eyes had settled on a nearby face he seemed to know. 'Good Lord.'

Moncrieff described what he'd found in the gloom of Barton's bedroom. The stench. The cat. The fact that she'd obviously been dead for some time.

'How long, do we think?'

'About a week.'

'Golly. That's truly awful. Any idea how she died?'

'None.'

'Nothing obvious? Nothing that caught the eye? She'd been under immense strain, of course. My fault, I suspect, and this bloody war of ours. She was a proud woman, Tam. Maybe she'd had enough.'

'Meaning?'

'Meaning she'd prefer to draw a line of her own before she went completely gaga.'

Moncrieff gazed at him for a moment, wondering whether to share the news from next door about a voice from her bedroom six days ago.

'Suicide seems unlikely,' he said instead. 'I found no signs, no empty bottle of pills, no note of any kind, nothing like that. The only oddness was a little keepsake under her pillow. Photographs.'

'Of?'

'Mildred Gillars.'

Liddell at last met his gaze. Mildred Gillars was one of two American women who'd broadcast German propaganda from Berlin throughout the war years. Together, they'd become known as Axis Sally.

'The Yanks will be issuing a warrant for her arrest,' a voice said. 'Are you aware of that?'

Moncrieff spun round. The last time he'd seen the Arab scarf was six days ago. Then, for Wednesday night's revels at the Tower of London, Philby had worn it as a headdress. Now it was looped artlessly over his shoulders. He's heard every word, Moncrieff thought. He's privy to everything.

Liddell had already drifted away to replenish his glass and accept congratulations from a passing fan. Philby watched him with an expression, Moncrieff thought, that was close to fond. Then he edged a little closer.

'They'll trace Gillars in the end,' he murmured, 'and then they'll try her for treason. One way or another, she may end up with a rope around her neck. Under the pillow, you say?' He was frowning now. 'Interesting.'

'Interesting how?'

'I suspect there were secrets that your Mrs Barton kept well hidden. Even from you.'

'Meaning?'

'Passion takes many forms, as we all know. Axis Sally wasn't to everyone's taste but even Mrs Barton might need a spot of consolation from time to time.' He wetted a fingertip and picked a tiny speck of cork from the rim of his glass. Then he looked up. 'Doesn't that sound plausible? Or am I being unduly harsh?'

Moncrieff held his gaze.

'Guy appears to believe this is some kind of suicide,' he said carefully.

'Suicide?' Philby was looking pained. 'I think he's suggesting your lovely Ursula had thrown in the towel. She lived alone, Tam. She had no friends that anyone was ever aware of, and I gather her family have mostly passed on. Solace, whatever shape it takes, isn't a crime. At least, not yet.'

'You're serious? You're really telling me she was in love with Axis Sally?'

'I'm telling you she'd lost her wits. It may be the same thing.'

'And after that, she ended it all?'

'After that, she saw no point in prolonging the agony. She was a woman of principle. You were very lucky to have her, indeed we all were.' He put his hand briefly on Moncrieff's arm. 'Is that a version you can live with, Tam? I do hope so.'

*

De Vries arrived in London the following day. Moncrieff was back at his desk in St James's Street and she phoned him from Salvation Army Headquarters.

'They've given me a room for as long as I need it,' she said. 'Which is very Christian of them.'

They met in a Whitehall pub later that same evening. Street cleaners were still attending to the aftermath of yesterday's celebrations, and Moncrieff apologised for being so late.

'The work's never ending,' he said. 'I thought war was bad enough but peace is far worse.'

De Vries put her arms around him, gave him a consolatory kiss. To Moncrieff's relief, she wasn't in uniform.

'Don't worry,' she said. 'I've already talked to the police. Tomorrow I'll be picking up the house key. Leave it to me. I probably knew her better than anyone. Tidying up is the least I can do.'

'And sending her on her way? Some kind of funeral?'

'That, too.'

*

Over the days that followed, Moncrieff kept in constant touch. Guilty that he couldn't offer more help, he wanted to know that De Vries had everything in hand. The answer, in conversation after conversation, was yes. She'd cleaned the house, emptied every drawer, disposed of all Ursula's clothing, been in touch with her bank manager, and talked at length to her solicitor. She'd even made time to borrow a mower from the man next door and tackle the lawn.

In her will, she said, Ursula had left everything to an obscure Dutch charity charged with protecting birds of passage in a corner of the Zuiderzee. This bequest would probably run into five figures, and the more she thought about it, the more De Vries had been touched. Back before the war, she said, the pair of them had spent many weekends prowling the Dutch waterlands in search of trophy shots for De Vries's camera, and the fact that these excursions had so obviously mattered had been a revelation, as well as a surprise. Birds of passage, Moncrieff had mused afterwards. Wildly appropriate.

*

Nearly a week later, Moncrieff found an opportunity to leave his desk at a reasonable hour and take De Vries for an early supper. He wanted, above all, to know about the police.

'They went through the house before they let me in.' De Vries was examining a plate of stew. 'Proper search, fingerprints, the lot.'

'And?'

'They say they found nothing.'

'Post-mortem?'

'Congestive heart failure. I've seen the death certificate. It's there in black and white.' She paused, looking up. 'What do you think she died from?'

'Disappointment.'

'You're serious?'

'I am. I think it started with a V-2 rocket. It blew up a market in Farringdon and killed a man she sort of knew.'

'Sort of?'

'She was a customer. He was a butcher, had a stall in the market. She must have seen him once a week but what she saw, she really liked, and that was enough. When he died, she was distraught, and after that she simply lost interest.'

De Vries nodded, said she understood.

'You mean that?'

'I do.' De Vries nodded. 'She believed what she believed. She was unbending. She set the bar very high. That can be hard to live with, especially if you happened to be Ursula. Disappointment is a good word. In fact, it's perfect.' De Vries gave the stew one last prod, and then pushed the plate to one side. 'I met the couple next door,' she said. 'They told me about hearing someone in Ursula's bedroom. Days and days before you turned up.'

'That's right.'

'So why didn't you tell me? And why haven't the police interviewed them?'

Moncrieff looked away across the crowded pub. London, in barely a matter of days, had come back to life again. Laughter, he thought. Opportunities. Even a little spare cash.

'You were in this game,' he said. 'One question answers the other. Ursula deserves a little peace. That's the least we owe her.'

Among the handful of documents De Vries had recovered from various corners of the house were instructions that she no longer wanted a Christian funeral. The flame that was her faith, she wrote, had flickered and died. Cremation would do fine, the hotter the better, and afterwards, if her friend De Vries was minded, she'd like her ashes scattered on the Zuiderzee, preferably on a day when the sun was out, and definitely in the company of tufted ducks.

De Vries, only too happy to oblige, had made arrangements for the cremation but had then discovered that taking a casket of ashes through customs wasn't quite as simple as she'd thought. After six years of slaughter, any evidence of the dead in transit had to be twice certified, once in the country of origin and again on arrival.

'So what will you do?'

At De Vries' insistence, they'd arranged to meet at one of London's many Salvation Army citadels. The closest was in Southwark, across the river, and Moncrieff had made his excuses at lunchtime to be there.

The citadel, when De Vries let him in, was empty. Her single suitcase lay beside a row of chairs at the back. She was booked on a ferry to Ostend which sailed at seven in the evening. Her train from Charing Cross left at half past two.

'I'll cheat,' she said. 'I managed to lay hands on a big tin of Cadbury's Roses. Soldiers in my line of work have a sweet tooth. I got rid of the lot in less than an hour.'

'And the ashes?'

'In there,' she nodded at the suitcase. 'I wrapped the tin up as a present.'

Moncrieff nodded. The prospect of Agent *Clover* smuggling her earthly remains into Europe in an empty tin of chocolates would, he thought, have amused Ursula Barton.

'So this is goodbye?' He was already stooping for the suitcase.

'Not quite. Come with me.'

De Vries extended a gloved hand and led him towards the stage. The big wooden cross on the back wall loomed over everything. Beyond the front row of seats, she nodded at the low padded bench.

'The Mercy Seat,' she said. 'Here's where we remember Ursula.'

'I have to say a prayer?'

'You have to give thanks. If not for God's benefit then for yours, and for mine. She was a good woman. We need to pay our respects. An adieu would be fitting, if you could manage it.'

Moncrieff didn't know quite what to say but then, unprompted, he sank to his knees. De Vries, beside him, had bowed her head. Her lips were moving and Moncrieff caught a whisper or two of prayer but nothing made much sense. Then he felt a stir of movement, and he accepted her hand again, and they both got to their feet.

'Easier than you thought?' She was smiling.

About the author

GRAHAM HURLEY is an award-winning
TV documentary maker and the author of
the acclaimed Faraday and Winter crime novels,
two of which have been shortlisted for the
Theakston's Old Peculier Award for Best Crime
Novel. His Second World War thriller *Finisterre*,
part of the critically acclaimed Spoils of War
collection, was shortlisted for the Wilbur
Smith Adventure Writing Prize.

www.grahamhurley.co.uk